AVELYNN

AVELYNN

MARISSA CAMPBELL

THOMAS DUNNE BOOKS

ST. MARTIN'S GRIFFIN   NEW YORK

THOMAS DUNNE BOOKS.
An imprint of St. Martin's Press.

AVELYNN. Copyright © 2015 by Marissa Campbell. All rights reserved. Printed in the United States of America. For information, address St. Martin's Press, 175 Fifth Avenue, New York, N.Y. 10010.

www.thomasdunnebooks.com
www.stmartins.com

Designed by Steven Seighman

The Library of Congress Cataloging-in-Publication Data is available upon request.

ISBN 978-1-250-08498-9 (trade paperback)
ISBN 978-1-250-06393-9 (hardcover)
ISBN 978-1-4668-6889-2 (e-book)

Our books may be purchased in bulk for promotional, educational, or business use. Please contact your local bookseller or the Macmillan Corporate and Premium Sales Department at (800) 221-7945, extension 5442, or by e-mail at Macmillan SpecialMarkets@macmillan.com.

First Edition: September 2015

10 9 8 7 6 5 4 3 2 1

For David, Lochlin, Aidan, and Brendan
With all my love

ACKNOWLEDGMENTS

I was in kindergarten when I decided I wanted to be an author. My life took a few twists and turns, but I never gave up on that mystical, magical dream. As I sit here and type these words, I am struck by a sense of humility, wonder, and awe. I am so grateful to be here, but I didn't do it alone. I've met some wonderful people along the way who were instrumental in helping me achieve my dreams.

I'd like to thank my agent, the incomparable Margaret Bail, who dared to take a look at an abysmal first draft, and saw enough promise in that jumbled mass of words to sign me. You've become a wonderful friend and mentor. Words cannot begin to express my gratitude.

To Barbara Rogan, Barbara Kyle, the wonderful staff at the Editorial Department, and Sherry Hinman, my fantastic editor. Thank you for wading through the early drafts and helping to shape and hone a rough, jagged manuscript into something polished and bright with promise.

To my incredible publisher, St. Martin's Press. To my editors, Toni Kirkpatrick and Jennifer Letwack, who took a chance on a debut novelist and guided me with their expertise and unwavering support. To Jessica Preeg, Angela Craft, and everyone else behind the scenes who rallied together to make *Avelynn* a success. Thank you for your confidence and trust. I am thrilled to be part of such a passionate and dedicated team.

To the amazing B7: A. B. Funkhauser, Susan Croft, Connie Di Pietro, Ann Dulhanty, Yvonne Hess, and Rachael Stapleton. You pushed, questioned, probed, and prodded, exposing plot holes, character flaws, and pacing black holes. Your dedication, support, and friendship mean the world to me. Thank you.

To the wonderful teachers and peers I've met through the WCDR, proving writing doesn't have to be a solitary act. Thank you for reaching out and enveloping me in a community of camaraderie and creativity.

To each and every one of my yoga students. You have touched my life in ways I could never have imagined. Thank you for your continued support.

To Carol and Bruce. Thank you for setting me on this wonderful path. To my friends old and new. Thank you for letting me drift off in conversations to stare out the window, for being my sounding boards, for standing by me during the long road to publication, and for understanding when I went AWOL.

To David, who told me to swing for the fences. You are my greatest champion, my dearest friend, and my one true love. To Lochlin, Aidan, and Brendan. You fill my life with endless joy and light. I am so proud of you. Thank you for your patience, support, and unconditional love. I love you all so very much.

Despite the world conspiring against her, Avelynn follows her heart and refuses to give up. Don't let anyone keep you from living your most passionate life. Do what makes you happy. Never give up on your mystical, magical dreams.

In gratitude,
Marissa xo

Avelynn

ONE

Sigberht gripped the hilt of his sword, and my heart quickened.

"Cut off his hand, lord," he said.

The boy's face waxed ashen, his hands kneading the front of his threadbare tunic. Only eleven summers old, he should have been out chasing chickens or helping his mother collect firewood for the coming winter.

Council was held once a year, and petitioners had been coming and going all day long, pleading their cases to my father, the Earl of Somerset. Sigberht, my father's reeve, was on hand to marshal out punishment. Almost everyone from the village was present, spectators and claimants alike crammed into my father's timber hall.

I had been silent, beyond the occasional grumble of dissent, and duly recorded each case and its judgment, but this last quarrel broke my tolerance. I put down my quill and rose, the hem of my dress brushing the freshly laid rushes underfoot.

I turned an appeal to my father. "The boy is merely a puppet."

My father sat in the lord's chair high upon the raised dais, his eyes hooded beneath waves of honey-blond hair, his face unreadable.

Sigberht stormed forward. "Surely Avelynn would be better suited to the weaving shed," he hissed. "Council is no place for a woman."

I scowled at him. "Apparently, nor is it a place for justice or common sense."

"Peace, you two." My father's tone was light, but the warning loomed heavy between us.

Sigberht's grip tightened on his sword. "The law is clear. Let me cut off the boy's hand."

"If anyone should be punished, it should be the tanner, not his son," I said.

"Your daughter needs a tighter leash, lord," someone yelled from the back of the hall, and was rewarded with a round of laughter.

Slaves scurried about with clay pitchers filled with mead, and the drink flowed into waiting bone horns. The central hearth, a long, narrow trough dug into the packed-dirt floor, burned bright, filling the hall with smoke and heat. A hole cut into the roof allowed some of the smoke to escape. The rest hovered over the crowd, filling the spaces between the large beams overhead. There were no windows, and shadows were deep. Pinpricks of light flickered from oil lamps suspended from the ceiling, and iron candle trees, scattered about the large open hall, sputtered in the constant drafts.

The tanner, his tunic smeared and reeking of dung—the perfume of his trade—addressed my father. "I swear my innocence."

"And who supports your claim?" Sigberht's grip on his sword never loosened.

"My brother."

A round, squat man stepped clear of the press, wringing a wool cap in his hands. "I stand up for my brother and his son, lord."

"You are a farmer?" my father asked.

"Yes, my lord."

I frowned. Judgment was made based on personal worth. The more status you held, the more influence your word carried. Though the farmer was a freeman, his oath would not carry much weight.

Eager to strike down the tanner's weak defenses, my father's master of arms approached the dais. Taller and thicker than most men, Wulfric looked like a bear. His shaggy mane and beard were blacker than pitch, and his eyes were hard and implacable. "Both my brother and I have seen your bastard lead your pigs into my keep." He spat at the tanner's feet. "The dog has been doing this all year, my lord. His pigs have grown fat off my land."

Wulfric and his brother, Leofric, were both warriors in my father's household guard. In a game of power and oaths, Wulfric had just won.

Sigberht withdrew his sword from its scabbard and grabbed the child's arm, hauling him toward the door.

The boy's eyes, as wide as a snared fawn's, pleaded with the cold, impassive stare of his father. He was trying to be brave, but a stray tear charted a wayward path through the grime on his cheek.

"Wait." I rushed forward. "I offer an alternative."

The hard set of my father's jaw warned of his abating patience.

"The boy will be twelve summers old, of age to hold a sword on his next birth day. Let Wulfric claim two swine instead, one for each of the boy's hands."

"I've only the five swine, lord. The boy will live with one hand," the tanner pleaded.

"What say you, Wulfric?" my father asked.

"That's fair compensation, lord."

"Done." My father waved them both away, ignoring the tanner's protests, and beckoned me closer.

I trudged the remaining few steps between us and stopped at his side. His head turned, but his eyes remained fixed on the crowded room. "The next word you speak, Avelynn, will see you bent over that bench, my belt your justice for all present to see. Am I understood?"

I nodded and sat back down, picking up my quill, my palms sweaty. After that small victory, I was not inclined to push my father further.

Sigberht addressed the crowd. "Demas of Wareham, nephew of the late Bishop Ealhstan, step forward and state your business."

Bishop Ealhstan had been an arrogant, dour little man, constantly voicing bleak Christian rhetoric. I never did have much patience for him or his litanies. I studied his nephew with curious interest.

He was tall and lean, not a strand of sleek black hair out of place, and his complexion was darker than any of the men in the village. He looked almost Saracen, exotic. His tunic and trousers were made from light brown wool, simple and unadorned, but he wore a purple cloak attached at his shoulder by a magnificent gold brooch. He made his way to the dais.

"Lord Eanwulf," he said, bowing to my father. "I've come to ask for your daughter's hand in marriage."

My quill floated to the floor.

I stomped over to a barrel of strong fruit wine, pried the lid off the cask, grabbed a cup, and ladled myself a good measure.

My father sat on a bench nestled up to the central hearth, his gray-blue eyes regarding me. "You are seventeen and unmarried, Avelynn. It is time you were wed." He straightened the front of his tunic. "Demas of Wareham comes from a respectable and wealthy family. He is a good match for you, and he has offered a generous bride price."

Ten generations ago, when the Goddess ruled the land, a woman was free to choose her mate, even casting him aside if the whim overtook her. But when the Christian church grappled England to her knees, a woman's rights began to vanish. I could own land, and my oath was respected, but decisions such as marriage were at the sole discretion of my father.

I walked back to the fire. Half a dozen small cakes of bread were browning nicely in the raked coals at the far end of the long, narrow pit. The comforting scent infused the air of my small wattle-and-daub cottage. My stomach growled.

"When you married Mother, did her interests affect you? Or could you have sat idly by and seen her married off to someone else just because he was wealthy or respectable? Or because he bribed you with a fat purse?"

"Mind your tongue, child." He grabbed my arm and pulled me to my feet. "You are not too old to be brought to heel."

I barely came to the middle of his chest, but that didn't stop me from testing him.

"God help me, Avelynn, you are as stubborn as your mother." And just like that, with the invocation of her specter into the room, he softened and let go of my arm. "Every day you look more like her."

I didn't think so. Where her hair had been dark and curly, mine resembled my father's locks, though mine trailed to the backs of my knees. I did have her icy-blue eyes and full lips, which were obstinately set at the moment.

"It is for her sake that I do not blister your ass." He dropped his hand from his leather belt.

"But I only want what she had. I want love and a man who will respect and honor me. Why is that not good enough for me? Why do you want me to be unhappy?"

"I do not want you to be unhappy."

"Then why do you insist on pushing me into the arms of a stranger?"

"I have given you leave for more than four years to make a choice. You have refused every suitor's attention. What father has given a daughter so much? You have been greatly spoilt, and I have been interminably patient. But your time is up."

"I will marry only when I'm in love. You cannot tell me who to love."

"You are right, Avelynn. I cannot tell you who to love, but on the other matter you are gravely mistaken, for I can tell you who and when you will marry. And I have decided to accept Demas's suit." He opened the door and stepped outside. "Demas will call later this afternoon. And you, my daughter, will be agreeable and charming."

I stood there frozen, rooted to the ground.

"Next fall, whether you like it or not, you will be married."

The door slammed shut. The veil of bravado drained from my body, and my legs became two limp strands of seaweed. I staggered backward and collapsed onto the nearest bench.

Dear gods, how had this happened? One moment I had proven myself equal to the men at council, even swaying my father's vote. The next, I was as insignificant as an ant underfoot. I stared at the door's weathered planks. Demas wasn't even a Saxon name.

There was a soft rap at the door. I sat up straight and wiped away all evidence of tears with the backs of my hands.

As old and wizened as the wrinkled oak trees he so admired, Bertram was my father's chamberlain, and my most noble tutor. He took one look at my face and nodded, as if affirming something, and then sat on the bench beside me.

"How?" I asked, looking up into his gentle blue eyes. "How could he do this to me?"

"His actions are not meant to be cruel. The Vikings have marched into East Anglia. He only wants you safe."

"Safe." I huffed. England was divided into several powerful kingdoms, each land ruled by its own king, governed by its own laws. Our village, Wedmore, was nestled deep in the heart of the Somerset Levels, on the western coast of Wessex—seven days' ride from East Anglia. "I'm protected here, now. He would never let anyone harm me. Who else could offer me such security?"

"Your father lost your mother, Avelynn, and there was nothing he could do—he couldn't save her, couldn't protect her, and he cannot bear to lose you, too. Your father would see you safely away from Somerset."

"So he wishes to see me shipped off to be someone else's responsibility, someone else's problem?" I started pacing the floor but stopped and stared at the bread. Forgotten, the bottoms had turned to charcoal. I grabbed my iron tongs and retrieved them from further destruction. "My mother died in childbirth. No man can protect against that."

"As far as your father is concerned, it was his seed that made the stillborn child grow in her belly. And therefore, in his mind, it was his fault—he was the cause of her death."

I gaped at him.

He nodded. "A man's pride is a haughty and pretentious thing. While only the gods and Goddess know each man, woman, and child's time and circumstances of death, when it comes to someone he loves, a man will inevitably blame himself for not being able to prevent it."

"But that makes absolutely no sense."

"When it comes to love, pet, very little makes sense."

I sat down and leaned against the wall. My head hit the wooden post with a soft thump. The smoke from the fire swirled and threaded up through the small hole in the roof until it escaped into the ether beyond.

Was the Goddess watching me? "What am I to do, then?" I said, looking beyond the rising smoke. I wasn't sure who I was asking, the Goddess or Bertram.

"Your only choice is to give Demas a chance. Perhaps he will ignite something within you that you have been searching for."

"Perhaps he will ignite a child inside me and kill me, too. Did my father ever think of that?" I knew Bertram had more sense than to answer my challenge. And in the end, what good would it have accomplished? Bertram wasn't the one I was angry at. "I'm sorry."

"It's all right, pet. These things have a way of working themselves out. You'll see." He gave my shoulder a reassuring squeeze and left.

I prayed Bertram was right, but what if he wasn't? I consoled myself with the knowledge that, at the very least, I had until the end of summer to try to change my circumstances. A marriage feast lasted several days. Despite my father's apparent urgency to see me married, he would never hold a wedding feast now, especially with the memory of last year's scarcity still fresh in everyone's mind. A week of feasting for hundreds of people would completely deplete our winter stores. He would wait until the crops and game were plentiful and the weather fine for travel before shuffling me off to Demas. I had time.

I turned to the small window. There was a lot of shouting outside, and the sound of approaching horses thundered through the courtyard. I leaned over the table and opened the shutters. People streamed through the gate. My brother, Edward, ran toward my cottage, his young face flushed.

He burst through the door. "Avelynn, Avelynn, the Vikings are coming!" He ran to me and pulled on my dress.

The last time Vikings had been seen in Somerset was more than twenty years ago, well before we were born. I looked at him for a moment. He was only nine and had a vivid imagination, but as I turned and watched everyone rushing for the hall, my heart quickened. I grabbed my cloak and let him lead me into the throngs of villagers.

TWO

My father and the king's brother, Alfred, walked toward the great fire in the center of the hall and stopped. The light from the blaze cast their shadows back to the door, where they were followed directly by their greatest warriors, leaving a trail of reverence and dominion in their wake. Behind the men, several young women entered. I caught sight of Ealhswith's brilliant smile and coppery hair and waved. She weaved her way through the press of people.

I embraced her. "What are you doing here?"

"I came to see you." She looked around. "Your father was receiving us at the stables when the sentry at the gate told us the whole town was buzzing like a hagridden hornet's nest. What's going on?"

I made to reply, but my father's voice filled the hall.

"What's amiss here?" He spoke to no one in particular but to all assembled.

A man stepped forward. He was covered in dried mud and dust, his cloak frayed and his tunic torn. "I have come with news, my lords," he replied, looking at both my father and Alfred.

"And who are you, friend?" my father asked.

"My name is Aelfgar. I was the armor-bearer for King Edmund, of East Anglia. I have come to spread news of his recent murder at the hands of the pagans." A communal gasp of shock echoed throughout the building. I looked anxiously at my father.

My father lifted his hand for silence, and the room hushed. He walked to the dais at the far end of the hall and took his place at the head table, inviting Alfred to sit beside him. He motioned to my brother and me.

Our position as his children granted us the right to sit on a bench just beneath and off to the right of the dais. We made our way through the crowd and sat down.

My father nodded to Aelfgar. "Pray, continue."

Aelfgar straightened his shoulders and projected his voice loud enough to be heard throughout the entire hall. "Almost a fortnight ago, Ivar Ragnarsson marched with his army into East Anglia. King Edmund offered terms, but when word came that Ubbe Ragnarsson had also come with a fleet to attack by sea, there was little reason for the Viking to negotiate."

Like lightning crackling across the sky, a sense of unease buzzed through the crowd. Ubbe and Ivar were two of the most feared Viking kings. I looked at the smoke rising from the hearth. If I tried hard enough, could I scry in the haze a vision of the entire Heathen Army lying in wait in East Anglia?

Aelfgar cleared his throat and spoke louder. "Our king was seized from his hall and dragged behind the pagan's horse to the forest's edge. He was tied to a tree, stripped, beaten, and whipped until his back was flayed open."

Whispers of outrage quivered through the room.

"Ivar then brought forth his best archers. He told them to make their mark anywhere as long as they did not inflict a fatal wound. Our goodly king was entirely covered with arrows, like the bristles of a hedgehog, yet he still lived."

The chorus of discontent grew louder. My father raised his hand in warning. The grumbling subsided.

"And what of King Edmund?" Alfred asked.

The strength of Aelfgar's voice wavered. "He was at length beheaded. Ivar left the body to rot against the tree and rode off with the king's saintly head."

I cringed. To a warrior, to be buried without one's head was to suffer the worst insult.

"Our country is now in the hands of pirates, our farmland seized, our women raped, our children sold into slavery. Our precious monasteries and churches have been burned—all the monks and nuns brutally killed."

A great uproar swept through the hall.

I chanced a look at Edward, whose blue eyes were as round as trenchers. I told myself firmly, this was naught but a tale of a distant king in another land. Surely we would be safe here. Wessex was the most powerful country in all of England, my father one of the most powerful men.

The Great Heathen Army led by the Ragnarsson brothers Ivar, Ubbe, and Halfdan had been in England for more than four years, but not once had they attempted to overthrow Wessex. Our country was stable, King Aethelred in firm control, our people strong and unified. Wessex presented formidable opposition, which gave me hope, for the Vikings were notorious opportunists. They preyed upon the weak.

When a hoard of Vikings had landed in East Anglia last spring, King Edmund had turned a blind eye, and the Vikings had grown fat and wealthy off his land. It was hardly surprising they came back to take what was clearly already theirs. And Northumbria was just as easy a target. The Vikings simply exploited the fact that Northumbria had been divided by political unrest for years and sallied in without so much as a fistfight—though they were fastidious in their murder of King Aelle. He was blood-eagled, a brutal form of torture in which they cut his back open, took an axe to his ribs, and threw his lungs over his shoulders to mimic the folded wings of an eagle. I shuddered. Perhaps they reserved their harshest cruelty for kings.

The outcry from the villagers rose to a heightened pitch. My father stood. "Silence!"

All fell quickly into acquiescence.

"Does my brother know of this news yet?" Alfred asked.

"Yes, my lord. I passed through Winchester and told the King of Wessex everything. He wishes to see you presently."

"Yes, I imagine."

"Avelynn." My father's eyes lighted on mine. "See that all the women and children in Alfred's retinue are properly housed. We must hold council on this news."

"Surely you'll want me to record the proceedings—"

"Father Plegmund has returned and will see to the documents."

"But—" His expression brooked no compromise. "Of course." I curtsied and made my way around the hall, ushering all the women and children to the door.

I ensured that Ealhswith and my brother, Edward, were in tow and headed outdoors to battle the unseasonably chilly November wind. Those who lived in town drifted back to their homes, while the members of Alfred's household were suitably lodged with families that would show them warmth and hospitality. When there were only the three of us left, we walked along the muddy road back to my cottage. It stood in a cluster of several outbuildings across the courtyard from the great hall.

Despite Bertram's age he belied all appearances and effortlessly caught up with us. Edward, seeing him approach, tried to look as inconspicuous as one of the many fence posts we had just passed.

"Young Edward, I am to take you back to finish your studies," Bertram said.

Edward turned in our direction, looking for some means of rescue. "I don't want to look at books. I want to fight Vikings."

Despite myself, I smiled. Visions of far-off battles and victories played across his innocent face.

Encouraged by my expression, he picked up a stick lying on the ground and, with a flourish, swept it through the air. "I'll slay them all with the point of my sword."

Bertram gave him a sharp rap to his head. "Foolish child. And how, at nine years of age, are you to take on a Viking? They would eat you for breakfast and pick their teeth with your skinny bones. Now, enough dawdling. Say good day to your sister and the lady Ealhswith."

Edward's shoulders drooped, but he gave a noble bow. "Good day, Avelynn. Good day, Lady Ealhswith."

We both dropped into low curtsies. "Good day, Master Edward," we replied in unison.

"Poor lad," Ealhswith remarked, watching Edward get hauled away. "Bertram is a tough teacher."

"He's not so bad. He's just teaching Edward some humility and giving him a healthy dose of common sense."

We turned and walked the last few yards to my cottage. The buildings scattered about the manor were all framed with large timber beams, but the walls varied between vertical planking and wattle-and-daub panels. Wheat thatch covered every roof.

"After you." I held the door open for Ealhswith to enter.

My chambermaid, Nelda, tended the fire. Squat and round with beady eyes and a long nose, she had the unfortunate luck of resembling a shrew. But despite her mousy looks, her smile was always welcoming and sincere. "M'lady." She curtsied.

I returned her smile. "Thank you, Nelda, that will be all for now."

She nodded, dropped her eyes to the floor, and scampered out.

Catching a glimpse of my windblown hair in the polished silver mirror, I tried to smooth the long strands into some semblance of order but gave up and hung our cloaks on hooks by the door.

"What do you think will happen with the Vikings?" I brought down an earthenware jug filled with mead and two fine silver cups from a nearby shelf.

"Honestly, Avelynn, I've heard enough talk of Vikings and their brutality to last me a lifetime. That's all anyone ever talks about." I passed her a full cup, and she took a hearty swig. "But I didn't come all this way to speak of Vikings. Let the men work that out. I came to see my dearest friend."

Ealhswith was always quick to brush off anything serious. And despite my longing to know what was being discussed in council, I had been dismissed from the hall, and there was nothing I could do about it. I tightened the grip on my cup. She was right—the men would handle it.

"Now, how are you?" She rested her cup on her lap.

"Don't ask."

"Whyever not?"

I slumped down beside her. "According to my father, I'm to be married."

For a moment she just stared at me, brown eyes wide. "To whom?"

"His name is Demas. He's Ealhstan's nephew."

"Well, you are seventeen, Avelynn."

If she was trying to make me feel better, she was failing miserably. Only a year older than me, Ealhswith had been married last autumn, a scant few days before her seventeenth birth day. "Maybe so, but I want to choose the man I marry, not be forced into a loveless contract like I see so many women at court endure." I wrapped both hands around the cup, the silver cool against my palms. "My mother knew the moment she saw my father that he was the one for her. I want nothing less."

"I understand your longing, Avelynn. The Lord knows you are

stubborn in your convictions. But you will be an old mare and completely unmarriageable if you continue to insist on this fantasy."

I could feel myself growing hot with indignation. I got up and went to the hearth. Nelda had set up a small iron cauldron on a tripod, and I ladled out two steaming helpings of pottage. I offered Ealhswith a loaf of bread, the blackened bottom cut away and discarded.

When we were younger, marriage had had a luster of promise and excitement about it. Getting married was what all respectable ladies did, and it was something we looked forward to. Ealhswith and I had spent so many days daydreaming and discussing the various details of marriage—what it would be like, what our husbands would be like, what the marriage bed would be like—that we anticipated the event with innocent enthusiasm. Of course, I had my parents to provide daily examples of what a loving marriage looked like. But one day, while accompanying my father on a visit to the smith's cottage, I witnessed the man beating his wife with an iron pan. When she could no longer raise a hand to try to stop him, he dropped the frying pan in the dirt. It landed with a hollow thud. He gestured to my father to step outside to finish their business and left her in a pool of blood—all because she burned his bread.

I looked down at the half-eaten loaf in my hand. A few smudges of black were still evident along the sides. A lump hardened in my throat, and I coughed hard, trying to swallow it.

Ealhswith rose to help me, but I raised my hand. "I'm fine," I said between breaths, my eyes watering fiercely. I had lost my appetite, and set the bread down on the table.

The worst part of that visit was that my father was powerless to stop it. The smith was entitled to beat her, for she was negligent in her duties. And when it was clear that she would never recover from her injuries, he tossed her like refuse and married another.

That was what marriage could look like when it was a match brokered by disinterested parties, and it was not to be my fate.

Despite being arranged, Ealhswith's marriage was a happy one. "You're lucky," I said, and tilted my cup in a toast. "Alfred adores you."

"Yes, he does." She smiled broadly and raised her cup in answer.

"What's it like being married to the king's brother?"

"Well, there are definite advantages. I have an entire household at my command, I'm privy to council secrets, and best of all, I get to tell my dearest friend that I am with child."

"How?!"

Ealhswith laughed so hard pottage came out her nose. She dabbed her face with the sleeve of her gown. "Avelynn, don't you know where babies come from?"

My face flushed in embarrassment. "No. I mean, yes. I know where babies come from."

I knew what went on behind the bed curtain. I had seen plenty of couplings amongst the animals scattered about the village, though I was thoroughly horrified at the notion of a man doing that to me. "I meant, how did this happen? You've only just been married. When is the baby due?"

"My sweet, virtuous friend, I've been married a full year." She set the bowl of pottage down. "But as to how—I can't wait till we can discuss in more graphic detail what the man does with his—"

"Ealhswith, you are positively lewd. I assure you, I have no interest in hearing the finer details, really."

"Oh, Avelynn, how I miss you." She wiped the tears of mirth from her eyes. "To answer your real question, then, the baby is due next spring."

I leapt up and embraced her. "I'm so happy for you. Alfred must be overjoyed."

"Yes, he is, though I told him he was sworn to secrecy until I spoke with you; then he may tell the whole world there will be a new addition to the royal house of Ecgberht!"

A rap at the door interrupted our celebration. "Come in," I answered.

The door opened and Bertram escorted Edward in. "Avelynn, Lady Ealhswith." He nodded in deference. "I'm sorry, Avelynn, but I must leave this willful scamp here with you." He ruffled Edward's sandy mop. "Your father requests my presence in council."

"Of course, Bertram, we'll take good care of him." The "him" in question was already helping himself to a bowl full of pottage and a cake of bread.

"Mind your manners, lad," Bertram reproved.

"Sorry," Edward replied, his mouth full of bread.

"Incorrigible." He closed the door behind him.

"How were your studies, Edward?" Ealhswith asked.

"Boring. I am made to sit down and read the dreadfully dull lives of saints and martyrs over and over again until I can't see straight."

"I suppose what you really want to learn about is Vikings and battle, then?" I asked.

Edward grumbled into his bowl. "I could beat Ivar, you know." He looked up. "One day I will be a great warrior and fight by Father's side, cutting down every Viking that crosses my path."

I walked to the far corner of the room and picked up a practice shield and sword. "Care to back up that claim?" I swept my sword in front of him.

Edward spent a great deal of time in my cottage. Before our mother's death, we had shared it with her. It was only recently that he had started sleeping in the hall with my father's thegns.

He jumped off the bench and grabbed his sword and shield.

"Ealhswith will be the maiden who has been taken captive by the Viking king Ivar," I said.

"Oh, help me. I need someone who is strong and brave to rescue me." Ealhswith swooned into a heap on the bench.

"But they must get past me first," I countered. "For I am Ivar Ragnarsson, and anyone who dares to face me will meet their end at the point of my sword."

"Fear not, fair maiden, I will vanquish Ivar and rescue you."

Edward moved fast and attacked, but I was ready and blocked the blow with my shield. Despite being thin and lanky, he was nonetheless quite strong. We were only playing with practice swords, but a solid whack from the wooden blade would leave quite a bruise if I wasn't careful.

I watched his efforts, genuinely impressed. He lunged and parried, turned and dodged, evading my attacks skillfully, and used his shield when necessary to press forward or block my blows. I smiled sweetly. While he had improved, I could still easily best him, but I was trying to be gracious. I was even giving him a sporting chance by fighting with my left hand. Truth be told, I had many years of battle training on him.

Wulfric, my father's greatest warrior and closest friend, had been my teacher ever since I learned to stand. He impressed upon me to use my natural talents to the utmost advantage. While petite in stature, what I lacked in height, I made up for in speed and agility. However, he was not above telling me to use my feminine curves as a thorough distraction—anything to exploit a man's weakness, he would say. But he also pushed me hard to develop strength, balance, skill, and cunning.

The battle was fierce. Red-faced, Edward's breath came in ragged spurts, and sweat wet his temples. His sodden hair stuck fast to his forehead. It was time for Ivar to be defeated. I waited for the next blow. Spinning on my heels, I pretended to lose my balance and gave Edward just enough time to thrust his sword toward my exposed stomach.

"Surrender!" he yelled in triumph. "One more move and I'll gore you through."

"Never. I will never surrender to a filthy Saxon."

"Then you will die."

He lunged, and I took the blade by locking it against my waist with my elbow. "Oh, great Saxon warrior, you alone have vanquished me." Coughing and sputtering for good effect, I fell dramatically to the ground.

Edward sauntered to Ealhswith. "I have rescued you, lady."

"My hero." She bent over and kissed his cheek.

From my vantage point on the ground, I watched as a crimson flush rose up Edward's neck to his cheeks, painted his nose with a vibrant swath of red, and then traveled outward in earnest, turning the tips of his ears a bright pink.

I stood, wiping all amusement from my face, and extended a strong hand to Edward. "Good battle, sir."

Edward beamed.

The door to my cottage opened suddenly. On impulse, I swung around, holding the point of my wooden sword directly at the Adam's apple of a stranger. I watched in amusement as the little lump bobbed up and down as its owner swallowed hard.

My father stood behind, gripping the door's iron handle like steel, his knuckles turning white. I withdrew my sword and set it against the wall beside me.

"Avelynn, you will remember Demas of Wareham. He has come to call."

THREE

I eyed Demas warily, prepared to make a considerable objection, but the look on my father's face made it clear any attempt would be unwise, so I curtsied with all due ceremony instead.

My father turned to Edward. "Bertram is ready to continue with your studies." He bowed to Ealhswith. "Lady, your husband awaits your company; he wishes to return to Winchester immediately."

I pleaded with my eyes, imploring Ealhswith to tarry, but she stepped to the door and grabbed her cloak. "I'll speak with you soon, Avelynn," she said, looking over Demas. She smiled brilliantly behind his back and retreated out of the cottage.

Wulfric stepped inside, ducking under the lintel, and leaned against the wall, arms and ankles crossed, hungry, predatory eyes fixed on the stranger. With a nod to his master of arms, my father ushered Edward out.

I rushed forward. "Wait. What news of the Vikings?"

"Wessex is safe. For now." My father's eyes held reassurance and trust, and a warning securing the abrupt end to any more discussion.

I nodded and stepped back. He shut the door behind him.

My heart hammered in my chest. Demas and I stared at each

other. Beads of sweat glistened on his broad forehead, threatening to drip into his hazel eyes.

"Would you walk with me, lady?" he asked.

The wind hissed through the thatch. It was cold, and I really had no interest in stepping outside. I pouted a plea to Wulfric, who merely shrugged and stood ready by the door.

"Of course. Let me get my cloak."

It was early evening, and Wedmore was lit softly by the pale autumn sun. There was one main road that flowed from north to south. At the north end was my father's manor, set high atop a hill. The manor, with all its yards and outbuildings, was surrounded by a wooden palisade, and there was only one way in or out—a guarded gate—which we passed through in silence. I waved limply to Leofric, the lone guard on duty.

Wedmore was one of the richest villages in the area. It boasted a tavern, blacksmith, glassmaker, metalworker, potter, and—rather astonishingly—a personable priest. The tavern demarcated the southern end of town, and in between the manor and the tavern, bordering the road on the west and east sides, were two neat rows of houses and merchant cottages. From the central hub of the village, precious hides of farmland stretched out like spokes in a wheel. Surrounding all of that was a wide, deep ditch and a great mound of heaped earth that encircled the ditch like a coiled serpent. Beyond the ditch, my father had also erected a wooden palisade.

I shook my head. My father never did anything in degrees—it was all or nothing with him—which brought my silent musings back to the man beside me.

Demas walked at a brisk pace, his head down, shoulders hunched. The wind whipped up from behind and sent a chill of gooseflesh up my back. I flipped my hood up and over my head and drew the cloak tighter.

Still bathed in thorny silence, we moved deeper into the village.

The press of houses increased, and the air grew thicker with the reek of habitation—running the gamut from the earthy smells of mud, straw, and cooking fires to the more noxious aroma of animal dung. In the spring, the refuse would be transformed into a commodity as valuable as gold, as its nutrients enriched the farmers' fields. Now, however, it sat fermenting in each yard. I could hear the occasional soft bleating of a goat or sheep and the staccato clucks of hungry chickens milling about within the fenced-in yards of each house we passed.

We continued to follow the road through the village, without speaking, our bodies braced against the lashing wind. The tavern appeared up ahead, and I spun around to look back at my father's manor in the distance. We had traversed the entire length of the village. I glared at Demas. He was the one who had come to call, the one asking for my hand in marriage. It was his responsibility to forge the conversation.

He cleared his throat.

Hoarse from inactivity, I thought tartly.

"Things are very primitive in England compared to Francia or Rome," Demas said, surveying the village.

"You've been across to the Continent?" For the first time, I realized he spoke with a considerable accent.

"I was born in England, but grew up in Rome. I was six when I was sent abroad to commence my education. I later became a scribe and worked under the recommendation of Pope Nicholas." The wind gusted, whipping his hair across his face, and he tried to smooth it back behind his ear. "When I received word of my uncle's death, and the large amount of land and holdings I inherited, I returned to claim my birthright."

If he thought wealth impressed me, he would be sorely mistaken. "What was it like in Rome?"

"Buildings tower above the streets. Tile and stone mosaics adorn walls and floors. Stately homes are furnished with the most opulent fabrics; their owners collect luxuries and oddities from around the known world." He shrugged. "It is rich beyond your imaginings—very different from here."

His tone was as cold and callous as the weather, and I sank deeper into my cloak.

"I lived in a small quarter of the papal suburb known as the Schola Saxonum, or Saxon village. It was not luxurious—the buildings were simple structures—but the roads were all lined with stone, unlike the perpetual mud here." He sidestepped a particularly deep and murky puddle. I squelched through it. He looked at me with an air of displeasure but continued.

"When I passed through Francia, I stayed at the king's palace at Verberie-sur-Oise. It was a magnificent stone building with terraced gardens, marble floors, and gilded furniture. Unlike petty kings here, King Charles does not debase himself and sleep on a wooden bench in a meager hall with his men, but sleeps in lavish splendor, in a luxurious chamber."

I narrowed my eyes at him. While I couldn't profess to know about King Charles's relationship with his men, I knew that the "petty king" Aethelred of Wessex slept in his hall with his closest warriors—as did most of the noble lords throughout England. But far from this practice debasing them, it fostered a sense of community and loyalty amongst the men in their household. I knew with absolute certainty that my father's men would die serving him.

"If Rome and Francia were so wonderful, why come back?"

"In Rome, I was a tool under my teacher's scrutiny and control. In England, I am no man's servant."

This definitely didn't warm me to him. I turned to look back at Wulfric, who followed at a respectable distance. The sun was setting, the rooftops behind us edged in fiery red. I should just say good night and be done with this.

"When did your mother die?"

"I beg your pardon?" Not only was the question itself and the careless way in which he stated it the very height of ill manners, but my mother was the last person I wished to discuss with the likes of him.

"I was young when I was sent away. I can't remember my mother. I thought perhaps you might have known her—or maybe your mother did?"

My pique softened a bit. "Who was your mother?"

"The Lady Mildrith of Wareham."

I thought for a moment and smiled. "Yes, I remember her, though I met her only the once." I had been sitting in my mother's cottage, pretending to be interested in a rather boring bit of embroidery while my mother, Lady Mildrith, and the queen shared a cordial cup of wine.

I struggled to bring his mother's image into focus from out of the hazy mists of memory. "She was very beautiful." I stopped for a moment and scrutinized Demas's features, searching for similarity between the two. "She had long brown hair, much lighter and curlier than yours, and beautiful eyes; I remember how they lit up when she laughed." I held his unwavering gaze. "Her cheekbones were high like yours, but her face was rounder, her skin like the inside of an almond: a creamy, milky white."

"How is it you remember her so well having met her only once?"

I resumed our walk. "I remember the scene vividly because it was also the first time I met the queen."

At the age of eight, meeting the queen was akin to encountering a Goddess. I had sat speechless as she bent down to say good-bye to me. My mother chastised me later for my discourteous behavior, but I was so enthralled that I couldn't manage a squeak in response. Time had done nothing to diminish my opinion of her, either—in fact, my respect and admiration grew even more reverential once I learned the whole inspiring story of Queen Judith's life. It was Judith's and my mother's passionate stories that fed my dreams about the future and its wondrous possibilities. I didn't want to settle, and frankly, standing here in the cold talking with Demas reeked of doing just that.

"What Saxon queen was this?" he asked.

"Queen Judith, the daughter of your illustrious King Charles of Francia."

"I've heard of her."

"Then you know the scandal her elopement caused?"

"I know she was once an English queen, and now she is not. My time in Francia didn't involve idle matters of gossip."

"Judith was England's *first* queen," I corrected him. "She was thirteen when she was given to King Aethelwulf of Wessex. But he died two years later, and she was forced to marry his son Aethelbald."

"Blasphemy!"

I glared at him. "It wasn't her choice. Aethelbald wished to possess her, and he did—despite the Church's and country's outcries." I didn't expect a man to understand. "Regardless, the offense lasted only two years and was remedied with Aethelbald's death. Judith was then free to return to Francia, where shortly upon her arrival she met the love of her life, Count Baldwin of Flanders."

I knew my eyes were glazing over. "A chance meeting sparked a love so profound that they professed their undying love right then and there. But when Baldwin asked permission to marry Judith, Charles refused, insisting Baldwin was beneath her station. So she took matters into her own hands, and in an act of great courage, she disobeyed her father's wishes and eloped."

I watched Demas for any betrayal of emotion. Judith's defiance set a bad example for womenkind everywhere. "After having to put up with pretense and propriety, her entire life arranged and bargained, she risked it all and chose love."

"Quite a risk. Not many women have such an opportunity." His gaze sent shivers up my spine. It was not a warm feeling. "Do you think you have a choice, Avelynn?"

"There are always choices."

"I wonder. Does your father share your conviction?"

If it were summer, I would have swallowed a handful of midges, my mouth hung so far open. It was time to leave.

I spied Wulfric and nodded. The sky was darkening. The last vestiges of sunlight quivered above the horizon.

"I'm sorry. That was callous of me." He hung his head in apology.

"This is where I bid you good night, Demas."

"Of course." He bowed. "Good night, Avelynn."

I watched in consternation as he turned, heading farther south along the path.

I lay back onto the down-filled mattress, furs and linen enveloping me, and watched as Nelda raked and banked the fire for the night before climbing into bed. She slept on a raised shelf along the back wall.

"What did you think of Demas?" I asked as she huddled under the furs for warmth.

"He's handsome . . ."

Under my administration for only a year, she was still reluctant to speak her mind. I put a lot of effort into making her feel at ease in my presence. "Yes, he is that." I flopped onto my stomach. "But what was your impression of him—the man, not his appearance?"

"He seemed nice."

"I don't know; I don't trust him."

She giggled. "You do not trust many suitors." Her hand flew to her mouth. "I'm sorry, m'lady. Please forgive me."

"It's all right, Nelda. Don't be afraid to speak your mind. I honor your opinion."

"You are most gracious, m'lady," she replied, her head duly bowed.

I sighed. So much for putting her at ease. "Sleep well, Nelda."

"Good night, m'lady." She blew out the large beeswax candle beside her bed.

I rolled onto my back and gazed at the ceiling. With only the dim light from the raked coals illuminating the room, deep shadows played across the uneven thatch.

I frowned and ran a tired hand over my face. Demas had seemed aloof and arrogant, bordering on hostile, but perhaps I was reading too much into his responses. After all, I had baited him with Judith's story. No man was going to approve of her actions or my fondness for the controversial tale. There were also the circumstances of his reintroduction into Wessex to consider. He was newly landed, his entire life altered, without any family to return to. I might grant him a little leniency. I could hear my father's booming voice accusing me of not giving suitors a chance. I groaned. While my parents had the good fortune of knowing nothing about each other when they met, I had to be guarded.

My father believed in sharing his wealth equally between his children—despite the abysmal failure of that same strategy carried out by his own father before him. Upon his death, my grandfather had entrusted the earldom to be divided equally between his two sons. But this act of good faith resulted in bloodshed and civil war throughout Dorset and Somerset, as jealousy, greed, and distrust raged between my father and his brother, Osric.

The conflict happened before I was born, and King Aethelbald had forced a peace between my father and uncle, insisting the terms of my grandfather's will and testament be upheld. I had never met Osric. He was not welcome in our home, and my father never spoke of him. Other than that he was the Earl of Dorset, I knew nothing about him.

But rather than deter my father, the conflict left him intent on overcoming the specter of the past. He was firm on his decision—Edward and I would both inherit an impressive amount of land and holdings upon his death. As part of this legacy, I was to receive Wedmore, and many suitors were eager to snatch a piece of the pie. I was merely a means to an end in their eyes.

I burrowed deeper into my cocoon of covers and closed my eyes, brushing my foot back and forth, a balm to my busy mind. What was Demas after? My father mentioned a generous bride-price. If Demas had wealth and status, he would make an attractive groom to any eager bride. Why pick me? There were plenty of unmarried women in England.

My thoughts reached out to one of my locked chests, and the silk pouch containing my divining bones concealed within. I wondered what the Goddess thought of all this.

FOUR

"Will you be long away, m'lady?"

At the stables, Marma waited for me, saddled and ready. A young page held her reins.

I smiled, taking the lead from his competent hands. "No, Bertram and I will be back by nightfall."

He nodded and walked back inside. The sounds of a rake grating against the hard-packed earth floor drifted toward the door along with clouds of hay and dust.

An impatient nose nudged my satchel. "Good morning, beautiful." I stroked Marma's strong, smooth neck. "Looking for a treat, are you?"

She snorted and I laughed, taking out one of the apples I had tucked away in my bag. I held it in my palm. Her soft lips parted and the juicy treat disappeared. I had been delighted when my father presented her to me on my seventeenth birth day. She was all white, with veins and flecks of gray, and I had called her Marma because she reminded me of the marbling in stone.

I checked the saddle's bindings, tightened the breast girth, and secured my sword to the side of the worn leather. I usually wore my hair braided when I rode, and I made sure its length was secured within the wolf-pelt cloak so it wouldn't get drenched. The morning had started dry, but dark shadows rolled overhead, buoyed by a sharp, damp wind. By the time Bertram arrived, a cold sleet had started to fall.

Enveloped in a mantle of white ermine, he stood out in stark contrast to the black gelding he rode.

"Thank you for accompanying me," I said.

"And miss the opportunity to ride in such fine weather? Perish the thought." He drew his hood lower over his forehead.

I nudged Marma ahead. There wasn't a lot of room to ride two abreast along the narrow dirt pathways that snaked through the manor, and Bertram settled comfortably behind. The damp weather would no doubt slow our course as dusty roads turned into troughs of mud, but it was only a two-hour ride to the edge of the swamps, and I was confident we would make Avalon in fair time.

Avalon was an enigmatic place, an island suspended between the lands of the living and the dead. King Arthur had spent his last few days on Earth there, shrouded in the shadowy mists of time and legend, hidden for centuries in the secret fae worlds of the Somerset Levels. From this strange, ethereal place, he would emerge triumphant once again to lead the people to victory and peace. At least, that is what the common folk believed—tenaciously. On some official map somewhere, my grandfather had labeled the island Athelney, but I preferred the mystery that surrounded the name and concept of Avalon better.

Even my father recognized there were mystical forces at work on the island and had presented the land to my mother as a wedding gift. She recognized its power immediately and was enchanted by both the sacredness of Avalon and the thoughtfulness of the gift. She had often taken me there. It was one of the few places safe enough to keep our religion alive. With England converted to

Christianity several generations earlier, the ancient Goddess religions, along with other forms of paganism, were mostly extinct and vehemently condemned by the Church. Some still believed and practiced the old ways, leaving talismans and offerings around sacred pools and knolls, but they were careful to keep their beliefs private. My mother wasn't born in England. She came from a powerful tribe in Ireland, where the Goddess was still reverently worshipped.

I smiled fondly. Bertram was the last of his kind in England, a mystical druid pretending to be a pious Christian.

We tethered the horses just inside the thickening growth and went the remainder of the journey on foot. It was surrounded by bog and marsh, and one had to traverse hidden pathways to arrive safely at Avalon's high and dry center. As the tide receded, platforms and passageways of stone materialized from under several yards of water. Only Bertram, my father, and I knew the way. Of course, my mother had known Avalon's secrets as well—it was also where she was buried.

We arrived a little before noon. That didn't give us a lot of time—the interval between high and low tide was only six hours.

Bertram wandered off in search of interesting tidbits of flora and fauna to collect, and I continued on to the heart of the matter. The island was heavily wooded, with a small clearing in the middle, marked by a solitary megalithic stone. That was where I was headed. I needed to speak with my mother.

For a moment, I stood and stared at the mottled gray surface of the stone, afraid I would glimpse an image of the beautiful woman buried in the dirt beneath my feet. No vision came, and I knelt in the soft grass. Reaching into my satchel, I withdrew my last apple. I placed the offering at the base of the stone to appease any restless members of the Otherworld and waited. The energy of the clearing shifted: a nod in acceptance of my gift. A token given in earnest was rarely rejected, and Avalon—the name itself meaning apple—was rife with apple trees. I felt the offering was fitting.

I removed my sword and knife and leaned them against a large ash tree. Implements of violence were not permitted within the ritual space.

I circled the grave, pouring powdered chalk from a small pouch, and then crossed the circle twice, dividing it into four quarters. I sat in the center.

I rested my forehead on the cold stone and took several deep breaths. I smelled the dampness of the earth, the fetid decay of death, and the sharp resin of rebirth that surrounded me in the swamp. The drizzle had stopped, and hazy rays of sunlight broke through the gray miasma hovering over the land. I could feel the sun's distant warmth spilling over my cloak.

With my finger, I traced the Ogham symbols carved into the smooth stone. I missed my mother with an ache that left me feeling segmented. She would have talked reason into my father, would have made him soften with her tenderness.

Out beyond the dense trees and boundless marsh lay the fury of the ocean that had brought my mother and father together. She had been traveling by ship from Ireland to Wales as a political pawn in an arranged marriage. She never told us the reasons for the arrangement or what benefit this marriage was to bestow upon her people, but in the end that contract was never fulfilled. A ferocious storm ravaged the seas, pitting the small boat against monstrous waves, pelting them with shocking gales and torrential rain. Many on board were lost, dragged down into the ocean's icy depths. In addition to Bertram and my mother, only a handful of warriors and a few servants survived, and the light of day found them marooned off the coast of England, stuck deep in thick mud when the tide withdrew.

My father, hunting with several of his men, was also caught off guard by the storm. Rather than return home, they were forced to wait out the storm inland. When morning broke, they rode out to the shore to see what damage the storm had caused. Great was their surprise when they saw a ship stranded without water and a beautiful woman standing on the bow.

So enamored was my father that he ordered his men to cut down a hundred trees and split them into planks so he could walk across the silt. Once he reached the ship, he dropped to one knee and begged for her hand in marriage. Besotted at once, she didn't hesitate. They were inseparable until the day she died.

Was it so hard to see why I wanted that kind of love too? I thought my father understood. Why was he pushing me away from something so wonderful?

I closed my eyes. "What am I to do, Mama?"

I listened, waiting for an answer or a sign to appear. I heard the abundant calls of birds, the soft rustling of a small animal rooting through the bushes nearby, but nothing sounded amiss. I felt the warmth of the sun on my head, a cold breeze nipping at my cheeks and nose, but I did not hear or sense any answer.

I opened my satchel and pulled out an earthen bowl. From a small stoppered urn, I poured in enough water until it quivered on the edge of spilling. I made a tinder nest of dried fungus and grass and struck the flint with the steel fire lighter until a spark teased the kindling and it began to smoke. Cradling the nest, I blew on it softly until the glowing ember surged and caught the grass and a hungry flame emerged. I placed the nest carefully under a handful of small twigs. I reached my arms to the sky and offered a silent invocation to the Goddess and my mother's spirit. I added an extra appeal to Thunor, the Saxon thunder god, Woden, the Saxon god of knowledge and prophecy, and Jesus, the Christian god, for good measure.

My mother and Bertram followed the Goddess, but since living in England, they readily adopted the English gods into their pantheon. As warrior and chieftain, my father—while a Christian—still held a soft spot for the powerful sky god, Thunor, so it was not uncommon to find the gods fraternizing with the Goddess in their worship and rituals.

I appealed to them all now. I needed to know what my future held and if I would be forced to marry Demas. I wanted to know if I would ever fall in love. And for these insights I needed the last item from my satchel—my divining bones. I opened the white silk pouch and tipped the small bleached bones onto the ground before me.

They fell into almost two distinct piles, with one small fragment traversing the void in between—a choice perhaps between two paths, or two sides. Each bone had an Ogham symbol carved into its surface. Huath/Hawthorn was turned upward—a test ahead, as was Tinne/Holly—attack or defense. Muin/Vine was also prominent—wealth . . . my inheritance, my legacy might be in jeopardy. I frowned. The most worrisome symbol was Ioho/Yew, for it stood for destruction and transformation.

I didn't like the message. A test or challenge ahead—where I was either being attacked or must become defensive. My legacy, my wealth, and my status might be threatened. And before transformation and rebirth, there would be destruction. I leaned over my earthen bowl and looked upon the water's reflective surface, hoping a clarifying image would appear.

A ruckus of thrashing and screeching emerged from behind me. I turned. A magnificent raven burst from a large ash tree, its wing injured as it tried to fly overhead. I watched its struggle in fascination, and several large droplets of blood fell onto my face. Startled, I blinked and jerked back as the warm moisture ran down my cheek.

The ground shook. A loud crash brought my attention back to

my mother's grave. A boar as large as two grown men barreled out of the woods, huge tusks extended from its long snout. I imagined those vicious points goring me through, and my hands grew clammy with sweat.

I held very still and tried to merge with the inanimate stone that hid most of my body from view. I prayed the beast would not see or hear me. My breath, shallow and quick, sent small puffs of mist billowing into the air above me. I became aware of each sound my body made—the rasping sound of my breaths, my heart hammering in my ears, the thundering of blood rushing through my veins— as my body prepared to either fight or flee. I prayed to the gods neither would be necessary, as the boar could easily outrun me if I tried to flee, and with my sword out of reach, there wasn't much opportunity to be victorious in a fight, either.

Cool perspiration prickled along my spine and pooled within my armpits and beneath my breasts. I winced. If the smell of the fire didn't reveal me, then the smell of my fear would.

The boar pawed at the ground and snorted as it sensed another presence in the clearing. It turned its beady eyes in my direction. I swallowed the bile rising in my throat.

The raven reappeared, careening out of the sky. With its claws exposed, it took a daring swipe at the pig. Distracted from me and infuriated with the raven, the boar gave chase, vaulting back into the woods in pursuit of the great black bird.

Seeing the angry twitching tail disappear into the undergrowth, I wasted no time and scrambled to my feet. I grabbed my sword and knife, stomped on the few remaining embers of the fire, and threw all my paraphernalia back into my bag, pausing only long enough to register a droplet of blood on the center bone.

I paced back and forth for what seemed like an eternity before Bertram appeared as if refreshed from a lovely afternoon stroll. He looked at me and at the marks around the clearing, where the boar's tracks were still fresh in the newly turned-up earth, and back as he surveyed the drops of dried blood clinging to my face.

"It's time to go," I said, grabbing his arm.

"Are you going to tell me what happened?"

I explained the events summarily, my feet keeping their brisk press forward.

He looked around at the blur of passing reeds and rushes. "You can let go of me now. I think we're safe."

With one final glance back over my shoulder, I released him and slowed my pace. "What do you think?"

His bushy white eyebrows meshed together in the center of his forehead. "What direction did the bird come from?"

"East."

"And the boar?"

"West; it came out of the woods in front of me."

We walked in pregnant silence for several more yards. Bertram's eyes focused on something in the distance. His voice startled me when he continued. "War is coming."

Sweat slicked my palms. "Why was I marked with blood?"

"That could be a very bad omen."

War, blood, death, and destruction—these were not things to look forward to in my future. I grasped for something—anything else—to take away from the day's events. Was it possible the vision meant something else? I was, after all, fine. The raven had saved me.

A familiar of the fourfold Goddess, the raven was a divine messenger. But why had the raven itself challenged the boar, an animal associated with Danu, Earth Mother and governess of fertility and marriage?

"I had also asked about Demas and love. Perhaps the vignette was to signify that if I give Demas one more chance, he may prove worthy of my heart and offer me security and protection . . . a way to avoid calamity—the boar—in my future?"

Bertram rubbed his snowy beard between his fingers. "It is possible, but we must proceed cautiously."

I nodded. A vision could have several meanings, but it was ultimately up to a priestess to decipher the signs and omens. I was far too eager to view the vision in a positive light rather than a negative one. Love, safety, protection. These messages were infinitely better than interpreting the situation as an imminent sign of bloodshed.

FIVE

As Ealhswith's friend, I was expected to attend the Christmas festivities, but Edward was too young to accompany Father and his thegns. With every muscle in my body protesting, I envied him his youth and freedom. The Nativity called for three masses—one at midnight, one in the morning, and still another again late in the afternoon. It was just after dawn, and I had endured one mass already.

I had been to Winchester several times, but the church itself never ceased to impress me. The building was made of hewn stone recycled from old Roman buildings and stood two stories high, the second story supported by arches and large square columns. The nave was long and narrow, the ceiling of which was painted in brilliant colors. Along the two longest walls, narrow windows sparkled with glass, filtering the weak winter sun. Each column, each polished surface was either etched or painted. Staircases led to private oratories upstairs with altars in honor of the Blessed Virgin Mary, St. Michael, St. John the Baptist, and other holy apostles and martyrs. The wonderful thing about each of those private altars was the addition of the blessed gift of a bench to sit upon whilst one prayed. In the wide-open nave, not a bench was in sight, and parishioners had to stand throughout each successive mass.

I yawned, eyes watering, and lolled my neck in an effort to revive my wavering attention. I had thought Demas's late uncle, Ealhstan, was verbose and rambling, but this perception was thoroughly supplanted upon meeting the Bishop of Winchester, Ealhferth.

The bishop was a corpulent little man, with piercing eyes far too small for his bulbous face. And since he spent the entire day lecturing on and ranting about humanity's immorality, he was perpetually red-faced. He reminded me of a crazed boar in rutting season. The short, sparse, and rather prickly shoots of bristles of his tonsure and beard did little to assuage the image.

I massaged the back of my neck, trying to work the strain out of the tight muscles. My back and legs ached from the interminable standing, and I still had another mass to go. I chanced a discreet look around the nave of the Minster. Everyone was wilted. Even King Aethelred's shoulders were slumped in defeat. I shifted my weight onto my other leg and tried to stretch, earning a reproving glance from my father. I slumped back into dignified piousness.

I returned my attention to the pulpit. Ealhferth was having quite a rant. "The Vikings have come as punishment for England's sins. Repent. Repent, before the plague of heathens descends upon us!" On and on it went, spittle flying in a continuous stream onto the poor parishioners in the front rows. "It's been four years since the Great Heathen Army descended upon this land. Hundreds of longships turned our horizon black as night, carrying the spawn of Satan forever to our shores. Northumbria has fallen, their lecherous ways leading them into the hands of the Devil. East Anglia has traded their virtuous robes for the cloths of sloth and greed, their saintly king tortured and defiled!"

I rolled my eyes. All the panic over King Edmund's death had come to nothing. The Vikings seemed content to settle down in East Anglia, marshaling out farmland and finding wives amongst Saxon women. They hadn't made any threats toward Wessex, and while spying eyes always kept wary watch, life had slowly returned to normal.

Ealhferth pointed a stubby, plump finger at his flock. "Wessex, your faith is being tested. Repent your sins, or feel the wrath of God!"

I groaned, earning glances from a group of ladies in front of me and a murderous scowl from my father. I cast my eyes downward, affecting pious contrition. The Vikings were not God's punishment for society's or man's weak, materialistic, and lascivious constitutions. They were not sent in retribution for not giving enough benefaction to the church, nor did they come as retaliation for celebrating and feasting for twelve nights at Christmastide, though the bishops would like everyone to believe that. The church's edict was clear—too much of earthly pleasures and God would smite you where you stood. Or better yet, he'd send the Vikings to do it for him.

The mass finally ended and everyone filed out of the Minster. I breathed in great gulps of cold, crisp air. While beautiful, Christian churches were suffocating. Unlike the Goddess faith—which celebrated the vastness of nature, in the vastness of nature— Christianity threw its followers into small, cramped churches and stuffed them together like rows of gluttonous piglets fighting for a teat. I was grateful to be back out in the open, despite the substantial nip in the air.

The morning was sullen and gray. A few flurries scurried about in the brisk north wind. November had been just a prelude of what this winter had in store for Wessex. It was, by far, the coldest December I could recall.

I caught sight of Demas walking out of the nave, and I smoothed down the front of my kirtle. I hadn't seen him since our first abysmal meeting a month ago, and I wanted to make a good impression.

I had spent a great deal of time fussing in front of my mirror earlier. I had picked a soft blue kirtle that suited the paleness of my skin and paired it with a deep indigo cloak that set the blue of my eyes sparkling. Near each temple, I had braided a length of hair, tying them together near the nape of my neck with a silk ribbon that matched the pale blue of my dress. Turning and turning, I had tried to gauge the effect from every possible angle. I felt confident that I presented an acceptable image.

I dropped into a low curtsy. "Good morning, Demas."

"Lady." He waved his hand in dismissal and continued on his way to the stables.

Taken aback, I stared at his departing form until he disappeared into the throng of men pressed near the king's stables. Wulfstan, the Earl of Devon's son, approached me and bowed gracefully.

"Lady Avelynn, you look enchanting this morning." Honeyblond hair hung in soft curls to his collarbone, framing high cheekbones and deep brown eyes.

"Thank you, sir."

"I hear you're betrothed." He looked in the direction of my intended.

"Yes, I hear that too," I said, following his gaze.

"I wish it was I who had stolen your heart."

I smiled weakly. He had been one of the most charming and handsome suitors to try to win my hand, and I enjoyed his company . . . but I never felt that spark of wanting, that fire of passion that I so desperately craved.

Reflecting on that terse exchange with Demas, I looked somberly at Wulfstan and wondered if my passionate longings and stubbornness were not going to be my undoing.

He extended his arm, and we walked together toward the stables. The air was alive with anticipation. A hunt had been planned for immediately following the mass. The king; his brother, Alfred; my father; Demas; and all of the noblemen of the court were to take part. There was organized chaos all around as men, stable lads, stewards, and pages readied horses, spears, and swords.

"How goes the news of the hunt this morning?" I asked.

"Superbly," Wulfstan replied. "Just before mass, the huntsman was scouting with his lymer, and the dog sniffed out a most noble quarry. A buck has been found, and the huntsman assured the king it was a hart of ten." He looked south into the wall of trees that bordered the courtyard, as if trying to discern the accuracy of the statement for himself. "A deer at this time of year is a great prize for any hunting party, but a mature one with ten points on his antlers . . ." He whistled. "That is game they will tell tales about for generations to come."

I suppressed a smile. While a hart of ten was magnificent, it wasn't rare or impossible. My father had caught one just this spring. But given the general buzz of excitement coursing through the crowd, I gathered all the men considered it a worthy challenge.

The women were adding their own distinctive touch to the frenzied energy, cooing and flirting until the atmosphere around the royal manor felt more like a Saturnalia festival than a pious Christian one. I caught a glance of Ealhswith doting on Alfred as he made ready to mount his horse. He wore a stunning red jacket with gold embroidery along the edges and a mantle made from the pelt of a bear. He laughed at something Ealhswith said, kissed her cheek, and then swung up into the saddle. He swept her a deep bow and took his place at his brother's side.

The Ecgberht brothers made quite an attractive pair. Aethelred was taller than Alfred, and wore his auburn hair slightly longer, but they both had the same warm brown eyes, slender face, and rosy mouth.

All around me, women were giving trinkets of good luck to the men of their choice. I had nothing to give Wulfstan, so I just smiled. "Good luck," I said as he pulled himself up onto his horse.

He flashed a brilliant smile. I kicked myself again for rejecting him. "Good day, Lady Avelynn," he replied, and spurred his horse into action, trotting away from me.

Demas was mounted next to my father. They were laughing. I scowled. Maybe they should be the ones getting married. I set my hands on my hips and brewed with righteous ire. A pair of familiar arms embraced me from behind. My annoyance melted immediately. I turned and grabbed the gloved hands in mine.

"How are you, my friend?" I asked.

Ealhswith always looked radiant. But now she positively glowed. Her skin was luminous, and her straight coppery hair, brushed to a brilliant sheen, contrasted vibrantly with the rich green of her dress. Unlike other married women, Ealhswith didn't hide her hair under a wimple. The only reason she wasn't reprimanded by the bishops was because Alfred liked her hair unbound. She had been right—being married to the brother of the king had its advantages. But not every custom was negotiable, and she did have to make one sacrifice. The church mandated that she cut her hair to the middle of her back, so all would know she was no longer a virgin.

"I'm much better than you, I think." She inclined her head in Demas's direction.

"Humph."

"I see." She grabbed my hand and pulled me to the main hall.

The huntsman blew his horn, and all the women bustled back away from the stables. The tethered hounds were released, and a host of fur and teeth started off in fervent pursuit of the quarry, barking and yapping in earnest. The huntsman and his dogs were followed by all the king's men, as they rallied with raucous shouts of anticipation, speeding off in search of their prey, a flurry of hooves kicking up turf and dirt in their wake.

King Aethelred's wife, Wulfrida, was rounding up the women, escorting them back to her chambers, where we were to await our heroes' faithful return from their quest. Ealhswith steered me in the opposite direction, and we ducked into the great hall.

The hall was decorated with fresh evergreen boughs and beautiful wall-clothing. The head table was at the east end on a raised dais, and there was a large space in front that would serve as the stage for this afternoon's entertainment. It sat empty save for a single lyre leaning against a stool in the corner. The feasting tables were placed around the room, several rows deep, so that they encircled the central hearth where the great Yule log burned steadily. Each table was adorned with rich, colorful linen and crowned with a magnificent centerpiece of wooden birds. Carved in a dizzying array of shapes and sizes, the birds were arranged in nests of dried and fresh greenery. A life-size swan embellished the head table, its stately presence peering over the table and stage below. Bread trenchers marked each man's place. Glass and bone drinking horns rested beside each trencher, and oil lamps and candle trees lit up the hall until it shimmered with elegance and finery.

"Wulfrida outdid herself."

"She's been preparing for the three-day feast for the past three months," Ealhswith said, and steered me away from the head table to one of the simple benches at the farthest end of the hall. These would be the seats for the lower classes and lesser thegns.

She yanked me down onto the bench. "What's going on with you? Last we spoke, you were determined to get out of this betrothal, yet today your father announces your engagement at court?"

"My father has been impossible. Marriage is his decision, not mine. However, I did come here willing to give Demas another chance."

She narrowed her eyes at me. "Really?"

I shrugged. "I received a vision and decided to proceed with the courtship."

"A vision?" She dropped her voice into a whisper. "Avelynn, you know I accept your faith, but there are others here, despite your father's position at court, who would see you hang for such talk."

I nodded, remembering my surroundings. "Regardless, while I may be willing to give Demas another opportunity to captivate me, I haven't agreed to marriage."

The look in Ealhswith's eyes told me she doubted I'd have a choice, but I chose to ignore it.

"Now, enough about me." I straightened, eyeing her slim figure. "How is my goddaughter ever to get big and strong if you don't get big and fat?"

She was reluctant to let the topic go, but a discussion about her unborn child proved too tempting to ignore. After a few moments of pleasant chatter, our hiding place was discovered by an austere and rather disagreeable matron charged with the task of commandeering us, and we were marshaled to Wulfrida's chambers to join the rest of the women.

Wessex was a large territory. It would take a stealthy messenger seven days to navigate from one end to the other. Feast days were an opportune time to catch up on the country's affairs, since noblemen and their wives attended from all over the region.

Stifling an epidemic of yawns, I learned who had given birth in the past year, who had died, how the harvest had fared in each part of the country, and how easily the taxes had been levied. It was a great relief to hear the huntsman's horn, heralding the men's victorious return from the hunt. Women scurried and bustled to grab cloaks and gloves, and the men thundered to the stables.

Under the watchful eyes of the stable marshal, grooms quickly whisked the horses away to be washed down and fed. Pages scurried to the kitchens. Two strapping young lads carried the prize to one of the cooking pits, the stag hanging upside down, its legs tied to spear shafts. Everyone else converged on the hall for supper.

Weapons were not permitted inside, save a small knife, which would serve as the only eating utensil. Spears, swords, shields, and axes were all left leaning against the outer walls, several armed sentries in charge of their keep. The atmosphere was jovial, everyone reveling in tales from the hunt as we followed the king inside. Cleaning bowls had been set up, and servants stood by with fresh towels so we could wash our hands before sitting.

King Aethelred and Wulfrida sat at the head table, Alfred and Ealhswith to their left, Bishop Ealhferth to their right. Our party sat nearest the hearth, and I was maneuvered diplomatically so that Demas sat immediately to my right, with my father, and Ealdorman Aethelwulf of Berkshire and his wife, Cyneburga, sitting in succession next to him.

Aethelred stood. "Welcome, friends." He spread his arms to encompass the entire hall. "May God keep you safe, healthy, and well this Christmastide and through the year to come." This oration was met with a resounding clamor as men pounded their fists on the tables, shouting, "Hear, hear!" or "May God keep you well, my lord!" or some such other apposite discourse.

Aethelred picked up his drinking horn and waited as Wulfrida came round the front of the table. She curtsied to her lord and husband and fetched a pitcher of wine from a waiting steward. She poured the rich garnet liquid into his drinking horn and he raised it high, waiting.

Ealhswith joined Wulfrida, and together with several pages,

they went from table to table filling drinking horns, each man standing in turn, holding his horn high in response.

The two women were complete opposites. Wulfrida was older, more matronly, with an austere countenance, her long black hair bound in volutes and hidden under her wimple. Ealhswith, on the other hand, chatted animatedly with the men she served, her hair flowing softly down her back.

With the first round of cups filled, Wulfrida and Ealhswith returned to the head table.

"Waeshael! Be well!" Aethelred hailed, and downed the contents of his horn.

"Drinkhael! Drink and be well!" each man replied. Horns lifted in unison and men swallowed, not stopping until they finished every last drop.

Once the toasting was completed, servants streamed in with plates of delicacies. The first course was an assortment of vegetables, including carrots, beans, and burdock flavored with imported ginger and wrapped in thin pastry. Next followed skewers of beef and pork spiced with pepper.

We had sweet courses of figs and grapes, honey and almond cakes, and apple-sloe purée served over cheesecake. From land and sea, we were served oysters, mussels, and lobster in a rich butter sauce; filets of trout and perch; and a pottage of roasted duck and vegetables. There were soft cheeses and bread and a collection of boiled eggs in a nest of shredded cabbage. A cooked plover—plumage reapplied—sat in the center.

Wine, ale, and mead flowed continuously. While I did a valiant job, I was only nibbling a taste of each offering after the fourth course. Demas and my father, however, did not hold back in the least. I couldn't tell how Aethelwulf's wife, Cyneburga, was making out, but Aethelwulf's hand kept reaching out for more as platters were brought past the table.

Conversation was at first limited to oohs and ahs—remarkably quiet for a gathering of a hundred people—but as the drink continued to flow, the conversations grew louder and more boisterous, and arms and hands gesticulated copiously.

After the first few courses, I tried to engage Demas in conversation. He sat with his back to me, his attention focused on whatever my father was saying.

Spying a page carrying a tray of honey cakes, I gestured him closer and grabbed two of the sticky treats. I placed one of the sweets on Demas's trencher.

He caught the movement out of the corner of his eye and turned.

"How did you find the hunt?" I asked him.

"Well."

"Did you get a chance to speak with the king?"

"Your father introduced me, yes." His body was still turned away from me.

"Did you have hunts in Rome?"

"No."

My father looked in our direction and smiled his approval of our engaging discourse.

I frowned.

"Is that all?" he asked.

"No."

It was his turn to frown.

"Is there any particular reason you're ignoring me?"

"Your father is more interesting." A twitch at the corner of his mouth lifted into a smirk.

"I am to be your wife, not him."

"Wives are meant to be silent and obedient. A lesson you would be wise to learn." He laid a hand on his belt and turned back to my father.

I prodded him on the shoulder. "Are you threatening me?" My

voice dropped to a hissing whisper. The man's audacity knew no bounds.

"I am merely reminding you of your place." He looked around. "Though perhaps we could continue this conversation later."

I followed his gaze. King Aethelred was watching us. I bit my tongue and bowed my head. He nodded and turned his attention to Alfred.

Sufficiently silenced, I vowed to confront Demas after the feast. If he thought he could speak to me, or treat me in such a dismissive manner, he was gravely mistaken. I was beginning to have my doubts as to whether or not the vision had anything to do with his pompous ass.

Unable to address the issue for the moment, I distracted myself, and my temper, by gazing around the room. Placated with liberal amounts of alcohol, everyone else seemed to be having a good time. Even Bishop Ealhferth's smile was jubilant. His paunch bulged under his long white alb, the fringed edges of his stole lying almost flat on the convex of his stomach. Ealhswith would occasionally catch my eye and gesture to Demas, but I shook my head, earning a reproving glower in response.

When the procession of foodstuffs was completed, the stage was set for our entertainment. Jesters and actors caroused and cajoled with great comedy, enacting skits of romantic mishaps and calamity, or juggling and dropping balls, sticks, and rings. Musicians proffered bagpipes, trumpets, flutes, and drums, and entertainers jumped and tumbled through the open space. Finally, the gleeman appeared with his lyre, while the scop settled himself on his stool, ready to enthrall the crowd with his esteemed storytelling.

It was always the same. Each story portrayed a brave and virtuous man who vanquished his enemies with skill and valor. He was able to do all this because he possessed the highest caliber of virtues and values of any man in the land, earning God's favor in all actions. The names, places, and dates were different, of course, customized to each wealthy benefactor, but the plotline was generally the same. In this instance, the stories praised our mighty king, Aethelred.

After the unapologetic adulation, the scop broke into well-known songs and poems of love, loss, and daring. By the time he finished, the entire hall sang along with him. A great cheer erupted when he finally bowed in closing.

With the celebrations winding down, we all headed back into the Minster for mass. Fortunately, the amount of wine Ealhferth had consumed softened his disposition. So, rather than dispense his usual threatening rhetoric, he was instead disposed to describe the beneficence of the Lord, recounting His loving, helpful ways and the manner in which we all could show Him our eternal love and gratitude. It was a much gentler mass and—thank the loving, kind, beneficent God—a much briefer one too.

The mass ended, and the men returned to the hall to continue the celebrations where they'd left off. Only this time, the plentiful drink was to be augmented with games of strategy, dice, and heavy gambling. The women were to bypass these baser aspects of the feast and, without much ado, were ushered to the guest building to pass the remainder of the evening in innocent slumber. I, however, was not willing to lay things to bed for the night.

I marched up to Demas, whose lips were miraculously not attached to my father's ass, and pulled hard on his shoulder. "A word, sir."

He looked at me and frowned. "Walk with me a moment."

I matched his pace, walking in silence until we were out of earshot of any other soul. Torches flickered around the manor, and he stopped just within the reach of their pale light.

"I had hoped to spare you this discomfort, but your insistence has made that impossible." He pulled his cloak tightly around his shoulders. "I sought marriage with you because it is what my uncle wanted. He felt our marriage would make a strong and powerful alliance. With the land bequeathed to you after your father's death, and the land I now hold, you would be one of the most powerful women in Wessex. You would oversee all responsibilities of the manor, its servants and its function. But," he said, glaring down at me, "you would be wise to remember your place. Your father has done you a great disservice by allowing you such a long lead. I will not tolerate your disrespect or your willfulness. You are to speak only when spoken to and do as you are bid."

Metallic heat burned in my cheeks, and I drew in a slow, steady breath. "I will not be treated like a slave. There are men here tonight who would give me their very heart and soul if I agreed to marry them. Why should I settle for less?"

"Those men you speak of, lady, tried to woo you, and look where it got them." He patted my head absently. "I'm not here to fill your mind with fanciful illusions. I'm here to make a profitable transaction. You can either accept my suit graciously, and with it a place of extravagance and enviable nobility, or content yourself with taking slop out to my pigs."

"I will do no such thing."

"You won't have a choice."

He turned to walk away, but hesitated and looked back. "After hearing tales of your capriciousness, I thought it was you who I needed to woo, but I quickly realized I was pursuing the wrong person." He smiled. "I pledged my allegiance to the master who truly controls your strings, little puppet, and whether you like it or not, your father will see us married."

SIX

———

Riding with a handful of my father's thegns and several pages, we made our way home, the Christmas festivities and Winchester a half day's ride behind us. I had asked Wulfric to maintain a pace several lengths behind so I could speak to my father alone.

"He's using me," I cried. "He'll toss me aside and steal your title and wealth."

"He will have a hard time at it, since I am still very much alive and breathing." My father looked sourly at me. His breath, plentiful and vigorous, puffed into great clouds of white in the frigid air.

"I beg you, release me from this betrothal."

"My decision is final."

"You're casting me into the lion's den, to be ravaged and ripped apart. Nothing will be left of me when he's finished taking what he wants."

"You are overreacting."

"No, I'm not. He's rude and arrogant. He threatened me."

"I saw the two of you speaking at the feast. He was nothing if not courteous and charming."

"Around you he is the shining, dutiful hero, but with me, he is the Devil incarnate. You've wronged me, Father, insisting on this farce of a marriage."

"Enough. You will marry Demas during the harvest festival and not revisit this conversation again. If you so much as mention it in my hearing, I will send you to Glastonbury to spend the next eight months of your betrothal in pious contemplation with the nuns. Am I understood?"

I gritted my teeth and nodded. I wanted to scream. He had raised me as equal to Edward, led me to believe there was nothing I could not accomplish, nothing I could not do. He molded me, instructed me, allowed me to entertain the fanciful idea that one day I, his daughter and eldest child, would take over the running of the estate. My mother had encouraged it, fostered it, and my father had agreed. He seemed to take great pride in my ability to read and write, in my sense of fairness and reason. But it was all a lie. He never had any intention of giving me the responsibility, the chance. That more than anything else hurt beyond all measure.

I spent the next few months dallying on long rides through the frozen countryside, visiting various cottages, doing whatever I could to help some of the poorer peasants make it through the harshest part of winter, anything to avoid the silence. My father and I were no longer on speaking terms. When I did see him, I turned and walked the other way. He never visited my cottage, nor did he send word to join him in the hall. It was a very lonely, dark, cold winter. And even with the arrival of warm March breezes and the new planting season, my bitterness did not melt.

Of course, the exasperating fire might have had something to do with that. I looked cantankerously at the hearth. Nelda had gone home to help her sister with the birth of her child, leaving me to my own devices, which suited my melancholy just fine but was rather inconvenient when I needed domestic assistance.

I tried to coax the fire to light and ran the jagged steel edge of the fire starter across my finger. "Damn." I pulled my hand back, dropping the flint as the sting hissed and the blood swelled. I staunched the flow with the hem of my dress and squeezed, my eyes filling as I stared at the unlit tinder. I brushed the moisture away irritably and slumped into a heap on the rush-covered floor.

"Why is this happening to me?" I yelled at the Goddess. I had long ago thrown out any notions that my vision at Avalon had been positive. Instead, I fortified myself for impending doom. I flung the steel fire starter toward my bed. "Why are you angry with me? Have I offended you in some way?" I looked up at the thatch, tarnished gray and black from years of smoky fires. "Do you even see me? Do you even know I'm here? I've sent prayers, and pleas, but nothing has changed. Why aren't you listening?"

Nothing stirred in the stagnant air around me. I sank my head into my hands. Nothing I did worked. I was still miserable—my father still adamant.

I missed my mother. I sniffed hard and stood up. I brushed the rushes from the folds of my kirtle, found the well-worn groove in the floor, and commenced pacing back and forth. The vernal equinox was fast approaching. Perhaps the Goddess was angry that I had only given her a cursory thought during the winter solstice. Traveling with my father's thegns to Winchester at Christmastide, my opportunities for worship had been limited. But my mother had always found a way to honor the sacred days. I would make it up to the Goddess this month. I wouldn't let my responsibilities slide further.

There was a soft knock on the door.

"Come in."

Bertram entered, carrying a folded piece of parchment. "Good morning, Avelynn. How are you feeling today?"

"Fine."

He lifted a bushy eyebrow. "Good, then you should be overjoyed to hear this news." He placed the parchment on a bench, walked over to the hearth, and knelt down, taking up my efforts to rouse the fire.

Very few people in Wessex, other than a handful of priests who acted as scribes for kings and noblemen, were gifted with literacy. Bertram was an accomplished scholar, and as his avid student, I took in everything he offered. I could read and write Latin, English, and Ogham letters and was fluent in Gaelic, Latin, French, Norse, and English. The advantage this afforded was not lost to me. Knowledge was power. And as a woman, possession of that knowledge provided me with a tremendous advantage over most of the noblemen in England. Even the king of Wessex was still trying to learn Latin himself.

I picked up the note. It was a royal decree from King Aethelred, ordering my father to gather men and travel to Rome to pay the church's tribute—a godly sum of gold and silver. Nothing like paying the pope to earn God's clemency.

"I don't understand. Why now?" Tribute was to be paid every year, and the king's most trusted thegns took turns transporting the precious cargo. But it had been several years since anyone had made that arduous journey.

"The Vikings have been silent. And fearing for his soul, Aethelred will delay the trip no longer." He gave a final flick of his wrist and a spark flew, landing on the tinder nest. The kindling caught. Tentative flames licked the air and Bertram blew softly until the fire surged. Satisfied, he placed a large log on the hearth and raked the burning kindling toward it. "I thought you might like to know that Demas, with his intimate knowledge of the Eternal City, will be joining your father's party. They plan to leave in two days' time."

The twitch of the first genuine smile to cross my lips in months lifted the corners of my mouth. Their journey would last well into the fall. Which meant there was not going to be a wedding, at least not until they got back. My chest felt a little lighter.

Bertram stood, his old knees creaking, and sat on a bench, patting the wood beside him. I sat down.

"Your father wants to know if you will manage the affairs of the manor and oversee the village's administration while he is gone."

"He wants me left in charge?" I narrowed my eyes at Bertram. It didn't seem possible.

"Sigberht's father died two days past, and he returned to Kent to settle his estate. Your father could have picked any number of men, but he chose you. Perhaps you will see this for what it is."

"And what is that?"

He rose to leave. "An olive branch."

I was silent a moment. "What of Edward?"

"He's to travel to Rome with your father."

I felt a fleeting pang of jealousy. My younger brother would see the world and travel in companionship with my father, a privilege I'd hoped to earn as his eldest child. But mostly, I felt loss. After Mother's passing, Edward came to me for comfort, and I welcomed his attentions and the chance to provide the reassurance and love he needed without restraint. I would miss him.

I went to the window where the shutters had been thrown back to let in the warm March sun and considered the offer. I suspected my father's decision to leave me in charge was heavily influenced by Bertram. He alone never doubted my abilities.

Outside, the manor was bustling with activity. Men carried barrels and crates filled with goods imported from overseas, women worked on vertical looms, bringing their craft outside to take advantage of the milder temperatures and longer daylight. Two old men sat on stumps, engrossed in thought, a wooden game table between them. Pages scurried and maids rushed back and forth between supply sheds and the kitchens, always prepping, always preparing meals for the manor and its wards. This was supposed to be my legacy, these people my responsibility. I wouldn't give it up so easily. I turned back to Bertram. This was the chance I'd been waiting for, the opportunity to finally prove myself as a competent leader—a leader who didn't need a husband to make decisions for her. "Tell him I will ensure everything is managed proficiently. He leaves Wedmore in good hands."

"Excellent."

The door opened, and Edward flew in.

"Avelynn, Avelynn, I'm to go to Rome with Father!"

"Yes, I hear."

"I'm to go on a boat, and climb over mountains, and see the pope."

"Minding your manners the entire time," Bertram said, looking down his austere nose at the jubilant sprite.

"Of course." Edward straightened.

"You represent the noble Saxons. You are our spokesman, our example. You must behave accordingly."

Edward puffed his chest and stood taller.

"Good day, Avelynn, Edward." Bertram nodded and left.

I turned my attention back to the beaming face in front of me. He would learn much on this trip and return a worldly young man. I would miss his tenth birth day.

"Father said we might even encounter pirates or Vikings on the trip."

"Well, you must be careful then. I want you to return in one piece."

He rooted through a cold pot of stew, turned his nose up at the congealed contents, and reached into the breadbasket, grabbing a small loaf. He poked the coarse crust with his finger and wormed his way to the soft center.

"Father is bringing lots of men to accompany us," he mumbled through a mouthful of bread. "We will be very safe."

Crumbs collected on the front of his cloak. I brushed them away. "I'll miss you."

"I know." He looked down at his feet.

I opened my arms, and he leaned into me.

"We shall have a fabulous feast upon your return," I promised, letting him pull away. Empty hands dropped to my sides.

"I will bring you back something from Rome."

"I'd like that."

He paused at the door, his hand resting on the iron handle. "I love you." His face flushed.

"I love you too," I said, letting him go.

My father was pacing, ticking off responsibilities with each finger as I made a list. "Council will be held when I return. Sigberht will collect the taxes from the shire when he gets back. You will oversee the household guard—Leofric will be left in charge. He will report directly to you. You will be judge in all disputes and must ensure all the manor's records are up to date. You will need to keep careful watch on our inventory and—"

"I know, Father, we've been through this." I read back part of the list. "Bertram, as chamberlain, oversees the treasury, is in charge of ensuring the manor has all the supplies that we need, and manages the servants. Father Plegmund will serve as scribe and record the day's transactions. Milo the seneschal and Walther his steward maintain the lord's table and keep a record of each individual grain of wheat, barley, oats, and rye that grows in Somerset." I put my quill down. "I understand." He had sat me down just after cock crow, and it was now early evening.

He stopped pacing. "I don't want any mistakes."

"I can do this."

He stared at me a moment, the stern lines of his face softening. "Your mother would be proud of you."

Wind rustled the thatch. Logs crackled on the hearth. The sound of my heartbeat echoed in my ears.

"Do well, and we will discuss your future when I return."

"And the betrothal?" I held my breath.

"We shall see."

Was it possible he was reconsidering? I ran to him and crushed myself against his chest. His arms closed around me. He smelled of woodsmoke and fresh air, the fine woolen tunic soft beneath my cheek.

"I miss her," he said softly.

My mother had died seven years before, on a cold March night just like this.

"I miss her too."

They left without fanfare. My father, flanked by Wulfric and Demas, inclined his head in my direction as he rode away. Edward waved animatedly, and I returned the gesture, waving until they rounded a bend in the road, disappearing from sight.

Early spring could be a dangerous time to cross the channel, but the weather was fine, and I prayed their journey across the ocean to Francia would be a safe one. Accidents happened all the time—a freak storm, a sailor's fateful mistake, a flaw in the vessel itself—but I chose not to dwell on misfortune. Instead, I visualized a successful journey.

A warm, luscious breeze blew from the south and brought a renewal of spirit and life back into the earth. My heart lightened, and I exhaled in relief. While my apprehension still lingered, my father's words had eased some of my fear, and the oppressive weight of the last two months flitted away on the balmy breeze.

Determined to prove my mettle to the people of Somerset, I spent two weeks traveling throughout the district with Milo and Walther, pulling up my dress sleeves whenever necessary and pitching in. I had spent the last few days alternating between encouraging the oxen to pull the single-bladed plow through the stubborn soil and trying to steer the heavy, cumbersome contraption. I was sweaty and filthy. I loved every moment of it.

I often helped in the large garden behind the hall, but apart from mixing manure into the soil with a small spade and rake and the constant weeding, there was little manual labor involved. Tackling acres of land with oxen and plow was quite another matter.

"You need to scatter the seeds like so." Milo gesticulated, swinging his hand back and forth, a steady stream of seeds flying into the newly dug furrow.

We were sowing barley. The stalks would be used for straw and bedding for the horses, the grain for bread and brewing.

"No, no, 'tis like this, m'lady," Walther countered, sweeping his hand as he walked beside the trench, each seed landing in the groove.

They argued amiably about proper technique. Though, in truth, I couldn't tell the difference. They were genial men, well into their mid-forties, and though distant cousins, the familial resemblance was striking. They could easily pass for brothers. Tall and lean, their necks and arms dark and sinewy from years of hard physical labor, they had worked for my grandfather before swearing oaths to my father.

As seneschal, or master of the feast, part of Milo's responsibilities involved determining which plants to sow, where, and when, so that the manor was never left wanting. Walther was his assistant. Walther could always be found carrying a tally stick, on which he kept careful account of the grain supply for the manor. A meticulous notch or slash, carved into each stick, kept his records up to date.

I grabbed another handful of grain from the pouch I'd made by folding up the hem of my apron and continued forward, emulating their steady swing. They nodded in encouragement and smiled at my technique.

Spring was a grueling time. The instant the ground became workable, every slave, freeman, woman, and child was set to task, toiling from sunup to sundown. It was unprecedented for a noblewoman to labor in menial work, and many of the townsfolk came out to offer suggestions, not passing on the opportunity to poke and jeer. I endured their lighthearted comments graciously, and at the end of each day sent for mead to be shared amongst my spectators and patient tutors.

With the barley laid and the furrows covered loosely with soil, I wiped the sweat from my brow and sat, eager to quench my thirst and wash the day's dust from my throat. The villagers had built a roaring fire to keep the chill of dusk at bay, and each person found a comfortable seat close to the warm glow. Mead was passed around to all. I raised my cup in a toast, acknowledging a hard day's work done well, but stopped midway, my lips set in a grim line. A horse and rider blazed toward the fields. It was Sigberht.

He dismounted and whistled for a lad to take his horse. "Let him graze while I speak with the lady." He handed the boy the reins.

"Sigberht," I said.

"I've returned from settling my father's accounts. You can return to your cottage. I'll finish things here."

"Finish what exactly?"

"The administration of the estate."

I left the fire and headed for a stand of hawthorn bushes, away from the curious ears and gossiping tongues of the villagers. Sigberht followed.

"You will do no such thing. My father gave me explicit instructions to see to the care of the estate in his absence."

"Only because I was indisposed. I am back."

"And what is that supposed to mean to me?"

"It means that you can finish playing at house. The men of Wedmore are warriors, not chambermaids. They need a man to advise and lead them."

"I am quite capable of running my estate."

The sun was setting, and a pale pink glow tinted the land, but Sigberht's color blazed red.

"For your mother's sake, your father has coddled you—letting you sit in council, giving you a taste of power. But he was wrong to do so. The administration of Wedmore will never be your job. Your new husband will see to that, and I for one look forward to the day when you are properly submissive."

My hands curled into fists in the folds of my dress. "I suggest you leave. And don't come back until my father sends for you. You're not welcome here while I'm in charge."

He laughed. "I am still reeve of this estate, lady. No one but your father can strip me of my title. I will not be going anywhere." He stormed back to his horse. As he tore off down the path to the manor, Milo approached me tentatively.

"Is everything all right, my lady?" he asked, watching clouds of dust billow behind the departing horse.

My mind was spinning. The equinox was in a few days, my course set. But how could I leave the estate with a viper circling, his fangs straining for my throat? I didn't know what was worse, missing another sacred day of the Goddess or leaving myself open for the beast's strike.

I smiled weakly at Milo. "Seems someone isn't happy with my current position."

"He'll come around, my lady."

"Are you not threatened by the prospect of me becoming lord of the manor?"

He chuckled. "My lady, your people love you. I've seen firsthand the good you do, how you help those less fortunate than yourself. Your father is fair and just, but in his stead, there are many here who would be honored to have you as their liege lord. I for one would lay down my life for yours."

The sincerity in his voice made my throat tighten. "Thank you."

He nodded and turned to leave, but I laid a hand on his arm. "Milo, can I trust the administration of Wedmore to your shoulders? I have a matter to attend to. It will take only a few days."

"I would be honored, my lady, of course. But what of Lord Sigberht?"

I followed his gaze. "I'll find something suitable for him to do."

As reeve, Sigberht's responsibilities included collecting taxes, exacting justice, and handling disputes throughout Somerset on my father's behalf. It was a position of influence and envy, and it was clearly time to deflate Sigberht's bloated head. While I couldn't overstep my father and cast Sigberht out outright, I could certainly make his quarrel with me a bitter tonic.

"Good afternoon, Sigberht. Please step forward." I had taken great pains to wear my richest kirtle of soft red linen, its embroidered bands of gold silk edging my sleeves, hem, and neckline, my wolf-pelt cloak, held at my shoulder by a heavy gold brooch inlaid with lapis lazuli and garnets, and my sword, the hilt and cross guard stamped with gold. Yesterday he had seen me in a simple frock, tending the fields like a peasant. Today he would know me for the authority of the manor. I sat in the lord's chair and looked down on Sigberht as Leofric escorted him into the hall.

Slightly younger than his brother, Wulfric, Leofric was as solid as a boulder, with the same dark hair and watchful eyes, but Leofric was more boisterous, with a charismatic and endearing nature. Today, however, he affected a severe countenance.

Sigberht scowled, but remained silent.

"The boundary lines need measuring. A necessary duty to quell any future land disputes. This task falls under your jurisdiction, does it not?"

Sigberht grumbled. Leofric nudged him politely with his shoulder. "Aye," he answered.

"Good." I nodded to Leofric, who stepped to the door and let in a small, wiry old man. His face was weathered and wrinkled, like an apple left out in the sun, but his eyes sparkled with intelligence. "You recall Eata, my father's butler."

Eata stepped forward. "I've brought the rope, m'lady, and the tablet."

"Thank you, Eata." I turned and smiled at Sigberht. "Before he became butler, Eata used to travel with Wiglaf, your predecessor as reeve. He knows each district better than anyone on the manor. He will accompany you and record each freeman's holdings on the tablet. You will of course be thorough and walk each and every boundary line, measuring it with the rope."

"That will take weeks," Sigberht hissed.

"Yes, there is an awful lot of boggy ground to cover."

"Your father—"

"Ah yes, my father. Since he also charged you with collecting the taxes, you can kill two birds with one stone. I'm sure he will be very pleased to hear of your resourcefulness and enterprise."

"You can't make me do anything, girl." He stalked closer.

"I believe she can." Leofric stepped between us. "You'll do as she says, or the priest here will record in the charter your willful refusal of a direct order by your lord."

Sigberht turned and glared at Father Plegmund, sitting piously at the table, recording the proceedings. Bertram stood nearby, leaning against the wall.

"That would be four witnesses to swear to the neglect of your duties as reeve," I said, resting my hand on the hilt of my sword. "A grave crime, the least punishment for which is to lose your position; the next penalty, your hand." I knew I was wading into dangerous territory. Sigberht was not likely to let this public humiliation go unanswered. But what choice did I have? If I could not earn his respect, I could only force his compliance.

He glared at me for a long moment, the only sound in the hall the crackle of the logs on the hearth. "Very well." He bowed slightly to me and the men present. "I will leave forthwith." He spun on his heels and stormed out of the hall, Eata scampering to catch up.

I let out the breath I'd been holding. My palm was sweaty where I held the sword, and my hands trembled slightly.

With the drama concluded, everyone left but Bertram. He studied me closely. "How do you feel?"

"Like a bully." I rose, releasing the cloak from my shoulders.

He nodded. "I can't say he didn't deserve to learn his place. I only worry that coming from you, he will not take the chastisement lightly."

"No. I imagine he won't." I sighed. "At least we can travel to the coast."

"Are you sure you need to do this?"

"I missed the winter solstice. I cannot let the equinox pass without honoring Her properly."

"Then we will leave on the morrow."

With only two days left before the twenty-fifth of March, I left Milo in charge of the estate, and Bertram and I headed to the coast.

In winter, the coastal areas of Somerset were sodden with brackish water, and vegetation was sparse, but in the spring, the water receded, and spongy marshland, full of rushes and withies, sprung up. A bit farther inland, heathland abounded with peat, coarse grasses, shrubs, and heather. Dense and sprawling woodlands intermingled with all, carving their way through the landscape. We were headed for a location almost a full day's ride from Wedmore. Bordered by thick forest, it was one of the few places along the coast that boasted a beautiful sandy beach.

Like Avalon, the coast was a mystical place. It was the farthest west we could travel before falling into the sea and was therefore the closest we would come to the mystical veil between the worlds of the living and dead. Since this part of Somerset was uninhabited, it was also sufficiently removed from cynical souls who would condemn me for my beliefs.

To the Christian church, March twenty-fifth was the beginning of the liturgical New Year—the day an angel appeared to a girl named Mary, informing her about an upcoming divine birth. In the pagan faith, it marked the vernal equinox—the juncture when day and night were equal. It was a powerful and auspicious time.

I had been raised to become a high priestess of the Four Directions. While I hadn't been able to officially achieve that illustrious status before my mother died, I was nonetheless an anointed priestess of my faith. I believed in one Goddess, She who has no name but has four parts, four personalities or manifestations that I could entreat—four Goddesses who guided us on life's path. Tomorrow, I would honor Her in a ceremony bound by beliefs and rites thousands of years old.

The ritual would take place at dawn, but we had to set up camp and gather enough wood for the ceremonial fire. The moment we left Wedmore, the sky clouded over. By the time we reached the coast, a misty drizzle veiled the land. We tethered the horses and assembled our tent on a relatively flat area of ground, just within the thick overgrowth of ancient forest. The canopy was dense. Ferns, their delicate fronds reaching out to capture the fleeting daylight, dominated the ground cover.

The light rain barely penetrated the trees, and we had little problem finding a large quantity of good, dry timber. We lit a fire to keep the chill at bay and ate a small snack of dried meat, cheese, and bread, treating ourselves to freshly roasted fiddleheads picked from the burgeoning shoots around us.

If I had been traveling with an entourage, my tent would have been grand. A bed, several chests, tables, and benches would have been brought and assembled inside. But with only Bertram and me, our lodging was primitive. I rolled out the woolen bundle that served as my bed and pulled the hood of my cloak up and over my head to stay warm, nestling between the covers.

Despite the meager comforts, I reveled in the freedom of being alone with Bertram—a woman in charge of my own destiny, away from the men who threatened to control my life. They were engulfed by ignorance and fear, and it was a blessing to know and experience my own power. And I would embrace that power tomorrow as a daughter of the Goddess.

I turned to Bertram to thank him for helping me, expecting to find him cocooned in his own bedding, but he was sitting against a log, his back rigid. "What is it?" I asked.

"I will not help you tomorrow."

I sat up. "What do you mean? It's the equinox!" As druid, his role in our rituals was just as important as mine as priestess.

"I mean, you will have to do this alone. I'll not encourage this any longer."

"Encourage what?"

"Following the Goddess is a path fraught with danger. The Christians do not tolerate our faith. I would see you turn your considerable talents and energy to something else."

We'd had this argument before, when my father wanted me converted. Bertram had refused my father's wishes, but only because I had been adamant. I would not be coerced into becoming a Christian. I had thought the matter closed. "You promised my mother to continue my learning."

"Yes, I did, and I've taught you all I know."

I doubted that and glared at him.

He shrugged. His mouth was set in a thin line. "With my drum, I will keep the rhythm. I will chart the pace, but you will have to do the ceremony alone. You do not need me for this."

I had watched my mother dance as Bertram chanted; I had even joined in, dancing as I grew older, but . . . "I've never done this alone."

He smiled. "You will know what to do." He wriggled into his covers and rolled over, his back to me.

I grumbled my dissent and begrudgingly settled down to sleep, my mind alternating between fits of confidence and doubt. I frowned, wondering if this was some sort of test. In fairness, I'd have to do this on my own eventually. I just expected more notice, more time to prepare. I had a rough outline of what was expected. The rest I would just have to improvise.

The drizzle stopped at some point in the night, and as the first hint of morning infused the darkness with the potential of shape and form, it revealed a heavy, impenetrable fog. Tripping over roots, rocks, and a terrain that had somehow sprouted treacherous mounds and divots overnight, we staggered back and forth from the camp to the beach, arms laden with firewood.

Protected within a small inlet, the air was still. Not a breath of wind stirred the thick wall of gray. Even the sea itself was calm, its soft murmur expanding and fading as the gentle waves ebbed and flowed. We arranged the wood to form a massive cone and lit the kindling at the base. A roar of flame erupted, licking greedily at the dry logs.

I was grateful for the sudden blast of heat. Prepared for the ritual, I had taken off my cloak and kirtle and wore only a thin, sleeveless white underdress, which I had rucked up above my knees, to allow for ease of movement. I had also braided my hair and tucked the ends under my leather belt to keep it from flying too close to the fire as I danced.

Bertram nodded, indicating all was ready, and walked away, disappearing into the fog.

Remaining on the inside, I used a stick to trace a large circle in the sand. "In the name of the one true Goddess, I cast this circle." Everything within this space was sacred. I walked the periphery, pausing at all four directions, invoking each Goddess.

"Aine, Maiden of the North, Goddess of the moon and stars, keeper of music, magic, and medicine, governess of the Mental Realms of enlightenment and wisdom, I welcome you. Hear me, beloved Maiden. Fill the body of this your priestess. Grant me your love, gift me your power.

"Macha, Queen of the East, Goddess of the sun, keeper of love, passion, and the rising of the dawn, governess of the Spiritual Realms of faith and righteousness, I welcome you. Hear me, sovereign Queen. Fill the body of this your priestess. Grant me your love, gift me your power.

"Danu, Mother of the South, Goddess of hills and plains, keeper of marriage, motherhood, and fertility, governess of the Emotional Realms of morals, virtues, and nurturance. Great Earth Mother who reigns over animals and humans, crops and forest, I welcome you. Hear me, luminous Mother. Fill the body of this your priestess. Grant me your love, gift me your power.

"Badb, Crone of the West, Goddess of oceans and rivers, keeper of power, courage, and perseverance, governess of the Physical Realms of death and birth, I welcome you. Hear me, great Crone. Fill the body of this your priestess. Grant me your love, gift me your power."

By the time I had finished the invocation, the sun had crested the horizon, its light permeating the shifting gray. The slow, steady rhythm of Bertram's drum filled the air. A haunting tempo echoed the rhythm of the waves, the heartbeat of the earth, and despite my reservations, my body began to move, urged on by the deep, throbbing bass of the drum.

Cool dampness caressed my bare skin as I danced around the sacred fire. With each pounding beat, I leapt and turned, stepped and dipped, arms reaching above me, honoring the Goddess. All I could hear was the resounding pulse of the drum. All I could see was the blazing fire. The fog engulfed me, cutting me off from the rest of the world. I was on an island as big as the earth itself. I was the earth itself. Beyond this moment, this circle, nothing else existed.

I sang a short verse of praise, then added a personal plea for my future happiness and the strength to conquer those who would oppose me—I envisioned a divine hand personally wiping the smug faces off both Demas and Sigberht; a prayer for my father and Edward—I would see them home safely; and the knowledge and skills necessary to run the manor in my father's absence. I also appealed to the Goddess's mercy and benevolence, imploring her to stave off the war, death, and bloodshed that were portended to enter my life and the lives of those I loved.

I felt the pull of tranquility. Thoughts and words slipped away, and a blanket of peace settled over me. My body moved as it wished. I was an instrument, the drum my master. Bertram beat louder and faster. It pushed and pulled, and I followed its summons, kicking up soft sand with my bare feet as I danced. I felt freedom, the boundlessness of eternity, and a connection to something greater than myself. I went home to the embrace of the Goddess, and I was rocked and soothed, supported and loved. Was my mother with me too? I wondered suddenly. I reached my arms out to her and danced, remembering when we had danced together, honoring the Goddess, keeping our faith alive.

A coarse, bloodcurdling shout reverberated through the mist. The drum silenced. I froze. My heart took up a thunderous beat as if a thousand starlings' wings beat in my chest. Something was terribly wrong. I turned my gaze to the sea, frantically scanning the swirling, ebbing mass of gray, willing the mist to lift.

Shades and shadows melted away. The outline of a Viking ship materialized before my eyes. A bloodred sail pierced the gloom, a black bird emblazed upon the fabric. A beast of a man ran toward me, a painted shield in one hand, an axe in the other. He stepped over the circle and grabbed my arms. I could smell the fetid reek of his breath, the unwashed sweat and sea spray on his filthy clothes. I screamed. He snarled, covered my mouth, and thrust me to the ground. I kicked and thrashed as he fumbled one-handed with the drawstring on his trousers.

Then he stopped, a look of surprise etched in his wide eyes. Blood sputtered out of his mouth, and he fell sideways. I scrambled back as his body twitched, my breath ragged. An axe was stuck fast in his spine.

I screamed again as another Viking appeared before me. Taller than Glastonbury Tor, he wore a silver helmet with nose and cheek guards and full mail. The same black bird as on the ship's sail stretched its wings across the battered wooden surface of his shield. A sword and a knife, cradled in their scabbards, hung from a leather belt on his waist. He grabbed one of the dead Viking's feet and hauled him out of the circle. He jerked the axe free of the body and tucked the weapon into a sling that hung on his back.

I found my feet, spinning to discover the extent of my trouble. Were there more invaders? Did the Viking know I was alone with no chance of aid? Were his men scoping the surrounding area even now? Did they find our campsite with only two horses and two bedrolls? Where was Bertram?

The Viking looked down at the circle drawn in the sand and bowed. With his body still bent, he raised his head, blue eyes regarding me. "I apologize for the disruption to your ritual, Seiðkana," he said, speaking in the Norse tongue.

I narrowed my eyes at him. Seiðkana? I wasn't sure of the translation of the word, but I thought it meant witch.

"Who are you?" I asked in Norse, earning a look of shock.

"I am Alrik the Bloodaxe, your servant."

Bertram appeared from out of the fog, his hands bound as he was tossed back and forth like a rag poppet between three brutes, each man armed with axe, sword, and shield. They turned their attention to me, leering, and made vile comments, grabbing and rubbing their crotches. Even if I hadn't understood the language, their sentiments were unmistakable.

I realized, belatedly, that I was completely exposed. I loosened my belt and the fabric dropped, covering my legs. I couldn't do anything about my bare arms, so I crossed them in front of my chest.

Alrik growled, and they stopped. He removed his axe and set it down beside a nearby rock. He then unclasped his cloak and tossed it within the circle.

I stood taller, lifted my chin, and didn't budge.

He grinned at me, revealing brilliant white teeth in a nest of neatly trimmed blond bristles, and then turned to one of the men. "Dispose of this rotting flesh." He kicked the dead man in the ribs. "And set up camp."

"What do you want with the old man?" another asked, and thrust Bertram in front of him.

"Bind him to a tree, but see that no harm comes to him. He carries the staff of a druid." He pointed to Bertram's worn staff, the smooth wood etched with Ogham symbols.

The Vikings were notorious for their penchant for slaughter, but they were also rumored to be extremely superstitious. The Ogham symbols may have saved Bertram's life. As for my fate, it seemed we were at an impasse. Alrik made no effort to cross the line, and I had no intention of stepping over it. If he truly thought I was a witch, he would not dare enter the circle, fearing a curse or other such malevolent treatment at my displeasure.

By late morning, the sun had long burned off the last remnants of fog. The sky was a stunning, clear blue, and the day—thank the gods—was blessedly warm. I sat in the sand between the smoldering fire and the edge of the circle. He sat on a rock.

After a short while, he had removed his helmet, revealing a mass of shoulder-length blond hair; a tidy braid hung on his right side. He placed his shield and weapons on the ground beside his axe, undid his belt, and pulled his mail coat up and over his head, adding these to the pile. He lifted his hands.

Since I was clearly unarmed, I emulated his gesture and lifted mine in response.

He laughed—a surprisingly hearty, warm sound. "Finish your ceremony, Seiðkana," he insisted, gesturing to the circle. "You would anger your gods."

I thought fast. Was there some way to evade him? "This is not a ritual for a man's eyes. I cannot close the circle with your eyes on me."

He stood and turned his back to me. "How is this?"

I studied his strong, wide shoulders. He looked like one of the fabled giants, a titan born of earth and stone. Could a mere mortal outrun a mythical beast? I doubted it. But maybe if I made it to the forest I could escape. I knew the territory, but he didn't. I wouldn't be able to free Bertram, but I could alert the countryside. It would take days on foot, but I could follow the River Avon until I reached Bath, a powerful royal village. There would be men garrisoned there. Perhaps they could prevent the Vikings from marauding farther inland?

I frowned. Even if the gods were kind and I managed to elude the Viking, how could I avoid getting caught by one of his henchmen? They had scattered into the wood heading south, probably in search of game. Perhaps if I stayed to the north. I eyed the line of trees. I certainly couldn't stay in this circle. If he didn't fear me, I was his prisoner, and I had no interest in finding out what he planned to do with me. I might be ransomed, raped, tortured, or sold—Saxon women were known to fetch a high price at the slave markets. I looked at the line drawn in the sand. Without the proper rites to close the ceremony, I couldn't voluntarily leave the sanctity of the circle either. If I did nothing, I was as good as trapped.

I judged the distance between the forest and my towering sentry. "Fine," I replied. "Stay there."

I made my way around the circle, stopping at each of the Four Directions, and thanked the Goddesses for their presence at the ceremony. Out of the corner of my eye, I never lost sight of the Viking, who, true to his word, remained turned. When I reached the most northern part of the circle, directly opposite where he stood, I murmured a hasty thank-you to Aine, the Goddess of the North, grabbed the Viking's cloak, and dashed for the edge of the forest.

SEVEN

Once embraced by the cool shadows of the forest, the sharp dampness of early spring seeped into my bones. It only worsened when the Viking's cloak snagged on a hawthorn branch. Rather than stop and wrestle the cloak free, I left it hanging, the branch bending under the weight.

In preparation for the ritual, I had left my sword and knife beneath my shoes and set them both beside my kirtle, all of which sat in a neat pile on my bedroll back in the clearing where Bertram and I had set up camp. A knot formed in my stomach when I thought of Bertram. I prayed his status as druid would keep him safe, but I had no way of knowing how he would be treated or if I would ever see him again.

I looked over my shoulder to gauge if anyone was chasing me and stubbed my toe hard on a rock. I yelped and hobbled awkwardly, limping until the pain subsided, cursing my lack of shoes. A breeze rustled the leaves overhead, and I tried to see past the thick canopy of shifting greenery. "Goddess, help me," I whispered.

For the next few hours, I continued to make progress, but much slower, navigating every carefully placed step. Part of my brain kept a vigilant focus on the sights and sounds around me. If the Vikings pursued me, I couldn't hear them.

In retrospect, while I realized it would take days for me to reach Bath, I hadn't considered that the Vikings could have burned and pillaged half the coast by then. My efforts to get help were most likely in vain. It seemed I'd only been successful at saving my own skin. I thought of Bertram again and swallowed the bitter taste of guilt that rose in the back of my throat.

The loud snap of a breaking twig sliced through the silence. I stopped and crouched in the ferns, my heart pounding. Cold perspiration pricked the back of my neck, and the hair on my arms stood on end. I felt the ground at my feet for anything I could use as a weapon. A heavy, jagged rock fit smartly into my searching palm, and I clutched it.

Running for help had been a terrible idea. Escaping, wandering off alone without food, water, shoes, a cloak, or weapons had been foolish; in fact, downright reckless. My eyes welled. Gods, what was I thinking?

A wolf's high-pitched howl echoed around me. It couldn't be more than a few yards away. I turned my head slightly, terrified to move or make a sound for fear of drawing further attention. Where was it? I scanned the clearing and locked onto two fierce yellow eyes glowing in the underbrush. My breath froze in my lungs. I stood and searched the wood. The nearest tree was a silver birch about five yards behind me. Even if I could make it, I wasn't sure I could climb it. It was tall and thin without so much as a lower branch to use as a foot- or handhold, and the only way to manage it would be to shimmy up the trunk. For the first time since I'd entered the forest, I was grateful for bare feet. At least they would give me better traction on the papery bark.

The wolf stared, assessing me, its massive tensile body waiting.

I didn't have a great deal of experience dealing with hungry wolves. I tried distraction.

"Bet you think you can just walk in here and eat me." I took a few slow, steady steps backward.

"I've been told I'm just skin and bones." I took another step toward the tree. "Not worth the effort."

I was only a yard away from it. Another step and I could start climbing.

The wolf growled a deep, menacing warning. Rusty-red and burnt-orange highlights flecked its thick brown coat. The hackles rose on the back of its neck. I searched for some other means of escape and panicked. If Wulfric or my father had been here, they would have wrestled the beast to the ground with their bare hands. I lacked their size and strength, and the odds were not stacked in my favor. I adjusted the rock in my hand, turning the sharp, jagged edge outward.

Another wailing howl in the distance snapped my head in the opposite direction—reinforcements. I pictured myself high in the birch tree, a pack of wolves circling hungrily below. Trapped in a horrific standoff until exhausted, I would fall asleep and drop like a juicy apple to their waiting teeth and claws.

The wolf pounced. A shadow of fur and vicious teeth flew through the air. I clutched the rock, aimed for the spot between its eyes, and swung my arm with everything I had. A blur of movement caught my attention, and I was knocked sprawling to the ground, the rock flying from my hand, the breath forced out of me. I rolled onto my side and gasped for air. My hands searched blindly for the rock.

Time slowed. Sounds amplified within the cavern of trees— a piercing yelp, a heavy thump, silence.

The soft, rich mulch of the forest bed cushioned my fall, its fresh, earthy scent clashing with the sharp tang of blood. My eyes watered but my breath had settled.

The wolf, very much dead, lay beside me, its glassy eyes staring empty and cold. I recoiled and scrabbled desperately away from it. Standing next to the wolf was Alrik, his sword stuck fast in the wolf's heart, the cross guard gleaming with inlaid garnets.

"You are strong for such a small thing." He presented his arm. It was bleeding and swelling rapidly. "If I had known you were going to hit me with a rock, I might have thought better of saving your life."

"Sorry," I mumbled, uncertain what else to say.

He leaned over the wolf. "Loyal protector, he who sits at the right hand of your master, Odin, go forth in spirit, my brother. His faithful servant Alrik the Bloodaxe sends you." He reached down and stroked the beast's fur tenderly, murmuring in soft, soothing tones before wrenching his sword from its body. He wiped the sword's surface with a cloth and slid the long blade back into its scabbard.

He removed his cloak and handed it to me. "You dropped this."

It was only then I realized I was shivering. Whether it was from cold or my ordeal I didn't know, but my entire body shook in earnest and my teeth clattered painfully together. I took the cloak without hesitation.

Another howl, this time closer, interrupted the fragile feeling of security.

"It is time to go." He looked down at me, crumpled as I was in a heap on the cold, moist forest floor. "Are you hurt?"

"I don't think so."

He took the edge of the cloak and wiped my cheek. "Blood."

I reached up and felt my cheek. "I don't think it's mine."

"No, it is mine." He pointed to his arm.

"Sorry," I grumbled again.

"Can you walk?"

"Of course I can walk. There's nothing wrong with my legs."

He bowed, granting me leave to get myself up, and leaned against the birch tree, crossing his ankles and arms.

I pushed myself up and promptly fell back down as my gelatinous legs gave out from underneath me.

He laughed and unceremoniously lifted me up and over his shoulder like a sack of grain.

"Put me down!"

He stopped. "Are you prepared to fight a pack of wolves, Seiðkana?" Several howls echoed in the woods around us.

"No."

He resumed his pace.

Resigned, I propped my elbow against his shoulder, rested my chin in my hand, and watched the world retreat away from me.

After a great deal of traipsing, he set me down in a small clearing.

"Do not move. I will gather wood for a fire and want you here when I return."

I nodded and watched his powerful body march back into the woods.

The clearing was bright. I lowered the cloak and let the late afternoon sun's warmth kiss the top of my head and shoulders. It looked much safer in the brilliant sunlight than under the dark canopy of trees, but I knew better. Suddenly leery, I told myself he wouldn't go far. A yell of distress would bring him quickly back.

I kicked myself for my helplessness. I had managed to ruin this day entirely. I tilted my head back. "Are you laughing at me?" I asked the sky, picturing the Goddesses upon their golden thrones, thoroughly entertained by my paltry human troubles.

I spread the cloak out underneath me and lay down on the soft grass. The day had started out so well but had deteriorated quickly. I had deserted Bertram in a vain attempt to save my own skin, I hadn't been able to alert anyone except hungry wolves, and now, not only was I still in the presence of a Viking, but I was also utterly lost in my own forests, defenseless and at his complete mercy. I buried my head in my arms at the humiliation of it all.

Sometime later I awoke. The sun had set, and Alrik was leaning against a rock, his long legs straight out in front of him. There was a warm, tidy fire burning between us, a hare roasted on a spit. I marveled that I hadn't woken, hadn't heard his comings or goings.

"Good evening, Seiðkana."

I sat up. "Good evening, Viking."

Succulent juices dripped and sizzled into the fire when he turned the spit, filling the clearing with the heavenly scent of roasted meat.

"Why did you not turn the wolf into a bird or a frog?" he asked.

I narrowed my eyes at him, trying to determine if he was serious. "Were you testing me?"

"I was trying to determine if you were a *völva*—a witch—or a Seiðkana—a priestess. You practice magic, but I do not think it is very powerful."

"Are you willing to take that risk?" Where my hair had come loose from its braid, it was disheveled, sticking out at odd angles, and my underdress was torn and ragged, my face filthy. I hoped I looked formidable.

He smiled. "Not just yet."

I watched him prepare his supper, powerful arms barely contained beneath his linen tunic. "Why didn't you attack me, on the beach?"

"I respect those touched by the hands of the gods." He turned the spit, and the fire sputtered as more fat dripped from the crispy carcass. My mouth watered.

"We heard the drum, and when I saw you dancing around a

sacred fire, I knew you to be one of the chosen ones. Ingolf was an ignorant fool for defiling your circle. I am sorry for his actions."

I nodded.

"It is a sacred time of year for our gods also. Though, our priestesses dance nude. A sight I would have been pleased to observe."

Heat rose in my cheeks.

He pulled the hare from the spit. "Come. You will be hungry."

I picked up the cloak, wrapped it tightly around my shoulders, and sat close to the fire's heat, opposite to where he sat. I eyed him curiously. He had saved my life, and now he shared his meal with me. He was the least threatening Viking I could ever have imagined. Yet I saw the long knife he wore on the right side of his belt and the sword that hung from the left. Both were innocuous, protected in their scabbards, but a mere flick of the wrist or sweep of the hand would produce their ruthless edges all too readily. I remembered his axe and the way the blade had stuck fast in the dead man's spine.

He cut the hare into smaller wedges, offering it to me first.

"Thank you," I said, surprised.

The heady scent of the crackled skin reached my nostrils, and my stomach growled noisily. I flushed in embarrassment.

He handed me another piece. "I cannot have you starving to death."

Watching him devour his food, I figured the chances of him starving to death were remote. He was the epitome of health, in peak physical condition. He must have weighed over fifteen stone and stood over twelve hands tall, with a broad chest and shoulders, and legs as thick as tree trunks.

"How's your arm?" I asked.

"Fine." He flapped it experimentally.

"May I see it?"

He proffered it without hesitation. It was swollen and bruising, the surface coarsely abraded, dried blood and dirt filling three deep gouges.

"Do you have any wine?" I asked.

He rummaged through a satchel and produced a leather flask.

"I want to use it to wash out your wound."

"Seems an awful waste of good wine," he said, watching me rip a length of linen from the bottom of my underdress. I poured the wine onto the cloth until it was soaked through and dabbed at the raw skin.

He jumped, caught off guard by the alcohol's sting.

I laughed. "I find it hard to believe a little wine could hurt someone as tough as you."

He smiled back, and I found myself growing very warm. Disconcerted, I concentrated on tying the linen around his arm and then shuffled back closer to the fire.

The air seemed charged as if it pulsed around me, and I became very aware of his presence.

"How is *your* arm?" He stood and closed the gap between us.

"My arm?" I asked, bewildered, conscious only of his intimate closeness, his thigh a mere hairsbreadth from my own.

"Yes." He lifted the limb in question.

Using the back of his palm, he brushed aside the cloak. Sparks shot along my skin from the center of his touch. I sat up very straight. My heart beat faster.

"You scraped it when I pushed you aside." His grip loosened until his hand slid down onto mine. He held it tightly. "I am sorry for that." He traced the outline of the scrape with the finger from his other hand.

I looked down and followed his finger with my eyes. I hadn't even been aware of hurting myself, but I was vividly aware of my arm now. In fact it had become the only thing I was conscious of—that, and his featherlight caress.

"It's fine," I heard myself say, as if from a distance. His touch moved in larger and larger circles, getting higher and higher toward my shoulder. My skin caught fire. My stomach cramped. Then something else, something much more powerful awakened. A deep, low tension, a stirring ember, hot and white, burned between my legs.

Startled, I pulled my hand and arm away and wrapped the cloak securely back around myself. "I'm fine."

He nodded and moved back to the other side of the fire. He had two bedrolls laid out as far away from each other as they could get. The fire would be closest to our feet, to prevent any accidental hair searing.

"Get some rest, Seiðkana."

"Avelynn," I answered quietly. "My name is Avelynn."

"Avelynn," he echoed, his voice deep, his accent foreign yet soft.

"I wanted to thank you, today . . . for the wolf . . . for saving my life."

"It was my pleasure."

We sat there silent, watching, waiting, neither one of us moving. The air was oppressive. Fear, uncertainty, confusion, hope, excitement, and arousal hovered like smoke from a peat fire, heavy and thick, choking my words.

"I will not hurt you," he said, as if reading my thoughts.

"What about my friend?" I wanted to hear impunity for the both of us.

"You are both safe. I give you my word."

Relief washed over me. I wasn't sure I could trust him, but I wanted to believe him. I needed to believe him.

"Why are you here, in England?"

He leaned back on his forearms, stretching out his legs. "We stopped to rest and replenish our supplies. We are on our way to Ireland. I was surprised to find you. I had thought this part of the coast uninhabited."

He'd said he respected those touched by the gods, and that at least explained his actions when he first saw me, but what of afterward when he followed me into the forest and killed the wolf? "Why did you save me?" I didn't think fear of being cursed could account for all of his actions.

"I like you," was all he said.

A tempest of butterflies took flight in my stomach, and any other questions I might have had evaporated on my tongue. My pulse charged forward, like a stallion given leave to run.

Was this how it was when my parents had met? Did my mother feel this kind of connection too, this bewildering tension between her and my father? Could it really happen like this—two people from disparate worlds colliding by chance in a moment that should never have happened? She had been shipwrecked, and I had picked this time to travel to the coast, to appeal to the Goddess. Was it fated?

I searched his eyes in the firelight. Guileless and infinite. "Good night, Alrik."

An enchanting grin lit up his handsome face. "Good night, Avelynn."

I lay down onto my back and gazed at the sky. The full moon was glorious. A pale orange light illuminated its mottled surface as it hovered in the sky. The night was clear and crisp. A few brilliant stars were visible, despite the moon's impressive glow. Tiny pinholes in a black blanket, each star flickered and shimmered in the translucent darkness, its silvery light reaching out to me. I closed my eyes and sighed in ludicrous contentment. He liked me.

"Having trouble sleeping?" He appeared above me, blocking the stars from view.

"A little," I replied, my heart pounding at the fright from his sudden appearance.

"Why?"

"Thinking too much," I said. He stood in profile to the fire, and I watched the shadows dance across his bold features. "Are you having trouble sleeping too?" I asked, trying to ignore the fact that he was breathtakingly close, and that we were completely alone—the trees, the moon, and stars our only witness.

"Yes." His voice was husky.

My body stirred. "Thinking too much?"

He sat down on the ground beside me. "Thinking about you."

I swallowed, my throat gone dry.

"I want you." He placed his hands on either side of my waist and leaned over top of me. His fierce gaze sent waves of heat and lightning coursing through my body. "But I will not force you. You may choose." He leaned closer.

When I didn't object, he leaned closer still. I could feel the warmth from his breath on my cheek. He stopped, searched my face in the pale moonlight, and waited.

I couldn't speak. I nodded.

He closed the gap. His lips, soft and full, brushed my cheek, and my lips quivered as his mouth covered mine. His beard tickled and brushed the smoothness of my skin as his kiss grew deeper. My body trembled. His tongue, eager and gentle, sought mine, and they met in the briefest of glances. I gasped and clutched the woolen blanket beneath me. Air became scarce, my breath fast and shallow.

Drawing his lips from mine, he dropped his weight onto one elbow and gazed down at me. He released my braid, his fingers twining and combing through the long strands until my hair pooled around me. "You are beautiful," he murmured. His finger followed the curve of my ear, trailed down the side of my neck and tucked just beneath the braided edge of my underdress. He continued his advance, sliding over my shoulder, and down to the rise of my breast. He hesitated, hovering. My breath hung suspended. *I want this. I've wanted this all my life.*

I felt him pull away, the warmth of his body replaced by a gust of cold air.

"Tollak," he growled.

"There's trouble, Alrik." Another Viking stood at the edge of the clearing, the full moon's light bathing him in a silvery glow. The effect was unnerving—he could have been one of the fae people. "When you killed Ingolf this day, his brother Ingvar banded with several men. They tried to burn the ship."

Alrik was already putting on his mail coat. "Stay with her." He pointed in my direction. "See that no harm comes to her in my absence." He laid his hand on the hilt of his sword.

"Of course."

Without another word, Alrik disappeared into the night.

Tollak sat on Alrik's bedroll. His hair was the color of freshly cut straw, and a tidy beard framed a full, bemused mouth. His clothes were well kept, and a gold brooch clasped the edges of his fur cloak. He was clearly of some importance. Other than this Viking and Alrik, the other members of the crew I'd seen looked more like an assembly of rabid dogs.

He gestured to my bedroll. I shimmied under the covers and pulled the wool blankets up to my chin.

"Peace," he said in perfect English, his empty hands raised.

I nodded.

He took his sword from its scabbard and began oiling and sharpening the edges. After what seemed liked hours, I decided he wasn't a threat and closed my eyes, the events of the day dragging me down into exhaustion.

I didn't know what to make of my torrent of feelings or this unfathomable situation. I was betrothed against my will to a brute, due to be married within the year, due to have an abysmal life of misery and inferiority, constantly wishing and hoping for some beauty, some passion in my life. And here it was, inexplicably before me—but with a Viking, the very scourge of England. It was an impossible, hopeless match.

I was wading into treacherous waters, but that just made it all the more enticing.

Dawn broke cold and wet. A fat raindrop landed squarely in the middle of my brow, waking me from a fitful sleep. I rolled my head to the side, brushing my face on the rough woolen blankets that cocooned me. I'd had a horrible dream.

I was falling through the air. There was blood everywhere. Ravens flew alongside me in hungry pursuit of the eyes of dead men on the battlefield. Off in the distance, shields clashed and men screamed.

"Fly with me," a raven called, gliding beside me, its wings outstretched wide as a man's height.

"I can't," I cried. "I'm not a bird!" I tried to stop my fatal fall, flapping my arms uselessly, but the ground approached fast, details emerging swiftly—a blanket of new snow, crisp edges of rocks, and divots of mud.

"Fly with me," it urged.

I continued my acrobatic writhing, my weightless dance, arms and legs flailing in vain. "I'm not a bird."

The ground approached with brutal finality.

There was no longer any uncertainty. War was coming. I sat bolt upright, remembering Alrik. I searched the campsite, but both Alrik and Tollak were gone. Alrik's bedding was rolled and leaning against his satchel, so he couldn't be far.

The fire had been relit. Raindrops sizzled as they burst on the blistering wood. I breathed in the fresh morning air and stretched. The ache of lying on cold ground grumbled in my cramped legs. I shrugged deeper into Alrik's cloak and rolled up my bedding, placing it beside his. Thirsty and wishing to wash my face, I wandered off in search of water.

Not far from camp, I heard a creek's gentle sloshing and followed the sound. I pushed through a clump of billowy reeds and froze. Alrik stood in the middle of the stream, rushing water up to his knees, his back to me. Sunlight gilded his naked body.

I stood transfixed, afraid to make a sound. I felt the full weight of his nakedness and drank it in. His body was firm, etched, rippling in hills and valleys. Shadows and hollows highlighted taut muscles that hugged his body like leather wrapped around hard steel.

He bent over to splash water on his face, granting me a most striking view of his behind. It was tight and wonderfully sculpted. He rose, shaking water like a wet dog from his blond hair, and turned in profile. I gasped. His manhood hung in plain view, resting against his thigh, and I found it difficult to avert my eyes.

He waded back to his clothes on the other side of the stream, where he stepped into a pair of tight brown breeches and slid socked feet into worn leather boots. Over his head, he pulled a crimson tunic trimmed at the neck, wrists, and hem with an embroidered pattern of animals and beasts in vivid colors. He secured his leather sword belt around his waist and pulled on a fine blue coat that fastened across his chest with strips, buttoned to either side. The cuffs of his coat he cinched with polished silver clasps. Sitting on a large boulder, he brought out a bone comb and brushed his hair, tying a new braid on the right side. With the end of a green hazel twig, he scooped out some paste from a small clay jar. After brushing his teeth with the pasted stick, he rubbed them thoroughly with a linen cloth and set about cleaning the dirt from underneath his fingernails.

I watched in fascination. Tales of heathen barbarians, filthy with the reek of dried Saxon blood on their ragged beards and yellow, broken teeth, contrasted sharply with this vision of Alrik. He looked more like a king than a vagabond pirate. And perhaps he was; after all, the Norsemen had kings and jarls—men like our earls—noblemen of great wealth and power. In order to command a ship and crew, Alrik must be well endowed with both wealth and power.

There was a fallen log spanning the brook, and he vaulted across it, making his way back to where I crouched in the reeds. My breath froze.

"Good morning, Seiðkana." He bent down, separating the thin stalks that had stood as my cover. A wide grin was plastered on his face. A florid blush covered mine.

"I'm sorry. I didn't mean to intrude," I stammered. "I merely came to the water to wash." I stood and pushed back through the rushes, but his hand on my arm stilled my escape. He crooked a finger, coaxing me closer, and the look in his eyes made my body stir.

Before I could move, he froze; his body tensed, alert. His grip on my arm tightened, warning me not to budge. A held breath later, he pulled me down, his body protectively covering mine.

"What—" His hand covered my mouth, and he brought his finger to his lips. I nodded, and he removed his hand. He tilted his head, listening. I tried to discern what he heard, but my heart pounding in my ears made it impossible to hear much.

"Alrik?" Tollak's voice drifted through the tall stands of grass.

Alrik pulled me to my feet. "Now what?"

"Ingvar," Tollak said.

Tollak stood only a few yards away. How was it I hadn't heard him approach?

"What about him?"

"He has killed Ohthere."

Alrik roared. "I spared the dog's life and this is how he repays me?" He opened his hand. "Give me Widow Maker."

Tollak handed Alrik his axe.

He turned on me. "Your gods mock me!"

"I don't understand."

"I spilled blood during your ceremony, and they have whispered words of battle in my men's ears, turning their minds against me."

"You saved me from being raped or killed . . . or both. The Goddess wouldn't condemn you for that." How could I possibly appease him? Convince him there was nothing sinister at work here? His own words "blood" and "ceremony" gave me an idea. "I think I can help. Let me make an offering."

Some of the tension left his body.

"Let me speak to your men. Bring them here to this stream, and bring the body of the dead man."

He narrowed his eyes at me. "What do you have in mind?"

My mother and I had sacrificed many animals to the Goddess. Rabbits, sheep, chickens, a pig. Surely a man wouldn't be any different? All that was needed was an invocation, a plea to the Goddess for her benefaction, and the sacrifice itself. I was confident the offering would be acceptable, but my performance needed to convince a group of Northmen of the Goddess's powers—and my ability to commune with her. I needed to appeal to their sense of superstition. This particular ritual would benefit from a little something extra, a sense of the otherworldly.

By the time I had hunted down a hare and bled it into an emptied wine flask, Alrik had assembled his men on the opposite side of the creek.

"*Völva!*" Alrik called.

Since I wasn't really a witch, I wasn't capable of real magic, but his men didn't know that. I upended the contents of the flask on my head and stepped forward. Blood ran in rivulets down my neck and shoulders, my dress stained red. I climbed on top of a large boulder and raised my arms. Crimson droplets fell onto the rock's marbled face.

A few men touched talismans that hung about their necks.

"You dare summon me?" I crouched low on the rock. "You have angered the gods!"

I scrambled off the rock and crawled on hands and knees to the water's edge. I stood and took a step into the stream. Every man stepped back.

I pointed to the corpse. "That maggot dared to defile me, a daughter of the gods. He must be sacrificed to Badb, the Goddess of Death, the Washer at the Ford." I took another step. Several men stepped back. "Take planks of alder and make a raft, then gather a garland of primrose. His body must be set to drift." Alrik had sailed with sixty men, and I held several terrified eyes in turn. "Badb, ruler of the underworld, Battle's Hooded Crow, will accept your gift and take his soul as payment. If you refuse, your journey across the sea will be cursed."

The air was still. Not a single breath was exhaled.

"Go!"

They scattered. Some ran back to the ship to get rope, others scavenged for flowers, a few cut down trees. When all was assembled, they placed the body on the raft.

"Ingolf has offended the gods. Is there any man amongst you who disputes this charge?"

No one spoke.

I raised my arms into the sky. "Goddess, Badb, ruler of oceans and rivers, gatekeeper to the Underworld, accept this sacrifice—a warrior's blood to appease your thirst. Release Alrik the Bloodaxe and his men from their bonds. With this offering, their debt is paid. As I will it, so shall it be." At that exact moment, the wind picked up and trees bent beneath the gale. A crack of thunder rolled overhead. I jumped. The water around my feet began to ripple, the wind churning the quiet surface. The few men who had waded into the stream with the body darted to shore. I looked at Alrik. His brows knitted together, concern on his face. Another bellow of thunder roared directly above us. A bolt of lightning flashed, a shattering *crack* filled the air. The bough of a large tree split, crashing into the water, pitching Ingolf's raft forward, pushing it into the current of deeper water so that it flowed downstream out of sight.

Common sense filtered into my addled brain, and I crept out of the water as the wind lashed and thunder rolled. The sky had turned a menacing black. Alrik's men seemed near panic, each having backed away from the water's edge. They huddled close together, fear etched on their faces, all eyes staring at me, pleading to end the onslaught.

Somehow I found my voice. It wavered at first, but I lifted it high. "Badb, destroyer, bringer of death, terror of men, still your anger. Accept this offering. Release Alrik and his men from your judgment, spare them your wrath. As your daughter and faithful servant, I beg you, hear my plea." I looked anxiously at the sky. The wind seemed to settle, the clouds continuing their brisk pace to the east. Thunder grumbled several more times, and distant lightning flashed as the storm moved on. My body trembled as if the ground beneath my feet quaked. I didn't know what had just happened—if the storm was merely coincidence, or the timing divinely auspicious. Either way, the effect was startling.

Alrik smiled broadly. I presented him with a wary one in return.

"You have done me a great service." Alrik bowed low before me.

"My pleasure." I still didn't know if I had actually done anything to cause the storm, but I liked the idea of pleasing him.

After the thunder and lightning passed, the sky had opened and the rain had fallen in sheets. His men had hastily returned to their ship, each murmuring a prayer to Thor. But the weather had calmed as fast as it had railed, and the sun peeked through the racing clouds overhead.

"You are a formidable witch." He kissed the furrow between my eyes.

I smiled.

He pulled me close. "I must go."

"I know."

We stood together in silence.

"Bertram?" I asked.

"He waits for you. I gave you my word."

I nodded and stayed with him a moment more before he pulled away. He lifted my chin in his hand and sought my eyes with his own. "I will come back in a month's time . . . on the next full moon. Be here when I return, and I will know you come to me of your own free will. But know I will have waited over a month for another taste of you." His gaze burned straight through me. "If we meet again, there will be no more disruptions. I will have all of you. Do you understand?"

I nodded. Words lodged in my throat.

He kissed me softly. "Until then," he said, placing the hilt of his knife into my hands. The cross guard was studded with garnets, just like his sword, the leather scabbard worn and smooth.

"Be safe," he said, and disappeared into the trees.

"You too," I whispered.

I put out the fire and waded into the stream, keeping an eye out for any strange or otherworldly ripples. Satisfied, I dunked my head several times. The water was frigid. Brushing my fingers through the stubborn tangles, I tried to dislodge the encrusted hare's blood. In time my hair softened, but I could do nothing about my blood-stained underdress. I tore two strips from the bottom and then took the garment off, leaving it in a sodden puddle by the bank. Using the fabric, I tied Alrik's knife to my thigh—no one need discover his gift—and wrapped his cloak around me. My leather belt held the thick wool firmly in place.

I followed the stream, knowing it would lead me back to the ocean. When I finally emerged onto the soft sand, the Viking ship had turned and was on her way out to sea. I raced down the beach in search of Bertram and found him sitting on a rock waiting for me. I ran, stumbling into his arms, and scanned him for any sign of harm.

He shushed me. "I'm fine, pet. The Viking said you would come; I need only wait." He pulled away and looked me over warily. "He assured me you were unharmed."

"Bertram, I'm so grateful to see you, to hear your voice again. Yes, I'm fine. The Viking, Alrik, he didn't hurt me." I hugged him fiercely. "Thank the gods you're all right."

We were silent for some time. After everything that had transpired, being here safe again, with Bertram at my side, felt like a dream.

The Vikings had left everything the way they had found it. Our horses, our bags . . . they had touched nothing, taken nothing. I changed into my kirtle and tucked Alrik's knife into my satchel. When I returned home, I would hide it away in one of my locked chests. His cloak I rolled up in my bedroll. The weaving wasn't any different from what a Saxon would wear, but my wolf-pelt cloak was much warmer.

We gathered our belongings and made ready to leave, both of us eager to get back home. But before we departed, I walked out onto the beach and stared at the gray-blue water, small whitecaps frothing against the shore.

A month's time.

How could I even entertain the notion of being here when he returned? He was a Viking. Yet I knew him only as the man who had saved me, and kissed me. My lips tingled at the memory. He was powerful—yes, dangerous—without a doubt, but there was much more to Alrik than met the eye.

Bertram appeared at my side, studying me closely. "The last time I saw a look like that, Avelynn, your mother was being carried away by your father."

EIGHT

It had been six days since the equinox. I didn't know what to do about Alrik and tried my best to put the encounter out of my mind. Even the offering of Ingolf faded to incredulity. I had awakened to raindrops the day of the storm. Clearly, I just hadn't noticed the thunderclouds roiling overhead. While it was fortuitous that the storm happened when it did, I had no reason to believe that I had caused it, or that the Goddess had somehow presided over the event; I wasn't that arrogant.

Since Bertram and I had no legitimate Christian reason for being at the coast, we kept our part in encountering Vikings silent. Bertram did, however, insist that we send a message to the king informing him that during our travels we met a trader who had recently seen a Viking ship off the western coast.

Bertram didn't know Alrik's plan to return in a month's time, and I wasn't about to enlighten him. Whether I was going to be there to meet him was another matter entirely.

When I was with Alrik in the forest, alone and brazen, lost in his embrace, I would have willingly given myself to him. Now, with time and distance between us, I couldn't picture myself going through with it. What would be the point? I could never be with him. There was no future for us. He was a Viking, I was a Saxon. Those two words hung suspended above me like a noose. It was best to put the entire experience behind me, forget it ever happened.

I walked to the hall, grateful to be in one piece and back to business as usual. I had asked Milo and Walther to meet me there—I wanted to settle the grain accounts. But as I approached the doors, I stopped, certain I had overheard my name spoken within. I listened but could hear no more. I stepped inside. Sigberht stood on the raised platform in front of my father's chair, looming over Milo and Walther. All three men were red-faced and huffing. Sigberht turned to me and frowned.

I walked to the dais and waited, my arms crossed in front of my chest. Sigberht moved aside, and I sat down on the lord's chair, taking my place as my father's voice and hand in his absence.

"What's happened here?" I asked.

"I'm sorry, my lady," Milo said, bowing slightly. "There has been some discrepancy over the final tallies for the month."

"We're being accused of mismanaging the accounts, m'lady." Walther stepped forward, looking at Sigberht tentatively over his shoulder. "We've worked for your father and your grandfather before him. Never have our accounts been questioned."

"Then perhaps it's time," Sigberht said. He was leaning his shoulder against the wall. "There are serious inconsistencies. I mean to make them clear to my lord Eanwulf upon his return."

"In his absence," I said, "I will address the matter." He grumbled under his breath. "Do you not have some ditches to measure?" Our eyes locked. "Or do I need to get Leofric to remove you from my hall?" He left, slamming the door behind him.

"My lady, please." Milo approached the dais. "When we did our final check on the winter's inventories, we noticed the amount left in the granaries did not match the account balances."

"We were on our way to see you, m'lady, when our lord reeve demanded to know the final tallies," Walther added.

"He accused us of misrepresenting the numbers, insisting we've been hoarding and selling seed to fatten our own purses."

"We've done no such thing, m'lady. 'Tis a mistake in numbers is all."

They stood side by side, sweat beading their wrinkled brows.

Walther dabbed his forehead with the wide sleeve of his tunic. "We asked him to turn over the accounts, to allow you to look 'em over—"

"Knowing how learn'd you are with the numbers," Milo interjected.

"He went into a fair temper, he did, said he was not disposed to do such a thing."

Listening to their exchange, my head jerked from side to side. It was like watching a leather ball being rallied between two bats.

"He accused us further of calling his authority into question and threatened to cut out our tongues for our disrespect." Milo winced.

"That was when you came in, mistress." Walther nodded solemnly. "He had hold of his sword and meant to silence us right then 'n' there."

"I see." I looked at the anxious faces before me, wishing I could give them reassurance. "Despite Sigberht's temper and his threats, no harm will come to you while I review the matter. But I won't be able to save you should I find something amiss."

Milo blanched at my words. "We ask only a fair and unbiased pair of eyes examine the accounts, my lady. Our innocence will be apparent." They both bowed and left.

I slumped against the high back of the lord's chair. Solid and heavy, made of thick oak, it was carved ornately with depictions of noblemen hunting bears, wolves, and deer. I didn't know how old the chair was. I had been told it was a gift to my grandfather's grandfather before him. I felt the weight of its presence, the responsibilities and decisions it had supported through the years. The edges were worn, the carvings almost imperceptible in places where hands had rubbed or legs or boots had brushed. I stroked the wood with reverence. This was mine, not Sigberht's—or Demas's.

I headed outside. Leofric stood near the stables.

He bowed and regaled me with one of his heartwarming smiles. "My lady."

"Leofric." It was impossible not to smile back. "I need you to summon Bertram. Tell him I seek his counsel. Then ask Father Plegmund to provide the grain accounts for the past year and bring them to my chambers."

"Of course."

I watched him depart and then made my way home.

Nelda had just returned to Wedmore, and upon seeing me chatted animatedly about the birth of her new nephew.

"You should have seen him, m'lady." She poured some grain into the hole of the handstone, grinding it against the quern until it turned into a fine powder. "He came out screamin' and red-faced, in a full fury, his little fingers balled into tight fists. He'll be a brawny young man one day."

"I'm glad to hear the child is well. And your sister, how does she fare?"

She collected the flour and placed it into a large bowl. She had been grinding all day. Her efforts would produce a dozen small loaves of bread. "She's doing very well. She was back up pesterin' her husband by nightfall. He said it was a good sign of her full recovery."

I laughed.

Bertram knocked and entered, preceding Leofric, who carried several stacks of parchment.

Nelda looked from the paper to me. "Should I leave, m'lady?"

"No, no. Keep to your baking. Bertram and I will set up near-est the window to help us see better."

I gestured to Leofric, who carried his burden to the table. "Thank you," I said.

He bowed and returned to the door, a mischievous grin on his face. "I'll be at the tavern should you need me further."

I smiled as he left. Leofric usually had a small flock of "hens" clucking at his heels, and the tavern was one of his favorite places to charm them.

Turning my attention back to Bertram and the task at hand, I opened the shutters on the small window. A refreshing breeze lifted and twirled the hazy smoke that filled the upper recesses of the small room. "The accounts have been questioned. I'd like your help."

Bertram nodded and grabbed an oil lamp and a few candles, placing them near the parchment. "In case we are at this late." He motioned to the copious, almost imperceptible small ticks and dashes of ink on each sheet of paper. I grimaced.

Sometime later, a page came in with Walther's tally sticks, add-ing to the dizzying array of numbers.

When we finally came up for air, Nelda had banked the fire and been to bed hours before. The candles had burned so low the oil lamp was almost empty. I rubbed my eyes and stifled a yawn. We had poured over every tally and matched them up to Walther's sticks. The numbers just didn't add up. We had only reviewed the records kept for oats. We still needed to sort through the accounts for wheat, barley, and rye.

Bertram stood and groaned, his body creaking and cracking. "The numbers are a cause for great concern."

I walked with him to the door. "I think we need to look at last year's accounts as well."

He nodded. "I shall inform Leofric to post a man outside each of the three granaries. Save ourselves, no one must be allowed access until we resolve the situation."

"I agree. Thank you."

"Good night, Avelynn." He bowed his head and left, closing the door quietly behind him.

I bolted it shut.

I turned back to the pile of parchment and frowned. Milo's and Walther's records were meticulous. Most of the tallies were recorded in sesters—a quantity of fifteen pounds. A mark or symbol accounted for every sester of grain produced or used on the manor: a dash indicated each sester collected at harvest, an *X* recorded every sester remitted for the king's tax. There were marks for grain paid against the church's tithes, grain set aside in seed stock for the spring sowing, marks indicating sesters used as food, and as fodder, quantities lost to moisture, pests, or rot, and any surplus that could be sold at market. There were also marks made for individual pounds that didn't add up to a full sester's worth. For oats alone there were thousands of tiny symbols—on both the parchment and the tally sticks.

I rubbed the back of my neck, soothing tight muscles that had cramped from bending over the accounts all day. If the numbers were accurate, my father's manor was being robbed of a substantial amount of grain. Wedmore was bleeding prosperity and wealth. The crime, however, did not necessarily lie at Milo's or Walther's feet. Someone could be walking into our granaries and pilfering grain right from under us. It was essential I discover the truth behind the incongruities, but it was also imperative that I get some sleep.

I tried to clear my mind of dashes, numbers, and conspiracies. From the cauldron that hung over the raked embers of the hearth, I ladled enough warm water to fill my small washing bowl. Testing the temperature with a cautious forefinger, I dropped a linen cloth into the bowl and then used it to rub the day's strain off my face, neck, and arms. I braided my hair for ease of sleeping and changed into a linen underdress. After brushing my teeth, I snuffed the candle stubs and climbed into bed.

The wood rattled, and the thatch rustled as a gust of wind disturbed the night. The room was dark, save a single slit of white moonlight that cut through a gap in the shutters to fall vividly across the foot of my bed. The beam ended atop the locked chest that held Alrik's knife.

I will come back in a month's time, on the next full moon.

I watched as the narrow band of moonlight slowly, almost imperceptibly, inched its way across the floor. The moon was waning.

I closed my eyes, remembering his smile and his smoldering gaze, and felt my body stir.

Absently, my finger traced the outline of a nipple. I could feel the ridges swell and harden beneath my touch. I bit my lip and rubbed the tip gently, tugging it slightly between thumb and forefinger. I shivered as heat filled me. My other hand drifted lower, sweeping over the smooth slope of my belly, until it found the moist heat between my legs. I sucked in a deep breath as my fingers found the hardened nub, and my hand slid between swollen folds.

I saw Alrik's face, his eyes, his powerful naked body, slick with water from the river. He moved toward me.

Sweat broke across my forehead and pooled between my breasts.

His fingertips caressed. His mouth brushed my lips, my neck.

I want you, he growled in my ear.

My hands moved with urgency. Yearning swelled within me.

I want you.

My breath came fast and ragged, my body wracked with desire. I felt the intensity build, my body hovering on the precipice of eternity.

I want you.

I crushed my face against the pillow, stifling my cries, my eyes tightly shut, my mouth frozen in exquisite pleasure. My breath hung suspended.

I want you.

I exploded into infinite light, pinpoints of desire, each one vivid and brilliant before flickering and fading. My body lay shaking, my heart pounding in my ears.

"I want you too," I answered dreamily, melting into the afterglow of warmth that enveloped me. *Gods help me, I want you too.*

After a light breakfast of bread with butter and smoked pork, a messenger arrived.

"My lady." He bowed. "Lady Ealhswith sends her greetings and intentions of visiting you this day. She will arrive shortly."

"Thank you," I said.

Relieved of his burden, he departed.

"Nelda, see to the kitchens and have them prepare a sumptuous meal for my friend and her retinue."

She curtsied and bustled out, the hem of her kirtle kicking up rushes as she left.

I eyed the stack of parchment on the table. I wasn't going to get any closer to discovering the secrets within the accounts this morning, and Bertram was too busy haggling with a merchant from the continent selling silk to offer any assistance. It would have to wait.

Ealhswith arrived before noon. Laboring toward me, her belly bulging beneath her dress, she stretched her arms to me, smiling. Grinning back, I embraced her. "You look beautiful." I pulled away and cradled her abdomen, placing my hands on the swell of her stomach, marveling at the solidness of the mound.

"I feel like an ox."

The child heaved underneath my hands, and I gasped.

She laughed. "It's only a shock the first time. After months of sharing the same body with him, I'm more than acquainted with his every twist, turn, kick, and jab." She took my arm in hers and directed me to the hall. "I do hope I've given you enough time to fix something to eat. I'm positively ravenous."

"Of course." I nodded to the young page who held the door and led Ealhswith into the hall, her retinue in tow. "I see you've decided my goddaughter is a boy now?"

"Alfred is heir to the throne." She stroked her belly tenderly. "Every king prays for a boy."

"What of Aethelred's two sons?"

"They are but babes with no claim to the throne. Alfred's father mandated the kingship pass from brother to brother. After Alfred, it will be up to our sons to hold the throne. A mother can never be too ambitious for her children's success and security."

"Nor too humble, I see."

"Pah!" She pouted. "You wound me. I'm the very epitome of humility."

I looked at her face—an expression of angelic innocence—and snorted with mirth. The humble lady wore a fine woolen kirtle, the neck and wrists edged in silk and embroidered with gold thread, while her cloak, trimmed with fur, was clasped with a gold brooch inlaid with pearls and garnets.

"So tell me," she said, dropping herself onto a bench, "what have you been up to these many days? How are the impending nuptials coming along?"

"My intended, along with my father, is away to Rome." I looked at her curiously. Surely she would have known that.

A servant placed a large platter of steaming food in front of us. Morsels of seared, roasted pork, the fat crispy and golden, glistened in their juices. With her knife, Ealhswith scraped half the platter onto her trencher. "I knew your father was commissioned for the task, but I hadn't realized Demas had accompanied him.

Pity." She smirked, grabbing some wine from a waiting maid. "You two looked so enamored with each other at the Christmas feast," she teased.

"You have two beautiful and shrewd eyes, Ealhswith; even you could see the ill match we presented. Though, on closer examination, in private of course, he revealed himself to be a horrible man."

"How so?"

Between mouthfuls, I recounted the discussion I'd had with Demas, listening to his threats and insults.

"Did you tell your father?"

"Of course. He told me I was overreacting and the betrothal stands."

"Oh, Avelynn, I am so sorry."

I shrugged. What more was there to say?

After three more courses of hard and soft cheeses, roasted vegetables, and a bowl of pheasant soup, Ealhswith assured me she was satiated. We left her entourage to lounge in comfort in the hall and strolled the road through the village. The sky was dull and overcast; puffs of cloud, in variants of gray, raced overhead, rolling to a gloomy horizon.

"Maybe you could leave? Your mother was a good friend of Lady Judith in Flanders; perhaps you could go there? Find an honorable position at King Charles's court?"

"I can't leave Wedmore. My life is here, with my stubborn father, and Edward." I swept my arm, indicating the small island of habitation around me. "These people will be my ward one day, this manor my own. I can't just desert them and run away."

"Avelynn, in your absence, Edward would rule Wedmore. He would treat the people with as much respect and clemency as you."

"My father has given me a great gift by including me in his legacy. If I run, what would I have to leave my children—the threadbare cloak off my back, a gaudy bauble or two? You spoke of security for your child. I want nothing less."

"But Demas will take Wedmore from you. Wouldn't it be better to leave England and ensure that the people you so care about are safe in Edward's hands? And who's to say you do not meet some handsome nobleman in Francia who can provide property and security for your children, and who also steals your heart and inflames the passion you so crave?"

"Perhaps."

I clung to the hope that my father might still change his mind. But if he didn't, if the months spent with Demas only hardened his resolve . . . I gazed into the leaden sky. But Francia was so far away, and I couldn't be certain Judith would take me in. And if she did, I would rank no better than a lowly chambermaid. No man of station would stoop low enough to marry a servant. As for stealing and inflaming my heart, a nobleman may debase himself long enough to entertain a bawdy roll in the hay with a pretty, young servant, but would I ever again feel the passion that I shared with Alrik?

A vision of Alrik, his lips full and parted, his clear blue eyes burning beneath white-blond lashes, flashed unbesought in my mind.

"You're blushing."

I turned away and stared at a large rock in the distance. The curve and contours of its surface made it appear to be a man hunched over in pain.

Ealhswith moved to face me. "What have you been up to?"

"Nothing."

"Nothing indeed!" She grabbed my hand and pulled me toward a field of burgeoning wheat, far away from prying ears and prattling tongues.

At the edge of the field she stopped. Tidy rows of new shoots peeked through the soil, their long, slender green leaves swaying in the cool breeze.

She crossed her arms in front of her chest and looked at me expectantly.

"I may have met someone."

"Really? I never would have guessed."

"He was just passing through . . . a merchant." I danced, walking a fine line between divulgence and full disclosure. "He was very handsome, and when we met there was a connection. I can't really explain it, except to say it was very powerful. It afflicted both of us . . . and we kissed." I squirmed under the scrutiny of her gaze.

"Avelynn! Who is he? Where is he? Is he coming back?"

"He promised to come back. But it doesn't matter. I can't possibly see him again."

"Why ever not?"

"Because nothing can come of it. I'm betrothed to Demas."

"So?"

I gaped at her, and she laughed. She tucked my arm in hers and led me to the large rock I had seen earlier. She hauled me down on its broad sloping surface. "Did I ever tell you about Regin?"

"No."

"Just after my betrothal to Alfred, but several months before our celebrated nuptials, my father sent me to Leicester to live amongst the nuns, in an attempt to further my refinement." She sniggered at the thought. "But alas, I wasn't there long before I became rather distracted with a handsome young rogue named Regin. He quite thoroughly dishonored me."

"Ealhswith!"

"I didn't know Alfred. I didn't know what my life was going to hold, and I was terrified. I hated my father for matching me with a complete stranger. I was angry and a little rebellious. Regin swept me off my feet. He lavished me with praise and flattery and quite literally charmed me into his bed." She stroked my hand. "I cannot feel what I did was wrong. The opportunity to experience life in all its passion and vivacity was too good to pass up. So I jumped in and savored every last drop."

"But you were betrothed."

"Who was hurt by my transgressions? Alfred doesn't know, and my father never found out. A little chicken blood on the marital sheets appeases even the most meddlesome priest. I had a beautiful, passionate love affair—a memory I will cherish all my life."

I fiddled with the fringe of my cloak.

"Why can't you have the same thing? In your heart, you know the type of marriage you will have with Demas. Why not pluck a little fruit from the tree of life and taste its sweetness before you commit your soul to hell?"

Gods, how easy it would be to give in to the temptation.

"What are you afraid of?"

"Everything. Getting caught . . ." Getting hurt.

"There's an old woman who lives near the swamps. She deals in secrets. She knows how to keep things hidden or stop them from ever transpiring. If you'd like to see your paramour again, you need to visit this woman first."

"Why?"

"The last thing you need is a child to announce to the world your indiscretions. The key is to be discreet, tell no one, and don't give anyone a reason to doubt you. She'll give you a tincture to stop the man's spirit from conquering yours, and no child will grow in your womb."

"I hadn't even thought about that." I groaned and dropped my head into my hands.

"That's why I'm here, to help you think of everything. Now, when's he coming back?"

"Full moon," I answered dismally.

"Then we have much to do between now and then." She rose. "Do you want to see him again?"

"I don't know."

"Really, you don't know? If he isn't worth it, then perhaps we should let the matter lie."

"But I'm afraid."

"That just makes it all the more thrilling." She pulled me to my feet. "I'll do everything in my power to help you. You can say you're coming to visit me. I'll go to the manor at Chippenham. That'll be near the babe's expected time of birth. It would be only natural that I would want you there. And once you arrive, I'll say you have taken ill and need bed rest. You can sneak away under cover of night and meet him." Her eyes gleamed with mischief.

"Chippenham is too far, it would take over a day to reach our rendezvous point." I closed my eyes. I couldn't believe I was considering this. "Bath might work."

She clapped her hands and embraced me. "Bath it is, then."

Ealhswith's words rang in my mind, swooping and diving, leading me in tangled circles. I clasped my head in my hands and moaned.

"Is everything alright, m'lady?" Nelda asked.

"I'm fine. Just a headache from staring too long at these records."

Afraid that Bertram would see through my erratic moods and start asking questions, I insisted that we divide the difficult task. While I tried to sort through this year's accounts, Bertram, comfortable in his own home, would see to last year's tally.

I rubbed the furrow between my eyes. "Nothing some fresh air won't cure." I stood, brushing down the wrinkles in my dress, and grabbed my cloak.

The sun was setting, a bloodred orb hovering just above the horizon. It had been more than a week since Ealhswith's visit, and I couldn't think of anything else, except of course our conversation's terrifying implications—I would see Alrik again. At the thought, my heart raced and my throat constricted.

The previous few days had been intense. Each of my senses was heightened. Colors were brighter, sounds louder, flavors and textures of food more pronounced. I felt the slightest stirring of the hairs on my arms, the restless brushing of my clothes against my body. And I felt as though everyone were watching me, as though they knew what I planned to do.

Black clouds clung to the sun, their dark razing claws piercing and dragging the brilliant red sphere from this earthly plane, pulling it to the underworld. Once the clouds vanquished the light, the world would remain in darkness. It was the new moon tonight—half a month had passed.

I wandered to the stables. Marma was nosing the straw when I entered, but her ears perked up when she heard me whistle. She turned and poked her head over the gate of her stall.

"Hello, beautiful." I patted beneath her forelock down to her muzzle. Her head bobbed up, lifting my hand.

I laughed. "I'm sorry, sweeting, I didn't bring you an apple."

She snorted her disapproval.

"How about a good brushing, instead?"

Her nostrils flared and she nickered. I took that as a yes.

I grabbed a metal curry comb from the bucket just outside her stall and started at her shoulders. The stable doors opened to the west, and the last rays of the setting sun bathed the space in a warm glow. I let myself relax with each long and languid stroke. Marma, too, seemed content, her dark eyes full of trust, her strong body easing into the rhythm.

But the distraction didn't last long. While dust motes flitted silently around me, my mind filled with noise. Try as I might, my mind was firmly fixed on Alrik.

Ealhswith had left me detailed instructions on how to find the mysterious old woman, and I was to set out in a week's time to procure her services.

"When did I decide to go through with all this?" I asked Marma.

The muscles under her coat shivered, rippling beneath my hand, and she whinnied. I sighed. I didn't know either. I tried to ascertain the exact moment that I had agreed to see Alrik again, and recognized with chagrin that for all my dismissals, I had only been fooling myself. I think I knew the first moment I saw him that I would do anything to see him again. I knew what he meant to do and realized I wanted quite badly for him to do it.

Marma stomped her foot, protesting my drifting attention.

I laughed. "Perhaps I should just bring you an apple."

She snorted her agreement.

Despite the late season, the storehouse held several crates of apples. Some of the fruit would be rotted, others soft, but Marma wasn't picky. I pulled a crate out and lifted the straw, rooting around until I found one. I returned to the stables, tossing the red sphere up and catching it, realizing sardonically that my own future was very much up in the air, but it, too, had the potential to be very sweet indeed.

I gave Marma her treat and headed home, visions and thoughts of Alrik dominating my mind. In only a fortnight, we would be together again.

Beyond the highlands, deep in Somerset's northern levels, I found the old woman's cottage. A towering oak stood sentry to the home. Hundreds of bones, dried and bleached by the sun, hung from its branches. They swayed and tinkled in the light breeze. No Christian would dare display such crudities. This woman was pagan. My heart skipped a beat. Other than my mother and Bertram, I had never met another pagan. I knocked on the door. A small stool sat beneath the single window; a knife, edged with blood, dripped soundlessly into the grass.

"Who's there?" a hoarse, crackling female voice called from behind the door.

I cleared my throat. "I hear you deal in secrets, mistress. I've come to procure your services."

The door opened a crack, and I heard shuffling as someone moved deeper into the home. I pushed against the heavy door. It was very dark inside; a single muted beam of light filtered in through a small hole in the roof. The air was thick with peat smoke, and the acrid smell of fresh blood reached my nostrils, coalescing with the unpleasant reek of at least one unwashed body.

"Close the door."

I reached behind me and swung the door shut. The room was muted into eerie silence. Only the sound of my own breathing, swift and shallow in my ears, disturbed the preternatural quiet.

"Sit."

I looked through the thick, gray haze. Near the middle of the room, I found a stool, the light leeching in from the roof just barely outlining it. I sat as directed.

"You're a pretty thing."

I had no idea where she was. Her voice floated in the gloom.

I tried to speak, but inhaled a lungful of gritty smoke. I coughed, my eyes watering. "I have come to—"

"I know why you're here," she interrupted. "Who sent you?"

"A friend."

I could hear more shuffling around the periphery of the large room.

I turned my head in an effort to follow the sound, but it was impossible to discern where the disembodied voice lurked or where the sounds originated.

A shadow passed in front of me right before something grabbed my arm. The sting of a hot blade sliced across the back of my hand.

I jumped off the stool, knocking it down in the process. "What are you doing?" I hissed into the shadows, wrapping my hand tightly with my cloak. The blood pooled and soaked into the thick fabric. Panic swept over me. I scanned the blackness, but couldn't find the door.

"Sit."

"I will do nothing of the sort. I demand you show me the way out."

"Can't do that."

"Show me the door."

"No."

"Then I shall find it myself."

I started to move, but something blocked my way. It was large—gigantic, in fact—shaggy, and reeked of fresh blood and dried urine. It growled. My heart hammered against my chest.

"Sit."

I backed up, fishing around the floor with a blind hand until I found the stool. Setting it upright, I sat back down.

"Good."

"I beg you, let me take my leave."

"Silence." Her voice echoed off the walls. "You'll get what you came for."

There was a great deal of rustling. I recognized the sounds of pottery being knocked about, a pestle grinding, a mallet pounding. When she finished her ministrations, she chanted in a strange tongue. I didn't recognize the language but sensed tremendous power in her words. The hairs rose on the back of my neck. Who was this woman? Why had I never heard of her before? Openly declaring oneself pagan was suicide. How had she kept herself hidden?

She appeared in front of me, holding a knife wet with blood. I scrambled back, standing. My mind raced to formulate a plan of escape or attack. I reached for the knife tied around my waist.

"Steel cannot help you."

I couldn't make out her face. It was shrouded within a black hood; only a few strands of long gray hair were visible.

"Your blood." Droplets fell from the knife's point into the bowl she held. "Now drink." She pushed the bowl into my chest.

"No." I adjusted my cloak so she could see the full length of the knife, its silver hilt visible in the murk.

"Steel will do you no good here. I have only to cry out, and my pet will make a quick meal of you." Her teeth clicked together, and the beast appeared by her side. It was a brown bear.

I had seen a bear only once before, in a passing caravan when I was young. Restrained by thick ropes, the beast had lumbered behind its master's wagon, and I had felt tremendous sadness watching the creature endure its keeper's relentless whip. However, seeing one this close up, its sinister, pointed teeth, its muzzle flecked with bloody gristle, I felt only terror.

"Drink."

My hands trembled, and I took the bowl from her thin, wrinkled hands.

"Drink."

I placed the bowl near my mouth, terrified to put the vile liquid to my lips.

"Drink. Or we'll mess up that pretty little face of yours, won't we, precious." She stroked the huge beast's head, its black, beady eyes watching vigilantly.

I tilted my head and downed the contents in one swallow, gagging on its foul taste. I heaved, but managed to keep it down, too afraid of what might happen if I brought it back up.

"Good girl." The beast disappeared back into the shadows. "Now, where's my payment?"

"Payment? For what? Intimidation? Threats? Injuring my person? Poisoning me?"

She laughed—a shrill, shrieking sound. "Silly child, I was merely toying with you. Had I meant to hurt you, you would be dead. A lesson." She waggled a pale, skinny finger at me. "You rush into things without thinking, girl. You are too willful. One day your behavior will get you into trouble." She shuffled back into the dark. "You won't ripen with child this month, and you have until the next new moon to do as you please; no babe will cling to your womb. I'll give you enough herbs to last the full lunar cycle. If you need more, you must come back."

I grabbed the small leather purse that hung from my belt. I shook it, coins jingling, and threw it onto the floor. "There."

She scuttled over to the purse, grabbed the bag, and opened it. She stepped into the light, her back to me.

"Hold out your hand," she croaked.

Afraid she was going to cut it again, I hesitated.

"Now."

I offered her my right hand.

"Not that one." She pushed it aside.

I thrust my left hand forward. It was shaking. I clenched my teeth while she rubbed some paste on the wound. It smelled sweet and fresh.

"That will heal by the morrow." She turned it over, palm up, and dropped four small linen packages into my hand. "Empty the contents of one packet into a cup of boiling mead and drink on each of the next four Sundays. Do this and you will stay barren." She disappeared again.

The creak of metal hinges and wood brushing over dirt caught my attention. I turned to find the source. A faint crack of daylight outlined the edges of the door.

"Go."

I edged closer to the door, petrified the bear would suddenly lunge at me and tear me to pieces.

I crept sideways until I had both feet on the other side, back in the daylight.

She swung the door open. I unsheathed the knife from its scabbard and held it in front of me, daring her to take a step closer.

Still shrouded in shadow, she laughed. "Headstrong and beautiful. Just like your mother. Good luck, Avelynn," she croaked, and slammed the door behind her.

"How do you know my name?" I yelled at the dark wood planks in front of me.

There was no answer. I waited a moment and repeated the question, banging on the door. "How do you know me?" Still no sound, no movement.

It was disconcerting enough to have a witness to my disobedience, but for this woman to know me, and possibly my mother, was entirely unsettling. But there was nothing I could do. I couldn't force the woman out, and I definitely didn't want to try to reenter the cottage.

The sky was darkening; a waxing quarter moon hovered above me. I needed to leave this wretched place. With a final glance over my shoulder, I left my question hanging in the air, mingling with the chattering bones, and mounted my horse, hell-bent for home.

NINE

——

True to her word, Ealhswith sent for me two days before the full moon, but I had one last matter to settle before I left. I needed to address the grain inventories and had called a meeting of the council, inviting the townspeople as witnesses.

I wanted a written record of the matter and had asked Father Plegmund to record the proceedings. He wore a monk's robe of brown wool with a simple corded belt. His head, neatly tonsured above a mass of bright red hair, bent over a small table to the right of the dais, his quill suspended over a crisp piece of parchment.

Leofric escorted Sigberht, Milo, and Walther into the hall.

I took my father's seat. "Thank you all for attending on such short notice. A great injustice has been committed against Wedmore and cannot wait for my father's return."

An excited hum rippled through the crowd. Appetites for gossip and scandal were gluttonous.

"After careful review of the grain inventory, I discovered significant discrepancies in the accounts. Over twenty bushels of grain went missing this year alone—that's equivalent to half an entire year's bread tax due the king. There were similar losses represented in last year's accounts as well."

The din of whispers increased, and I raised a hand. My pride swelled, and I stifled a smile as all fell silent. I hadn't realized until that moment how badly I wanted the villagers to accept me. I set my shoulders. A great deal rested on today's outcome.

"I have posted a guard at each granary, and this practice will continue for the foreseeable future. Anyone wishing to have access to any of our food stores must seek my permission. I will review all transactions from this point forward."

I swept my hand, indicating the men standing before me. "Sigberht of Otford, reeve of Wedmore; Milo, seneschal of Wedmore; Walther, steward of Wedmore, you are each hereby accused of mismanaging the accounts."

Sigberht's scowl only deepened, while Walther's mouth went slack. Milo approached the dais. "My lady, please." I raised my hand, and he stepped back.

"However, due to the nature of the losses, it is impossible to lay the blame on anyone present."

Milo's and Walther's faces regained some of their color.

"While I cannot prove who has committed the crime, someone has been stealing from Wedmore, and it is imperative that we all work together to ensure this does not continue."

Milo and Walther rushed up to me, grabbed my hands, and knelt on the ground.

"Thank you, my lady." Milo bowed his head.

"Yes, thank you, m'lady," Walther echoed. Both men looked up, and their eyes shone, their faces glowing with a relief only those skirting possible execution could know.

I nodded to Leofric, who escorted them back to their positions. Sigberht's eyebrow crested his forehead.

"I am not finished."

I could feel the thrum through the crowd. Anticipation buzzed until the energy in the hall near prickled with it.

"Given that you have all been remiss in your responsibilities, I have no choice but to revoke your privileges as esteemed members of this court and suspend your duties until further notice."

Sigberht lunged. "You have no right."

Leofric positioned himself in front of Sigberht.

"Would you like to make a statement, Sigberht, before I suspend your duties?" I sat back and waited.

"Milo purchased a cow this year, and Walther bought a fine new sword for his son. How did they afford such luxuries? Your guilty party stands before you." He waved in their direction. "If your father were here, he would have them killed." He laid a hand on his sword, and his voice dropped, laced with venom. "If you haven't the stomach for the job, step aside. Your weakness is a disservice to this estate and a disgrace to your father's good name."

The villagers tittered, and for a moment, I sat speechless, his contempt and disrespect disarming me of a response.

Milo rushed forward. "My lady, Father Plegmund will swear to our arrangement. Walther and I have been assisting the monastery at Glastonbury with their inventories. The cow was a gift in exchange for my services, and Walther received the sword for his son from the Abbot Herefirth himself."

Father Plegmund stood. "It is true, my lady."

I nodded, sufficiently recovered to find my voice. "Your accusations are refuted, Sigberht, and as overseer of the accounts, you have been found negligent. My verdict stands." I watched his jaw clench. My gaze locked with his. "In addition to the suspension of your duties, you are hereby charged six hundred silver shillings. Your disrespect for me will not be tolerated. Leofric, escort him from my hall."

The hall erupted as Sigberht was forcibly removed. The wergild was usually reserved for matters of injury to person, like death. In forcing Sigberht to pay for an insult, I was setting a new precedent. The charge was equivalent to six hundred sheep or twenty cows.

I turned to Eata, whose job as butler was to ensure the adequate libation of all present. "Inform the kitchen to serve the feast. Make sure everyone here has a cup filled with mead."

I stood and smiled, shaking hands with those who approached me, and gratefully accepted their praise.

Bertram moved to my side and surveyed the crowd. "Quite the spectacle."

I grimaced. The proceedings hadn't gone quite as planned. Sigberht's disrespect rubbed like a goat's-hair tunic, but I wondered if perhaps I had overreacted. Surely, I needed to set an example, to prove I was in charge, that my authority was not to be questioned.

Bertram seemed to sense my doubt. "You did well today. Your father will be proud."

Gods, I hoped so. "Will you accept the title of reeve?"

He rubbed his beard, considering. "That is a lot to take on."

"What if Leofric assists you? I need someone I can trust in this position."

He nodded. "Very well." He accepted a horn of mead from one of the servants. "Who will you find to replace Milo and Walther?"

That was trickier. "Eata is shrewd and keen to earn my favor." He had done a thorough job of measuring the boundary lines with Sigberht, and, like Milo and Walther, he had been involved in the manor since the days of my grandfather. "If I find a young man to assist him, they might manage until my father returns. Milo and Walther could continue in an advisory role." I sighed. "In my heart I believe they are innocent."

"And what does your heart tell you of Sigberht's innocence?"

"Given his desire to silence Milo and Walther by cutting out their tongues, he might have been trying to keep the thefts hidden. Unfortunately, I have no proof." If Sigberht was capable of such an act, what was to stop him from threatening them further, demanding their silence? The discrepancies might never have been discovered.

The more I thought about it, the less I trusted the man. "Regardless, I want him as far away from Wedmore as possible. Leofric has assigned someone to escort him to Kent, where he can await word from my father. I can only hope that the time away softens his disposition, rather than strengthens his resolve." Little pinpricks of cold swept across my neck, and I shivered. Retribution, I feared, would be swift and brutal.

The next morning, I left Bertram in charge of the manor, and Leofric and I rode for Bath. After my experience with the old woman and her harrowing judgment of my character, calling me willful and reckless, I thought perhaps a pair of strong hands on the road might be prudent. I would dismiss him when I reached Bath and return home with one of Ealhswith's guards instead, decreasing any chance of someone keeping tabs on me while I was there.

A royal village, Bath was quite large, boasting more than four hundred souls, including a thriving monastic community. Lying just north of the River Avon, it was surrounded by lush farmland, worked by bondsmen and their families who were charged with ensuring the royal manor's considerable demands were always met.

Markets were held frequently, and trade goods from all over the continent found their way into prosperous hands. A water mill was in use at all times to grind flour, and bakers churned out fresh bread for the manor and villagers who could afford it.

We were met outside the city's large earthen rampart by one of Ealhswith's guards and escorted to the royal manor near the southwest edge of the village. Once we were inside the walls of the manor grounds, our horses were whisked off to the stables, and I parted company with Leofric, instructing him to return home on the morrow after he was sufficiently rested and fed.

The manor was in a flurry of activity, and the lady in the center of the upheaval stood holding one hand against her lower back, while her other reached out to take mine.

"You look well," Ealhswith remarked.

"And you, my friend, look as though you are about to burst."

"And feel it too." She wrapped my arm in hers and led me to the hall. "I know it's well past supper, but I thought you might be hungry after your travels, so I had the kitchens prepare a grand feast for you. I admit the gesture wasn't entirely altruistic."

We ate companionably, catching up on innocent and unremarkable gossip—anything and everything but the real reason for the visit. When we finished, I watched her rub her lower back and groan.

"Are you well?"

"I grow tired of carrying this child around. Everything aches. I don't believe there's a spot on my body that hasn't made its presence known. Come." She drew me to my feet. "My bedchamber is filled with thick cushions and soft blankets to ease my cantankerous body."

At the far end of the hall, we made our way through a narrow passage that led to Ealhswith's chambers. Upon our entrance, she dismissed her maids, shutting the door behind them. It was a beautifully furnished room with carved panels and vibrant wall-clothing. The herb-scented rush floor was crowded with couches and chairs, which in turn were burdened with pillows of every shape and size. A handsome bed, carved with swirling vines and animals, dominated the far wall. With a grunt, Ealhswith dropped onto the bed, puffs of fabric billowing around her.

I rearranged some of the copious pillows to find station on a chair. "How does Alfred fare?"

During their wedding feast, Alfred had been stricken by a strange ailment. The court leeches couldn't discern what had caused the sickness, and there was much speculation that he might have been poisoned. In the end, no one knew the reason, and it had been some time since I had asked of him.

"He fares well enough, I suppose. He's still plagued by griping pains in his belly, but he tries to make light of them. No one at court is the wiser to his discomforts." She rolled onto her side and grimaced. It looked as though the babe could come at any moment.

"Perhaps I should stay here with you. Not leave for the coast."

"Having come this far with the ruse, my dear friend, I won't allow you to fail now. Besides," she added, rubbing her lower back, "I'm living vicariously through you and am in need of much distraction."

"Speaking of ruses, how do you know the old woman you sent me to see?"

"I've used her services in the past. Why?"

"Because she's a raving witch."

She sat up and shrugged. "Perhaps. But her medicines work."

"Do you know she has a pet bear for company?"

"A bear? How wonderful."

"You wouldn't say so if it had sized you up as its supper."

She propped her elbows on her belly and rested her chin in her hands. "Sounds positively thrilling."

"She knew my name."

"I assure you, she didn't learn it from me. I sent a message to my contact in Congresbury. But all it relayed was, 'Tell your mistress a friend comes to call. She must not have children.'"

I rose and poured us both a cup of ale from an olive-green clay pitcher, its neck stamped with circles and notches. "That at least explains how she knew the reason for my visit." I handed Ealhswith a cup. "She knew my mother."

"That's not too surprising, is it? After all, there aren't many pagans left wandering about England. It makes sense they would perhaps know one another. Did you recognize her?"

"No, I couldn't see her face. She kept to the shadows the entire time."

"Now, that's interesting. I wonder if you've met her before, and she wanted her identity concealed from you. Avelynn, you do get into the most fascinating situations."

"Humph." I wouldn't have been in that particular fascinating situation if it hadn't been for her, nor would I be in this one presently if I hadn't confided in her and agreed to see Alrik again. "What's the plan for this evening?"

"You'll retire to my guest cottage. There will be a black cloak hidden beneath the mattress of your bed. Three bells will toll, each marking the hours of the night office. On the third bell, it will be midnight. Leave the cottage at that appointed hour, and there will be no sentinel guarding the gate."

I felt my throat tightening and took a healthy swallow of ale.

"On the southern side of the main road you'll find a horse saddled and ready. He'll be tethered by the King's Oak. You cannot miss the ancient tree. It is gnarled and massive; its twisted body stands sentry at the road's edge."

"Should I be taking notes?" There seemed so many details.

She laughed. "All you need to remember is the cloak, the bell, and the tree. I've even taken care of equipping the saddlebag, so there's nothing to worry about." She leaned back, a wall of pillows between her back and the thick oak headboard. "I've also included a flask of my finest wine—a gift to help get the festivities under way."

"What was I thinking?" I muttered into my cup.

"You've nothing to worry about. I've covered every aspect of your disappearance. No one will see you leave. No one will know you're gone. And when you return, all will be well . . . though you must return at night. I'll leave a dove tethered to a stake behind the King's Oak. Release the bird and it will alert me to your return. Once you see a candle burning in the gatehouse, it will be safe to make your way back to the cottage."

Fear blazed in my veins and gripped my stomach.

"Return at night, release the bird, and watch for the candle. That's it." She rested her hands primly on her belly.

"This is madness."

"Nonsense, I've thought of everything."

"I can't do this."

"What are you afraid of?"

I grabbed one of the colorful pillows and studied the detailed embroidery. Where to start? "I'm not afraid of the deception. Believe it or not, your plot doesn't concern me—much," I added honestly. "I knew you would have thought of every possible scenario, and in that regard, you've outdone yourself."

"What then?"

I traced the embroidery with my fingertip. "I'm uncertain what to do when I see him." I could feel myself blushing. "I don't know what will happen . . . I don't know what to expect when he . . . takes me." I'd heard enough bawdy remarks from the women in the village to know being with a man could be satisfying, and I was no stranger to exploring my own body and its pleasures, but I also knew lying with a man could hurt. I'd heard women whisper about bruises and being unable to walk for days afterward. Women also screamed and cried out. I'd heard my own mother often enough, and she sounded as if she was in terrible pain. When I asked her about her nightly sojourns, she just smiled and said it was a good sort of pain and that one day I would understand. But I didn't understand and, hidden behind the bed curtains, I couldn't see what they were doing, though in truth, I was too terrified to look.

"Come here." Ealhswith patted the vacant spot on the bed in front of her. I lay down, facing away from her.

"There's nothing to be afraid of," she said, stroking my hair. Her fingers brushed and lifted the long strands, and I felt myself relaxing.

"That's easy for you to say—you've been with a man." The occasional sweep of her fingers across my back sent shivers up my spine.

The bed shook with her laughter. "Yes. I've been with a man and, really, there's not much to it, after you get over the initial shock of how the bodies fit together and where everything goes."

I groaned and buried my head in one of her pillows. "I don't want to know."

"If a man is gentle, there's no reason it should hurt. Unless his manhood is very large, in which case you will feel considerable discomfort until your body learns to ease and accept him. However, once your body becomes accustomed to his, you may find yourself quite appreciative of his considerable attributes."

"What of the blood?"

She started braiding small sections of my hair. "That's more of a man's dream than a reality. Men like to judge a woman's chastity by the presence of blood, but chances are you bled when you were younger, galloping over hill and dale on your horse. You're not likely to bleed now." She paused. "Though it's still possible you might, in which case it will hurt."

"You're not helping."

She laughed. "Close your eyes. Let me paint you a picture."

I did as instructed.

"Does your paramour have a name?"

I hesitated. Alrik wasn't an Anglo-Saxon name, but I had told her he was a merchant . . . "Alrik."

She shifted closer until I could feel the press of her belly against my back. "Good. Now I want you to imagine Alrik's kiss, imagine how it made you feel."

That wasn't hard to do. I had replayed our encounter over and over again in my mind until I felt faint with desire.

"Keep imagining his kiss, his lips, his tongue, his breath heavy and hot against your skin."

My body stirred. The embers of desire, so quick to light, caught and blazed through me. Her hand ran down the length of my leg until it found the hem of my skirt. Setting the cloth aside, her fingertips brushed the skin above my ankle.

"He's kissing you, but his touch, hungry and eager, conquers your body." Her hand moved higher up the indent of muscle that outlined my calf, over the side of my knee. "His body aches for you." Her fingers trailed along the length of my thigh, her breath warm and moist against my neck.

"Have you ever pleasured yourself, Avelynn?"

"Yes," I whispered.

Her hand slid between my legs and I gasped.

"So you know what this feels like?"

"Yes."

"There's a sweet channel that the man enters when he takes you. Do you know where that is?"

I shook my head.

"Sometimes he will use his fingers to help prepare you." I felt her fingers glide through the wetness and then one stopped, teetering on the edge, just barely slipping inside me. "Does that hurt?"

"No."

Her finger slid a little deeper. "How about now?"

I shook my head.

Her finger probed a little farther. "Now?"

"No." It came out in a hoarse whimper.

She pressed down harder. I inhaled sharply.

"If this doesn't hurt, Avelynn, there will be no blood. If he's slow and careful, you should feel only pleasure." She held her hand very still. "Do you want me to stop?" Her lips tickled the edge of my ear.

"No."

Her hand moved in a slow steady rhythm, her lips caressing, her teeth grazing my ear and the side of my neck. I held onto the quilts as sensation overtook me. Awareness fractured and my mind stilled, my body pulsing with pleasure. There was no end to my being, no beginning to my flesh. Everything was sensation, and I floated blissfully above the world.

From somewhere far beneath me I heard her say, "It just gets better and better."

I spent the rest of the night alone. I'd never had a friend like Ealhswith. We lived in a world that crushed passion, but Ealhswith refused to let that dissuade her from living her life the way she wanted. I supposed that's why we were such good friends. We supported each other in a reality that couldn't live up to our wishes and desires. It was a dangerous path. I could be killed for what I believed in, and she could be killed for her own secrets.

She had given me a precious gift tonight: confidence. I was no longer afraid of what would happen when Alrik and I met, and I looked forward to our rendezvous with anticipation.

I laid the dark cloak over the back of a chair and waited anxiously for the third bell to toll. There was a large silver mirror in the room, and I busied myself fussing with my appearance. I kept one of the small braids that Ealhswith had tied, and let the remainder of my hair flow softly over my shoulders and down my back. I had picked a forest-green kirtle and a pale yellow woven belt for my clandestine outfit.

I sat down on the chair, got back up, straightened and brushed down the creases in my dress, and walked to the small window. I peered through a crack into the blackness beyond. Unable to will the bell to sound, I turned and started all over again. Finally, after wearing a tread through the rushes, the bell tolled midnight.

I slung my sword over my shoulder, ensured that Alrik's knife was fastened securely to my belt, and wrapped the cloak around me, making sure every lock of hair was concealed. Opening the cottage door, I slipped into the night. The guard's keep was empty, so I scuttled to the main road until I found the King's Oak.

It was a clear evening; the moon, almost full, was high and bright. I had no problem seeing where I was headed. Just inside the cover of trees, I found the horse waiting patiently for my arrival. It snorted and nudged my arm as I untied it. "Shhh," I cooed, and smiled into its dark, trusting eyes. I was wary of staying on the main road long, lest someone see me, but with the dark cloak, no one would recognize me, and I had to stay on the road for only a short time. Once I crossed the ford over the River Avon, I could veer off and follow the Wansdyke—a monstrous earthen rampart that ran parallel to the river, snaking its way for miles to the coast. It would lead me straight to the eastern edge of the forest, and I had only to follow the tree line south until I found the trail that would lead me back to the very place I had met Alrik almost a full month ago. I wouldn't get to the coast until early afternoon.

The going was easy, the moon lighting the way, the rampart free and clear of obstacles. When I finally reached the forest, it was mid-morning. I stopped by a narrow creek and let the horse drink and graze in the burgeoning meadow. The dull, dried brown of winter was slowly being replaced by the verdant, soft green of spring, and the horse munched happily on succulent shoots of heather. I followed the horse's lead and ate some of the food Ealhswith had packed for me. My body and mind had grown tired from the long sleepless night, so I splashed cold water from the creek onto my face. The sky was a bright, clear blue. White clouds, like strands of fleece, drifted lazily to the horizon. I was sorely tempted to just sprawl out under that azure sky and fall blissfully asleep, but the full moon was this evening, and I wanted to make sure I was at the coast in plenty of time. I reined in the horse and finished the last leg of my journey.

When I arrived at the exact spot where Alrik had materialized out of the mist, the beach was deserted save a few squawking and circling gulls. He hadn't arrived yet. Thank the gods. I was exhausted and that made me feel scattered and on edge. I trudged to the clearing where Bertram and I had last made camp and tethered and wiped down the horse. I rolled out my bedding, tucked Alrik's knife beside me, and collapsed into a sound sleep.

When I woke, the sky was dark and the full moon, stoic in a swirl of ever-changing clouds, illuminated an empty beach and bay. The water, inky and endless, blurred into the expanse of sapphire sky.

I scanned the beach in both directions. No boat, no Vikings, no Alrik. Only sand and driftwood. He said he'd be here. He said he'd come back. I moved a little way down the beach, looking for any evidence of landfall—footsteps, a fire pit—but found nothing. Did he think I wouldn't be here? Or did something happen to prevent him from returning?

I searched the cold, indifferent water. What if he did make landfall but landed in the wrong spot? Was there even now, somewhere along the coast, a conflict happening, swords and shields clashing, Alrik fighting for his life?

I lit a large fire. If he had yet to arrive, he might be searching the coast for the right inlet. The fire would guide him.

Arms crossed, I stood staring at the ocean. The tide was out. Perhaps they were waiting until daylight. I frowned. But they'd been here before; surely they knew the bay was free of boulders and debris. I studied the taciturn water. The moon was brilliant, illuminating much of the land surrounding me, but its radiance couldn't penetrate the jet-blackness of the ocean. Maybe he would be here in the morning.

Like a thread that begins to unravel, so did my thoughts. He'd been here before. I remembered him saying they had stopped here for rest and to replenish their supplies—that they were on their way to Ireland. But what if he was hiding their true intentions? All his men had been armed to the teeth when they arrived here. There could be no doubt that Alrik was leading a war band. But what were they doing on the western edge of England when every other Viking was supposed to be holed up in East Anglia or Northumbria? The vision I'd had at Avalon returned unsought to my mind: the raven, the blood—Alrik's ship, the sail. I thought about the dream I had had that morning in the forest, the sounds of shields clashing thundering through my mind. Was Alrik scouting for the coming war? Would he return on the morrow with a hundred warships to launch an assault on Wessex? Lost in naive lust and folly, I'd never questioned his motives. Concern had seemed unwarranted— there had been only one ship, and they had left peaceably. I'd been reckless and foolish.

The blood drained from my face. Gods, what was I doing here?

TEN

It was time to leave. I kicked sand onto the fire, suffocating the flames. The musky traces of burnt wood dissipated into the darkness. I ran back to the clearing, gathered my satchel, and rolled up my bedding, tying it haphazardly to the saddle. I reached for the reins but stopped dead.

"Going somewhere?" Alrik's hand held the horse's bridle.

I stifled the scream lodged in my throat. "Yes," I stammered, taking a step backward. I had tied my sword to the other side of the saddle, but his knife hung from my belt.

His eyes flashed to my side and then back to my face. "You are alone, unprotected." He took a step closer.

"But not helpless." My hand rested on the hilt of the knife.

He stopped. "You think you can sting me, little bee?"

I crouched, ready.

"I did not come here to fight."

"Then why did you come?" I asked.

"To be with you."

"Where are the others?"

"My crew? Out there." He pointed to the ocean. "I did not want anyone interrupting us this time." He flashed a devilish grin, sand-wiched between a neatly trimmed beard and mustache. He took another step closer. I withdrew his knife, its blade gleaming in the radiant moonlight.

"What is all this about?" he asked.

"Why were you here?"

He furrowed his brow.

"Last month, what were you doing on the west coast of England?"

"I see." He turned and walked away from me. I could hear the scraping of steel across flint. Sparks flashed in the darkness like fire-flies blinking. A flame surged, having caught on a bundle of kin-dling neatly arranged under a tripod of waiting billets. He sat down on a fallen log. "You mean to interrogate me?"

"Yes."

"Very well." He removed his sword and leaned it against the log and then unclasped his belt, placing it beside him. "I was visiting your fine country on my way to Ireland." He removed his cloak and placed it on top of his belt. "We had been raiding the coast of Fran-cia all winter, and I had agreed to sail to Dublin to help my brother quell an uprising come spring." He reached behind the log and pulled out a conveniently stashed bedroll, which he arranged on a patch of lush ferns near the fire. He then grabbed a second roll, plac-ing it directly beside the first. "I decided to stop for a fresh meal, since we needed to make repairs to the boat." He slid off the log onto the woolen blanket and pulled his tunic up over his head.

Devoid of a shirt, his flesh drew my eyes. His chest, golden and smooth in the firelight, progressed from massive and wide at his shoulders to slender and chiseled as it merged with the rippling muscles above his waist. He leaned forward and removed his boots and socks.

"Thinking this part of the coast uninhabited, imagine my sur-prise when we heard drums." He slid off his trousers, revealing long muscular legs glinting with fine, flaxen hairs. In only a pair of baggy linen shorts, he crossed his ankles, leaned back, and draped his arms across the top of the log. He smiled. "I met a beautiful woman and came back to see her again." The air was cool and crisp, and his nipples stood tight and erect. "Come. Sit beside me." He patted the vacant blanket. "You are cold."

Fully dressed and wrapped in my cloak, I was not cold, but I was trembling. I stood frozen. "Are you here to start a war?"

His eyebrows knitted together. "I am here to see you. Nothing more. Once this night is done, I am bound to return to Ireland."

I alternated between hesitation and compulsion until I was certain my insides would tear apart. Why had I come? Even if I did believe him, what was I hoping to accomplish with this tryst—a fast and furious tussle in the grass? On the surface, and in an entirely selfish, impulsive manner, Ealhswith's advice to live before ceding to marriage with Demas certainly had its appeal, but was it really worth it? I felt cheated. What was one night compared to the rest of my life? Could it possibly make any difference?

Shadowy leaves rustled softly in the light breeze. Beyond the brilliance of the fire, the forest disappeared into a void of shadows and secrets. It was here that we had first kissed—a kiss that had sent shock waves through my body and pulled me back a month later, like a moth to a flame.

Heedless of consequence, I had sneaked and connived, stealing away in the middle of the night to be with him. I had spent a month longing for him, waiting for him. I'd endured a bear and a witch and risked the potential wrath of my father and condemnation from my people. All to stand here, petrified, conflicted, and out of my right mind with desire.

I took in the scope of his beautiful, muscular body. My legs, iron anchors weighed down by doubt, plowed slowly through the sand.

He stood. "Trust me. I will not hurt you."

I stopped in front of him. His hands smoothed the hair away from my temples and stayed there cupping my face. "Do not be afraid."

"I'm not," I lied.

He drew me close. Our lips touched, and the kiss blossomed like a rose unfurling in the summer sun. After a month of imagining, I was finally here, engulfed in his arms, and for a wondrous moment time slipped away.

He pulled back and regarded me with critical discernment. "This will not do." He lifted an edge of my cloak, letting the hem drop from his fingers. He unclasped my brooch, and the heavy wool slipped from my shoulders. Folding it neatly, he placed it on the log. His steady hands removed the corded belt from my waist.

"I see you kept the knife."

"I brought it back for you."

"It is yours now, Seiðkana."

I'd forgotten his term of endearment. "You're not afraid I might turn you into a frog?"

He smiled. "No, but I will think twice before angering you."

I remembered the tempest and the churning river, the raft with Ingolf's body speeding downriver, but as he helped me shimmy out of my kirtle, pulling it over my head, thoughts melted away.

"You are the most enticing present I have ever unwrapped."

He nuzzled my neck, sending walls of inhibition crashing down around me. I drew in a sharp breath.

My underdress came off rather suddenly, and I found myself on the ground, Alrik straddling my thighs, his hands braced on either side of my body.

He leaned down. "My beautiful Seiðkana." His tongue traced my lips, and I met him boldly, my own brushing and grazing his. He groaned and opened his mouth to mine.

His hands explored my flesh. Fingernails trailed, leaving shimmering waves of gooseflesh behind. His caress was purposeful in its avoidance, determined and merciless in its course—a little here, a little there, but always evading where I most craved to be touched. His fingertips graced the tops of my breasts, the curve of my belly, the length of my thigh, until my entire body convulsed with each brush, each touch, each stroke.

"Please," I begged.

He removed his shorts and guided my hand to him. The torrent of sensation ebbed for a moment while I considered this new development. He positioned my hand, and I wrapped my fingers around him. He slid my hand up and down and let out a deep moan. Fascinated, I reached out with my other hand, studying him. I played with the coarse hairs that cradled him, the tight, rigid sacks that caused him to inhale sharply when my fingers brushed against them. I traced the outline of his stomach and his waist, running my fingernails up along his broad back, smiling when he arched and twisted away from my touch.

"You're ticklish," I marveled.

"So are you." He nuzzled his beard into my belly. I squealed.

He sat up with a wide toothy grin. "I wonder where else you are ticklish?" He grazed his beard along my side, from hip to ribs. I screamed and squirmed until his mouth found purchase on a nipple, arresting my breath. His tongue brushed gently back and forth and his hand cupped the moist heat between my legs. I clung to him, my eyes fiercely closed.

"Do you want me?" He held his hand very still, a taunt, a promise of more withheld.

"Yes." I sounded desperate. I wanted to arch my hips upward into his hand.

A low rumble caught in his throat, and he chuckled, but his next words were thick with hunger and longing. "Touch me."

I reached a trembling hand back down between his legs. With admirable patience, he instructed me how to stroke him powerfully and then resumed his own ministrations, slipping his finger deep inside me.

"Oh, gods."

His attention was reverential. His lips paid homage to mine, his hand worshipping my breasts, while his fingers delved into my soul, parting and coaxing my surrender. I lost the last tenuous grasp of rationality. My body shuddered and writhed beneath him, my hips pressing, my hands grasping. I knew only his touch, his mouth, his tongue, and his breath, and I gave back in kind, wanting and needing more until I was dizzy, my fingers and lips tingling.

"I want you. Now." He lowered his hips, hovering, waiting.

I opened myself to him and he entered me slowly.

I sucked in a deep breath and winced, pushing against his chest as a sharp pain ripped through me. "It's not going to fit."

His eyes crinkled at the sides. He stroked my hair away from my face. "I will be gentle." He waited for a response. I nodded.

He was very attentive, reading my body's secret language— stopping when I tensed, resuming when I let go—all the while nuzzling my neck or caressing my breasts, until at last he settled deep within me, filling me, and I thought I might disintegrate into oblivion, melting formlessly into the ground. But then he moved, a primordial rocking that pierced the very core of my being.

I shattered into a million dazzling pieces, ready to float for eternity amongst the stars. But it lasted only a moment, for the pieces coalesced, bringing me back to my ecstatic body, a body on the peak of rapture. He moved faster and deeper. Feeling myself dissolving, desperate for an anchor to this world, I wrapped my arms tightly around his neck and held on. He kissed me thoroughly, stifling my cries.

My hips rose. My body arched. My nails grazed his back. I cried out and merged with the matrix of life, joining the land of the gods.

A strangled cry escaped his own lips, and he collapsed onto the ground, drawing me on top of him. He grabbed one of the bedrolls and wound the heavy wool blanket around us.

We lay there panting, still joined, his pulsing echoing in the throbbing of my own body.

A sated grin fixed on my face, his arms enveloping me, I started to drift off, lost in the embrace of languid contentment.

"Thank you," he said an eternity later.

"For what?" I stretched and nuzzled closer.

"For coming back."

"I almost didn't." I looked past him into the forest's shadows. "I almost left."

"Why?"

"I was beginning to question my motives . . . and yours. Several months ago, I had a vision of war coming. I thought perhaps you were here to start it." I glanced in his eyes but turned away, suddenly shy.

"I told you why I came back." He got up and added more wood to the dwindling fire. He started to dress.

Was that it, then? Having gotten what he came for, he was leaving? I felt exposed. Vulnerability crept in like a horde of insects crawling and scratching beneath my skin, scampering their way to my stomach, where a large knot was forming.

What had I expected—the world to shift somehow? That our encounter would alter fate, negate my upcoming marriage, bring my father and brother back safe and sound, and somehow allow me to live happily ever after, Alrik by my side? I pulled the blanket around my acute nakedness. "Leaving so soon?"

He stopped in mid-dress, one boot on, another hovering in the air. He looked from me to the boot and back again. "I left our salmon hanging in a tree. I thought you might be hungry."

"Oh."

He lifted my chin with his hand and kissed me. "I will be back."

He swung on his boot and disappeared into the darkness. I stared at the fire and then dropped my head in my hands. Gods, I was being a fool. The light of the moon threaded through my fingers. Perhaps the Goddess Aine had cast a spell over me, blurring the edges of wisdom with her lunar magic. I climbed back into my clothes, self-conscious that he should find me naked.

He returned with the fish, deboned and filleted. "I caught these earlier today." He placed them on the fire.

I retrieved the satchel from my horse and presented Ealhswith's wine. "This is a gift from a friend." I set the flask down on the log. "To celebrate our . . ." What—tryst? Future? I grimaced. "To us," I ended succinctly, picking the flask back up and taking a healthy swig.

"To us," he said, taking the proffered liquid and downing a good measure.

We ate and drank in silence.

By the time the wine was finished, I was feeling warm and languorous. "You've been to Francia and Ireland, but where is home?"

"I am from Västergarn, Gotland, an island off the eastern coast of Sweden. My grandfather is jarl there." He leaned against the log, the fire between us. "And you are from England."

"I live a day's ride from here. It was quite the adventure to meet you this evening." I proceeded to tell him about Ealhswith and her daring plan to help me with my deception.

"I am forever in her debt." He poked the fire with a stick, sending a procession of hot orange embers floating upward. "I had not thought of the means necessary for you to meet me. I was focused solely on what it took to make my way back to you."

It hadn't occurred to me there would be challenges for him, either, but I felt rather pleased with the notion that he had gone to some length to see me again. "What could possibly stop a Viking from getting what he wants?"

The distance between us evaporated, and he pulled me onto his lap, my skirt rucked up to my waist, his intentions hard and clear beneath me.

"Nothing," he said, and proved it.

When morning intruded on our sanctuary, the sun blazing a reminder that our time was up, I hadn't slept a wink, greedy to hold onto and savor every drop. Alrik, however, was fast asleep.

I shifted as silently as I could, placing my elbow just beside his ear. Watching his breath for any sign of waking, I lifted myself until I could rest my head in my hand and gaze down at his beautiful face. He was absolutely perfect. I could easily imagine the gods creating him in their image, carefully chiseling each feature out of the earth. Methodically carving the oval curve of his face, sculpting his high cheekbones, dipping their quills, and anointing his face with golden highlights, frosting eyebrows, lashes, upper lip, and jawline. My gaze lingered on his neatly trimmed beard, a beard that, only moments before, had been grazing my neck. That slight divergence in thought sent shivers up my back. I drew my attention higher, admiring his soft, full mouth. Lips that had kissed every inch of my body, leaving no freckle or mole undiscovered.

Desire kindled and I shifted, brushing my thigh against his. He roused slightly at the touch, and a stray tendril of hair fell across his cheek. I reached out and tucked it behind his ear, letting my finger chart a path along the side of his neck.

I sighed in repletion and settled back under the blankets, drawing myself closer to his body. He stirred and pulled me tighter to him. He smelled of musk, and leaves, the ocean, and the night. He was a creature untamed and wild, and his raw energy roused a constant wave of passion in me. I traced the outline of a small scar on his chest. His body quivered from the touch. Emboldened, I ran my finger down the middle of his chest to his stomach and the mass of flaxen curls that betokened possibilities slumbering mere inches lower. I paused, resting my hand on his stomach, feeling the rise and fall of his breath.

A sign of great encouragement rose up from those curls. I laughed. "You weren't asleep, were you?"

"No," he admitted, rolling on top of me.

Cupping my breasts, he leaned down and paid considerate attention to my nipples. His tongue circled and flicked the tight, strained tips. His mute kisses moved thoroughly down my body until they reached my right thigh. He slid down, lying between my legs, his breath hot and moist against my skin. His fingertips brushed up and down my leg. I shivered with anticipation.

"Are you cold?" He looked up at me over the gentle slope of belly and breasts.

"Yes."

He blew softly between my legs. "Would you like me to make you warmer?"

I nodded. My voice escaped me.

His tongue caressed me slowly but purposefully.

Fever surged through my body. I closed my eyes. Red flames danced beneath my eyelids. I didn't think I would ever be cold again.

"I don't want this to end." My ear rested on his chest, and I snuggled into his side. Lying on his back, he held me firmly to him with one arm. His hand, fingers splayed, was planted squarely on my rump, cupping it effortlessly like it belonged there.

We were silent for some time. The ocean breeze, laden with damp and heavy with moisture and brine, lifted the forest's leaves in its embrace and left them quivering in its absence. The birds sang, calling out in eager anticipation, waiting for a lusty reply. All around me life ebbed and flowed. The world was moving, getting on with its day, but I wanted to freeze this moment forever. I wanted to lose myself in the rhythm of his heartbeat, the texture of his breath.

He pulled away. "It is time to go." He got up, his broad back to me, and started to dress.

I retrieved my clothes from the log, breaking the spell and closing the door on this fantasy once and for all.

After disbanding camp, we sat down to eat a light breakfast of bread and cheese. He didn't say a word. In fact, he didn't even look at me.

I wasn't sure why he was being so cold. I had thought this meant something to him, that perhaps I had meant something to him. But the more I watched him ignore me, the more determined I was to leave, to put this whole disorienting experience behind me.

We had shared a thrilling moment in time, and I would never regret it, but I tried to make this assignation into something it wasn't. This connection was merely a fleeting, visceral experience. No ties, no questions, no commitments. Being with Alrik was wonderful, but we started and ended with one night, nothing more than that.

The sun had risen higher, the brilliance of morning done. If I left now, it would be dark enough by the time I returned to Bath. My eyes swept over to where he sat, still silent, still rigid. He was right. It was time to go.

I tucked the rest of my uneaten breakfast into the satchel and fastened it to the saddle. I led my horse out of the clearing, back to the beach, away from his silence.

Near the edge of the tree line, his hand reached out from behind me and grabbed my arm, spinning me around.

"I cannot let you go." He grasped my other arm and held me there, searching my face. "On Odin's eye, I do not know how to make this work, but I must see you again."

The look of pain and urgency on his face made my heart beat faster. Hope surged to the surface. "I want to be with you. But it's impossible." He drew me forward, the soft wool of his tunic warm against my cheek.

"Come with me."

"Where?"

"To Sweden. Be my wife."

I backed away from him. "I can't leave England."

"I can give you a good home, a good life."

"I . . ." I faltered. This proposal, this man was everything I had ever wanted. But it meant traveling to a distant land, away from my family, my people. "I can't."

He paused. "I will sail back to Ireland, band with my brother once more in his fight against the Irish, and in three months' time, I will return." He grabbed my horse's reins and led us both onto the beach. "That will give you plenty of opportunity to pine for me and change your mind."

His ship was drawn up on shore. Its crimson sail was furled, and thirty shields painted in brilliant reds, blues, and yellows covered the oar ports. Several men milled about on the beach, others were engaged on the boat, and all were just as frightening as the ship. Large, unshaven, and unkempt, each man carried some sort of implement of mortality. I looked at them warily. Could this be my fate?

I rested my hand on Alrik's arm, making him pause. "I promise to be here when you return, but I won't leave England—not in three months' time, or six."

He flashed a confident, knowing smile. "We will see." He lifted me onto my horse and laughed. "I will see you on the third full moon, Seiðkana." He slapped my horse's rump, and I sped off, blazing down the beach—away from the Viking ship, away from Alrik, and away from a potentially glorious future.

ELEVEN

Ealhswith's face was flushed and damp with perspiration. "Where is the rutting swine? I'll rip his cock off!" She collapsed back against the pillows, the contraction easing.

It had been a fortnight since I was with Alrik, and much to Ealhswith's dismay, the babe had taken its time arriving. The midwife attending the birth was a spritely woman. Round, squat, and rosy as an apple, she whistled tunelessly, fussing over Ealhswith, propping and fluffing pillows, fetching water, and feeding the hearth.

The room was stifling. I wore a thin underdress, but the soft linen clung to my back, and sweat dripped between my breasts. The walls of Ealhswith's room were covered in thick woolen wallclothing, dyed in brilliant reds, yellows, and greens. They were a godsend in winter when drafts threatened to chill every inch of your skin, but it was May and, combined with the heat of the hearth, the extra insulation made me feel like a pillar of wax melting onto the chair. Formless, I sat beside Ealhswith's bed, caught in the throes of anxiety and her relentless grip on my arm.

I felt helpless, unable to ease her pain, and I was terrified. Thoughts of my mother holding the lifeless body of my newborn brother, her weakened body caught in the grip of death, were embedded in my mind. I watched the midwife carefully, judging her reactions and mood for any signs of alarm. As long as she was happy and calm, I could maintain a shred of composure.

"Get it out!" Ealhswith curled into a ball on her side. I brushed sweat-soaked hair from her face and stroked her hand.

"Isn't there anything you can do?" I mumbled to the midwife as she whistled by.

"M'lady is doing just fine. Won't be long now."

No sooner had Ealhswith stilled than she was writhing again. "I'll make him a eunuch. As Christ is my witness, I'll tear it off with my teeth!" She leaned forward on the bed and screamed to wake the dead.

My heart leapt into my mouth and hung there, pounding. The midwife merely laughed.

"Changing my mind, m'lady—'tis time." She moved to Ealhswith's side and helped her down onto the floor over a soft pile of clean linens. There was a rope looped over a beam in the ceiling and she handed the ends to Ealhswith. "Up on your feet, m'dear." She positioned Ealhswith into a low squat, with me sitting and supporting her from behind. "Let's bring this willful child into the world."

After a half hour of insults, threats, blasphemy, and pushing, Aethelflaed, a beautiful baby girl, was born.

With mother and baby wrapped up in blankets, the one cooing, the other suckling, I removed the sodden underdress, pulled on my kirtle, and left the confines of the room, seeking fresh air. The sky was overcast, but there was a warm breeze coming from the west. I filled my lungs gratefully and leaned against the wall.

The manor at Bath was bustling. Men repaired fences and buildings, the woodworker turned bowls on a pole lathe, selling his wares near the gate. Several women worked outside on standing looms at the weaving shed. Children laughed and squealed, chasing frantic chickens. Cattle were milked in their pens, pages scurried to the kitchens with jugs so the maids could churn butter and form cheese. And pacing back and forth outside the main entrance to the hall was the new father, Alfred. He had arrived a few days before, expecting to see his newly delivered child. I waved in his direction, and he bounded toward me.

"How does she fare?"

"Both Ealhswith and your daughter are resting well."

His shoulders dropped away from his ears. "The midwife came and announced the birth in the hall but would not permit me to see them." He looked longingly at the door, but then something changed. He inhaled sharply. Sweat gleamed on his forehead and his pallor washed ashen white.

"Are you all right?" I asked, reaching out to him.

He placed one hand against the wall; the other gripped his middle. "Just a small discomfort."

I was about to run for the manor leech, but the pain seemed to pass as quickly as it came on. He took a moment to compose himself, brushing down the front of his vibrant orange tunic, and then his eyes once again focused on the door to his wife's chamber.

"Come," I said, taking his hand. It was cold and clammy. "I'll sneak you in. The midwife has gone to harry the kitchen for some pottage."

"Thank you." His smile was full now, and I couldn't help but appreciate how handsome he was. His hair was the color of chestnuts. His beard, a shade lighter, was flecked with blond. He had a youthful exuberance that twinkled through his eyes.

I opened the door to Ealhswith's chambers and gave a cursory look around. Certain the way was clear, I turned to her. "There's someone here who wishes to see you."

She looked up from the bundle asleep in her arms, and her eyes alighted upon her husband. A tender smile graced her face as she reached out her hand. He seemed to float toward it. Taking her hand in his, he kissed her forehead and knelt at her side, eyes fixed on the face of his new daughter. I closed the door behind me.

"Mistress Avelynn."

I turned to see Aluson, Wedmore's messenger, approaching me. "A letter has arrived from Francia for you."

He handed me a well-traveled piece of parchment. A feeling of dread settled in the pit of my stomach. With a slight tremor, I opened the letter. It was written by a monk at the St. Denis monastery.

> *Dearest Lady Avelynn, Daughter of Eanwulf, Ealdorman of Somerset, I am writing to inform you of a sickness that has afflicted your father's party. It is my sincerest regret to inform you that two men have succumbed to their illness: Wulfstan, son of Wulfstan, the Earl of Devon; and Willibald, son of Willibroad, ironworker of Wedmore. Your most noble father, humbled before the most glorious God, prays for the deliverance of their souls unto Him, asking for His beneficent mercy. He asks you send his sincerest condolences to the families of these brave men, who in selflessness served Him and His humble servant, your esteemed King Aethelred, here on this earthly plane. May God receive their souls.*
>
> *It is also with great sadness that I inform you that your brother, Edward, has taken ill and is too weak with fever to continue on to the most Eternal City of Rome. Your betrothed, Demas of Wareham, has also been stricken. I have taken it upon myself to see to their recovery, or if it be His will, their passing. If by the grace of God they should be healed, they will return home. I ask for your prayers and thoughts for their welfare and hastened recovery.*
>
> *Farewell in Christ,*
> *Brother William, St. Denis*

I slid down the wall, my skirt crumpling onto the dusty sand.

"Are you well, my lady?" Aluson stepped forward, but I raised a hand, imploring a moment.

Dear Gods, this letter would have taken over a fortnight to reach me. While I was lost in Alrik's embrace, Edward could have been struggling for his last breath. He could right now be dead, buried in foreign soil far from home.

I rubbed a rough hand across my face. And Wulfstan, the sweet, kindhearted boy who had sought my hand . . . dead. I thought about when I had seen him last at Christmas, eager to embark on the hunt. How full of life he had been. How was this possible?

A light mist had started to fall, just enough to dampen my up-turned face and make my hair heavy and limp. I closed my eyes. I knew I should feel concern for Demas; after all, he was suffering too, perhaps teetering upon the edge of death, but deep inside I felt a sense of hope. That didn't mean I wanted him dead—I wasn't that cold and heartless—but perhaps he could be too weak to return to England. Maybe he would head back to Rome, where the clime would better suit his weakened condition. Maybe he would stay there.

I exhaled, chastising myself for my insensitivity and selfishness, and promised to say a prayer to the Goddess for his soul and well-being.

I opened my eyes and peered through the tiny droplets that hovered on the edge of my lashes. The sky was darkening. I needed to get home. I had to inform Wulfstan's and Willibald's families of the men's death, and I wanted to be there in case Edward returned.

I turned to the young man waiting patiently for my response. "Aluson, get to the kitchens, take what sustenance you need, and have them pack two satchels for us. Inform the stable master that we will leave at first light on the morrow. You can sleep in the hall tonight."

"Of course, my lady." He bowed and ran off.

Aluson and his twin sister Dearwyne had been orphaned when they were only seven years of age. My father had taken them in and found a place for them in the manor. Aluson was lean, tall, and restless—admirable traits in a swift messenger—while Dearwyne had a keen eye and a quiet, serene focus that belied her years. At fourteen, she was better than many of the older women in weaving and embroidery.

I knocked softly on Ealhswith's door. Waiting a moment, I opened it fully and stepped inside. The room was still stifling and the small family remained intimately absorbed in one another.

I cleared my throat. "I must leave."

Ealhswith turned in my direction. "Why?"

"A letter has arrived from Francia. My father continues on with his journey, but my brother has fallen ill."

"Oh, Avelynn, I'm so sorry."

Alfred rose and clasped my hands. "May God watch over him. I will say a prayer for Edward's health."

"Thank you." I walked to Ealhswith. Aethelflaed's little hands were balled tight, her ruby-red lips pouting as she slept. I kissed Ealhswith's forehead. "Take care of yourself, my friend, and spoil my goddaughter until I can get back and do it myself." I looked at her pointedly. "I will visit here again in July."

The royal entourage grazed from manor to manor, depleting each royal village's resources before moving on to the next. This way, the burden of supporting the crown was shared amongst the shires, and the nobility managed to keep a close eye on their subjects. Not knowing where she might end up, it was essential that Ealhswith found her way back to Bath.

"July?" Her eyebrows shot up and a huge grin crinkled the edges of her eyes. "Really?"

I had doggedly avoided the topic of my paramour coming back.

It was one thing to tumble into one night of logical impairment, but to willingly engage in the activity again—it was hard for me to rationalize, never mind talk about. But I knew I would need her help.

Alfred was looking directly at me and couldn't see his wife's salacious look of mischief.

My cheeks reddened. "Until July, then," I said, and retreated quickly.

Seeking the guest cottage, I prepared myself for a night of listless sleep. A vision of Edward cloistered and scared, alone and sick in a dark, damp room far away from home, alternated with an image of his small, emaciated body, black earth packed tightly around him, his vacant eyes open, eternally searching for peace.

TWELVE

JUNE 870

A month and a half passed without word from Francia or the arrival of my brother. I had written back at once, asking for an update on Edward's and Demas's progress but had yet to hear any news. I tried to keep my mind from dwelling on Edward's condition and on my upcoming meeting with Alrik by busying myself with manorial tasks.

The granaries were still being guarded. So far, no word of bribes or treachery had reached my ears, and the inventory was being checked consistently for any signs of theft. Milo and Walther seemed grateful to retain honorable positions at court by acting as advisors, and I had assigned Aluson to assist Eata. I was very pleased. Aluson was a fast and eager learner.

In his role as head guardsman, Leofric continued to oversee the remaining warriors of the estate and proved skilled at tackling the added responsibilities while helping Bertram as reeve.

Most encouraging of all, Sigberht had stayed in Kent—not a wisp of malevolence to disturb my fledgling calm. He had even made his first payment of one hundred pence without so much as a grumble. All seemed well, and for that I was grateful.

The fields were sowed, children assigned the task of keeping hungry birds away from the newly laid seed with slingshots; hay was scythed, dried, collected, and placed in byres; cows were milked, pigs were fattened, sheep were sheared; fields kept fallow were plowed, manure mixed into the hungry earth; and gardens were tended with as much care as the larger fields of cereals, beans, and peas.

Along with several other women, I spent a great deal of time fussing in the large garden behind the hall. Fenced off from the surrounding area, so no wandering sheep, cow, pig, or deer could trample or eat the tender shoots, the garden included a large variety of vegetation—from foodstuffs to culinary herbs to a few common medicinal plants.

I knew very little about leechdom. My practical knowledge and experience with healing were pitiful at best. I knew simple cures for wounds and fevers, but anything more that I might have learned from my mother, she never got the opportunity to teach me.

There were several leeches in Wessex, but many, if not all, revolved around the king's court. Some of the more powerful monasteries had monks adept at healing, and they were charged with caring for the poor. However, the monasteries were crowded and often had to turn people away, and most villagers didn't have the means of transport necessary to make the trip, nor did they have the money needed to send for a royal leech. Most preferred to die at home in their beds. If a situation looked dire and I was informed in time, I would personally send for the leech and pay for his services. At worst, I would stand with Father Plegmund, offering my own silent prayers to the Goddess if they passed into the afterlife.

The more I weeded around the various medicinal plants, pulling out roots, or cutting the noxious stems close to the earth, the more I wondered what the witch had given me: both to ward off pregnancy and for the wound on my hand. Despite my trepidations, I was leaving on the morrow to attain more of her curious decoction. I wasn't looking forward to stepping foot again in that squalid hut, but my fear of ripening with child and the scandal it would create, not to mention the terror of childbirth itself, more than outweighed my fear of her—and her beast.

I pressed a leaf of sage between thumb and forefinger, inhaling the faintly musky aroma. Perhaps I could entreat her to share her knowledge? Maybe there was something I could offer her in return. I thought about the purse I had thrown onto the floor. She definitely liked coins.

Before I left for the witch's cottage near Congresbury, I sent a message to Ealhswith, informing her of my intent to visit in just over a fortnight. I would arrive two days before the next full moon.

Part of me wanted to stay at Wedmore in case word of Edward arrived, but I had waited in vain since early May, and it was now the end of June. With the manor running smoothly, it seemed an opportune time to leave. Bertram sensed something within my elusive moods, but my answer to his unwavering questions was always the same: I wanted to commune with the Goddess . . . alone.

I needed to fend off his suspicions for only a little while longer. I knew this relationship with Alrik couldn't last. This rendezvous was most likely the end of it. But I desperately wanted to see him again. I wanted to feel his arms around me, his body pressed against mine. I wanted to collect each sensory experience, each vibrant moment, and hoard them away, ready to relive again and again whenever I needed them. If Demas returned, I knew I would need all the inspiration I could get.

As I drew farther from Wedmore, the noxious fumes of the

tanner's trade assaulted my senses. Pits of urine were used to help remove the hair from the skins, and vats of dog and animal dung were used to soften the hides. I raised my arm to cover my nose as Marma and I passed. I wondered what ever had become of the tanner's son. He had kept his hand thanks to me, but I imagine my interference had not spared the lad other insults or injury. I glanced around but didn't see anyone. It wasn't necessary to constantly watch the pits, as each hide could sit in the mixtures for weeks or months at a time, the tanner removing them only to knead or scrape as needed before plunging them back into the noxious liquid. Spurring Marma forward, I encouraged her to set a brisk pace until we were no longer downwind.

After half a day's ride, the road through the highlands alternated between thick gravel tracks and narrow dirt trails. As I rounded a bend, vibrant green hills inclined away from me on my right, while a narrow band of grass and low scrub blended into the thicker forest to my left. I had made good time and allowed Marma to meander at a snail's pace while I collected my thoughts. I was determined to gain the witch's confidence.

A muffled shout filtered through the trees. I reined the horse to a stop, scanning the path ahead. There were no signs of habitation nearby. Marma sensed the tension and pawed anxiously at the ground, pulling on the reins as she tried to convince me to leave.

"Whoa, beautiful," I soothed, stroking her strong, smooth neck. I dismounted, and despite her apprehension, tied her to a tree. While thieves and outlaws were uncommon since Aethelred's reign had begun, the forests still held deep and dark secrets. I couldn't walk away if someone was in need of help. No one else was likely to come upon this spot for hours, if not days.

Unsheathing my sword, I followed a deer track, pushing through the dense undergrowth, moving deeper into the forest. A lone horse snorted and shifted at my approach. I brought my finger to my lips, shushing the horse, and made my way forward, tiptoeing through slender saplings and leaf mold. The hairs on my arms bristled as the row of thrashing and grunting increased, the sounds of struggle carrying me to a clearing.

I froze, the view before me opening. Two men were engaged in some sort of sexual act.

One was bent over a large log, while the other, his trousers bunched around his thighs, thrust and groaned. Realizing my error, I tried to flee, but was stopped short by the presence of a sharp blade pressed against the small of my back. My sudden intake of breath seemed to echo through the clearing, and the men, stopping their horseplay, turned to face me.

I blinked at the apparition, my mouth dropping in shock. Standing with his weight resting softly against the other man's bare buttocks, Demas stared back at me.

"I thought you were dead," was the first thing that escaped my mouth.

He looked down at his hands, turned them over, and shrugged. "Apparently not. Sorry to disappoint you."

The men disentangled themselves, the other extricating himself up off the log and hastily pulling up his trousers. Demas just stared, his eyebrows creasing. "I was on my way to see you." He stroked the man's cheek. "But I became rather distracted with my handsome friend here."

"I didn't mean to interrupt." The blade still pressed firmly into my back, discouraging any attempts at turning tail and fleeing, and a hand squeezed my arm until I relinquished my sword. A moment later, a hard tug pulled at my waist, and my knife followed.

Demas shrugged. "It is nothing that cannot be finished later." He pulled up his pants and righted his tunic.

The man laid a hand gently on Demas's shoulder, his face turned away. "I should leave." He spoke in French.

Demas leaned his cheek into the man's arm. "Wait by the horse."

The man nodded and kept his head down as he slid past me. I studied him carefully. Warm black hair, bound by a thong, hung past his shoulders, and like Demas, his skin was darker. His clothes were made of fine material, and a gold brooch crafted in the likeness of a stag clasped a soft wool cloak.

A shove from a large hand pushed me deeper into the clearing.

Demas stumbled to a flask and swilled the contents. He wiped his mouth and regarded me. "You shouldn't have seen that."

I didn't care about his proclivities, it mattered not a whit to me whom he slept with as long as it wasn't me. What shocked me most was seeing him here, in Somerset, when last I heard he was stricken ill in Francia.

"How did you get here? Where's Edward?"

Demas retrieved his belt and sword. "On Edward, I cannot say. I left him in Francia with the monks. As for my part, I was just visiting our fine king in Bath, delivering a message from your father." He swayed violently.

"What message from my father?"

"That he has been delayed. Something about Vikings."

"Is he well?" My heart was pounding in my chest. I could hear its echoes booming in my ears.

"Better than you."

I narrowed my eyes at him.

"Gil, my bodyguard." He swept his hand, and I turned slightly to regard the man behind me. Gil cracked a toothless smile; drool dribbled from the corner of his mouth. One side of his face was badly disfigured; his forehead, eyelid, and cheekbone all dripped and oozed together, collecting in a sagging jowl.

Demas took another swig from the flask and belched. "Where are my manners? Please, have a seat." He motioned to the log that had only a moment before been used for matters other than sitting.

Not wanting to give Demas any further ideas, I moved to a small boulder instead.

"I am suddenly thinking that your presence today was divinely inspired, and I can use this occasion to my advantage, taking the opportunity to solidify our pending nuptials. While he may not look the distinguished gentleman, I assure you Gil is quite literate, reading and writing Latin with ease. As our witness, he can testify to the consummation of our marriage. Our arrangement will then be quite binding. A convenient happenstance to tie up loose ends."

I stood, my breath coming heavy. "You're drunk and a fool if you think I'm consummating anything with you."

"Choice." He scoffed. "You seem to think you are in possession of this illusive creature, but tell me, how has that worked out for you?"

"I've always had choices. I could have run away, left England at any turn."

"Ah, but you didn't. Could you really have chosen that, or was fate just toying with you, giving you the illusion of choice?" He sat on the log and upended his flask, tossing it with disdain when it emptied. "In Rome, I had no choices. Instead, I came here to this wretched hole looking for opportunity. Yet I find myself in no better position."

"You have wealth; you have enviable position. How is that not better than being a scribe?" I chanced a discreet look at Gil, whose attention seemed to be wavering as he leaned his bulk against a tree. Was it possible to keep Demas talking and distracted long enough to catch Gil off guard? "Why does this marriage matter so much to you? You could have any woman in Wessex. Why me?"

Demas's eyes hardened. "If it were solely up to me, puppet, I would have never pursued you to begin with. We are both pawns in a greater game, and since I have no choice in the matter, neither do you." He stalked closer.

I crouched low, ready. I may not have had my weapons, but I'd be damned if I let him touch me.

"Tsk tsk. Two against one." The edge of Demas's lip curled upward.

"One of you is drunk."

"Yes, but one of us is a giant with a slingshot. Gil, try not to kill her, please."

I spun toward the troll of a bodyguard in time to see his hand release.

A blow glanced off my forehead, just above my temple, and I stumbled backward. My legs crumpled and curled, dropping me like a stone into the coarse grass at my feet. Warm rivulets ran down my cheek and neck. Arrows of silver flashed before my eyes. The forest blurred.

"Nicely shot, Gil." Demas's voice was low and garbled.

Something grappled with my wrists. I fought the rising panic and squirmed away, shuffling on my knees until I fell on my side, my face pressed into the ground, my hands tightly bound. One well-polished leather shoe stopped in front of my face.

"Oh, look, Gil, my wife has finally learned her place."

"I am not your wife. I never will be." I struggled to bring my knees underneath me and pressed my shoulder into the ground, desperate to right myself. I pushed through the throbbing in my head, kneeling before I found my footing and stood on shaking legs. Nausea pitched and heaved, tossing me in its swells.

Gil lumbered over and placed a knife in Demas's hand.

"Why must you make everything so difficult?" He ran the back of the blade along my cheek and left the point hovering over my throat.

I swallowed hard, my face flushed with sweat. "I'll tell everyone you raped me. That you held me against my will." I had a hard time keeping my focus on Demas's face. His features pulsed and ebbed.

"And who will believe you?" He trailed the blade between my breasts and down to my navel. A rough tug cut through the simple fabric belt around my waist, and the yellow silk floated to the ground.

I was dangerously close to fainting. "You're drunk. Please . . ." I lurched sideways, leaning into a large tree. Pinpricks of light danced through my vision. The world spun away from me. I fell to my knees and threw up.

He recoiled away from me. "If your father had agreed to my insistence that we be married immediately, instead of waiting until the fall, we could have avoided these unpleasantries. But you would have fought the matter even then, isn't that right?" His face turned a motley shade of red. "No matter what I do, you manage to foul everything. You're the only thing standing in my way."

"I don't understand. I don't know what you want," I sputtered. My head felt like it was going to be sliced in two.

He stormed over, fisted a handful of my hair, and yanked me to my feet, his hazel eyes filled with hatred. "I don't need you to understand. I need you to shut up and do as you're told."

I spat at him.

"You spoiled little whore."

I closed my eyes and waited for the blow. But it didn't come. Instead he released me. I opened my eyes, dazed.

He slunk backward, creeping to the opposite end of the clearing; the blood had drained from his face. Gil appeared beside him and the two men stood stock-still, staring into the trees behind me. Fear spread its icy tendrils throughout the clearing. My heart strained against my chest, my palms slick. Another wave of nausea crested. I used the tree to hold myself upright. The world tilted and twirled. Something very large moved through the trees. I could hear the heavy breathing as it snorted and sniffed the air. Something massive and black lumbered forward, its shaggy body inches away from me. It stood on two massive legs, or maybe it was four. I blinked hard. It lifted itself as high as a tree and roared. It pounced, and something powerful swiped sideways, catching me in the ribs, hurtling me back against the tree. Everything went black.

THIRTEEN

I looked into the boughs of a flowering crab apple tree. Delicate white petals fell softly on my cheek. The shadow of a woman's head blocked the blossoms from view. "You've broken some ribs, I imagine. And that lump on your forehead's going to need tending."

The shadow receded. I could hear the woman rummaging in the foliage around me. A hand gently turned my chin. She clicked her teeth and went back to her ministrations. I lifted myself up on my side and winced while the world spun. I leaned back against the tree. My head pounded, the left side of my ribs burned, and pain stabbed with each heartbeat. A wave of nausea rose, the heat filling my cheeks. Oh, dear gods, please no. I breathed slowly through my nose. In, out, in, out. The thought of vomiting with the pain in my ribs . . . in, out, in, out. I focused on my breath, full of relief as the nausea receded. I scanned my surroundings. I was in a clearing. How did I get here? Who was the woman?

A long braid of snow-white hair fell to just above her waist. Her face was pale, etched with years of living. Wrinkles upon wrinkles settled deeply around her eyes and across her forehead. She wore a pale green kirtle and a faded brown cloak. If she pulled the hood over her hair, she would disappear into the woods around us.

"Leaves of common plantain." She picked at a squat green plant. "For the cuts on your face." She looked off into the distance. "And some calendula, yes." She bent back over, studying the flora. "Did I not say your recklessness would get you into trouble?" She shook her head. "They never listen."

Recklessness? Trouble? The witch! I stared at her white head in amazement. The only part I'd seen in the cottage was her long, thin hand. And the images my mind created for the rest of her were certainly not favorable, nor did they remotely resemble the woman standing in front of me. While thin and elderly, her face had a regal, almost delicate quality to it—she might even have been beautiful when she was younger. I had been on my way to see her. But where was I? Where was her cottage?

My memory snapped back like a bent sapling let go. Demas. Gil. The beast. Gods, it was her bear!

I closed my eyes. I was reckless, but being called upon it left a bitter taste in my mouth. I had stepped into that clearing with Demas, thinking only to help whoever was in trouble. While noble, it was foolish. I had seen only the one horse and drawn the conclusion there was only one miscreant. It didn't occur to me there might be more, or that I could possibly become disarmed or overpowered. I'd been arrogant and naive.

"Can you walk?" Her face hovered inches from mine.

"No." I didn't think I could ever move.

"Why? Forgot how?"

"Yes."

"Time to get up."

"Leave me be, witch." I wanted to sit and wallow in self-pity.

"Witch? Is that what you call me? Name's Muirgen. I'd prefer you use that." She stood, placing her hands on her hips. "You can come, or you can take your chances alone."

"Come where?"

"You need care, and I can't help you here." She waved her hand, indicating the wilderness around us.

The thought of entering her cabin made me remember my earlier strategies. "My horse . . . my sword."

"I imagine they're either in the possession of your attacker or remain where you left them. You can look to them after I've treated you. Until then, you're coming with me." She grabbed my arm and looped it over her shoulders. "Ready?"

"No."

"Good. Here we go." She pulled me upright with considerable strength, my legs doing only half the work, and I almost buckled under the pain.

She waited a moment. "Ready?"

I shook my head no.

"Good." She stepped forward, dragging me with her. The pace she set was slow, but my body reeled from the impact of each and every step.

By the time we reached her cottage, I was covered in sweat and shaking with the effort. She led me inside. My first impression was that it smelled fresh, like linens washed in lavender and dried in the sun. Not the oppressive stench of unwashed bodies or wet bear that had impregnated the cottage when I was here last.

Leaving the front door wide open to the hazy late-afternoon sunlight, she sat me on a bed thick and soft with a feather mattress. Near the door, she pushed aside a heavy tapestry, tucking it behind a hook on the wall, revealing a large window. She opened the shutters. I stared at the scene before me. Along the farthest wall, opposite the door, a long, wide table stretched from one side to the other. It was cluttered with jars, bottles, boxes, knives, candles, and plant odds and ends. The central hearth, glowing a warm red, was raised on a large stone slab. A huge iron cauldron hung from a tripod above it. Several boxes and baskets lined rows of shelves opposite the bed.

"Thank you for coming to my aid today," I said.

"I don't care for men who abuse women. He's lucky there were two of them. Coward ran off like the filthy rat he is." She poured the contents of several bottles into a large bowl. "Do you know him?"

"He's to be my husband."

She stopped what she was doing. "Not a happy marriage, I fear."

"No."

"Well, let's get this dress off. I need to wrap your ribs."

After much struggle, starting, and stopping, we were both left sweating, my face covered in tears.

She clicked her tongue. "Only one rib is broken, the rest are bruised."

"That was from your bear."

"Well, he wasn't perfect." She grabbed some cooled fat and scooped it into a bowl with the liquid, mixing it thoroughly with a knife. "He gave his life to save you from a terrible fate."

Chastened, my tone softened. "What happened?"

"The ogre cut him down."

"I'm sorry."

She grunted and let the matter drop, applying salve to my ribs. I flinched.

"Be still."

I grimaced, but complied, watching as she worked. "What are you using?"

"Horsetail and calendula. Good for broken bones and swollen, hot skin."

She wrapped my ribs with long strips of linen and then ladled hot water from the cauldron into a wide wooden cup. She rummaged through the clay jars on the table, deciding finally on one, and placed some of the contents into the cup. She pulled down a large stoppered pitcher from the shelves overhead and poured a ladleful of the liquid into the strange concoction. "An infusion of wood betony for your head and fermented hops to help you sleep."

After a thorough examination and treatment of cuts and bruises, she handed me the cup. "Drink and then rest."

I sniffed the muddy-looking liquid and frowned.

"Drink."

I downed the contents as fast as possible to limit the contact with my tongue. It was foul, but warm, and by the time it was finished, I felt relaxed and sleepy. I lay back onto the mattress, grateful for the tight wrap around my ribs because it seemed to help ease some of the discomfort. Or perhaps it was the drink. I placed the cup down on the floor beside me and rolled gingerly onto my side, covering myself with a wool blanket. I knew I should be angry with myself for getting caught off guard, for allowing Demas and his henchman to disarm me, but I was feeling oddly at peace with it all. Everything was going to be all right. I drifted off to sleep, thinking of summer meadows in a distant land and a handsome young Viking standing on the bow of his longship.

I vaguely remembered being woken often by Muirgen. She made me sip more of her foul potions and asked me bizarre questions like what my name was, or my mother's name, or where I lived, but after a while, even her questions stopped, and I was left to sleep unmolested. I don't know how long I was out for, but when I woke, it was to a loud growl of protest from my stomach.

I rolled out of bed, pleased that my ribs felt much better, and retrieved my kirtle. Muirgen was nowhere to be found. I wandered over to the hearth, where something was simmering in the cauldron.

I peered inside. While it smelled like porridge and looked like porridge, I wasn't willing to take the risk.

I stepped outside. The air was warm. The sun shining straight
overhead was hot. The bones swung eerily in the breeze, chinking
and clacking softly, but in the dazzling brilliance of the summer
sun and the presence of a neatly tended garden, lush with flowers
bobbing in the wind, the cottage looked almost quaint. I paused,
ear tuned to the back of the dwelling, where a woman's voice rose in
perfect pitch, singing in a foreign tongue.

I followed the sound, poking my head around the back of the
cottage. I was a little light-headed and felt close to swaying to one
side, but the sunlight felt wonderful on my face and spirit.

A large garden etched into the earth stretched beyond me, and
in the middle, naked, with her back to me, Muirgen was plucking
weeds.

"Good morning," she called, her voice high and piercing, losing all of its previous beauty. "Grab a spade. There are plenty enough
weeds here for two." Her long, slender finger pointed to a row of
garden implements leaning against the cottage. Her hair was loose.
Long, wispy, silver-white waves tumbled to her low back. Her skin,
wrinkled and thin, was tanned a light bronze and her frame was
lean and wiry. I could count each bone in her spine as she bent over
the dry, dusty earth.

I stood there.

"A spade. The garden won't weed itself."

"But I'm hungry. . . ."

"There's porridge in the pot. Eat and then weed. You need to
earn your keep."

Earn my keep? I had thought her kindness genuine. "I can pay
you in coin for your efforts."

"Don't want your coin. Eat and then weed."

I stomped back into the cottage and ladled out a bowlful of oats, eating and grumbling under my breath at her audacity . . . her insensitivity.

When I finished, I grabbed the spade and started in on the opposite side of the garden. I couldn't bend over, but I could loosen the soil around the roots, making it easier for her to pull the weeds out.

"Your mother never liked gardening," she said, pulling a noxious corn cockle out by its stem and tossing it aside.

"How did you know my mother?" My spade froze in midthrust.

"I know a great deal about your family." She grunted and pulled at another weed. "Carry on." She gestured to my shovel, hanging in the air.

I brought it down hard into the earth, jarring my ribs in the process. I took a deep breath, as deep as the bandaging would allow, and wiped the sweat from my brow. The sun was blazing down, melting me where I stood. "How do you know my family?" I knew nothing of this woman, and it was unsettling that she claimed to know me.

A man's voice called from out front.

"Back here," Muirgen's voice pitched.

Bertram rounded the side of the cottage.

"What are you doing here?" I asked.

"I've come to bring you home."

I turned to Muirgen. "How does he know I'm here? What have you told him?" My temper flared.

"Bertram, give us a moment."

Bertram nodded and retraced his steps out of sight.

I turned on her. "What have you done?"

"I merely informed your household of your safety. They sent messengers throughout the countryside looking for you. You've been gone five days."

"Five days?"

She stood up straight, her back cracking and popping. "Yes, and it's time you headed back home."

"I can't."

"Why not?"

"Demas threatened to rape me. And while he didn't succeed, it won't stop him from telling everyone we slept together. We will have to be married. It will be his word against mine. Everyone will think I am a whore."

"Well, you are."

"Excuse me?"

"Demas didn't take your virginity—but someone else did. You were on your way to see me so that you could meet him again, were you not?"

Any words I might have said dried up, and I stood there with my mouth open.

"Demas didn't take your virginity, and he knows that. What he doesn't know is that it had already been taken. An advantage you can use—if you continue to play the role of virgin. He has no proof and therefore will not bring up the encounter. Your family believes you were thrown from your horse and that I took you in."

"Play the role of virgin?"

She slapped her hands together, sending small clouds of dust into the air. "Look pious. Keep your eyes downcast when men are around, act humble and chaste." She regarded me and smirked. "Not an easy role for you."

Words evaporated on my tongue, and I closed my mouth.

She laid a hand on my shoulder. "That man from the clearing is a beast, a horrid, evil man. I've seen the shadow of death and sorrow around him. He will cause you only pain. Do whatever it takes to break free of his grasp. If you've found love, let it carry you away from this place. Leave England. If you stay, I see heartache and suffering for you ahead."

"How do you know these things?" Fear gripped my stomach.

"I'm a high priestess. I make it my job to know. And I care what happens to my granddaughter." She left to join Bertram, leaving me standing in the middle of the garden, watching the pea pods shimmer in the breeze.

"Granddaughter?" I burst into the cottage.

Muirgen, who was now fully dressed in a pale green kirtle, sat at the table with Bertram, the two companionably drinking from fine glass vessels.

"Wine?" Muirgen asked.

"No. Explain to me how you're my grandmother."

Muirgen looked at Bertram as if expecting him to answer for her.

He sighed. "Muirgen and I were involved in a sacred fertility ritual that begot your mother."

I stared at him. "You're my grandfather?"

"Yes."

"Wine." I sat down on a sturdy chest behind me.

Muirgen handed me a glass. "During the spring equinox, before the planting, we were chosen to unite and bring forth a child, a gift from the Goddess, a promise of fertility for our crops and health for our livestock. Bertram was the highest druid; I was high priestess. We were both virgins."

Bertram continued. "If our coupling had not succeeded in producing a child, our village would have suffered dire consequences. There had been two years of drought, and a sickness in the cattle that killed half the herd. It was a blessing when your mother was born. While your grandmother swelled with life, our crops prospered, and our animals grew healthy and strong."

I looked at Bertram. "Why didn't you tell me?"

"You're being raised in a Christian world, Avelynn. It didn't seem appropriate to complicate matters with the story of your mother's pagan birth."

"I'm a priestess, a follower of the Goddess. You promised my mother to teach me all you knew. Yet I know nothing of my mother's family. Don't you think I would have wanted to know? To understand where I came from? You never thought this information would have helped me?

"And you . . ." I turned to Muirgen. "Why have I not known about you? When my mother died, why didn't you make your presence known? I've felt alone, adrift, without anyone who understands me. Bertram was the only person I knew who was pagan, but he's a man. I could have learned so much from you."

Bertram nodded. "Perhaps we were wrong in keeping these things from you. Our only thoughts were to help you fit into the world around you."

"But I don't fit in. Every day I walk a fine line between my beliefs and the ignorance of others. No one understands me." I set the glass down and walked to the window. I gazed at the bleached bones. An image of a body hanging from the tree, shriveled and old, flashed into my mind. I blinked, but the specter was gone. Had I only imagined it? Feeling disoriented, out of time and place, I turned back to the two strangers in the room.

Muirgen studied me closely.

"You see where I live," Muirgen said. "Would you have preferred to live this type of existence? I chose to withdraw myself from the world your mother embraced rather than give up my faith."

"But she didn't give up her faith. She still performed rituals, she still prayed to the Goddess."

Muirgen frowned. "She practiced only at feast days or at the equinoxes. She had to hide that side of herself. I would not." She moved a few jars on the table and pushed an object to the front. It was a stone carving of a small, very pregnant woman. It looked old, the face distorted with the softening of time and handling. "There's more to our faith than a token ritual. I will teach you if that's your choice. But understand—the more you know, the more you risk. The Christians will not hesitate to kill you for your beliefs."

Bertram sighed. "I would caution you, Avelynn. This part of your life was kept from you in order to protect you. Pagans are not welcome in England. You are young, with a life of promise ahead of you. You would be wise to distance yourself from your past."

"I can't do that."

"I've done all I can. If you wish to continue, your grandmother will be the one to guide you on this path. I cannot."

I had so much to ask, so much to understand. A thought struck me. "You were both on the boat when my mother decided to stay here?"

They nodded.

"Is there anyone else I should know about?"

"You may have a cousin somewhere," Muirgen said.

"A cousin?" My head swam. I wasn't sure if it was from the news or my injury, but the room tilted away from me, and I reached a hand out to the windowsill to steady myself.

"We're not certain," Bertram added. "It was a long time ago, and his body was never recovered."

"When your mother agreed to stay in England, there were many who stayed with her. Your aunt—" Muirgen said.

"My aunt?" I dropped back down onto the chest and stared at them.

"Her name was Leenan, and she was murdered, left for dead along the roadside. Her son, only a babe at the time, was never found."

"But he was not only your cousin on your mother's side," Bertram added. "Leenan had an affair with your father's brother, Osric, the Earl of Dorset. That relationship is what killed her."

"What happened to her?"

Muirgen reached above my head and pulled a small chest down from one of the shelves. She removed a fine gold brooch and placed it in my palm. It was intricately carved with vines and animals. It was very heavy. "This was Leenan's. When we found her body, the bastards who killed her didn't bother to take this. It wasn't an act of robbery. It was murder. Cold and simple." She sat back down by the table. "I knew Leenan had met someone, but she tried to conceal his identity. She was eighteen. You turn eighteen this summer, don't you, Avelynn?"

"Yes." I avoided her eyes.

"I discovered who the man was and told her to end it. I knew your uncle was only using her to get back at your father, by hurting your mother. She refused to listen. She was deeply in love, she said. When she learned she was with child, she was certain he would marry her. Foolish girl." She sighed. "But the pregnancy was a hard one. She needed to remain in bed or risk losing the child. He was born healthy and strong, with hair the color of dried leaves in the fall and pale blue eyes. As he grew, his eyes darkened and changed color, as did the birthmark on his chest. Once a faint pink line from nipple to umbilicus, it thickened and darkened into a cherry wine color. He was a handsome lad. But he wasn't with us long enough. When she regained her strength, she set up a meeting with Osric behind my back. Taking the babe, she raced off to meet him and never came back."

Bertram stood. "I know this is a lot for you to take in, but we must get back to Wedmore before nightfall. I'll make ready your horse."

"My horse? Marma?"

"Muirgen retrieved her, and your sword, while you were healing."

I studied Muirgen. I couldn't figure her out. Her manner was curt with a hint of impatience and arrogant indifference, yet her actions were kind.

Bertram inclined his head to Muirgen and stepped outside. I felt incapable of following.

She retrieved the brooch and dropped a small packet into my other hand, closing my fist around it. It was the herbs I had come for. "For love," she said.

After everything that had happened, love seemed so far away. "I'm not sure I should see him again. My father would never accept him. It's pointless."

"Demas seeks to break you. If you stay, I see only suffering and pain. Your father cannot help you. Nor can he hinder you. Follow your heart, Avelynn. Don't let anyone stop you."

"But if Leenan hadn't followed her heart, she might still be here."

Muirgen shrugged. "We all have choices to make. Leenan's fault did not lie in following her desires, but in refusing to acknowledge what was happening around her. I could only guide her, try to show her the danger in her actions. But in the end, it was her life. Her decisions were right for her, and she made the right choice."

"But she died."

"Yes, but up until that moment, she lived."

FOURTEEN

It was two days before the full moon in July. I sent a message to Ealhswith. I would not be coming to visit. After countless sleepless nights, churning over everything Muirgen had said, I had decided to leave England. I filled my purse with coins, hoping Alrik would give me passage. I didn't know where he was headed next, but for the right price he might be willing to take me across to the continent. I didn't expect him to want me still, not after I told him the truth of my betrothal. Like my father, Alrik struck me as a man of honor. I was promised to someone else and had willingly broken that pledge. Worse, I had lied to him, at least through omission. In his place, I wouldn't want me, either.

I didn't want to think about my father or Edward. I didn't want to think about whether Edward would come home. It made me sick to think about deserting everyone, but once my father returned, Wedmore would carry on without me. Everyone was replaceable.

I shoved some clothes into two large satchels and upended the contents of my locked chest, sorting through my most precious possessions. I left much of the jewelry, packing only a few pieces, more in case I needed their weight in gold than their ornamentation, and carefully hid my pouch of divining bones inside the sleeve of one of my kirtles. I stared at the packets of herbs Muirgen had given me and then locked them back inside the crate. I had no need of them now. I scrawled a hasty note to Bertram, entrusting the estate to his capable hands until my father's return, and headed to the stables.

Macha, the Goddess of Dawn, spread her golden cloak across the sky. I had wanted to leave before first light, but I stalled, taking my time brushing and stroking Marma. "I'll miss you, girl." I laid my forehead against her neck. Her velvety nose nudged my arm, and I hugged her fiercely. I was being selfish, and I knew it, but I couldn't risk marrying Demas. I had seen the monster lurking behind those hazel eyes. The shadow of suffering and pain Muirgen had seen hovering around him was real. I understood that now. The vision I'd had on Avalon—the raven and the boar, the promise of death and bloodshed in my future—would come to pass if I stayed. It was never about Alrik, or war. The message was far more personal. The Goddess had sent her sacred messenger, the raven, to warn me. A caution I would finally take seriously. Demas was the beast, and he had the ability to gore me through. I didn't plan to stay long enough to give him the chance.

Unwilling to risk leaving Marma to find her way back home, and knowing I couldn't expect Alrik to give both me and my horse passage, I saddled a sprightly bay mare instead and headed to the coast. The morning had started warm and clear, and by midafternoon the sun held council; not a cloud dared defile her court. It was stifling. The slight breeze was humid and did nothing to lift the hair clinging to my neck. There had been several days of blistering heat, and the leaves on the trees were wilted as they baked under the demanding sun. As I approached a dense hawthorn bush, a startled crow squawked in alarm and set off in a flurry of feathers. I jumped, pulling a little too hard on the reins, and the mare huffed in protest. I wiped the sweat from my brow. My nerves were frayed.

It was late evening when I reached the coast. The sun hung heavy in the sky, infusing everything with a muted pink hue. I set up camp in the clearing where Alrik and I had last been together and waited. It was cooler near the ocean, but still too warm to be comfortable. I thought about Muirgen weeding her garden, her bare body offered up to the sun, and felt a stab of regret. I had just gotten to know her and was leaving her behind.

I rolled out my bedroll and lay down. I watched as several large ants marched up the stem of a nearby gooseberry bush, investigating its burgeoning fruit. How easy it was to just reach out and end life with as little effort as it takes to bring a thumb and forefinger together. I reached into the satchel at my side and grabbed a loaf of bread, crumbling some of the coarse grains into my hand. I crouched near the shrub, placing my hand alongside one of the leaves. After a few moments, a curious ant wandered onto my outstretched palm. The industrious feet tickled as the inquisitive black body explored the lines of my flesh. I lowered my hand to the earth and let the ant and crumbs go.

I retired to my bed and fell into a restless sleep. When I next opened my eyes, my breath was shallow and rapid, my pulse galloping as the specter of the dream faded. I was tied to a tree. Demas was striking me over and over again. I had been torn apart, ripped in half. He laughed. Gil drooled. I couldn't breathe.

I moaned and rolled onto my side, curling into a ball. My ribs ached. The bones were healed, the bruising gone, but sleeping awkwardly on the cool ground had irritated them. The moon was full now. A few wisps of gray, as fine as horse hairs, drifted across the brilliant mottled surface. Aine was the Goddess of the Moon. I wondered if she watched me from her throne of silvery light. "Aine, please help me. Show me what to do."

When I awoke the next morning, a seed of thought had been planted in my mind. A filament, thin and tenuous, but glimmering with hope. The moon was gone, replaced by the dawning sun, but I had no doubt Aine had sent me the idea: the Witan.

The Witan met twice a year, once during Christmastide in December, the other during Whitsuntide in June. It was an opportunity to bring before the king disputes that could not be settled at each individual council of the shires.

I envisioned myself standing before the great men of Wessex, asking to be released from my betrothal. It was not without precedent. A noblewoman of Berkshire had appealed to the Witan only last year, demanding release from her betrothal—an arrangement her father had orchestrated without her consent. She claimed that her betrothed had committed incest with his sister, the other woman's swollen belly a testament to his lechery. The court demanded an ordeal by fire, where the accused had to walk across red-hot plowshares without injury. When the man's feet puckered and wept with blisters, he was found guilty. The court released her from the contract and set her free to marry a person of her choosing. She was even able to collect the dowry her espoused had promised.

I wondered if perhaps I might persuade the Witan to grant me a release. But what would I base the charge on? While Demas had threatened to rape me, the mere threat would be useless as a case against him, and I would not lie and say he had succeeded. I thought of the handsome Frenchman. While I held no judgment on their actions, the Christian church condemned the free expression of lust between men and women, never mind partners of the same sex— that act was reprehensible and strictly forbidden. I thought of Ealhswith. Bringing up the charge would make me a hypocrite, but what choice did I have? Demas had left me with little recourse.

The allegation would certainly be sensational enough, but to stand up in front of the king, the bishops, and my father's peers without proof? I ran a hand over my face. It was a terrible risk. Dear gods, what would my father say if I went behind his back like this? He said we would talk when he got back, but I now suspected those were merely words spoken to assuage me. There were too many uncertainties, too much left to chance. I'd rather leave than take that risk.

The sea was calm. Waves lapped softly onto the sandy beach. Alrik's ship sat high on shore, a beehive of activity swarming its hulking wooden frame. When Alrik approached me, I barely recognized him. Gone was the polished, meticulous leader of men, and in his place was a warrior, a barbarian. His hair and beard were longer, his clothes stained, and his face wore an air of savageness.

His expression lightened. "Avelynn." He lifted me off the ground and kissed me thoroughly.

I stiffened.

"What is it?"

"I need passage to Francia. I know I have no right to ask, and no reason to expect you to help me, but I've nowhere else to turn. I have to leave England." I offered him a purse filled with coin. "I have more than enough to cover the inconvenience. Please."

"When last we met, you said you would never leave England; now you cannot get away fast enough. What has changed?"

"I wasn't truthful when first we met." I lowered my head. "I'm betrothed." All I could see was his feet. Worn leather boots caked in dried mud, metal buckles clouded with grime. They didn't move. "I should have told you. I'm sorry."

A red-tailed bumblebee thrummed around my shoes. Its bright fuzzy backside hovered above the worn leather before venturing off in search of pollen.

His silence was deafening, and I continued quickly, desperate to fill the void. "I let him catch me off guard. He disarmed me, threatened to rape me. He would have succeeded, too, if the bear hadn't stopped him." I knew I wasn't making any sense.

Rage contorted his face. "Did he hurt you?"

A tear slid down my cheek. "No."

"Who is he?" He rendered each word with extreme control.

"His name is Demas. He owns a manor in Dorset called Wareham. The betrothal was my father's decision. I have no choice but to marry him if I stay. I have to leave." I lifted the purse, hands shaking. "I don't expect you to still want me after this. . . ."

"Did you love him?" His face was hard, expressionless.

"No."

"Do you love me?"

Did I love him? Gods, I loved him with an ache that made my chest seize, my stomach flutter, and my mind spin. "Yes."

His fist clenched and then he turned his back to me and walked away. "I can't help you. Not now."

I ran after him. "I don't blame you for hating me. . . ."

"Hate you?" He turned to face me, his eyes filled with pain. "I swear to Thor and his father, Odin the Furious, I will kill the bastard for threatening you. But your betrothal changes nothing. I said I wanted you for my wife. I still do."

"You do?"

He lifted my chin in his hand. "Was any of it your choice?"

"No."

He nodded, and sadness clouded the light in his eyes. "The Norns, the Goddesses of fate, brought me to you. I am not about to let you go so easily." He kissed my forehead. "But I cannot bring you with me. I am sworn to help my brother in Ireland. I cannot leave until he bids me go."

"But I'm to be married in the fall."

The words hung between us. The sound of my heart pumped in my ears. The waves whooshed to shore. A gull flew overhead.

"I will seek release from my oath and return in September," he said.

I didn't know if I could wait that long. "I can come with you to Ireland. My mother's family has roots there."

"My brother has sworn vengeance against all Saxons. I cannot take you with me."

"I could slip away at night."

"You know nothing of Ireland. The country is torn apart by civil war. Norsemen maraud, rape, and torture for the sheer pleasure of it. Slave traders prowl the countryside, looking for women to sell to the highest, cruelest bidder."

"But what of my mother's people?"

"Assuming they are still alive?"

I swallowed hard and nodded.

"If they are fortunate, they will be under the protection of an Irish king. There are territories to the north and west, away from the coast, that my brother has yet to penetrate, but I have no means of finding your kin or ensuring your safe passage. I cannot effect a homecoming."

I felt lost, for myself and for the family I'd never met. "Is there nothing you can do?"

"No."

Individual grains of sand blurred into a soggy yellow mash as tears welled. What was I going to do?

Alrik lifted me, one arm beneath my knees, the other wrapped around my shoulders. He smelled like salt water and fresh ocean breezes, and my body fell limp against him.

He carried me back to the clearing and set me down on my bedroll. He sat beside me. I hugged my legs into my chest and rested my forehead on my knees. I felt like a fool—a fool for asking, a fool for crying, a fool for subsiding into such a weak, pathetic creature. "I shouldn't have asked."

He looked at something in the distance. "I watched my mother suffer under my father's tyranny. I felt helpless then too." His shoulders collapsed in defeat.

I rested my hand on his forearm, faint blue veins threaded through the hard muscle. He laid his hand on mine. It was warm, his touch deeply reassuring. "Let us walk," he said, rising.

Ivy sprawled along the ground, its pungent, bitter scent enfolding us as our footsteps crushed the soft, hairy leaves. Slender stems of wood anemone and bluebell, long past their flower, swayed in our wake. The woodland was alive with birdsong and chatter. The *tser-err-err-err* of a blue tit and the loud *pitchoo* of a marsh tit joined in chorus, their calls conducted in an ancient rhythm by the busy staccato taps of a woodpecker.

He held the hilt of his sword. The garnets on the cross guard, dark as blood, gleamed scarlet whenever a flash of sunlight caught their angled surfaces.

"Can you tell me about your mother?" I asked.

"She lives in Gotland with my grandfather, but owns a prosperous trading center in Denmark—a gift from my father."

"Was your father cruel?"

"My father was a warrior, a king. His life was battle. My brothers have carried on in his image. I had envisioned a quieter life for myself, but . . ." He shrugged. He lifted a hazel branch out of my way. "My mother was his mistress, but she wished to be more. He always promised she would, but he came around only when he wanted her, and like an obedient, submissive dog, she rolled over and begged." He almost spat the last words. "He was king. Whatever he wanted he got. She had no say in the matter. She meant nothing to him. She was merely a pretty little diversion, and everyone in Denmark and Gotland knew it."

I reached out, turning him toward me. "I don't care about the past."

He held my gaze, placing his hands on my shoulders. "Nor do I." His voice was husky. "I have no right to ask, no claim on you, but I have only the one night. And by Odin's eye, woman, I cannot bear to leave without having you."

Muirgen had said to follow my heart, and it had led me here, to this moment, to this man. I refused to let anyone or anything take this away from me. If I couldn't go with him, I had him still. As to my future, I would chart my course. I would figure out a way to rid my life of Demas forever, and I wouldn't do it by running away.

I lifted my hand to his face and guided his lips to mine. This was the man who loved me, the man who had saved my life, who asked for my permission, who waited on my answer. And I gave my heart to him completely.

He stepped away, removed his tunic, and laid it across the ferns. He lay down and rolled onto his back. I knelt beside him.

I ran my finger from his temple to his jaw. He closed his eyes, and I kissed the soft lids. My lips skimmed and my teeth grazed his neck, my body responding to the change in his breathing. It was restrained, shorter, faster. The tip of my nose brushed his ear, and a shiver passed through him. I kissed the tiny lobe, nibbling it with my teeth. He inhaled sharply. I alternated between his ears and his neck while he kept a firm hold on the moss growing along the ground. I took my time, enjoying the gooseflesh that erupted on his arms, his quickened breath.

His nipples were erect and hard. I brushed my finger over one and he jolted, his eyes flying open in surprise. I flicked my tongue around the small nubs and sucked gently. His body went rigid; his trousers bulged, tenting high in the middle. I hesitated. Demas's ghost hovered close—a reminder of my weakness, of what had almost happened.

He sensed my trepidation. "I will not demand anything of you, ever. You have my word. It might kill me to stop"—his mouth curled into a half grin—"but the choice is yours, Avelynn, always."

I stood and removed my linen kirtle, dropping it on the ground beside me. The cool ocean breeze tightened my nipples, and my body erupted in gooseflesh. I lay down beside him. "I won't have you die on my account."

Sometime later, drowsy and content in his arms, I asked, "What's Gotland like? Is it very different from England?"

He stretched his arms and clasped his hands behind his head. He was naked, sprawled out on the forest floor, his legs twined with mine. "It is beautiful. Towering cliffs rise above rocky shorelines, windswept grasslands roll into neatly tended farmland, and forests of ancient oak are blanketed with orchids and wildflowers in the spring."

"Were you born there?"

"Yes. I was born near Visby, on my grandfather's manor. My grandfather, Herraud, controls most of northern Gotland. He was furious with my mother's treatment, but my father always placated him with gifts of livestock, ale, and slaves. He quickly stopped complaining."

I chased away an inquisitive fly from his chest and let my fingertips brush the toned ridges of his belly. I smiled as his muscles tensed and flexed. "Did you spend much time with your father growing up?"

"As king, he spent most of his time in Lejre, and when he was not in his hall there, he was busy invading and conquering other countries. For the most part I was left to my own devices. Though my mother was implacable when it came to my learning, she called my father an ignorant heathen and demanded the opposite of me."

My fingers stopped their explorations. "You're not pagan?"

"I was reared by my mother and a Christian priest who taught me Latin and English, astronomy, mathematics, spiritual morality, and jurisprudence. My father discovered my learning and fell into a rage. He beat my mother for making me soft and killed the priest. I was twelve."

Several birds hopped from branch to branch above us, happily chirping amongst themselves. "From that point forward, my father ensured I was raised properly. He dragged me to his hall to learn a real man's education of fighting, drinking, and cruelty. He also insisted I embrace the faith of my forefathers. I am as pagan as any other heathen barbarian you are likely to meet." He smiled broadly.

I laughed. "Good."

He kissed my neck and blew softly into my ear. I shivered. I could feel my body awakening again. "So, that was it? You went to Lejre and became a ruthless warrior?"

"I wanted to be a shipbuilder." He rolled onto his side and looked at me sheepishly. He caressed my arm, running his finger slowly up and down. The soft, delicate, downy hairs stood on end with each pass.

"I made my ship."

"Why did you stop? It's beautiful."

"A ship is an extension of a man's soul. *Raven's Blood* is my most valued possession. I would die before I let another man sail her. But owning a ship is different from building one. Shipbuilding is an honorable craft in most men's eyes, but not in my father's or my brothers'. It was a warrior's life or no life at all. When my father was killed, my brothers swore vengeance. To them, a shipbuilder was weak and useless. They left me behind, unable to avenge his death." A shadow passed over his eyes.

"Their intent was to dishonor me. But their cruelty made me

stronger, and their impressions of my weakness were gravely mistaken. I have since proved them wrong."

I wasn't sure I wanted him to elucidate that, and he didn't. Instead, he shook his head, as if emerging from under water, and brought his attention back to my naked flesh. A twinkle once again sparked in his eyes.

"Tell me about England." His finger resumed its course, moving up my arm, over my collarbone, and down between my breasts. He traced the outline of one breast, circles moving higher and higher, closer to my nipple.

An orange-tipped butterfly flitted overhead.

"I was born in a manor called—" His finger reached the nipple and he tugged gently on the tip. His finger brushed back and forth. "—Wedmore," I managed to push out.

"What was it like growing up in Wedmore?"

I inhaled deeply as his mouth replaced his finger. He had disentangled his legs from mine and climbed on top of me, his legs straddling my thighs.

"I'm the daughter of a powerful . . . earl." His teeth grazed the tightened skin, and he pulled gently, taking my nipple into his mouth. Wetness surged between my legs, and I shifted my body as tension mounted.

"I have a younger brother. Both my father and brother left some time ago for Rome." "Rome" came out as a squeak. I didn't want to think about where they were or what might have happened to them, for I'd still heard nothing of Edward's health or received any missives corroborating Demas's claim that my father had encountered Vikings. Fortunately, Alrik's tactics were very distracting, and I pushed the uncertainties from my mind.

"Mmm-hmm," he mumbled, his tongue charting a path lower until he was lying between my legs.

"I just found out I have a grandmother, and maybe even a cou—sin." His tongue probed between my legs.

He lifted my leg onto his shoulder. His fingers slid through the moist heat and his tongue worked furiously. My body arched. My hips rose.

His fingers slipped inside, stroking, pushing deeper. He lifted his head. "You were saying?" His pace quickened.

"Oh, gods," I cried out but then was unable to utter one coherent word more.

Just before dusk, we made our way back to the beach. Alrik had asked me to intercede with the gods and bestow a blessing upon his crew, granting them success in battle. I stood, a roaring fire at my back, and had each man line up and kneel before me. I whispered a charm over every sharpened blade they presented to me. Axes, spears, swords, knives, and arrows each received their own blessing. Then I laid a hand on each bowed head and called on Macha and Badb to bring swiftness to their blades and fearlessness to their hearts. I added an appeal to Odin and the Valkyries, Odin's maidens of death, to take the fallen to Valhalla so that they might dine amongst the valiant warriors at his high table.

The entire crew came forward, save one. He loomed near the ship, a hulking shadow outlined against a darkening sky. Alrik, having caught the man's absence, stormed toward him. I couldn't hear what was said, but it wasn't long before the man stalked over, his face hard, his body tense. He knelt at my feet and thrust out his sword. I looked down at a crop of wayward brown hair tamed only marginally by a ragged middle part. I drew my eyebrows together.

"What's your name?" I asked.

"Ingvar."

My next words caught in my throat. It was the dead man's

brother, the man who had met his death by Alrik's axe when we first met.

"Get done with it, *wyrt-gaelstre*."

Witch! He had called me a witch, and in my own tongue. "Who are you?"

He looked up, cold hatred in his wide-set eyes. "You killed my brother, *wyrt-gaelstre*. Do you know what we do with your kind? We break their legs and tie their hands. Then, one shovelful at a time, we bury them alive, gritty earth filling and choking their open mouths as they scream."

I knew only too well what the Saxons did with a woman they suspected of witchcraft. Alrik saw I was shaken.

"What has he said?"

"He's Saxon."

Alrik nodded. "He was a slave and should have been killed, but he surrendered to my brother and swore allegiance." There was a hint of disgust in Alrik's tone. "He has fought well for us and has not caused any trouble until recently."

"You may trust this *wyrt-gaelstre*, but I do not." He made to rise, but Alrik put a hand on his shoulder and shoved him back down.

"She has assured us victory and safe passage. You will not jeopardize that. Kneel and accept her blessing." He gripped the handle of his axe, cutting short any further objections from Ingvar.

Ingvar knelt, and I invoked the Goddess. A deep unsettling crept through my veins. I couldn't explain it, but at that moment, I wished Alrik's brother had killed Ingvar when he'd had the chance.

After the ritual, they invited me to dine with them. We sat on logs around a roaring fire, sharing mead and rabbit stew. Nervous after all they had seen me say and do, the men relaxed as the consumption of drink increased. By the time the moon descended in the sky, they had regaled me with stories of valor and mishap from

their travels, the laughter and ribald comments growing more boisterous as the hour increased.

At length, Alrik and I left the beach and sought the privacy and
solitude of the clearing. We dozed off now and then, slipping noc-
turnal sojourns in between fervent and desperate lovemaking.
Knowing that this might be the last time we were together, we clung
to each other, imprinting each moment, savoring each sensation,
each touch, each kiss, each word.

He would try to come back at the full moon in September, but
couldn't promise. His brother's struggles in Ireland would keep him
occupied for quite some time. And then, after September, the seas
would start to get rough and the window for sailing would soon
close. And in the undercurrent of silence and desperation that
swirled around us lurked four words that were never spoken. I would
be married.

Come morning, dark clouds threatened on the horizon, black
against the brighter sky before it. Standing on the prow of his boat,
Alrik waved, his blond hair lifting in the rising wind. The bloodred
sail, the raven's wings outstretched, its claws hooked, ready to snare
the souls of the dead, billowed as it caught the lusty gales. I watched
long after the boat had sailed out of sight.

Behind me, the forest danced in anticipation of a coming storm.
The leaves quivered in the moisture-laden breeze. The parched landscape rejoiced as the rain came. It lashed and it wailed, but I stood
there, a wall against its torrent, dry and barren as a desert, with no
hope of relief. Thunder clapped. Lightning flashed and a blazing
fork landed nearby. My heart pounded, beating out the thunder in
its clamor. The sea turned a dark, angry gray. The waves frothed
and crashed to the shore.

Be safe, Alrik, I pleaded into the fury. *Please come back to me.*

FIFTEEN

August and September came and went without incident. The harvest was plentiful; grain was collected, threshed, and winnowed. The granaries were bursting, the inventory balanced. Orchards abounded with ripe, juicy fruit, their succulent yields overflowing in baskets and crates; nuts were collected, larders were filled. Abundance swarmed around me. Everyone smiled, their mood joyous and thankful. I searched but could find nothing to smile about—the full moon waxed and waned, but Alrik did not return.

There was one flicker of light, however. I had not seen Demas since the confrontation in the forest, and Sigberht had also remained absent, keeping to his estate in Kent. While I was not one to overlook my blessings, when autumn passed without any word from my father or news of Edward's well-being, anxiety mingled daily with my already dark and melancholy mood. Any crossing of the channel now meant the men would be taking great risks. Winter storms were savage and swift, coming out of nowhere to drag a ship down to an icy grave.

I had taken to visiting Muirgen often, as she was teaching me how to develop my gift of prophecy, but I had not been able to see—in the bones, or the water, or the fire, or the Ogham—what had become of them.

With the fae night of Samhain approaching, Muirgen summoned me. It was a powerful time of year for divination, and perhaps I would finally get some answers. Chasing the setting sun north and then westward, I arrived at her cottage late in the evening to find it in complete disarray.

"What are you doing?"

She shuffled about, dragging and setting aside numerous crates and boxes, sorting through their contents.

At last she stood and held up a red gown.

It was a beautifully woven garment with gold and silver thread twining along the hems and up the sleeves, which fluted slightly.

"Should fit nicely." She circled me, studying, her eye critical. I felt like a prized sow at market. "Try it on."

"Was it yours?" I removed my kirtle and slipped the dress over my head. The neckline scooped low and the waist hugged tight to my body. I brushed down the fabric with reverence, smoothing the skirt as it settled lightly around my thighs.

"This was made for your great-great-grandmother. Each woman of our family has worn this dress during her initiation as high priestess."

I ceased admiring the dress and stared at Muirgen.

She nodded. "It is time."

"But I'm not ready!"

"You are eighteen, Avelynn. This can wait no longer."

"But I have so much left to learn."

"You know what is necessary. The rest will come. In time."

"That's not good enough. You said you would take over my learning, guide me."

"And I have."

"Give me until the spring. I'll work harder, visit more often."

"No. It must be tonight."

"Why?"

She sighed and motioned to the table. "Sit."

I relented and she pulled up a stool opposite me. "What does it mean to be a high priestess?" she asked.

"It is the greatest honor in our faith, bestowing upon the anointed the ability to commune and intercede with the Goddess Herself."

"But you can divine the future, see visions, and you are but a lowly priestess."

"Yes." I wasn't sure what she was asking.

"The Goddess already speaks to you, reveals to you the future. Where then is the difference?"

"I don't know."

"The difference is responsibility. In times of old, people came to seek the counsel of the high priestess. She would oversee all ceremonies and rituals, she would initiate young women into the faith, and she would use her gifts in the service of others. Never causing harm, she was a guardian of the earth, protector of her people. Her visions were respected and sought by kings. And while times have changed, our numbers diminished, there will always be those who seek the truth. As high priestess it is essential, now more than ever, to keep our faith alive—to find believers, to teach and inspire by example. Your faith is strong, Avelynn, your heart true, your gifts divinely given. If you are ready to accept the responsibility, then you are ready to assume the role you were born for. I will not force you. But after tonight, the opportunity will not present itself again."

An ominous warning. Like frost, frigid and swift, it spread under my skin.

"You must choose."

I wanted to sound strong and assured, but my pitch wavered, the volume barely above a whisper. "I accept."

"Good." She rose. "From this point onward, you may not speak until I call upon you at the sacred well."

I nodded.

She loosened my braid and grabbed a fine bone comb. Brushing out the soft curls, her fingers were soothing, her touch gentle. An aching familiarity clamped around my heart, the scene reminding me of my mother. She should have been here. A tear slid down my cheek.

"Shush now. Your mother is with us."

I searched the room, desperate to see her face, to look into her eyes once more. Why couldn't I see anything? If she was truly here, wouldn't I at least be able to feel her presence? I slumped on the stool.

Muirgen laid a hand on my shoulder. "One day, your gifts will surpass even mine. Give it time."

She had taught me that gifts like divination and the ability to commune with the dead were akin to an artist surrendering to the muse in order to create epic poetry or sculpt wondrous pieces of art from simple metal or clay. Each of us is born with the innate knowledge to learn these skills, yet some possess a higher degree of aptitude and hone and practice their craft until they become masters. Effort and persistence would pay off, she'd assured me. I need only be patient.

Starting near my temples, she braided two sections of hair, the strands circling my head like a garland. The ends she tied with ribbon, and then she placed several dried rose blossoms in the wreath of hair, weaving another red ribbon throughout. After poking and primping, she must have been satisfied with the results, for she left off fussing and retrieved a bone cup, its murky liquid sloshing within.

"Drink."

I inspected the contents carefully, wrinkling my nose at the strong alcoholic smell.

"To prepare you for the ritual."

I eyed her dubiously.

She smiled. It was such a rare occurrence that my stomach clenched. This couldn't be good.

With an impatient lift of her eyebrow, I swallowed my reservations and downed the measure, the substance burning a trail to my stomach, where it sat hot and heavy. I breathed deeply, my eyes watering.

She removed the cup and placed in my shaking hands the stone Goddess figurine that always sat squat in the middle of her table. Without another word she left, shutting the cottage door behind her. Several candles on the table flickered as the air stirred, and the hearth fire, burning warm and steady, filled the room with a soft glow.

I turned the figurine over in my hands. A great weight settled on my shoulders. I always knew this moment would come. I was raised to become a high priestess, but now that the time was upon me—I was at once terrified and exhilarated.

I glanced along the shelves and caught the spine of Muirgen's book. Bound and glued with thick sheets of parchment, it was the illuminated equivalent of a pagan bible. It was filled with detailed accounts of rituals and chants, and I had spent the past several months poring through its pages, yet the more I learned, the more questions unspooled. An intricately detailed cipher, it had taken me several visits to grasp the meaning behind the gibberish, let alone conceptualize and memorize the array of knowledge the tome contained.

I set the figurine down and slid the book free, opening it carefully. One of the larger sections was dedicated to the rituals and festivals revolving around the sun and moon. I leafed through, stopping at the entry for Samhain. The ceremony called for a great fire and a blood sacrifice. Cattle were the offering of choice, a gift to

Danu. Samhain heralded the coming winter, resting halfway between the autumnal equinox and the winter solstice, and marked
the transition to longer nights. Badb was especially revered on this
hallowed eve when the dead could walk freely amongst the living
and the fae slipped through the worlds eager to trick humans, ferry-
ing them away to be lost in the mists forever. I shivered. It was not a
night to be traipsing around in the dark. I closed the book, placing
it back upon the shelf, and walked to the door, suddenly anxious
for Muirgen to return. Before I could reach the handle, the room
tilted away from me. I stumbled, gripping the frame for support.

What was in that drink? I blinked hard, trying to focus my
vision. I opened the door a crack and peered out.

A disembodied light floated toward the cottage, flickering in and
out as it weaved through the leafless trees. I held my breath. My
heart galloped, my palm sweaty as it gripped the iron latch. The
radiant orb stopped as if suddenly anchored to the earth yet hovering above it. An ethereal figure dressed in white robes moved in
the blackness, its gauzy silhouette undulating in the otherworldly
light. Surely it must be Muirgen. Leaning against the wall, I shuffled back a step in case it wasn't. Muirgen had been wearing her
green kirtle and a dark cloak when she left. I wanted to admonish
myself for my foolishness, but couldn't quite manage it. Instead I
closed the door quickly and practically crawled back to the stool.

Reconsidering my options, I snatched my sword from my belt
and laid it beside me. I wasn't sure it would be much use against
spirits of the dead, but if there really were faeries or mystical crea-
tures wandering about, I would be ready. The latch turned, and I
gripped the hilt a little too tightly. Would the dead not just float
through the door? What need did they have for locks and handles?
I swallowed, willing my imagination to settle, shaking my head,
desperate to clear it. The door opened and a swish of white robes
billowed into the room as the wind gusted. I may have stood, pos-

sibly even taken a step backward. The robes vanished, the doorway empty. I craned my neck to look around the frame in time to catch the outstretched hand of an old woman beckoning. I didn't dare move.

She stepped fully into the room, a wraith of a thing, the white robes flowing around her thin body, her face pale and wan in the faint candlelight. A cloak of white ermine draped from her bony shoulders. She wore her silver hair garlanded like mine, the roses bloodred in contrast.

Her voice startled me. "It is time. Come, child."

Did the dead talk? Was she one of the fae sent to lead me to my death?

"Do not be afraid." The apparition wavered, and a small child stood before me, her smile welcoming. I took her outstretched hand.

I followed the girl as she weaved through the trees, her footfalls silent as mine crunched over fallen leaves. She stopped just within the torch's light, the warm glow highlighting the soft cheekbones and gentle eyes of a woman, her beauty luminous, as pure and fresh as the morning dew. She pointed. Beyond the first torch lay another, and another, illuminating a narrow path.

"Where does it—" I turned but she was gone. A violent shiver passed through my body as if I had been hit by a cold gust, yet the trees did not move. I spun on my heels, trying to determine the way back to the cottage, but the whole world flexed and coalesced, light and dark playing and turning in my mind. Panic seized me.

"What's wrong?" Muirgen's eyes looked deep into mine. "Come, we're almost there."

Had she been there all along? Had I just imagined the apparition? I didn't trust myself to speak and followed blindly, clinging to her hand.

Shadows danced, the mist ebbed and flowed, breathing, opening onto eternity, swirling around my feet, grounding me, lifting me. Time stopped and Muirgen followed, her movement halting. Torches encircled a pool of water. A rushing brook cascading over rocks burbled downhill just beyond the wreath of stones protecting the pool's shelter. I stepped closer, drawn by the shimmering surface, the moon's silvery light shivering as if from a lover's touch. I reached out, trying to catch it, but came up empty, droplets sluicing through my fingers.

Muirgen helped me forward, and I stood in the center of the pool, water lapping around my thighs, my dress billowing bloodred in the inky blackness. In the cradle of my arms she placed a large tray, burgeoning with acorns, seeds, apples, jars of milk, and honey on a bed of dried greenery and flower petals.

She raised her hands heavenward and walked the circle of stones, stepping from one smooth surface to the next. "In the name of the one true Goddess, I cast this circle.

"Aine, Goddess of Winter, Graceful Swan, Innocent Maiden, I welcome you. Winds of the North, Darkness of Days, Ice and Snow, embrace Avelynn. Guide her on her journey so that she might honor you as high priestess in all her words, thoughts, and deeds.

"Macha, Goddess of Spring, Noble Horse, Sovereign Queen, I welcome you. Fire of the East, Promise of Plenty, Seeds and Furrows, embrace Avelynn. Guide her on her journey so that she might honor you as high priestess in all her words, thoughts, and deeds."

I tried to impart every word, but no sooner had she spoken them than they drifted like smoke from a candle, light and tenuous until they dissipated into air. I should have been cold standing in the water, the wind gusting through the skeletal trees, but I felt cocooned, bathed in a warm light.

"Danu, Goddess of Summer, Abundant Calf, Plentiful Sow, Regal Mother, I welcome you. Rock of the South, Deliverer of

Abundance, Earth and Womb, embrace Avelynn. Guide her on her journey so that she might honor you as high priestess in all her words, thoughts, and deeds."

I fell to my knees, the tray slipping from my hands. I stared at my reflection in the tranquil water. My face shimmered in the moon's glow. An acorn bobbed out of sight.

"Badb, Goddess of Autumn, Wise Raven, Loyal Wolf, Noble Crone, I welcome you. Spirit of the West, Battle's Messenger, Decay and Restoration, embrace Avelynn. Guide her on her journey so that she might honor you as high priestess in all her words, thoughts, and deeds."

She began to sing, a soulful keening that stirred my heart as it raised the hairs on my arms. I tried to push myself out of the water but failed, my limbs grown heavy, my head fogged.

An insistent voice called to me, summoning me, pulling me away from my silent contemplation as I studied the distorted image of my fingers rippling under the smooth surface of the pool. "Avelynn."

I looked up, unable to focus on Muirgen's face, which seemed to blend and blur, becoming all at once young and old.

"Do you accept the title of high priestess?"

I managed to press out the words "I do," though they sounded distant and strange to my ears.

"Do you promise to keep your faith, honoring the Goddess above all others?"

"I do." I braced my hands against one of the stones.

"Then so shall it be."

I heard a calf bleating, and then all was silent. There was blood. Everywhere blood. I was anointed. I bathed in it. I swam in the bloodred water, my dress mixing and merging with the elixir of life. I beseeched. I cried. Chanting. A great fire blazed. Howling.

The moon descending. Flames rippling, distorted underwater. My breath taken. Air. Water. Blood. Fire. Earth.

Then all was darkness.

"Good morning." Muirgen held a cup in front of her, offering.

I closed my eyes, wanting nothing more than to burrow back under the covers. "I am not drinking any more of your noxious potions ever again."

"This is mead, nothing more."

I groaned and sat up, listing a little to the right. "What did you give me?"

"An ancient tonic to help open you to the divine."

Split open would have been more appropriate. My head felt as though Mjölnir pounded inside, Thunor himself wielding the mystical hammer. I took a tentative sip of the drink, testing, swirling it around my mouth before swallowing. Satisfied it tasted like mead, without a hint of anything nefarious, I took a liberal mouthful.

She laid her hand on my shoulder. "You are a high priestess now, Avelynn, a sacred gatekeeper of our faith. Guard your heart and your secrets well. I see great challenges ahead. Your will be tested, but you must persevere. Use your gifts wisely."

I started to sweat, from the aftereffects of the ritual or her warning, I couldn't tell. "What is it? What have you seen?"

"The Witan. You appear before them. You are standing on higher ground, but there are lampreys undulating in the water. They want your blood."

SIXTEEN

November heralded warnings and suspicions. There were hints that the Vikings were preparing to move, but no one knew where or when they might attack. Despite the flurry of missives and reports burying England under parchment, I received only more silence from the Continent. I had written numerous letters to the monks of St. Denis imploring answers, but none came, nor was there any word from my father. If he had met with trouble as Demas had hinted, I had no idea of the outcome.

December brought everything to a head. As my concern for my father and brother swelled, so did Demas's ambition. In the dread of silence, he saw opportunity. When the Witan met before the twentieth of December, Demas beat me to the strike and approached the tribunal, seeking approval to proceed with our wedding. They granted his request, giving me one night to prepare.

The ceremony was to take place in the magnificent two-story hall at Winchester. Downstairs, supplicated with a steady supply of mead and wine, the lofty men of the council waited in leisure for the wedding to finish and the business of the Witan to resume. Upstairs, King Aethelred, Wulfrida, Ealhswith, and Alfred sat at the high table. Another table along the sidewall was occupied by various clergymen, but the only one I recognized was Ealhferth, the Bishop of Winchester, whose massive swath of belly made him impossible to miss.

Wulfrida and Ealhswith had decorated the hall with swags of greenery. A huge arrangement of autumn leaves, willow branches, and feathery grasses hung suspended from the massive beams overhead. Directly beneath it stood Aldulf, the Archbishop of Canterbury, ready to join our hands in marriage. I was supposed to be honored that the archbishop was presiding over the service himself.

Demas stood on the opposite side of the hall from me. His hair was trimmed to just below his jawline, and he had grown a mustache since I saw him last. He wore a purple tunic and a pair of pale brown trousers, his legs wrapped with leather banding.

In a pale green kirtle devoid of any ornamentation, my long blond hair unadorned, I sat with my back against the wall, my hands clasped and resting on my lap. Sweat pooled cold and wet between my palms.

"Demas and Avelynn, please step forward," Aldulf said.

We both moved, joining Aldulf in the center of the room. Deep lines fanned out from the corner of the archbishop's eyes and the skin beneath them sagged into pouches of purple and blue. A halo of gray hairs peeked through his blond tonsure.

"Avelynn, please repeat after me: I take thee, Demas, to be my wedded husband; to have and to hold; at bed and at board; for fairer, for fouler; for better, for worse; in sickness, in health; till death us do part."

"No."

Aldulf's gray-blue eyes blinked. "No?"

"I refuse to marry this man."

Moments before, the hall had buzzed with the sounds of revelers below, but as word of my declaration spread, a heavy hush settled around me. The wood floor creaked beneath our weight. Shuffling and stomping followed as ravenous spectators ascended the stairs, their ears tuned to succulent scraps.

I knew it would come to this. From the moment Aine had planted the idea in my mind, it was only a matter of time before the thought blossomed into reality. When Alrik told me he couldn't take me away from England, I knew what had to be done. I was tired of running, of blindly accepting my fate.

Muirgen's warning had been fortuitous. It had given me the time I'd needed to prepare. I was ready. The day of reckoning had come. "I wish to exercise my right to terminate my engagement."

"On what charge?" Aldulf asked.

"On the charge that my bridegroom is a sodomite."

The momentarily silent hall erupted into sentiments of shock, outrage, and disbelief.

King Aethelred stood. "Silence!" he barked, and then turned to me. "This is a serious charge, Mistress Avelynn."

"I know, my lord."

He looked at Demas. "What say you to this charge?"

"I firmly deny it, sire."

"I have a witness," I offered. The crowd began to hum with speculation.

Demas narrowed his eyes at me. "Mistress Avelynn has refused to marry, going against her father's wishes for several years now. This is merely another one of her tactics. The claims are false."

Aldulf approached the head table and bent his tonsured head to Aethelred. The two whispered in conference. Aethelred nodded and Aldulf addressed us.

"It is the lady's right to a trial. We will reconvene the Witan and address this matter presently."

While the men of the council sorted themselves, Ealhswith marched over and grabbed my arm, pulling me aside.

"What are you doing?"

"I'm getting out of my marriage."

"How?"

"By proving he's a cretin and a cur."

"By charging him with sodomy? I know you had words, but if you go through with this you'll ruin him."

"Good."

She studied me, eyes filled with concern. "What has he done?"

"Aside from binding me and threatening to rape me, you mean? I caught him with his pants down, engaging in carnal activities with another man."

Her face paled, and she made the sign of the cross. "Jesu, Avelynn." She looked around anxiously, her voice low. "Could we not be charged with the very same thing?"

I held her hands, giving them a reassuring squeeze. "You know where my heart lies on the matter, but his aggression and threats have left me little choice. I needed a charge strong enough for the Witan to grant me a release." My eyes pleaded with hers for understanding. "I cannot marry him, Ealhswith. What would you have me do?"

She pulled me close. "I'm sorry. It is dreadful what he has put you through. I'd no idea things had gotten so out of hand."

Out of the corner of my eye I caught the purple of Demas's tunic as he pushed his way forcibly to the stairs. What was he up to? I withdrew from her embrace. "Will you stand for me and swear to my character?"

"Of course. I will support you in any way I can."

"Thank you." Demas disappeared from view. "I'm sorry. You'll have to excuse me." I slipped my hands from hers. "I'll be right back."

I maneuvered through the press of bodies and reached the stairs in time to see Demas step outside. The lower level was almost empty. Everyone crammed upstairs to see the spectacle first hand. I peeked out the door just as Demas slipped behind one of the outbuildings. Borrowing a heavy wool cloak that someone had left lying over one of the benches, I followed. I nodded to the guards who kept vigil over the weapons and retrieved Alrik's knife. It was the only thing I had left of him, and I refused to hide it any longer.

I reached the building I had seen Demas disappear behind, but he was nowhere to be found. I scanned the area. He couldn't have gone far. I might be overreacting, but the way he left the hall, the urgency in his step, made the skin on the back of my neck prickle.

I wandered the grounds until I heard voices, one of which was very loud and very angry. I followed the confrontation to a small sunken building and crouched near the window. Demas was inside. I could hear his rich Roman-accented voice raised in defense, but I didn't recognize the other speaker. I lifted my head and tried to see inside. There was a small crack around the frame of the shutters. I closed one eye and peered into the gloom beyond. It was a weaving cottage; two large looms leaned against the wall farthest away from me. Demas was standing by the door. I couldn't make out the man looming over him, his back to the window.

"You did what?" the man spat.

"I was drinking."

"Drinking?" He moved so quickly, I only had time to see Demas's reaction to the swing. Demas stumbled backward and hit the door with a loud thud.

"In Rome, teachers shared more than manuscripts with their young acolytes. It was not a sin." Demas picked himself up off the dirt floor.

"You foolish ass," the man hissed. "This is England. Not some cesspool of depravity. You would risk everything we have worked for." The man turned. I slid down and pressed my back against the wall, my heart pounding.

"I hadn't expected to meet anyone. I made a mistake."

"A mistake?" The voice moved away from the window, and I chanced another look.

I didn't have to see the blow—I heard it. Demas went down like a sack of grain. Why wasn't he fighting back? The man kicked him several times in the ribs, causing Demas to emit a grunt of pain but no resistance.

"Get up."

Demas stood, using the wall to brace himself.

"You will do whatever is necessary to convince them of your innocence. If you fail, you will not live long enough to regret it." He opened the door and left.

I scrambled to the back of the building and peered around the corner as the man made his way to the hall. He was a tall, thickly built man with wavy blond hair and wide shoulders. He wore a red tunic, his waist cinched by a thick leather belt. It would certainly be easy enough to determine who he was once we were all back inside.

I glanced back at the window of the weaving shed. The council would be assembled by now and wondering where we were. I couldn't leave until Demas was gone. I couldn't risk getting caught listening.

When Demas finally stepped outside, his face was red, and a line of blood clung to his chin, dripping from the side of his mouth. He wiped his face, straightened his tunic, and walked a little gingerly to the hall.

"What are you doing lurking about?" a woman's voice chastised me.

I spun around, startled, but relaxed when I saw Muirgen.

"When did you get here?"

"Just now."

"But I didn't hear you." I regarded the stables behind me.

"I suspect you were otherwise preoccupied."

"Yes, I guess I was." I watched Demas disappear into the hall. "Are you ready?"

"Humph." She fussed with the costume I had insisted she wear. The men of the Witan needed to take her testimony seriously. Beneath her fine wool cloak, she wore a pale yellow kirtle. Her hair was bound and hidden beneath a wimple, a large wooden cross hung prominently from her neck. She tugged at the cross in distaste.

"You need to look the part," I said.

"Are you sure you want to go through with this? If you should fail—"

"Absolutely," I said gaily, ignoring the knots tightening in my stomach.

"Well, come then, let's get this over with."

They were all waiting on me, and as Muirgen and I entered the hall, I scanned the room for the man I'd seen in the weaving shed with Demas. I found him upstairs, leaning against a wall, but I didn't recognize him. I'd never seen him before. His eyes lighted on mine. Cold dread swept through me, and Muirgen's grip tightened on my arm. Demas sat on a bench to one side of the head table, and Aldulf indicated I should wait on the other side, opposite him. Muirgen sat beside me.

"We will now address the matter of marriage between Avelynn of Wedmore, daughter of Eanwulf, Earl of Somerset, and Demas of Wareham, nephew to the great Bishop Ealhstan. Please state your charge, Mistress Avelynn," Aldulf said.

"Thank you, sir." I curtsied to the head table. "Sire, distinguished and honorable men of Wessex, I request you release me from my betrothal to Demas, based on his proclivities toward young men."

The hall exploded in reaction.

"Silence," King Aethelred bellowed. "I will not have the tribunal disrupted by outbursts. If you are not capable of restraint, I will see to it that everyone is removed save the parties involved." When he seemed satisfied with the effect of his words, he sat back down. "Please continue, Archbishop."

"Demas." Aldulf motioned to the center of the room. I sat down.

"Thank you, most honorable Archbishop Aldulf." He bowed to the head table. "My good and godly king, Aethelred, fellow God-fearing men of Wessex, I am innocent of all charges and demand that the wedding proceed as Eanwulf, the Earl of Somerset, had intended. Eanwulf is a great man. I had the pleasure of accompanying him on his commission to Rome, and he was adamant that this wedding take place in the fall. My intent is to fulfill his wish and see this wedding completed." Demas sat down.

"Avelynn, bring forth your first oath taker," Aldulf said.

I stood, Muirgen beside me. "I was on my way to visit Muirgen, a respected healer of Congresbury, when I heard a struggle in the wood. When I happened upon the scene, a young man lay exposed, bent over a log. Demas stood behind him with his pants down. Muirgen, coming to meet me, also witnessed the event."

Muirgen stepped forward. "I swear, my lords. What Avelynn said is true. But, what she failed to mention is that after the biddable gentleman withdrew from the scene, Demas then restrained Avelynn and threatened to rape her."

Muirgen's admission caused another round of gasps and murmurs. My stomach churned, as if wrung inside out. I hadn't planned on ceding that much information.

"Is this true?" Aldulf looked to me.

I nodded.

Aldulf produced the Book of the Gospels. "Do you swear it by all that is holy? By God the Father, God the Son, and God the Holy Ghost?"

I placed my hand on the book. "I do so swear."

He repeated the same oath to Muirgen and she, too, swore on the Christian book. Watching her act so serene and righteous, I would have laughed if this hadn't been so serious.

The next few days passed with each of us calling members of the community forward who would swear to our character. Alfred and Ealhswith stood up for me, as did each of the warriors left behind to guard Wedmore. Bertram, Plegmund—even Milo and Walther vouched for my virtues.

Breaking his exile, Sigberht stood up for Demas, painting a picture of my headstrong ambitions in matters best left for men, and my constant refusal—supported by Nelda, my chambermaid's, testimony—to get married.

I didn't know what they had threatened the girl with, but she refused to meet my eyes and cowered limply beside Sigberht.

After Sigberht, the man I had seen in the altercation with Demas addressed the Witan. "Osric, Earl of Dorset, stands for Demas of Wareham. The charges are false and seditious."

I stared at Osric. So this was my uncle? I had never seen him before. He had never been to any of the Christmas feasts, and he certainly would not have been invited to any of our family gatherings or celebrations. I could only assume that he was here because my father was not. He returned to his place, sitting at a table opposite the king.

After what I witnessed in the weaving shed, I was more than a little surprised when he stood for Demas's character. In fact, Demas had the support of several powerful earls. I couldn't fathom how he had managed to earn the favor of so many influential men in such a short period of time in England. I suspected it had everything to do with my uncle. There was a clear division at this tribunal between the men who supported the Earl of Somerset, and by virtue his daughter, and those who supported the Earl of Dorset and his interests, whatever they might be.

It soon became clear, however, that it was a matter of his word against mine, and since we both had the backing of some very powerful people in Wessex, the Witan was at an impasse.

I had hoped for a firm, decisive solution to the matter, for everything to be settled by a vote. My victory rested on being able to provide Muirgen as witness to the event. But Demas supplied his own alibis, and, through deceit, managed to throw my account into question. Unless I was able to produce the young man implied in the charge, I had no proof.

"The matter will be determined by a trial of boiling water," Aldulf said.

Pages scurried to and fro, and the central fire was stoked hot and glowing. A large cauldron was placed over the fire, and water was poured to a depth fitting of the crime. In this case, it was filled near to the top. A piece of iron was placed at the bottom of the cauldron. Once the water began to boil, everyone was asked to leave the hall save those directly involved—except of course the king, who remained seated. The rest of us stood in a circle around the cauldron. We were allowed to retain one witness. My uncle stood up for Demas; Muirgen stayed with me. The only other persons in the hall were two members of the clergy—Aldulf, who would preside over the trial, and Ealhferth, the Bishop of Winchester, who would assist if necessary.

"You have the right to assign a deputy," Aldulf said to Demas.

"I will prove my innocence with my own flesh," Demas answered.

"Very well." Aldulf sprinkled everyone with holy water until we were satisfactorily doused, and had us each in turn kiss the Book of the Gospels and a large wooden cross.

"Bend your heads silently in prayer and ask the Father to reveal to us the truth in this grave matter."

To a pagan, Christian rhetoric and symbolism were nothing more than mist in the wind. They held no substance, no tangibility. But if this pageant was to continue much longer, I was worried Muirgen might say something aloud. I could tell from the rigid set of her shoulders that the archbishop was trying her patience.

Aldulf began a long, steady chant in Latin, singing the litany— a repetitive petition to our lord God.

Muirgen looked at me, her lips set in a grim line. I pleaded with my eyes. She nodded and looked heavenward, her eyes large and reverent.

Demas was to reach into the cauldron of boiling water and pull out the iron. The priests would then bandage his wounds. In three days, if his arm festered, he would be found guilty. If the wounds were clean and healing, then he would be proved innocent by the grace of God. I had taken a huge risk with this ordeal. If the marriage proceeded, I was lost.

Aldulf stopped his droning and gestured to Demas. "Please remove your shirt."

"That is not necessary." Osric laid his hand on Demas's shoulder. "He can merely lift his sleeve."

"The law states that the accused must bear his heart before God. The shirt must be removed."

Demas looked at Osric, who huffed but nodded.

What a bizarre exchange. The man was about to stick his entire arm in a vat of boiling water, and they were concerned about the removal of a shirt?

Demas undid his belt, handing it to Osric, and then lifted the tunic over his head. I inhaled sharply. There on Demas's chest, from nipple to umbilicus, was a birthmark, thick and garnet red, just like the one Muirgen had described when speaking about my cousin, the babe who was never found. Osric's son! I glanced at Muirgen, who stood rod stiff with a blank expression. When I turned back to Demas, both he and Osric were watching me, their faces unreadable. Oh gods, did they know I knew? I lowered my eyes in an act of humility, trying to play the role of virgin as Muirgen had once suggested. This seemed to please Aldulf.

"Not a sight for an innocent," he said to me. "You may keep your eyes averted. When you are ready, Demas, you may proceed."

A loud bang reverberated through the hall as the main doors slammed heavily. We all turned. My father bounded up the stairs.

My heart at once leapt for joy at the sight of him, and then dropped liked the iron bar at the bottom of the cauldron. His eyes blazed hotter than the central fire, and he was headed straight for me. Instinctively, I stepped back.

Aldulf stepped between us, partly obscuring the force of his rage. "Lord Eanwulf, we are in the middle of a trial. I request you wait outside."

"I will not." His face was red from the cold. He was dressed in full mail, and his helmet was dented and tarnished.

"You will give me a moment with my daughter, priest."

Aldulf deferred to Aethelred, who had moved to stand beside the archbishop.

"It is good to see you returned to us, Lord Eanwulf, but this is a formal trial. You cannot intervene. As your king, I demand you do as the archbishop requests and step outside."

My father turned to Aethelred as if seeing him for the first time. He blinked, and an expression of careful control shifted his features.

"My king." He bowed slightly. "I bring news."

Aethelred looked at him curiously. "Yes?"

"The Heathen Army has crossed into Wessex."

I was segregated from the other female guests sleeping in the women's quarters and squirreled away in one of the small guest cottages. It boasted a raised shelf against the far wall for sleeping and a small trestle table nestled between two benches. A raised-slab hearth in the center of the packed-earth floor served as the only source of heat and light. The lime-washed wattle-and-daub walls did little to keep out the frigid December cold.

Muirgen had informed Ealhswith of the situation thus far, and the two of them sat across from me, pity and concern written in their eyes.

To all but the women in front of me, I was a pariah—ambition and vanity raising me too high. God would see me harshly punished. Most hoped my new husband would beat me into submission, or in lieu of that, they expected my father to do it. Regardless, the Witan had moved on to more pressing matters, and the charges against Demas had been thrown out. I had lost, my life forfeit.

My only ray of sunshine was seeing my brother's face. While thin and pale, he was here—home, alive, and well. I hugged him briefly, aware of each rib beneath his tunic. He smiled, but his eyes were distant, and his face wore a look of heavy weariness. I learned that the monastery at St. Denis had come under attack by Vikings during his time there, and I desperately wanted to speak with him, but I didn't have time. My father demanded his presence at council.

All of the men were holed up in the hall, discussing the news my father had brought. Despite the implications of imminent war, the archbishop was adamant that the Nativity still be celebrated, and he instructed Wulfrida to continue with her preparations. The Christmas feast would start tomorrow.

Ealhswith brought my attention back to the present moment.

"Marriage between two cousins is forbidden by the Church. Surely they will grant you a release now."

I rested my head in my hands. "And how do I prove he's my cousin? Muirgen is my only witness, and we know how well that tactic works." I didn't even have the energy to cry. "Why does this marriage mean so much to him?"

"It's obvious," Muirgen said.

It certainly wasn't obvious to me.

"Your uncle's using Demas as his pawn."

"I don't understand."

"When your grandfather's will divided the earldom, your uncle's greed and ambition caused a bloody and vicious civil war. While he's been quiet these last years, it's clear his lust for power has not been tempered. With your marriage to his son, Osric will be one step closer to ruling both earldoms in all but name. If something were to happen to your father, Osric would become the most powerful man in Wessex, save the king himself."

Ealhswith's mouth hung open. "But Demas cannot claim to be Osric's son, or the marriage won't take place."

"I suspect he'll wait until the marriage is signed, delivered, and consummated before he reveals his true parentage."

"And what of his claim to be the lady Mildrith's son, Bishop Ealhstan's nephew?" Ealhswith asked.

"A lie."

Ealhswith laid her hand on my shoulder. "You must leave."

"And go where?"

"Francia?"

"And what is a disgraced lady to do in Francia? Prostitute myself for my bread and water? I might as well stay here and do that at my husband's court."

"It won't come to that, yet," Muirgen said. "The war you foresaw is upon us."

"What have you seen?" Ealhswith asked.

"Remember when I mentioned I'd had a vision and agreed to give Demas another chance?" I cringed.

"Yes."

"Well, I misinterpreted the signs."

"I gathered that."

"I saw a raven and a wild boar. They were fighting each other. At the time, I was looking for something, anything, other than the struggle and pain the vision portended. In the end, I realized Demas would be the cause of that suffering, and everything I've done—resisting his betrothal, charging him at the tribunal—has been in an effort to escape my fate. However, there was much more to that vision than could be gleaned at first glance; an entire manuscript was written in a passing moment. The meaning behind the animals fighting is obvious now. War *is* coming."

"But you saw more," Muirgen said.

"Not on the same day, but later in a dream. I fell through the sky, surrounded by ravens. Battle raged beneath me. Men were dying, their bloodied bodies littering the snow-covered fields, turning the ground into a rusty sludge. Their cries were horrible." I shivered. "I was falling and there was nothing I could do to stop it. I was going to die." The last words came out in a whisper.

"That's nothing but a nightmare brought on by Mari, the sorceress of dreams, to frighten you," Ealhswith said.

"While my part in the coming violence is elusive, these visions have come to warn me that I will be affected by it in tragic ways."

"Ealhswith is right, Avelynn. The war has been foretold, but your part in it has yet to be written."

I gave Muirgen a droll look. "You are far too wise to believe that."

The door to the cottage flew open, and my father stepped inside, his hulking frame taking up the entire doorway.

"You, *wyrt-gaelstre*." He scowled at Muirgen.

"Hello, Eanwulf."

"You have placed these ideas in her head." He slammed the door and stalked closer.

"You need to hear what your daughter has to say." Muirgen stepped in front of him. She barely came to the middle of his chest. "You would be wise to listen."

Something passed between the two of them—a flicker, an unspoken current. He glared at Ealhswith.

"I should go. Aethelflaed will be needing me." Ealhswith grabbed her cloak and maneuvered around the standoff, casting me a look of sympathy before slipping out the door.

I turned to face the wrath of my father.

SEVENTEEN

My father may have taken off his mail coat and helmet, but he was ready for war. "You have shamed me."

"You don't understand—"

"You stood in front of the most powerful men in Wessex and spewed lies, all to disobey my wishes." He pulled off his belt. "By God, your new husband will beat you senseless for this, but he will have to wait his turn."

"You will not touch her," Muirgen said.

"Stay out of this, *wyrt-gaelstre*."

"I will not."

"Move out of my way, or I will knock you down where you stand." He raised his hand as if to strike her.

"I'm warning you." She glowered at him and yanked the cross from her neck, throwing it into the rushes on the floor.

He hesitated.

"Demas's intentions were to take your daughter and force her hand in marriage. If I had not happened upon the scene, she would have been raped."

"Liar."

"I may be many things, Eanwulf, husband of Aileen, most esteemed high priestess, but I am not a liar." She scowled at him. "Is your pride so blind that you would condemn your daughter to this marriage? It was Demas who schemed behind your back, arranging the marriage at the tribunal. Your daughter merely protected herself and her legacy."

I watched doubt flicker in my father's eyes.

Muirgen continued. "You'll remember my daughter Leenan and the babe fathered by Osric, a child born with a scar across his chest?"

"What of it?"

"Demas is that child."

"Impossible; the babe was killed."

"No, the child was never found. Yet he stood here today a man. There was no denying the birthmark."

"That cannot be proven. Only a handful of people saw that scar, and most are dead." He flashed a look at Muirgen that seem to imply he wished she were one of them.

She ignored it. "And if it could be proven? If they knew something we did not? Once Demas is married to your daughter, Osric will, in all but name, control Wedmore. You and your son, dear Eanwulf, will be the last things standing in his way. Did you not run into trouble on your journey to Rome?"

"Vikings and pirates."

"Yet where did they attack? A monastery where your son lay ill? A convenient way to dispatch the last heir to your great fortune— a monastery where presumably Demas also lay ill." She shook her head. "You are blind and foolish."

Could Demas have orchestrated the Viking attack? How was that even possible? I watched my father and my stomach clenched, waiting for him to strike out, but he stood there.

"And since we're sharing in an environment of acceptance and honesty, you should also know that your daughter is now a high priestess. I have ordained her." A smirk edged the corner of her thin lips. "War has come, Eanwulf. Your daughter has foreseen it."

He blanched white as newly fallen snow and looked at me with an expression somewhere between terror and disbelief. When he spoke, his voice sounded hollow, lacking any of the depth and conviction I was used to hearing. It sent chills up my spine. "Aethelred has sent an envoy. He's prepared to pay the Vikings to leave Wessex," he said.

"Money will not save Wessex this time. Prepare your men, Eanwulf. You'll ride to war before the calends of January."

He looked back and forth between us, his eyes wild like a cornered stag, and then spun on his heels and left. The crackle and hiss from the hearth was the only sound that remained in the vacuum of his departure.

"Dear gods." My stomach lurched, and heat flushed my face. I held the back of my hand against my mouth as a wave of nausea threatened.

"It will be all right now."

"How can you say that? Didn't you see the look on his face?" I collapsed onto a bench. "And when did you come up with the first of January for war? I've never seen a date."

"You saw snow. A storm is coming." She grabbed her cloak. "I must go, Avelynn, but before I leave, I ask only two things."

I waited.

"Keep my book safe."

I furrowed my brow.

"And bury me under the large oak."

I leapt to her side. "Are you unwell?"

She laid a withered hand on my cheek and smiled. "I'm fine. I ask only so that when my time comes you honor me with a proper burial, in the old ways."

I studied her face for any sign of imminent illness. "Of course."

She moved to the door but paused. "When life seems at its darkest, those are our most powerful moments, moments when the Goddess shines through us, offering us an opportunity to embody our fullest potential. Choose wisely, Avelynn. Always remember your strength."

I grew increasingly anxious with each word she said. "What is it, Muirgen? What have you seen?"

The specter of sorrow flitted across her face. "Be well, child." She smiled weakly. "The war has come. Right now, the Vikings march to Reading."

Reading was a rich and prosperous royal village in Berkshire, only a day's ride from here. "You need to tell Father . . . the Witan . . ."

"They'll find out soon enough."

It was the twenty-eighth of December, and we were still at Winchester, assembled in King Aethelred's hall for another feast. The Christmastide festivities would continue until the Epiphany, the sixth of January. Edward sat to my left. He had been quiet and reflective since coming home, and when I looked in his eyes, shadows hovered above the dark blue beneath. I tried to engage him in conversation, but he answered only in short yes-or-no quips and would say no more. My father, stiff and silent, sat on my other side, his eyes never drifting far from his brother, Osric. He hadn't spoken a word to me, hadn't even looked at me since that day with Muirgen in the cottage.

The place next to my father was empty. Demas was still curiously absent. I hadn't seen him since the trial. I looked farther down the bench. Ealdorman Aethelwulf of Berkshire and his wife, Cyneburga, sat at our table just as they had a year ago. My shoulders dropped as if under the pressure of a thousand sacks of grain. One year had passed. So much had changed, yet here I was, still stuck in the exact same position.

A young boy ran into the hall and bowed before Aethelred. "The Vikings have taken Reading, my lord. The emissary you sent to offer terms has been beheaded. His head is mounted on a spike overlooking the old Roman road."

The hall exploded into action as men stood, preparing to fight.

"Hold!" It was Aldulf, the Archbishop of Canterbury.

"God is testing our faith. He has brought the heathens to our door during our Lord's, the Savior Christ's, most holy week. We must spend time in prayer to seek our Father's guidance. We must not rush, lest this be a trap from Satan."

"But they have taken Reading, my lord," the messenger said.

"Then there is nothing we can do to root them out now. If we attack without God's favor, we risk certain failure."

Nervous whispers filled the room.

Aethelred, our noble king, stood. "I will not risk earning God's displeasure. Wulfrida, see to it that the Christmas feast continues without interruption. Alfred, send messengers out to the shires— tell them to prepare for war. I will join the priests in silent contemplation and prayer. Once we have word from God that it is an auspicious time to attack, we will march."

I stared at them in disbelief. Aethelred and his priests left the hall, while the men of Wessex stood around, helpless. My father exchanged glances with Aethelwulf, who nodded and left, his wife clinging to his side. Despite the pious praying that the king would undertake on our behalf, Aethelwulf was clearly a man of action.

Three days later, word came that Earl Aethelwulf had ambushed a large Viking raiding party. Two powerful Viking leaders were killed, and the stragglers who escaped hobbled back broken and dejected to the fort. If this was the mystical word from his God, only the deity knew for sure, but Aethelred took it as a sign and ordered the Wessex fyrd to march for Reading.

"I will fight alongside Father," Edward said, and put on his new helmet and padded leather coat.

We had returned to Wedmore yesterday so that my father could levy the men of Somerset to his side. Edward had come to my cottage to say good-bye.

"You shall do no such thing. You are to stay at the back of the flanks and observe so that when you're old enough you'll know what to do. Besides," I said, straightening his coat, "leather will not protect you from a Viking blade."

"A coat of mail wouldn't be a bother to me. I'm ready to fight— I want to fight. Father is being unreasonable."

Even soaking wet and with a full stomach, Edward would be outweighed by a mail coat. "You're still too weak from your ordeal in Francia to wear a coat of mail."

"I am not helpless." He ripped off his helmet and threw it on the floor. He sat down in a huff on my bed and looked distractedly at the smoke rising from a single beeswax candle on the bedside table.

"Edward, what happened in Francia?" During the raid on St. Denis, the Vikings had taken Edward prisoner, holding him for ransom. Upon receipt of the news, my father and his men returned from Rome and chased the pirates to a small town in northern Francia. With a contingent of men from King Charles's court, they defeated the Vikings and rescued Edward and several monks unharmed, including the abbot of the monastery.

He continued to stare.

"Please, talk to me." I knelt at his feet.

"The Vikings tortured the monks. They made me watch," he said quietly, never taking his eyes away from the curling smoke.

He opened his palm and held it above the orange flame. "Men of God, good and holy men. They scalped one young acolyte—just cut along his forehead and pulled. Blood poured everywhere."

I could smell his skin burning. He pulled his hand away from the candle and rubbed at it absently.

He looked at me, his eyes rimmed with red. "Remember the blood eagle we heard about? That thing the Vikings did to King Aelle of Northumbria? It wasn't a myth or a tale to scare children. I saw them do it."

He grew silent again. The wind whipped around the cottage, wheezing and whistling. Snow was coming.

"Some monks lost their eyes or their tongues. Others had their hands or feet cut off. I could do nothing to help them."

"You cannot feel guilty, Edward. Those men were monsters. They would have hurt you or worse if you tried to stop them."

"I'm of no help to anyone." He picked up his helmet and pulled it onto his head. "God keep you safe, sister," he said, and left.

I grabbed my cloak and opened the door, ready to chase after him, but my father's shadow blocked my way, and he advanced into the cottage. He walked over to the fire, removed his gloves, and warmed his hands. He was wearing his mail coat, and soft blond waves stuck out from underneath his helmet. His bear-pelt cloak draped off his broad shoulders, and his sword and sax hung from his belt. He was ready for war.

"I have come to say good-bye."

"I'm sorry," I said.

"It is I who am sorry."

My breath stopped.

He turned to me. "I have done you a great disservice. Will you forgive me?"

I ran forward and crushed myself against him, my heart bursting with gratitude, relief, love, and happiness. He reached around and held me.

"What of Osric?" I asked. If everything Muirgen said was true, Demas and Osric were a sinister threat to our family.

He released me and walked to the door. "I have no proof of his deceptions, but I can put a stop to this betrothal. It is a start."

He waited a moment, and a knock sounded. He opened the door. Wulfric and Sigberht shuffled to the central hearth. Dressed in full mail, their sword hilts clanked softly against the linked metal as they moved. Father Plegmund followed and sat at the table, producing an inkwell, a feather, and a swatch of parchment. With all these stalwart male bodies in my small cottage, there was little room to maneuver.

We'd not spoken since the scene in the cottage, and I'd had no opportunity to fill my father in on what had happened during his absence. As acting reeve, Bertram must have informed him of the situation with the grain accounts and my judgment in the case. I was furious that Sigberht was once again in my father's good graces—especially given his testimony against me at the Witan.

My father cleared his throat and nodded to Plegmund. "I hereby call off the betrothal of my daughter, Avelynn of Wedmore, to Demas of Wareham." He turned to me. "These men will sign as witnesses and swear to my decree."

Plegmund produced the newly writ charter and each man penned his name. My father moved to the bedside table and poured hot wax from the candle onto the folded parchment. He waited a moment and then pressed his gold ring into the cooling wax.

He stepped in front of me, forcing me to look into his eyes. "Sigberht has been charged with delivering this letter personally to the king. He will not let me down again or he will lose his position here as reeve."

Relief surged through me. He understood. He approved. I would have jumped and thrown my hands around his neck had it not been for the audience. Instead, I smiled. He nodded and handed the letter to Sigberht, who bowed slightly and left. Plegmund and Wulfric followed closely behind.

I was filled with a giddy lightness. I looked upon my father with a sense of awe and adoration. He was fair but firm, gentle but ruthless when crossed, and like the man I remembered from my childhood, he was once again my greatest champion and hero.

He lifted my chin. "You are so much like your mother, Avelynn." He kissed my forehead. "She was bloody headstrong and single-minded too."

I hugged him fiercely, the tiny circles in his mail coat blurring through my tears.

"Now, wish your father well."

"God keep you, Father."

"It is not God I ask." He pulled out an amulet of amber that my mother had given him. It was tied around his neck with a leather thong.

In my wildest dreams, I couldn't have imagined this moment. He accepted me, all of me, for who I was, for what I was. For all that I had done. The world, my future, seemed brighter. "I will pray to the Goddess every day that you come back to me safe and sound."

He inclined his head slightly. "Thank you, priestess."

Nine months had passed since I'd stood outside my father's hall, watching them leave for Rome. Now my brother and father were marching off to war. The uncertainty that surrounded their last departure had been nothing like it was now.

The wind was howling from the west, bringing icy fingers to bear on exposed flesh. I drew my cloak tighter. The sky was dark and foreboding, and white flakes swirled through the air. My father had to muster the men of Somerset to action. Wulfric, Leofric, and his household warriors rode at his side. All around me, women stood in clusters to keep warm from the wind, clutching crosses, tears falling. All the freemen of Wedmore would march to Reading, save Bertram and a small contingent of slaves who would stay behind to help maintain the efficiency of the manor. I was pleased Sigberht would be joining the cause after he delivered my father's decree to Winchester. Wedmore would be left undisputedly to me.

Edward gave me a brisk hug. He had the promise of our father's height, and with a sword by his side he looked every bit the warrior he was destined to become. "I'm sorry for my outburst."

I pulled him to me and hugged him proper, hard enough to make him groan. "I'll miss you."

"I'll miss you too," he said. He shuffled his feet, the toe of his leather boot disturbing a few drifting snowflakes.

"What is it?" I asked.

"I hate Demas."

Startled, I stared at him.

"I hate what he tried to do to you. He's a monster. He's worse than the Vikings. I'll kill him one day if I get the chance."

His desire to protect me filled me with love, and my heart ached. I had two champions this day.

"I love you, sister." He kissed my cheek.

"I love you too, Edward."

As he mounted his horse, a cold chill crept up my spine. I turned to find Demas standing at my side. The blood boiled in my veins and my face flushed red. "Get away from me, you rutting bastard."

"I love it when you're angry. Such passion, such fire. Makes it all the more enjoyable to snuff it out."

I refused to give him what he wanted.

He straightened. "A storm is coming. Terrible day to ride. A bad omen, I think."

I bit down hard on the inside of my cheek and ignored him.

"If you believe in such things, which I think you do, don't you, Avelynn. Omens and other forms of witchcraft."

I turned.

"What do you want, Demas?"

"I was merely wondering what you foresaw for me?"

"I don't know what you're talking about."

"Your friend, what was her name, Muirgen? She seemed to know an awful lot about what was going to happen. She was after all a witch . . . and so are you."

I glanced around to see if anyone had overheard his statement. We were alone.

He leaned down, his cheek resting near my ear. "No simple trial by water for you, witch. They will bury you alive."

I stiffened.

He pulled away. "I have a gift for you."

"I don't want anything from you."

"You wouldn't want to disappoint your husband."

"You are not my husband, nor will you ever be. My father has called off the betrothal. His decree will be in Winchester by the morrow. You can't touch me."

"Much can happen in war." He clicked his tongue in mock sympathy. "So much confusion." His voice grew cold and low. "People are lost. Some are never found, just like pieces of parchment. I hope for your sake that your father returns unharmed to your side." He started walking away.

I grabbed his arm. "And just what do you mean to insinuate with that threat?"

He brushed off my hold as if swatting a fly. "I was merely

pointing out the risks of war. If your father does not come back, Avelynn, I will have my way. Nothing will stop me, and you will rue the day you tried to cross me."

He tossed a leather pouch in my direction. It fell onto the ground. "A lesson," he said, and slinked away, disappearing into the throng of warriors ready for battle.

The men spurred their horses onward. Both my brother and father turned back and waved. My heart swelled. No matter what happened next or what had come before, in this moment I was loved.

They bounded out of sight, the thunder of hooves fading into the howling wind. I looked down at my feet and picked up the leather pouch Demas had thrown at me. I pulled open the drawstring and peered inside. It appeared to be strands of fine wool. I drew them out. The smell of rotten flesh assaulted my nostrils. I threw the pouch and its contents onto the ground and backed up. My hand flew to my mouth, stifling a scream.

It was Muirgen's silken white hair, scalped right off her head.

EIGHTEEN

Bertram and I pushed onward, heads bent to the wind. The horses' breath raised plumes of shadowy mist into the swirling white air, their hooves pounding through the accumulating snow.

It was only the day before that I had watched the men depart from Wedmore. I would have left for Congresbury immediately if I thought I could reach it before nightfall.

As soon as dawn broke, so did the storm. We hunched into tightly wrapped cloaks and raced headlong into the worst of it. Despite nature's fury, I was determined to reach Muirgen's cottage. I had to honor her last wishes.

By noon, our pace had slowed almost to a crawl. The going had become treacherous, the trail lined in places with ice hidden beneath the snow.

When we finally reached the village, nightfall was approaching, and we sought hospitality in one of the more prosperous churl's wattle-and-daub cottage. The farmer tended to our horses in one half of the home, while his wife, a small, thin woman with missing teeth and wiry, russet hair, offered us bread and pottage.

"What brings m'lady out in this terrible storm?" she asked as she stoked the fire hotter. A long rectangle, their cottage was a meager one. The shallow central hearth dug into the dirt floor divided the byre from the living space, a wattle fence the only thing standing between us and the cow, the pig, a few chickens, and our two horses. On this side of the fence there was a raised platform built into one of the longer walls closest to the hearth. It held a thin straw mattress and a few linens folded neatly on top. The only other furniture in the room was a table and the two stools we sat upon. Our hostess stood and smiled as we ate her humble offering gratefully.

"Have you any word of Muirgen, the healer?" I said.

"The witch?"

I nodded.

"Last I saw her she was headin' into town for some big trial."

"Has your husband had word of anyone coming to visit her lately?" Bertram said.

"Not that I know." She called across the fence, "Wolfstan, you know somethin' about the witch these last few days?"

He came to the fence, a sallow stick of a man, and brushed his hands against his worn trousers. A cloud of dust mixed with the heavy smoke in the air. The couple burned peat, which was wonderfully warm, but terribly smoky. Their cottage had a miasma of gray so thick that if you stood up, your eyes watered and your chest tightened.

"No one's come by here savin' yourself, m'lady." He inclined his head slightly.

I frowned. Did Demas catch her on the road? Did she even make it home? Was she left at the edge of the road, her frail body a feast for wolves? I pressed my thumb and forefinger above my closed eyelids. I didn't want to think about it.

The next morning, Wolfstan accompanied us to Muirgen's cottage. Her home was surrounded by dense woodland, and since I was not sure who or what might greet us when we arrived, I welcomed the extra company.

The storm had stopped overnight, and weak sunlight struggled to break through the thinning clouds. The world was blanketed in white. A hand's depth of snow had fallen since the previous morning, and trees and bushes hung heavy with their accumulated burdens.

As we neared the cottage, the acrid stench of burnt and wet timber began to grow stronger. I spurred Marma forward. An image flashed into my mind. Thickly corded rope looped around the central beam in the roof, the ends binding Muirgen's wrists, her arms stretched above her, her head bent. Blood dripped from her mouth. She had been tortured.

I shook my head, determined to clear the image that blazed in front of my closed eyes. I prayed to the Goddess that she hadn't suffered long.

At the footpath leading to Muirgen's cottage, we tethered the horses and walked the remaining way, our footprints marring the virgin white landscape. Streaks of pale sunlight filtered through the skeletal branches of the large oak tree, illuminating the disembodied bones that shivered with the weight of newly fallen snow. In the middle of the boughs, hanging from a noose tied around her neck, swayed Muirgen, her naked body defiled and ravaged by carrion. She was frozen and stiff; her blue-gray skin, ripped and torn in places, hung loosely in thin shreds. Both her feet had been chewed off. I didn't know what I had been expecting, but it certainly wasn't this.

"Blessed Goddess," Bertram whispered beside me.

Wolfstan crossed himself. "Mistress, I think it best if I wait by the horses."

"Of course." I watched him retreat, practically tripping over his feet in his haste.

Behind Muirgen, the scene was just as bleak. The cottage itself was burned to the ground, a blackened scab in the middle of the pristine forest. Her book—the rituals, the incantations—all lost. *Oh, Muirgen, I'm so sorry.*

I surveyed the wreckage. The fire hadn't been hot enough to melt the cauldron, which still hung suspended over what was once the hearth. I riffled through the soot and ash, looking for anything I could use for her burial. I found an iron mortar unscathed and tucked it into my satchel. Everything else was destroyed.

"There is little we can do here." Bertram placed his hand on my shoulder.

"We have to bury her. We can't leave her. . . ." My throat tightened.

"Then we must gather supplies." He shrugged deeper into his cloak. I looked into his face. Muirgen and Bertram had known each other in another life—in a time before England. They had conceived a child together, but I knew nothing about their relationship. Did he care for her?

He sighed. "Her death is a great loss."

"Were you close?"

"I respected her as a healer, as a priestess, and as a woman. Your mother had a trace of Muirgen's spirit, but you possess the full measure of her strength, her tenacity, and her power. You are very much alike. Goddess keep her."

I looked back at her body. It was impossible to imagine this decayed vessel as the woman I had come to know. Anger swelled within me. I felt helpless. I wanted Demas to pay for what he had done, but, again, I was left without any proof. I had her scalp, but no one had seen Demas give it to me. I could insist he felt threatened because of her testimony against him at the trial, but the charges had been thrown out—there was no reason for him to hurt her, except to hurt me.

Jostled by a frigid northern gust, Muirgen's body swung slightly.

Something flashed as it caught the sunlight. I moved closer, peering upward. The sun glinted off a brooch that had been stabbed into her shoulder. The silver was intricately forged in the shape of a stag. A sharp breath ripped through me. The Frenchman.

A vision blazed. A young man, his throat slit. A man standing behind, his knife slick with blood. Demas prostrate beside the dead body. I shook my head. "No."

Bertram moved to my side. "What is it?"

"I saw him." My breath was shallow and rapid, my chest heaving as my hands shook. "The man in the forest with Demas. He's dead. Osric killed him." There had been love in Demas's eyes, and pain, tremendous pain, as he lay at his lover's side. I looked at Muirgen. Tears streamed down my cheeks, and my gut wrenched as I thought of the way Demas had tortured her. "My actions have killed them both."

"You could not have known it would come to this."

"But I should have. I should have looked beyond my own selfish ends. I should have contemplated the consequences."

"When a rock is thrown into a lake, the ripples cast a wide net, each wave affecting new and smaller ripples until even the memory of the rock disappears. The events leading to this moment were set in motion long before you made the decision to stand before the Witan. Demas knew his actions were wrong in the eyes of the Church. That is why he hid in the forest. He made a choice and in doing so accepted the risks. The weight of those consequences lay squarely on his shoulders. Muirgen knew what would happen when she stood for you at the Witan, yet she insisted on going."

"Why didn't she tell me? I would have stopped her. I would have found another way."

He shook his head. "Even when you can see what lies ahead, there is often little that can be done to change it, and perhaps we are not meant to."

"Is everything fated, then? Is choice only an illusion?" Demas's words to the same came poignantly to mind. I refused to believe it.

Bertram shrugged. "I am an old man. I have pondered these questions for a lifetime. Would Muirgen have averted her fate by staying at the Christmas feast and returning to Wedmore with you? Or would she still have met her death? What I can tell you is that she chose to ride home alone, knowing she would be overtaken."

"Why would she do that?"

"Perhaps there was a higher purpose to her sacrifice."

I waited.

"The vision you just received was powerful, the images clear, were they not?"

"Yes."

"There will be great trials ahead. You have both foreseen that. I suspect Muirgen has passed her strength on to you so that you might be ready."

"But I'm not ready. There was still so much for her to teach me." I sank against the oak. "I've lost everything."

"No. Not everything. You have her book. It has been tucked safely away with your divining bones."

I gaped at him. All that time. They both knew she was going to die and still they remained silent. I glanced at Muirgen's lifeless body. I could have averted this. If they'd just told me, if I'd known the consequences, I could have found another way. Instead, together, they cast their rocks at fate, setting the future.

"You chose this path, Avelynn, despite my warnings and encouragement to the contrary. You are high priestess now. The desires of one must never outweigh the needs of many. The ripples have already been set in motion. Ready or not, there is no turning back."

———

Guilt and uncertainty plagued me as the three of us headed back to Congresbury, but no matter my internal struggle, I needed to lay Muirgen to rest, and for that I needed supplies to tend her body. In addition to Wolfstan's home, there were several other cottages scattered along a worn dirt path, and I paid handsomely for a small wooden cup, a linen winding sheet, two shovels, and a pickaxe.

By the time Bertram and I had returned to Muirgen's cottage, it was almost noon. The forest blocked the worst of the wind, but when it gusted, it cut through me, leaving a persistent shiver in its wake.

We lit a fire on the cold hearth. When the water in the cauldron had heated sufficiently that my hands would not freeze to work with it, we cut down her body and laid her on the ground. I washed her frail, brittle skin, drifting to thoughts of my mother. I hadn't washed or prepared her body. She had been laid out in her finest gown. A rich gold-and-amber brooch fastened a fur cloak, and her fingers were heavy with gold rings. Long dark hair tumbled in waves over her shoulders. My newborn brother, swaddled in furs, lay gently on her stomach. At the time, I had no idea how much her death would affect my life, how large a hole would be left. No one could replace my mother—that cavern would never be filled—but somehow Muirgen had softened the jagged edges, and now she was lost to me too.

When her body was ready, I reached into the pouch Demas had thrown at me and removed her scalp. Before we left Wedmore, I had washed the blood from her hair and brushed the strands until they shone. I set it back onto its rightful place.

With her body as whole as I could make it, we wrapped her in the winding sheet.

I handed Bertram a shovel, and we started digging beneath the large oak tree, choosing a spot far enough from the trunk to avoid the thick, fibrous roots. Protected by several inches of leaf mold, the ground was hard but not impossible. It was nonetheless back-breaking work. After several hours of hacking in the dirt with the pickaxe, we managed to dig a respectable grave—deep enough to dissuade any hungry wolves from disturbing it.

Oak was a magical tree, its properties revered and respected by my grandmother's people. I couldn't take her home to Ireland, but I could at least give her a proper burial here beneath her tree.

We placed her into the ground, feet facing west, and I tucked several amulets of amber around her body to ward off any evil spirits that might take advantage of a newly departed soul. We filled the grave back in, mounding the earth above it.

The wind had picked up, the gusts furious and unrelenting. Blowing snow from the trees and ground whipped my face and hands, leaving them chapped and frozen. At Wedmore, I had asked Bertram to perform the burial ritual. I had never done one, nor had I ever seen one performed. I had only a cursory understanding, a lesson in theory. But since I was ordained, he insisted it was now my duty. He would merely accompany me, and offered to bring his drum.

My chest was still tight with reservations as I looked at the freshly mounded earth. I didn't want to let Muirgen down.

"You are ready," Bertram said, his hand on my shoulder offering comfort.

I nodded, unable to find words.

Bertram found a sheltered spot in front of some low-growing hazel and began to beat his drum. I took a deep breath, centering myself.

"Aine, Goddess of the North, of the deep snows and the long nights of the northern lands, Goddess of Winter, wisdom, magic, and medicine, I ask you to bless this rite." From my satchel, I removed a bundle of feathers tied with a strip of leather, an offering representing air, and set them onto the ground, placing Alrik's knife on top so the offering wouldn't fly off in the bitter wind. I moved to the next aspect of the circle.

"Macha, Goddess of the East, of the rising dawn, the fire of the sun, Goddess of Spring, desire, love, and passion, I ask you to bless this rite." I lit a small fire of kindling, waiting until the smoke began to rise before adding a few small twigs.

"Danu, Goddess of the South, the Earth Mother, the keeper of virtue, the judge of vice, Goddess of summer fields in bloom, the harvest of plenty, I ask you to bless this rite." I placed the small iron mortar at the southernmost aspect of the circle and filled it with a handful of herbs, representing earth.

"Badb, Goddess of the West, guide to the dead, champion of the newly born, Goddess of Autumn, courage, and strength, I ask you to bless this rite." I placed the wooden cup on the ground and filled it with water from my leather flask.

I couldn't form a funeral procession. There would be no drinking, feasting, or wailing lament over her body, but there would be a blood sacrifice. I had bought one of Wolfstan's chickens. It was pecking and clucking nervously beside me inside a wooden crate.

I reached inside and pulled the chicken, squawking, from within. I grabbed its legs with one hand, with the other I pushed down on its neck, and in one swift motion, I pulled hard, twisting upward until I heard the snap. Its wings flapped wildly, though it was dead instantly. When the death throes subsided, I grabbed Alrik's knife and slit its throat, letting the blood soak into the mounded grave.

"Blessed be the sacred blood, the channel of spirit. As this precious river ebbs from life, so it ferries the promise of life in the hereafter. Spirits of the Otherworld, accept this offering and grant protection to this soul as she walks the plane between life and death." I placed the carcass at Muirgen's feet to the west, an offering for Badb.

The wind swirled around my legs. The snow, drifting lazily into piles, was caught in the movement and began to circle in a funnel upward. The drum's mournful pulse grew quicker, louder.

"Goddess, blessed on your golden throne, all powerful in your caer in the sky, mother of all, giver of life, bringer of death, destroyer, welcome your daughter Muirgen. Deliver her safely to the underworld."

The wind ripped through the clearing, and any hair exposed and unbound whipped my face, the icy ends like razors on my chapped cheeks. The boughs on the trees leaned heavily in the gusts, the snow billowing off the branches as it caught in the wind's embrace, pelting me as if formed of sand. I shielded my eyes with one arm and staggered backward in the strength of the gale pressing against me. Fear leapt to the surface. What was happening? I could no longer see the cauldron that stood only a few feet away. The wind, gusting and blowing, drowned out any sound of Bertram's drums, and I fell to my knees. "Goddess, I beseech you. Muirgen is come home. Welcome her, your noble priestess and valiant keeper of our faith, welcome her at your table. Ease your grief, hold your anger, I beg of you."

The winds stopped. The snow settled and fell.

Bertram appeared at my side. "Muirgen taught you well."

I stood on trembling legs. "What in the Goddess's name just happened, Bertram? That is twice I have witnessed such an event." My hands shook as I glanced around me. Not a breath of breeze stirred.

"It was merely a blustery wind, from the icy mountains far in the northlands beyond the seas."

"But to have stopped so suddenly?" I had never seen anything like it. "Surely the Goddess caused this."

His voice was stern. "In my long life, I have seen many things, Avelynn, but to think a Goddess or a god causes events to happen, whether for good or ill, is foolish and ignorant. You would be no better than the Christian priests and their damnable rhetoric to believe so. Instead put your faith in what you can see, hear, taste, smell, and touch. That is real. There is little that cannot be explained."

I would have pressed him further, for I was certain more was at work here than could be so easily explained away, but the wind picked up again, tossing the snow about in circles, sending it chasing its tail, the gusts catching me off balance, forcing me backward. While it would have been nice to know the Goddess was here for Muirgen, to mourn for her, to grieve for her, I conceded that perhaps I had looked for something that wasn't there.

There was nothing left to do here, and against the lashing winds, we gathered our supplies and mounted the horses. I turned Marma to leave but the frozen, desolate landscape held my gaze.

Beyond the gray smudge of Muirgen's cottage lay a garden hidden beneath the snow. I sighed, remembering the months I had spent weeding beside her while she taught me about the plants she grew. I tried my best to remember all their medicinal and magical properties and the phases of the moon in which to plant and pick them, but knew I had only a fraction of her vast knowledge.

"It's not fair."

"Life rarely is," was Bertram's sage answer.

Nudging Marma over to the sentinel oak, I pulled down one of the small, bleached bones that danced amongst its branches, and rubbed the smooth surface between thumb and finger. I tucked it into my satchel and laid my palm against the deeply grooved bark, bowing my head. *Good-bye, Muirgen.*

We headed back to Congresbury; the bones raised a chorus of lament over her grave as they tinkled softly against one another in the wind.

———

Dawn broke crisp and clear. We thanked our hosts for their kind hospitality, leaving them with several coins for their trouble, and raced back to Wedmore. When I arrived at the manor, I invited several ladies from the village to join me in my father's hall. While awaiting word of the war, it was easier to pass the anxious hours in company than be left to my own thoughts, alone in my cottage. Most brought some project to work on: basket making, embroidery, or single-needle knitting.

I had tried idling away the time by taking up a strip of purple silk and envisioning a twining design of ivy in gold thread for the neck of my newest kirtle, a dress of soft lavender. But domestic pursuits were not my skill, and despite my halfhearted efforts, I couldn't force my mind to focus on the mind-numbing repetition.

Aluson burst into the hall. "M'lady."

I placed the cloth across my lap and waited, heart pounding in my ears.

"The Saxons have been routed. King Aethelred has fled. Each man left for himself."

The ladies jittered.

"My father? Edward?"

"No word, m'lady. I'm sorry."

"What happened?"

"The king besieged the town. The Vikings appeared weakened and began to retreat behind their walls. Our men gave a great cry of victory and rallied after them. But it was a trap."

One of the ladies swooned. I turned to help but saw she was well attended by the other women.

"Aluson, pray continue."

He looked to the stricken woman but then pulled his attention back to me. "The Viking numbers were larger than we thought, and they swooped down upon us like demons, screaming and yelling. 'Twould've made your hair curl, m'lady." He shuddered. "They slaughtered anyone who stood in their way. We ran, but they chased us down. One by one, men fell—a sword or axe thrust through his back. I lost your father and brother in the melee. I'm sorry."

"It's all right, Aluson. I'm glad you're safe. Get yourself to the kitchen, take what you need, and rest. Tomorrow you can head out again, but return at once, as soon as you hear any word about my father, or Edward, or the men from Somerset."

I watched him leave. The women clutched their crosses and began to rock back and forth, chanting to their God for protection of their loved ones. I envied their ability to profess their faith in public. I sank into the chair. Would I know if something happened to them? Would I feel it? Would a vision come? *They're well*, I told myself firmly. My father knew the lands of Wessex better than anyone. He would have found a way to evade the Vikings and bring our men to safety.

The women were almost hysterical. What would happen if their men didn't come home? If my father didn't come home? How could I protect Wedmore and its people? What would become of us if the Vikings prevailed and laid waste to Wessex?

I looked across at Dearwyne, Aluson's twin sister. After Nelda, my previous chambermaid, had stood against me at the tribunal, siding with Osric and Demas, helping them paint a picture of my recklessness and disregard for authority, I had relieved her of her position and offered the prestigious post to Dearwyne. The twins were fiercely loyal, and I needed those near me to be people I could trust.

Long dark curls flowed over her lap as she worked on a wall-clothing for my cottage. She was quiet and reserved, with thick eyelashes demurely set above limpid brown eyes, her face as delicate and pale as a snowflake.

"Dearwyne, fetch Bertram. Tell him to meet me presently in my cottage."

"Of course, m'lady." She curtsied and left.

I turned my attention back to the frightened women. "Ladies, keep to your sewing. My father will bring your men home. Be patient. Word will come of their well-being."

"What'll we do, m'lady, if our husbands don't return?" one of the merchants' wives asked. Her knuckles were white from clutching her cross.

"I'll make sure you're provided for. You'll not go without."

"Bless you, m'lady," the tanner's wife said.

"How does your son fare?" I hadn't seen him since council, the day I saved his hand.

"He's well, m'lady. Thanks to you." She hung her head. "My husband was right sore after. I'd never say so in front of him, but I can't thank you enough for your mercy."

There was a mutual murmur of consent from the mothers present.

I laid my hand on her shoulder. "I'm glad he's well."

Excusing myself from the hand-wringing, I returned to my cottage and started pacing.

Bertram knocked and let himself in.

"What's the plan for Wedmore should the Vikings win?" I asked.

Thick white eyebrows knitted together. "We haven't any."

"All this time, with the threat of war hanging over us, has no one discussed an escape route, or a means to get the people safely away?"

"Where would we go?" He removed his heavy cloak, hanging it on a hook near the door, and sat down. "If Wessex falls to the Vikings, there will not be any place safe from their wrath. Each county, each city, will have to defend itself as best it can."

"But other than a few slaves, there are only women and children here. How are we to defend ourselves against a horde of Vikings?"

"I suspect we can't. If it comes to that, we can only hope for their mercy."

"Mercy?" I remembered what Edward had said about the Vikings' penchant for amusement by torturing the monks of St. Denis. "I'd be responsible for leaving lambs to the wolves."

He rested his hands in his lap. "What would you propose we do?"

I slumped onto a bench opposite him, defeated. "I don't know, but I can't sit by and do nothing." I searched his eyes. "I wouldn't be able to live with myself."

"War is not a time for guilt, Avelynn. Too much is beyond our control. The outcome of this conflict is the will of the gods. Each man, woman, and child's fate rests in their hands."

"I refuse to leave them helpless to the gods' whims. There must be something we can do." I tapped my foot impatiently and scanned the room for inspiration. My mother's psaltery hung on the wall. An expert craftsman had made the harp for her, and when she played it, it was as if the notes moved you to another time and place, the music stirring your soul into a world of beauty and promise. She played it almost every night, and I would often accompany her on the tabor— Bertram wasn't the only one skilled at drumming. I smiled, remembering those long-lost evenings, but then something sparked. The psaltery made me think of my mother, which made me think of . . .

"Avalon! We'll take them to Avalon." I turned to Bertram. "No one else knows about it or how to reach it. We can build a new life there, a life safe from Vikings, safe from torture or rape, the children safe from the slave markets."

"And if no one agrees to go?"

"If it comes down to such a decision—to stay and face death or worse, or take a leap of faith and save themselves and their children—I don't think there'll be a contest."

"We would need to start making preparations."

"Agreed." I felt much better now that I was doing something. Waiting helplessly for word of my father and brother was gut-churning.

"Speak with Father Plegmund. See if you can persuade him to support our cause. We can use the weaving sheds to assemble all the supplies and foodstuffs we would need to see us through till the next harvest. I'll speak with the women and ask that they each assemble a crate of clothes, blankets, and essential household goods to be ready should we need to depart hastily."

Bertram stood and laid a hand on my shoulder. "I hope it will not come to this, but if it does, you may have saved many."

"M'lady." Aluson bowed. "I've word of your father."

It was late evening, a full day since we first received word that the army was routed, and I sat in my cottage, preparing a list of what would be needed should we be forced to flee. I had already visited each of the homes in the village and asked them to spread word: should Wessex fall, or the Vikings march to Wedmore, we would meet at the gates and flee into the marshes. I assured them I knew of a place hidden from danger. I was pleased that most of those I spoke with were readily in agreement. I could do nothing for those who chose to stay.

I put down my quill and wiped my face, realizing I had probably just smeared ink across my forehead.

I looked at Aluson and held my breath. "Yes?"

"He fares well, m'lady."

"And Edward?"

"They're both safe."

I let out my breath, and my shoulders dropped away from my ears. "Thank the gods." Heart pounding, my gaze locked with Aluson's. His eyebrows creased in confusion. "I mean . . . thank the merciful God. What news?"

The uncertainty on his face relaxed, and if he thought any more of the heretical statement, he gave no indication of it. It was after all a term that hadn't been uttered aloud for hundreds of years. Affecting calm, I eased myself back, leaning against the table.

His news continued unabated. "The king and a large portion of the army made their way to a small ford across the River Thames. They retreated to safety, not stopping till they reached Windsor. The army is regrouping. Many didn't escape the slaughter. Ealdorman Aethelwulf of Berkshire lay amongst the dead."

"Aethelwulf?" I thought of Cyneburga, of the two of them together at the Christmas feast. Would Berkshire fall? Would Cyneburga and her young children perish next? My thoughts flowed to Wedmore and its people. I wouldn't let them down.

"The Vikings will not rest, m'lady. Already Halfdan Ragnarsson and Bagsecg march toward Wallingford."

Wallingford was home to one of the richest monasteries in Wessex. Outside Wallingford was a wide causeway of stone and rubble that allowed people to ford the Thames. The pass was a crucial link in one of the most valuable transportation networks through southern England. To lose that strategic and economic post would cost Aethelred and Wessex dearly.

I sent Aluson off to scout more news while I turned my attention back to Wedmore's plan of escape and waited, like everyone else, for further word.

Two days later, on the eighth of January, Aluson returned. Another battle had raged in Berkshire on the plains of Ashdown.

Everyone in Wedmore was assembled in the hall to hear the news. And like the gleeman who enjoys the rapt attention of all who hear him sing, Aluson appeared to enjoy the crowd's absorption in his words as he acted out events and raised and lowered the inflection of his voice as all good storytellers are wont to do.

"We were entrenched high above the old Roman road, on

Kingstanding Hill, waiting for the Heathen Army. The Vikings came over the ridge and saw us spread out before them. They split their army—one force commanded by Halfdan and Bagsecg themselves, the other by several powerful jarls. Each division formed a shield wall and began hurling taunts and jeers at us as they advanced."

The shield wall was a ruthless and bloody business, and the military formation of choice. Standing shoulder to shoulder, warriors formed a defensive line, several rows deep, and slowly marched forward until the opposing walls collided.

"King Aethelred split his forces to meet the Vikings head-on. Alfred was in charge of one division, our good king the other. Eager to crush the heathens, Alfred raced to the field, his men lining up their shields in opposition. The Vikings advanced toward Alfred until they closed in on him from both sides. It was a terrible racket, everyone banging their swords or axes against their shields, yelling and taunting one another."

I thought of Ealhswith and her babe, Aethelflaed. Dear gods, if anything should happen to Alfred. I gripped the arms of my father's chair. "What of Alfred?" I asked.

"Alfred was in a dangerous position. He was going to have to retreat and give the Vikings considerable gains, or press forward and fight."

"Where were Aethelred and his division?"

"He was praying, m'lady, for a favorable outcome."

My mouth gaped, but all around me people were whispering in reverential murmurs.

"You mean to tell me that he sent his brother into the fray and held his men back while he prayed?"

"Yes, m'lady. Alfred was alone on the field. But he took matters into his own hands and charged at the Vikings with the courage and valor of a true chieftain. His shield wall crashed into theirs. I could hear the impact from where I stood. 'Twas a most noble act!"

"Jesu," one of the women nearest me whispered, and crossed herself.

I echoed her sentiment, if not her words, and sent a silent prayer to the Goddess for his safety and the welfare of Ealhswith and their child.

"Alfred stood strong for a time, but by noon his shield wall was crumbling; the piles of bodies lay several corpses deep."

"Where was Aethelred? Couldn't he see his brother was in danger—that they were losing? Where was my father during all this?"

"I was with your father as he waited on word from Aethelred. We could see the bloodshed but could do nothing till we received the king's command. We watched both divisions of the Viking army close in on Alfred. He was surrounded."

I was furious. So much wasted life, for what—a sign? "Dear God, Aluson, what happened?"

"When all seemed lost, the king gave the command to charge. The Vikings were caught off guard. Having thought Alfred was all that was left of the Wessex army, they left themselves open for Aethelred's attack." His eyes shone with awe. "The battle raged for several hours until the Viking king Bagsecg fell, and then five more jarls met their deaths at the end of Saxon blades. The Heathen Army was put to flight, and we gave chase until nightfall, cutting down all who stood in our way. The Viking dead lay in the thousands. It was a valiant victory for Wessex! The fyrd is heralding Alfred as a hero, but in his humility, he raised the first toast to his brother, our noble king."

Everyone cheered, and I slumped back in my seat with relief. I sent for barrels of mead to be fetched from the storage room at the back of the hall. We would celebrate.

"What of Halfdan?" I asked over the jubilant cheering.

"He limped back to Reading with a handful of men. The Vikings are ruined." A brilliant grin fixed on his grubby face.

"Mead for everyone!" I yelled.

Harps, lyres, psalteries, pipes, and tabors appeared, and the hall erupted in music. I had the kitchens prepare a sumptuous feast.

After several hours of revelry and a steady supply of mead, pages brought in a roasted pig festooned with garlands of greenery. They placed the meat on a large table and began carving it out to all present. Breads and cheeses, apples, and nuts were passed around, each person taking his fill.

"M'lady?" Aluson appeared at my elbow. I sat at the head table, tapping my foot to the music.

"Did you help yourself to enough mead and meat?" I asked, my eyes fixed on the merriment.

"Yes, m'lady."

I turned and looked at him. His face was washed of its ruddy glow. My heart began to flutter. "What is it?"

"A messenger, m'lady. He's waiting outside."

"Well, send him in, Aluson. It's freezing."

"He asks to speak with you . . . alone. He says it's urgent." He stepped back, waiting for me to rise.

"Very well."

I retrieved my cloak and stepped into the frigid air. A young boy stood beneath the porch's overhang. He was dressed in a ragged cloak, torn gloves, and a hat far too small for his long, narrow head. It didn't even cover his vibrantly red ears.

"M'lady Avelynn?" He bowed.

"Yes."

"I bring news of greatest sorrow. A funerary cortege makes its way west to Wedmore. Your lord father has been killed."

NINETEEN

"How is this possible?" I demanded of Wulfric. "You were sworn to protect him with your life."

"Be still, Avelynn," Bertram soothed.

I was pacing the floor of my cottage, the rushes pressed flat beneath my relentless feet.

"Aye, and I was beside him the entire time. I didn't see him suffer so much as a scrape. He was a valiant warrior. I know no man his equal." Still dressed in full mail, Wulfric and Leofric stood near the door.

After the Vikings had been routed, Wulfric found my father leaning against a tree. When he slapped him on the back in congratulations, my father fell forward and rolled lifeless to the ground, blank eyes staring upward into the beech's naked boughs. Blood poured from a gaping sword wound to his belly. His mail shirt was the only thing keeping his intestines from spilling onto the snow.

My chest shook with the effort of restraint. Confined tears blurred the corners of my eyes, but I refused to show weakness in front of my father's men.

"And Edward? Who was protecting Edward?" I asked.

Leofric removed his helmet. "He was told to remain at the back with the priests. No one knows what happened. We scoured the dead, but could not find his body."

I sniffed back a choking sob. He had wanted to fight the Vikings. Gods, what had he done? "No one can just vanish," I stammered. "If he's not amongst the dead then someone must have taken him. Have the Vikings sent any demands for ransom?" A wave of nausea flushed my cheeks, and I reached out to lean against the table.

"We've not heard of any, no," Wulfric answered.

"Send men to scour the slave markets."

"We cannot spare them, my lady," Leofric answered.

"Avelynn, sit." Bertram motioned to one of the benches near the hearth.

I didn't want to sit. I hugged my arms tight around me.

Bertram frowned but didn't press the issue. "The war is not done, Avelynn. Already reinforcements have arrived to join Halfdan. Viking warships are choking the Thames estuary, sailing toward Reading. Their numbers will swell, where ours have diminished. They will be thousands strong with fresh warriors, while our army, battle weary and cold, cannot hope to add more to our numbers. Somerset is the only county that has sent levies to support Berkshire. Other shires are merely watching and waiting. And despite the need, Aethelred is not in a position to argue. He requires the shires to be ready lest the Vikings change course and set upon another area. Wulfric cannot spend time searching for Edward. Wessex can spare no one."

"You will find someone to search. I don't care if it's a slave. I refuse to give up so easily." I glared at them.

Bertram nodded. "Very well."

I sat down.

"Avelynn," Wulfric said, bending on one knee. "The funeral

must proceed today. We can't wait on word of Edward. My men and I have to return to the king."

"But you have no one to lead you."

"We'll fight under the banner of Dorset and Wareham."

"Osric and Demas?" Fire sparked from my eyes.

The giant man recoiled and stood up hastily.

"You'll not fight under them, ever." I'd die before I saw my father's men, my men, led by those usurpers. "You'll stay here until my father is buried. Then . . . then, I will lead you."

"My lady, please." Leofric appealed to Bertram.

Bertram moved to my side. "You're ill with grief. Let me fix a tonic to calm you."

"I'm not ill, nor do I need a tonic. Like all the great shieldmaidens who have fought and led men in ages past, it's my right to avenge my father and take his place." I turned to Wulfric and Leofric. "Hasten to the church and prepare my father's grave. Then bring Father Plegmund to the hall so that he may oversee the procession."

I grabbed my cloak and stepped outside, heading to the hall where my father's body lay upon a pallet. It was near noon, but the world was shrouded in a veil of darkness as clouds, heavy and black, menaced the sky above.

"Avelynn." Wulfric caught up with me. "War is no place for a woman. Stay here and mind the manor—"

I spun around on him. "How dare you question me. I'm the Earl of Somerset now. Through my father you are sworn to serve me."

"I only meant—"

"Are you not sworn to serve me?"

"Yes, but—"

"Are you not sworn to obey me?"

"Yes," he growled.

"Are you not sworn to protect me?"

"Aye, and that's precisely what I'm trying to do. The shield wall is no place for a woman." He had risen to his full height and loomed over me.

Wulfric had always been like an uncle to me. All through my youth, he was as constant as a rock and fiercely loyal to my father. Despite my surge of anger, I was fond of the old churl. He had taught me how to fight, and until this moment, had treated me no differently from the scores of young men he'd helped train for my father's household.

"You've taught me as well as any of your warriors, and despite your well-intentioned concern for my welfare, you cannot deny my skills." I crossed my arms. "Will you not stand beside me and protect me with your very life, Wulfric, as you would my father?"

"Aye, of course I would, but this is folly—nay, 'tis madness. You've no experience in battle."

"And how much experience does a young boy of twelve have when he is given a sword and thrust into a shield wall for the first time?"

"That's not the same—"

"You're right—it's not. I've been trained for this since I was small. The poor farmer's son has never held more than a wooden hoe." I glared at him. "My mind is set. Bring me the priest." I walked into the hall, shutting the door behind me, leaving a dazed and belligerent Wulfric to cool his heels in the snow.

The hall was empty save for Dearwyne, who sat near the light of the central hearth, scrubbing and polishing my father's helmet and mail to a brilliant sheen. Glistening new links hid the fatal rent in the otherwise innocuous mail coat.

"Leave me," I said.

She placed my father's belongings on the table beside the pallet, nodded, and left.

I leaned against the wall and let my head thump softly against the wood. I closed my eyes. Wulfric was right. I could fight, but leading men in a shield wall was madness. What was I thinking? And yet, it was as clear as a cloudless sky after a summer's storm. No matter how much Demas or my uncle Osric wanted my father's lands and title, as long as I still had breath within me they would never have it. Entreating my father's warriors to fight under their banner was a backhanded, devious way of getting them to pledge allegiance to a new lord. That would leave Wedmore and Somerset with nothing—no warriors of our own, no form of protection. I would have to beseech Demas or my uncle for aid. I shuddered, imagining the price I would have to pay for such consideration.

And what if I didn't survive the fight? With my father gone and my brother presumed dead, I was Earl of Somerset, Lady of Wedmore. Who would lead in the case of my death? As our closest living kin, would my uncle be granted my father's estate by the king? I wasn't willing to take the chance.

I would ensure that Osric and Demas never saw a piece of my father's legacy. Upon my death, I would give everything to my goddaughter, Aethelflaed.

I dragged my steps forward and gazed down at my father's exanimate, vacant face. The leech at the battlefield had washed and prepared my father's body, sewing up the gaping wound, and Wulfric had dressed him in his finest clothes—an azure blue tunic, light gray trousers that were cross-gartered to his knee, and his bear-pelt cloak. The cloak was clasped on his shoulder by a heavy gold brooch, and the long fingers of his strong hands were heavy with rings. A brilliant gold buckle cinched tight his waist. His hair shone like gold thread, while his gray-blue eyes lay closed forever.

At some point in the fighting, the leather thong that held the amulet my mother had given him must have loosened, for it was gone. I wondered if this ill luck had hastened his death, and I quickly tucked other small amber talismans around him. I pried the fingers of one of his hands loose enough to enclose within his palm a small stone carving of Thunor's hammer, a token of his favorite deity.

I ran the backs of my fingers along his cheek and smoothed his hair over his shoulders. Hot tears blazed down my face.

"Why?" I asked the Goddess in a choked whisper. "I just got him back. Why have you taken away everyone I love?" I thought of my mother, Muirgen, even Alrik—all lost to me forever. And Edward. My heart ached. Had he been taken from me too?

"What have I done to deserve this?" I slammed my fist down on the table and collapsed onto the bench. I clung to my father's body, my head resting against his chest. I missed the way my life had once been—when I wasn't worried about betrothals, or leading men into battle.

"It's not fair," I yelled to the unseen world above me.

"It only seems that way," Bertram said. I hadn't heard him enter. "No one knows the will of the gods, Avelynn. Not you nor I. But they do not act out of spite or vengeance. Every man, woman, and child has his or her destiny. Your father has fulfilled his. Now it is your turn to embrace yours."

"What if I can't?"

"Come," he said, placing his hand on my shoulder. "Everyone is waiting. It is time your father was laid to rest."

I sat up and wiped the tears with the backs of my hands.

Bertram opened the door to admit Wulfric, Leofric, and two other men.

They picked up the pallet and laid my father inside the coffin. A warrior must always be buried with his sword, but I stopped them from placing his helmet and shield beside him. I wanted to honor him by wearing his armor into battle.

Most of the Somerset levies were still with the king in Windsor, but everyone remaining in the village and surrounding countryside attended my father's wake. As they entered the hall, I received their condolences as stoically as I could. Twenty of my father's closest warriors each knelt before me, swearing their fealty, and kissed the ring on my finger.

Wulfric's great black mane bent forward at the last. "I swear to our lord God and His son, our savior Jesus Christ, to serve and protect ye till the day I die—even if ye are a right stubborn maid." He kissed my ring.

"I accept your pledge. Now go eat, you old bear, and honor my father with tales of victory and daring."

A feast had been prepared, and when all had eaten and drunk their fill, each of my father's thegns passed the harp, singing songs to celebrate my father's valor. Then they regaled us with capers and stories from his youth. I had never seen this side of my father and laughed along with the others as they shared tales of innocent pranks and boyhood antics.

Plegmund said a prayer and mass over the body and then placed a small chalice of holy water inside the coffin to protect the newly departed soul from evil. I watched as the lid was lowered and felt each strike of the hammer, each driven nail, as an assault on my heart.

Plegmund led the procession, and we made our way through the blowing snow to the small churchyard. It was fully dark now, and we moved slowly down the main road, carrying torches, the flames slapping and twisting in the bitter January wind. The coffin was placed into the ground, and after Father Plegmund said a final prayer entrusting my father's soul to God, everyone departed. I stood there frozen, shivering, until the last spadeful of dirt was mounded above the grave and a small stone marker placed on top.

"Come inside," Plegmund offered. "There is warmth by the fire."

I let him lead me into the small nave of the chapel. Barely able to hold more than fifty people, it served for small masses. On special feast days, services were always held in my father's hall, where there was room for hundreds. I stopped. My hall. My throat constricted, as the weight of those two words rested on my shoulders. The church's doorkeeper nodded as we passed and went back to laying fresh rushes. The room smelled of dried grass and hay.

Plegmund led me through a vestibule into the cramped church office.

"Please, sit and rest a moment." He gestured to a low stool nestled up to a small trestle table and then shuffled over to the hearth, adding another log to heat the room.

Along the farthest wall was a pallet for his bed and several locked chests piled high with sheets of parchment. A large wooden cross hung on the wall.

"How are you, Avelynn?" he asked, sitting across from me and resting his hands on the table. The worn wooden surface was scarred with ink stains and globs of wax from two rancid-smelling tallow candles.

"It hasn't been the easiest of days. Or months, for that matter."

"No, I imagine not. I'm sorry for your loss."

"Thank you."

He picked at a mound of cooled wax. "I understand you wish to take vengeance into your own hands."

"I do."

"I cannot blame you for wanting justice, but it's dangerous for a woman to tread into men's waters."

"I'm quite capable of leading the cause." I felt like my brother having to defend his desire to fight Vikings. The thought of him brought a quiver of pain as sorrow shot through me.

"I'm not questioning your abilities or your rights. I'm merely pointing out that you will not make any friends with this venture."

I eyed him curiously and waited.

"There are factions at work in Wessex, and I fear you may be baiting lions with this action."

"I don't understand. What have you heard?"

"Just whispers, rumors, of powerful men making pacts with the Devil. There are no names of course, but perhaps you should remain here and see to your people. What will happen to Wedmore if you are lost?"

"That's what I was hoping you could help me with. I wish to make my will."

"I cannot sway you from your course?" He looked at my unmoving face. "Very well."

He selected two pieces of parchment and waited.

"In the event of my death, I wish to give everything—Somerset, Wedmore, all my chattels—over to my goddaughter, Aethelflaed. She is to be named earl in my stead. My keys and locked chests are to be given only to Ealhswith. And Ealhswith, as Aethelflaed's guardian, is given control of running the estate until Aethelflaed comes of age."

He nodded and drew up the document on one piece of parchment, copying it on the other. The doorkeeper was called in to witness my signature.

"On the morrow, I will send one copy to join Wedmore's official records in Glastonbury. The other will abide here." He nodded to one of the large chests in the corner of the room.

"Thank you." I rose to leave.

"God keep you, Avelynn, and pray be careful."

I stepped out into the night's blackness, buffeted on all sides by the cold, merciless winds of fate and snow.

By the time I reached Windsor, messengers had already informed the entire Saxon army of my intent to fight. Along with Aethelred and Alfred, both Osric and Demas were waiting in Windsor's grand hall for my arrival.

"Avelynn, go home," Alfred insisted.

"I will not."

King Aethelred eyed me curiously. "Wulfric tells me you are well trained with sword and shield."

Wulfric was leaning against the thick planked wall, scowling into his cup of ale.

"I've been trained as well as any of my father's thegns."

"Sire, she makes asses of us all," Osric spat. "A woman on the battlefield! She'll curse us with her very presence."

The idea of being cursed clearly didn't sit well with Aethelred, and he squirmed uncomfortably in his seat on the raised dais.

"I invoke the blood feud," I said, glaring at my uncle. The blood feud was an ancient rite of revenge, allowing a family member to avenge any wrong done to their kin. This was a sacred tenet of our society, and by invoking it first, I'd hoped it would give weight to my cause.

"As Eanwulf's brother, it is my place to exact retribution from the Viking bastards." Osric stormed over to me. "You will turn about and go home."

"Since when have you spared one thought for my father? I'm his rightful heir. The feud is mine. I'm not leaving."

Osric's face turned crimson. A vein bulged along his forehead.

"Avelynn," Alfred said, stepping between us. "Osric will provide justice in the name of your father. Leave vengeance in his capable hands. The shield wall is no place for a woman."

I was getting tired of hearing that. "Draw your sword, Alfred. The first to yield or fall wins."

I caught a smirk on Wulfric's face, but he covered it quickly in his cup.

"I'll not fight you." Alfred looked at me aghast.

"I will." Demas stepped forward. "Allow me to be your deputy in this challenge, my lord."

All eyes waited on Alfred, who in turn looked to his brother, the king, for guidance.

"Very well." Aethelred sighed and stood up. "The first to fall, be rendered unarmed, draw blood, or step out of the circle loses. If you fail, Avelynn, you will return to Wedmore and give up any claims to this cause in the future. Demas, if you fail, Avelynn maintains her right to avenge her father and earns a place in the Wessex fyrd. Are you agreed?"

"Yes," we both answered.

"Osric, make the circle." Aethelred waved his hand limply and then sat down.

At the far end of the hall, benches were pushed aside and the rushes swept away from the dirt floor. Osric grumbled but did as ordered, fetching some chalk and marking out a circle.

I stepped into Wulfrida's chambers and pulled on a pair of brown trousers and a yellow tunic, marveling at the unfamiliarity of wearing a man's garments. Borrowing a leather thong from Wulfric, I braided my hair, tucked the long tail under the tunic, cinched it in place with a belt, and then slipped on a leather helmet, graciously provided by Aethelred. My father's head was much larger than mine and his helmet would slide down my face without the extra padding.

By the time I returned to the hall, we had amassed a rather large crowd of spectators. At least forty of my men and twice as many of Osric and Demas's numbers were present for the show. Everyone was in a festive spirit, and mead flowed liberally. With all the benches pressed and stacked against the walls of the hall, people crammed shoulder to shoulder, the toes of their boots nudging the white chalk outline. Additional oil lamps had been lit, and they hung from the rafters above, illuminating the battlefield.

"Now, remember what I've taught ye," Wulfric said, putting on my helmet. The contest was to be fought with full mail and regalia. "Stay low 'n' watch for any opportunity to knock him off balance. He has a wide swing. That'll come in handy if ye watch him carefully."

"Thanks."

"You're a bloody-minded daft woman, but your father would be proud."

I would have hugged him if Alfred hadn't spoken.

"Avelynn, Demas, step forward."

Alfred waited until Demas and I stood nose to nose. "This is a friendly contest. The first to draw blood will automatically forfeit his—or her—cause and the opponent will win the field. Are you both clear on the rules?"

We nodded.

Aethelred stood. "Begin!" He raised a cup of ale and drank heartily as everyone cheered.

I took a step back, crouched low, and watched, waited. Demas crossed his feet one over the other as he walked the periphery of the circle. I matched his progress step for step. He leaned in with a slow drunken swing and smiled. Everyone laughed. He hopped from foot to foot and then poked his sword at me and smirked. I hit it hard to the ground.

I slashed at his waist. He backed up and scowled. I smiled charmingly at him. My men hooted and hollered, heckling Demas on my behalf.

With two hands, he brought his sword down toward my waist. I swerved from the blow and aimed high. My sword grazed the mail on his shoulder, earning approval from my men, as Demas received more jeers. The humor left his face.

His next blow glanced off my helmet with a loud twang and

sent me staggering backward. My ears buzzed. A hush descended on the room. The fight was on.

"You continue to overstep your place." He circled around me.

"And you're a weak fool, controlled by Osric's strings."

Our swords met in a clash of steel that sent shock waves up my forearms. He swung again, the point just missing my chest as I leaned backward. I lunged and aimed low, slicing at his shins with the flat edge of the sword. He saw the volley, blocked the strike, and then cut toward my helmet.

I lifted my sword, blocking the blow, but he barreled into me, knocking me off balance, forcing me to take a few steps backward, my heel just a hairbreadth from the line.

"You will learn to be properly submissive," he said.

"Like you were in the weaving shed at the Witan? You're just Osric's little bicche."

His wide hazel eyes focused in realization.

"Yes, I saw. I saw you grovel and fall under my uncle's yoke."

He lunged, swinging in a blind rage. Any impression of this being a friendly contest vanished. Spittle flew from his lips. "How is Muirgen?"

"Bastard." I rushed forward, my sword's deadly precision aimed at his neck. He ducked and thrust at my stomach. I turned away from the swing and connected with his mail coat near his kidney. He growled and dove. I leapt aside, and he staggered back, his sword swinging. I dodged the blow and stayed low, using my weight to ram into his side.

Several vats of ice water were thrown at us. Aethelred stood before us. "Hold!"

We both froze, panting.

I ripped off both my helmets and knelt before Aethelred. Demas dropped to his knee.

"I'm not sure what we have all just witnessed. But by God, it stops here."

"I'm sorry, my lord," we both mumbled.

"Stand and shake hands. I will have no animosity in my fyrd," he said.

We did as ordered, and I resisted the urge to wipe my hand against my sleeve. "The fyrd? Does that mean I can fight?"

"A shieldmaiden is welcome in my army."

"This is madness," Osric spat.

"The matter is settled," Aethelred warned.

"Then promise me, my liege, that should Avelynn fall, her lands, her title will be awarded to me as her closest kin."

"I'm afraid that can't happen," I said, looking at Aethelred. "I've already written my will. Aethelflaed, my goddaughter, has been named as my heiress. The charter lies at Glastonbury."

"Is this so?" Alfred asked, his eyebrows raised in shock.

"Yes, my lord. All that I have will be hers."

"A most noble and charitable gift," Aethelred said.

Osric's gaze pierced my mail. "A most noble gift indeed. May God keep you safe, niece," he said in a voice as controlled as a coal maker's fire.

Within a few hours of my arrival, word came that the Vikings marched to Basing, another prosperous royal village. If the Vikings were able to seize control of the center, they would be a direct threat to topple Wessex's capital of Winchester.

By the time the fyrd had arrived, Basing was deserted. No smoke rose from cooking fires, each hearth empty as families packed up what possessions they could carry and headed for the forests or to nearby churches to await the battle's outcome. The weatherworn and sun-bleached planked buildings, dark and brooding in the surrounding snow and sleet, looked like the charred remains of a once fat and cheerful body. We had drawn our line just south of the village in a wide, empty field. No side had the advantage of hill, valley, river, or crag to aid their fight. The blood from the battle would nourish the soil underfoot, and the grain would prosper when planted in the spring. If there were still men to tend it.

Wulfric helped me into my father's mail, and I secured my sword to my waist. I called upon the Goddess in a silent plea, praying for strength and protection, and then fastened my helmet, grabbed my spear and shield, and led Somerset into what I thought would be the hardest battle of my life.

My first impression, after staring into the crazed eyes of a Viking berserker, was that a shield wall was no place for a woman. I was terrified. Wulfric had been right. None of my training had prepared me for this. But fear was a luxury I could ill afford. My men looked to me to lead, and my father's shadow cast a wide net. I would not let him down. I swallowed and took my place in the line.

That was in the morning. By noon the toll to both sides had been great. This was the third wave of attack in a battle that had started just after dawn.

"Stand!" I yelled for what seemed like the hundredth time that day.

Everyone leaned their weight forward and waited. Wulfric was to my right, Leofric to my left. Two hundred men made up the front row of the shield wall. We stood side by side, everyone crushed together, shoulder to shoulder. Hundreds more filled the rows behind. Saxon shields pressed tightly against my back. My contingent comprised the farthest right-hand side of the wall. The two brothers had once again split their defenses in answer to the Vikings' charge, and Somerset was under Alfred's command.

The weather was suitably miserable for early February. All night it had drizzled—a cold, wet sleet—and dawn brought more of the same. I had spent the night in a tent, tossing and turning, with only a few blankets and my cloak. The tightly woven fabric walls kept the water out, but did nothing to block the dampness and chill in the air. Standing outside all morning long in the freezing onslaught ensured I was soaked through. A constant wave of shivering threatened to knock the spear from my hand. My feet had been numb since we left Windsor.

I wiped the moisture from my face. The Vikings hurled endless threats and jeers, and we answered back with insults and goading of our own. There was no open hand-to-hand combat. The two sides stood apart from each other as in a childhood game, each taunting the other, but slowly the forces—the entire wall—advanced until they crashed shield to shield.

Despite our bravado on the surface, everyone was exhausted. The Vikings were slower in their attack, and we were less anxious to press ours. It was now a waiting game to see who would crack first.

"Stand!" I yelled to steady my men.

Pride flared with each taunt. It was getting harder to keep the men in check.

"Shields at the ready," I ordered as I noticed the Viking line take a step closer.

They tightened their overlapping shields.

"Spears ready." A line of steel points thrust through the wall of bodies.

"Hold!" I ordered as the lines of men behind me pressed forward. The recent snowfall had turned to slush, and the ground was a field of slippery mud. Maintaining footing was becoming harder and harder as the morning wore on.

The Vikings moved close enough for us to smell their sweat. They were ferocious, their beards unkempt, their hair and eyes wild. They smeared the blood of the dead on their faces and advanced with a fearlessness born out of a religion that honored bravery and shunned weakness. They welcomed a warrior's death. To them, death was a reward. The bravest men would feast at Odin's table.

I studied my men. Hair cut just below the shoulders, beards and mustaches trimmed. No god would toast their bravery if they fell. And worse, unlike the Vikings, who had nothing to lose but their lives, these men would leave their farms and families unprotected, with no one to provide for them.

A Viking shield crashed into mine as their wall closed the gap. The impact shot deep and thrummed in my bones. My father's shield, which I held in my left hand, covered me from shoulders to knees, while the spear in my right hand jabbed furiously at any exposed flesh. I glanced at the overlapping shields of the enemy. The tight wall of shields made a direct strike difficult, but a spear could gore above the shoulders and a sword could hack away below the knees, and that is where everyone's ministrations were aimed.

It was a vicious and bloody pushing-and-shoving match as shields rammed against shields, and axes, swords, and spears maneuvered around their heaving neighbors to swing, jab, and thrust toward the enemy at will. Wulfric lifted his shield to block a blow from a sword that was aimed at my skull, and I drove my spear into the groin of my attacker, pulling it back sharply. He fell and was trampled, his face pressed into the squelching muck, as another Viking took his place at the front of the line.

A large weight fell against my right side as Leofric collapsed into me. Another blow from a Viking axe came down, cleaving his helmet in two. Half of his good-natured face stayed momentarily on my shoulder while the rest of Leofric slumped to the ground. Blood pooled around him, turning the muddy slush a rusty shade of red. For a second, I stared, stunned that such a great man could fall. Demas appeared at my side and raised his shield to block the axe from inflicting the same mortal wound on me.

"Watch what you're doing," he hissed.

I blinked at the apparition. "Kind of you to be concerned with my welfare." I grunted, thrusting my spear forward, looking for a soft spot to impale.

"Personally, I'd rather see you dead," he yelled over the battle cries. "But your little ploy with the will has caused me to reevaluate things." He shoved against a Viking shield.

I clenched my teeth, wishing I had enough room to turn my spear sideways. Demas's waist was wide open. "You'll never have Wedmore or Somerset," I spat. I wondered if Wulfric had seen his brother fall. My heart ached for them both.

"You're a considerable hindrance," he grunted, thrusting his sword into the man pressed up against him. "Like a louse I can't crush." He pulled his sword back, the blade thick with blood.

There was a loud commotion coming from the wall farther to the left. I chanced a quick glance. The Saxon wall had been breached in the middle, our straight line buckled, like the V in a formation of geese, and the Vikings pressed their advantage, concentrating their efforts on the fracture. We were losing ground rapidly.

Taking advantage of the Vikings' momentary diversion, Demas turned slightly to face me. "You're the last of the vermin to affect our plans. Your brother was easy prey. And your father?" He laughed. "He screamed like a suckling maid when I gutted him through."

"My father, Eanwulf, the Earl of Somerset, the king's most trusted and revered warrior, was not brought down by a flaccid little sack of grain." I refused to believe it. His words were meant only to hurt me. He was playing me. My father died honorably in battle, and my brother would be found safe and sound.

Demas pulled a leather thong from around his neck. My mother's amber amulet glinted like molten steel against the pale silver of his mail. The numbing cold disappeared, and a burning fury consumed me.

"Bastard," I roared, and turned on him. Wulfric noticed the change of my focus.

"Avelynn," he yelled. "Steady!"

A Viking shield shoved hard against my side, knocking me off balance, and brought my attention back to the immediate threat at hand.

A Viking spear point clashed with the bronze boss of my shield, and I spun around to face my attacker. While the Vikings had redirected a lot of their energy to the breach in our wall, there were still plenty of them left to occupy my efforts. "Hold!" I yelled to the men behind me. With the chaos of the wall splitting farther down the line, men were dropping away from behind me, either turning to run, or trying to aid those who were taking the brunt of the fight.

I dropped my spear and unsheathed my sword. I swung hard over top of my shield, meeting Viking steel in a clash of sparks.

"You must be careful. I'd hate for anything to befall you before our wedding day." Demas pressed his body tightly against me, his shield overlapping mine. I could smell the stench of ale on his breath.

"I'll never be your wife. My father's decree was sent to Winchester. You'll never touch me again."

"About that message . . ." He inclined his head behind me to the right. "You remember Sigberht, my associate. He never made it to Winchester—he brought the note straight to me. And, of course, I disposed of it promptly and thoroughly." He swept his sword up and over his head. A yelp and barrage of insults assailed us, along with a disembodied hand that someone threw at Demas's head.

I didn't dare look behind me lest I open myself to a fatal blow, but I knew Sigberht was there. I could sense his malevolence. "I have witnesses," I said, feeling the cold seep back into my pores. Black ice filled my veins. Suddenly the Vikings didn't terrify me nearly as much as the man to my left.

"Oh, yes, about them." He looked across at Wulfric. "You remember my other associate, Gil?"

This time I did turn. The toothless, drooling bodyguard didn't look any worse for the wear after his encounter with Muirgen's bear. My heart sank but then began to hammer madly against my chest as I saw a flash of steel.

"We can't have any witnesses," Demas said.

"Wulfric! Watch out!" I screamed, but Wulfric merely looked up, thinking a Viking sword or axe was bearing down on him. He didn't expect the blow to come from behind. Helplessly, I watched Gil's knife sink deep into Wulfric's back, slicing upward to his kidney. Gil held him up momentarily.

The crux of the battle and everyone's attention had moved off to the left. No one noticed Demas's treachery.

"Wealth buys formidable allies," he said, leaning in close. "Your own missing grain accounts have purchased your fate, lady." He pointed to a fearsome Viking with blazing red hair. "We have a little arrangement, Halfdan and I. By the time he's finished with you, you will beg for me."

Gil dropped Wulfric, who fell hunched to the ground, and then reached around and pulled off both the leather and my father's helmet, yanking and twisting my head painfully upward. Something brushed against my back, slicing through the thong that bound my hair, and hands pulled hard on the long waves, wrenching them from beneath my belt. Waves of gold whipped around my face in the wind.

"Just so there's no mistaking you," Demas said, and the three of them disappeared into the chaos behind me.

The Saxon wall had fallen apart. Men were fleeing in all directions. I tried to turn about and run, but the Vikings plowed through the remaining stragglers, ending any attempts at escape. A few of my men noticed my state of distress and turned from the crumbling wall, encircling me. We tried to hold our ground, but Half-dan sliced and carved his way toward me as if my father's greatest warriors were no more than butter for his bread.

Then it was finished. I was surrounded. The Saxons were gone. The Vikings had control of the field. My men were slaughtered.

I wiped the sodden hair away from my eyes and crouched, waiting. My shield had been lost, and I held my sword with both hands.

"I admire your courage, maiden." Halfdan spoke in Norse as he stepped closer to me. Blood caked his axe.

"You are like a wild filly. I look forward to breaking you." He licked his lips, and the Vikings laughed.

"Alrik, take care of her," he said flippantly, and walked away, celebrating and cheering with his men.

I turned to the man charged with my care. He barreled toward me, but stopped, his body inches from mine. Azure eyes looked down at me, and my breath stilled. I would know that face anywhere, high cheekbones, golden beard and mustache beneath the silver helmet. I never thought I'd see him again. I reached out, but something made me pull back. Alrik's expression of shock turned hard, a cold malice clouding his eyes. And I watched, as if in a daze, as he raised the familiar garnet-studded hilt of his sword.

"I am sorry, Avelynn," he said, and brought the pommel down hard against the back of my head.

TWENTY

Nausea washed over me, and my head pounded as if a hundred blacksmiths' hammers were forging my skull. I was draped over something, lying on my stomach, being jostled and banged about. I opened my eyes. The ground moved slowly beneath me. A leather boot rested in a stirrup along a horse's russet flank. I admired the tightly bound laces and then vomited all over them.

The horse stopped.

"I see you are awake."

I tried to lift myself to see who was speaking, but pain swelled behind my eyes and clamped tightly around my head. I thought better of it.

My companion slipped off the horse and landed with a soft squelch. I was lifted up and placed unceremoniously on my own two feet. I swayed, listing heavily to one side, and clung to the large arms supporting me.

"It will pass," he said.

The harsh accented English sounded vaguely familiar, but I couldn't quite place it and let the thought pass as another wave of nausea overtook me. Backing away, I stumbled to a small oak tree and retched into the flattened and dead foliage around its trunk.

Leather boots, considerably worse for the wear thanks to my unsettled stomach, appeared in the grass beside me. "You will need to walk now."

I leaned against the tree, trying to stop the swirling dots in my vision. He reached out and enclosed one of my hands in both of his. They were rough and calloused but welcomingly warm. He grabbed my other hand and began binding them with coarse rope.

Despite my discomfort, my indignation soared, and my gaze flew upward. I found myself staring into Alrik's clear blue eyes. For the briefest moment there was a feeling of elation at seeing him again, but then it all came crashing back to me—meeting him on the battlefield, his assault knocking me unconscious.

"You bastard!" I tried to squirm free of his hold.

His face hardened, but he continued to secure my wrists.

"Let me go!" I twisted, pulling against the rope, but stopped when I felt it pinch even tighter.

"I cannot," he said simply, pulling me to his horse.

"What do you mean you cannot? What are you doing?" I grabbed the rope with both hands and tried to tug myself free. This was about as effective as trying to budge a mountain.

"You are being held for ransom by my brother Halfdan."

Brother? He was a Ragnarsson! Of all the Vikings on the earth, I had to meet the son of one of the most reviled and vicious Vikings ever to have lived. While Ragnar was dead, his sons, Ivar, Ubbe, and Halfdan, had taken up where he left off, and Alrik was their brother!

We were on the old Roman road heading east to the Viking stronghold of Reading. "Alrik." I glanced around nervously. "Where are we going?"

I froze, hearing the approach of horses. He pulled the rope, yanking me forward, and leaned in close, a death grip on my arm. "Do not say a word." He straightened.

A towering Viking in full mail stopped his horse beside us. A grizzled brown beard lifted the cheek flaps of his dented helmet.

He took in Alrik's appearance and laughed. "I hope you had the Saxon wench at your cock till she retched." His large belly shook with the effort of his mirth. "Best hurry along, boy. Halfdan'll be returning to Reading." He nudged his horse and sped off.

"Charming company you keep."

"It would have been better for you if you did not know Norse. I expect you will hear a great deal more and worse." He tied the other end of the rope to the back of his saddle and mounted his horse.

Goddess help me. He was going to drag me to Reading!

"I will keep the pace reasonable. I advise you to keep up."

"How dare you treat me like—"

The horse started forward, and I slipped, sliding on my knees. I struggled to regain my footing, grabbing hold of the rope to help pull me up. The effort to stay vertical quickly assumed all my energy, and any choice words I might have had for the man in front of me remained unspoken.

I had been stripped of my armor and weapons, a cloak the only outer clothing left to me to help fight off the frigid cold and damp. My hair had been tucked beneath the cloak, presumably to keep from ensnarling the horse's legs, but the long ends swung free and were soon caked in mud.

For the most part, Alrik kept the pace manageable. But even the slowest march would have proven difficult. After the drizzle and sleet, coupled with the vigorous travel the old dirt road had seen in recent days, it was a mangled, churned-up, muddy mess. I was on my knees almost as much as I was on my feet. In no time, I was soaked through and covered with thick, rancid sludge. My teeth were clattering so hard my jaw ached.

Every so often, another Viking would pass us, taking the time to either spit in my direction or make a bawdy threat or ribald remark. Alrik said little in response and maintained his pace.

Left to my own thoughts, the long, arduous journey to Reading lent itself to a great deal of silent reflection. For me, the war was over. I had no idea if the Saxons had recovered or if Wessex was finished. I thought of Alfred and Ealhswith, of my goddaughter, Aethelflaed. Were they safe? Perhaps escaped to Mercia in the north to seek aid amongst Ealhswith's family. Would Bertram have had time to get the women and children of Wedmore safely away, or were they right now being slaughtered at will? I cringed as an image of Demas flashed into my mind.

I hoped, somehow, someone had seen what he did and twisted his spineless neck. But there had been so much confusion on the battlefield, steel flashing everywhere, so many men dying in the mud. I suspected no one was any the wiser to his treachery. And even if someone did see something, would they have understood in the heat of battle what they really saw? You don't expect murder and sabotage from one of your own.

The Berkshire woods surrounded us on both sides and dusk closed in, hastened by thick gray clouds that filtered the pale winter sunlight.

The equinox was only a month and a half away. Soon the ground would be workable and the fields would have to be plowed for the spring planting. My brows pressed together. Were there still fields to sow and people left to tend them? If the Vikings didn't eradicate us, famine and sickness would, as families fled to the forests and fens. It felt as though an iron weight had been placed on my heart.

I looked at the man before me. What had I been thinking? How could I have had feelings for him? He was a Viking, one of the ruthless barbarians destroying my homeland and murdering my people. I searched for some connection, some glimmer of hope, but I no longer saw the man I had known last summer. When he had first appeared out of the mist, I'd been at once terrified and awed. I had felt so many other things for him since then, and for what? Heartache and betrayal?

"Who do you think you are?" I spat in Norse. I slipped, and the horse dragged me several feet before I caught my footing. "I was just a Saxon whore to you," I half shouted, half cried at his rod-straight back. "You disgust me! You miserable—"

He reined his horse to a stop, dismounted, and stalked over to me. "I told you to be quiet." He scanned the road in both directions, untied the rope from the saddle, and led both the horse and me to a large stand of oaks. He weaved us through the thickening underbrush until we reached a small stream. Tethering the horse, he dragged me deeper into the woods.

He stopped and pulled me to him, crushing his lips against mine. I struggled madly against his hold.

"Get your hands off me!"

He let me go.

I wiped my mouth furiously with the edge of my cloak. "Don't touch me, you filthy—"

"You dare speak to me with hostility?" His eyes flared with anger. "What were you doing fighting in a shield wall?"

"That's not your concern."

"On Odin's eye, woman, it is my concern. You could have been killed, or raped, or worse! Your actions have jeopardized us both."

"Us?" I stared at him, incredulous.

"Because of your recklessness, I am to sit and watch my brother make an example out of you. How am I supposed to tolerate that?"

"You're not. Save us both the trouble and let me go."

"I have been charged with delivering you to Reading. A Ragnarsson does not break his word."

"So you're a weak fool who does his brother's bidding?"

"I am saving your life."

"It looks as though you're saving your own selfish skin."

His face turned a furious shade of red. "You want to go? Fine." He untied my hands. "Go. I will not stop you."

I rubbed the burned and chafed skin around my wrists and looked down the river.

"There is not a Saxon within fifty miles of here. Norsemen lay thick in these forests. They command the roads. How far do you think you will get before someone finds you?" His voice was hard as steel. "What do you think they will do with you once you are caught? Or perhaps I should have just left you on the battlefield, to be assaulted by every rutting bastard in Halfdan's army."

The shadows became menacing. Fighting in the shield wall, I had come face-to-face with hundreds of Vikings, the lust of war and blood drunk in their eyes. The gods only knew the depth of abuse I could have suffered at their hands. And now I was deep in their territory, with no hope of finding my way back to the Saxon fyrd. I sat down, sinking into the mud, my legs suddenly too weak to bear me up.

I hadn't thought things through. I had been so eager to lead the charge, I didn't think of the consequences. A woman in a shield wall—gods, what was I thinking? I wrote my will, preparing myself for the possibility of death, but being captured, raped, or worse had never even crossed my mind. I closed my eyes. If Alrik hadn't been there . . . "I'm such a fool."

Powerful arms enfolded me and drew me into a fierce embrace. "No, Seiðkana, you are brave. But you are in great danger."

I was getting very tired. "What does Halfdan want with me?"

"He is holding you for ransom. He has made a lucrative arrangement with a Saxon."

"Demas."

"The man who threatened you?"

"He did worse than threaten me. He murdered my father and brother, and scalped and tortured my grandmother. He's a spineless pawn in a political gambit to take over my estate and make me his wife. Now it appears he's enlisted the aid of pirates to further his cause. He's even used Wedmore's wealth to secure my capture." I felt light-headed. I wanted to curl into a little ball and fall asleep. Perhaps I would drift into unconsciousness and freeze to death. Oddly, I didn't really care.

"That will never happen." He must have felt the spasms of shivering wracking my body, because he covered me with his cloak. Heat radiated off him in blissful waves. "I swear to Thor and Odin, I will protect you."

I drifted into a dreamy state of weariness. "And how exactly do you plan to manage that?"

"I have saved enough gold, twice as much as the Saxon has offered. Halfdan is a greedy man. The extra coin will persuade him to consider other offers. But I must get it to someone you trust, someone who will take the money and offer it to Halfdan for your freedom."

"Ealhswith would help," I said groggily. "But I don't know where she is. She's probably been sent as far away from the conflict as possible, maybe to Bath."

"Your king was injured in the battle."

That sobered me up a bit. "Is he dead? Did we lose?"

"No." He pulled me closer. I could feel the steady beat of his heart against my cheek. "Your men regrouped and rallied around your king. They were successful at keeping Halfdan at bay. Both sides have agreed to a temporary peace, offering up diplomats as ransom. If the peace is broken, those ransomed will be killed."

I tensed. He kissed my forehead. "For good or ill, Halfdan has other plans for you. You will not be included in that lot."

I might have dozed off momentarily, but he pulled away. "When we get to Reading, you must not let them know you understand the language. Norsemen do not tolerate spies." His gaze turned in the direction of the road. Stark and barren tree limbs stood silhouetted against a darkened sky. "We have to leave. I have stalled long enough."

If he expected me to jump up and follow him, he was to be disappointed. My body had no will to move.

He lifted me in his arms. The rhythmic pace of his stride lulled me into oblivion, and my head nestled into the hollow between his neck and shoulder. I remembered lying like that once before, but that was another time and place.

The clamor around me was a mixture of laughing, shouting, and boasting, all in Norse. I didn't have to open my eyes to know where I was: Reading. I tried to cover my ears to lessen the din, but my hands were once again tied together. I groaned. A large weight leaned against my shoulder and garbled in stentorian snores. Reluctantly, I opened my eyes and turned my head toward my companion. I couldn't make out more than the top of his disheveled brown mop. Following the outline of his hunched body brought my attention to his foot and the heavy chain clamped around his ankle. The black iron lay limp between us, encircling my ankle and locking me in its jaws before snaking its way along the ground, joining five more prisoners.

We were bunched together in a corner near the front of a hall.

I could make out Halfdan, with his unmistakable red head, sitting in an ornately carved chair on the dais. There was a stone table in front of him, the surface divided into dark and light squares. Halfdan's hand hovered over the game pieces. He stood suddenly, his face flaming in color to match his hair. "Loki's spawn!"

His opponent stood, glaring. Half Halfdan's height but just as wide-shouldered, the man gave no quarter. "I won fairly."

The crowd separated, backing away from the conflict, and the surrounding chatter quieted into snickers and murmurs.

"You are a whoreson cheat!" Halfdan said.

"You are a sore loser." He turned to leave.

Halfdan growled, the deep bass of it thrumming through my chest. He lifted the stone table and brought it down squarely onto his opponent's head. The skull caved in and blood sprayed out amongst the shattered pieces of stone. The man crumpled, his body splayed across the dais.

"I see you still have not lost your love of chess," Alrik said, stepping around the carnage. He was taller than Halfdan and notably younger. His face, smooth and slightly bronzed, contrasted sharply with Halfdan's ruddy pallor and the deep-set lines on his forehead.

"Well, if it isn't the runt come sniffing around the alpha's ass!" Halfdan's anger dissolved, and he turned and embraced Alrik heartily.

"Brother," Alrik replied.

"Up for a match?" Halfdan asked.

"I do not care much for the odds."

Halfdan laughed and slapped Alrik hard across the back. "Ale for everyone!"

Banter and drinking resumed as if nothing out of the ordinary had happened, while pages rushed in to dispose of the offending victim.

My companion started at the resumption of noise and lifted his head. Relieved of the burden, I stretched out my cramped neck and shoulder.

"Sorry about that," he said.

I recognized him, but couldn't place where I'd seen him before.

"Britnoth, master of arms for the lord Berkshire, at your service."

"You're Aethelwulf's man?"

"Was, m'lady. Berkshire is now in the hands of his brother, Wulfstan." Britnoth stretched his long legs as best he could, given the chain joining our ankles, and leaned against the wall.

"I was disheartened to hear of his death," I said, remembering him and his wife at the Christmas feast.

"'Twas a loss indeed, but Wulfstan fought bravely yesterday in Aethelwulf's stead."

"Yesterday? The battle was yesterday?"

"Aye, lady."

Had I slept that long? The hall was lit by oil lamps and candle trees. Without any windows, it was impossible to judge the time of day.

A long shadow crept over top of me. Halfdan, Alrik, and the large, dark-haired Viking I had had the pleasure of meeting on the road earlier approached.

The Viking kicked Britnoth's foot, insulted him, spat into his face, and then knelt down in front of me. He pulled out a knife.

I held my breath, my heart pulsing wildly in my ears. He grabbed my hands, slipped the knife between my wrists, and gave the steel a quick jerk. The rope fell limply onto my lap. I rubbed my wrists, attempting to ease some of the discomfort from the angry, raw friction burns. He inserted a key into the barrel lock clamped around my ankle and released my foot from the chain.

Grabbing one end of the iron links, he stood and yanked hard, causing the other six prisoners to yelp and jolt forward onto their hands and knees for balance.

"Saxon dogs!" He lifted his axe as if to strike. Britnoth and the others couldn't understand what he was saying, but they recognized the threat in his voice and its implications in his axe. All six men cowered. The hall burst into laughter.

"The wench has more balls than they do," someone yelled.

"Can they do tricks, Gorm?" another quipped.

"Aye, they can do tricks!" The giant Viking grabbed Britnoth's hair and pushed his head into his crotch. "Look here. He can suck his own cock!"

Amid the joviality this spectacle generated, Britnoth and the others were hauled to their feet. Gorm led them from the hall, kicking and shoving at whim, while others threw bones and garbage at them. I remembered what Alrik had said about Saxon prisoners being held for ransom and wondered if they would make it out of Reading alive.

The Vikings resumed their merriment and drinking. I scowled at the two men hovering over me.

"What will you do with her?" Alrik asked.

"I've readied a cottage for her. You can throw her in there. I want two guards posted outside at all times." Halfdan looked me over appraisingly. "She's a spirited wench."

"What is she to you?"

"I have an arrangement with a Saxon. I'm just holding her for him."

"Halfdan brought to heel by a Saxon." Alrik shook his head.

Halfdan's face turned a menacing shade of purple-red. "Do not press me, boy. You're only half my blood, and I'll not bat an eye tossing you from this hall without your head." He gripped the hilt of his sword.

"Peace, brother," Alrik soothed. "I merely inquire if you have considered other offers. I overheard the Saxons talking. She is of great importance, kin to the king. Did your Saxon buyer mention that? Perhaps you could make more if you ransomed her to the highest bidder."

My eyes widened in shock. What was Alrik doing? I was fairly certain any connection with King Aethelred wasn't going to win me favors here. I remembered belatedly that I wasn't supposed to understand the Norse tongue, but Halfdan wasn't looking at me. He was studying Alrik.

"Kin to the king? Are you certain of this?" Halfdan's high color retreated.

"I heard it personally." Alrik reached down and lifted my chin as if to get a better look at me. I twisted it out of his hand. "And she is a virgin, no less, look how she wears her hair long and unbound. If you keep her chaste and untouched, she will be worth more." He leaned his shoulder against the wall, crossing one foot over the other, and took a thoughtful drink from a silver cup. "The slavers would offer a pretty penny for her. Perhaps Ubbe can take her to Ireland. He is certain to get a king's ransom in gold for her at the slave markets. And if not"—he shrugged—"then he can return and you can sell her to your Saxon."

Ireland? Slave markets? Alrik promised to get in touch with Ealhswith. Had he changed his mind? Was this a new ploy to get me out of Reading?

Halfdan stroked his thick red beard. "Won't hurt to see what the wench is worth. I could exact double from the Saxon dog." He smiled broadly. "Speaking of Ubbe," he said, dropping his hand from his sword, "have you word?"

"A Florentine merchant bought several sacks of wool from Ubbe at his hall in York, not more than four days ago. Give me leave to sail, and I will bring him to Reading."

Halfdan nodded. "Very well. I want him here when we attack Meretun. He has promised me a thousand more warriors. The Saxons think we will honor their peace." He laughed. "Their king is weakened, his brother still young and inexperienced. With new forces, Wessex will fall."

Alrik lifted his cup. "To victory."

A thousand more warriors! Our fyrd was depleted, our men on the verge of exhaustion. They needed time to return home to rest and see their families. Fields needed to be plowed and seeded. If the Vikings pressed another battle, Wessex would suffer famine and sickness. Goddess help them.

Halfdan grabbed a horn out of someone's hand. At first the Viking was disgruntled, but seeing who it was that had stolen his beverage, he nodded in deference.

"To victory." Halfdan drained the horn dry. "More ale," he bellowed. A serving lad dutifully appeared at his side with a pitcher.

He wiped his mouth on the sleeve of his finely woven orange tunic. His blue-gray eyes traveled lasciviously over my body. Catching his brother's gaze, Alrik grabbed my arm roughly and yanked me to my feet.

"I will take her to the cottage now." He pushed me in front of him. "And I will send Hilde along to distract you."

Halfdan smiled, his beard framing thick, wet lips. "Ah, Hilde. Yes, a distraction would be welcome." He gave another hearty whack to Alrik's back and then rejoined the festivities.

It was late in the day, and the sun hung low in the sky. Small mounds of crystalline snow dusted corners, while the rest of the compound was a layer of thick, icy mud. I had been to Reading once before with my father, but that was several years before. Around the periphery of the hall, outbuildings were scattered haphazardly. I needed to get word to Aethelred. He needed to know about Meretun, the additional Vikings. I tried to make out the stables but suspected they were in the opposite direction from where we were headed.

Alrik nodded to more than two dozen men on our short trek. I frowned. Vikings, like fleas on a dog, were everywhere. A thousand warriors in a single town meant that any chances of escape to warn Aethelred were slim to none. I thought of Britnoth and the other prisoners. When the war started, they would all be killed.

Alrik led me into a small cottage and shut the door. It had a single bed and a central hearth, which blessedly had been lit, but that was all. No window, no table, no shelves—nothing I could use as a weapon or means of escape. I turned on Alrik and inhaled a lungful, ready to unleash a torrent of iniquities, a thousand words and disparate thoughts competing to find purchase on my tongue, but his hand clamped firmly over top of my mouth, his calloused palm pressing against my lips, and he pulled me into him, my back resting against his chest.

He whispered in my ear, "I will sail tomorrow with enough gold to make Halfdan mad with greed. I will find your friend and ensure she sends a messenger with her offer. He will not turn you over to Demas yet—we have bought ourselves time." He turned me around to face him. His eyes locked with mine. "Do not do anything reckless while I am gone. Sit and be patient."

I squirmed free of his hold. "You mean to leave me here?" I hissed.

"You will be safe until I return. Halfdan will not touch you and risk a drop in selling price."

"And if I'm not willing to take the risk?"

"What I said in the clearing stands. I have assured your safety and fair treatment. If you leave this cottage, you are on your own."

Deep down I knew he was right, but I was furious at my helplessness. "Why do you cower to him?"

The bronze glow of his skin flushed with anger. "You know nothing about me or my life. Loyalty and blood are valued above all else to a Norseman."

"Your brother doesn't seem to share your ideals."

We stood toe to toe, glaring at each other. "I have worked hard to earn respect from my men and from my brothers. I will not jeopardize my position for—"

"A Saxon whore?"

"For a hopeless cause. What good would it serve to anger him? You would be sold to Demas, and I would be killed and could do nothing to help you."

I turned away from him in defeat. I was fighting the wrong man. Gods, why was I being so ungrateful and hurtful? I closed my eyes. The next words were no more than a whisper. "Why didn't you come back in September?"

"I returned too late. I wanted to come earlier, but I had given Ivar my word."

"You gave your word to me." A tear burned the crease of my eye, threatening to fall. I swatted at it furiously, but another took its place. After all I had been through, being here with Alrik, captive and helpless, was breaking the last of my reserves.

He took a step closer. "I could not promise I would be back in September, but I promise you now. I will not let you down. You have my word. I will see you safely delivered to your people."

Delivered to my people. He wouldn't be with me. He would never be with me. The tear fell.

His arms encircled my waist, and his lips met mine. I pulled away. I was angry—angry that he left me, angry that he returned.

"I will not force you, Seiðkana."

My eyes involuntarily traveled down to the tent in his breeches. His words awakened months of unrequited passion. I shoved it away and crossed my arms in front of my chest.

He looked to the door. "We do not have much time."

"You hurt me, let me down, and then brought me here . . . dragged behind your bloody horse!"

"Of that, I had no choice. To all we passed on the road, you were my captive. Though, I cannot say it did not serve to wake you to the danger you were in." His eyebrows creased, but he pulled me back into him. The soft wool of his tunic brushed my cheek.

I could smell the musk of his scent, and my legs trembled. "Why didn't you just let me go? Why did you have to come back?"

"Because I love you."

Tears blurred my vision. "I hate you."

His mouth found mine, forcing my lips to part, his tongue demanding my surrender. My hands groped blindly for his neck. My tongue slid over his teeth, grazing the roof of his mouth, devouring him. Gooseflesh rippled along my skin. My breasts swelled, the tips straining against his chest.

He forced me against the wall, my back pinned against rough wooden planks. His hand traveled down my body, slipping inside my trousers, searching and finding the desperate wetness there. I inhaled sharply as his fingers slid along the sensitive flesh.

My own hands tugged the drawstring at his waist. His breeches slipped over his hips. I ran my fingernails down his thigh and brushed them lightly against the rigid sacks between his legs, cupping and massaging them in my palm before grasping the length of him. A rumble deep in his throat escaped, filling my mouth with heady vibration.

His teeth grazed my neck, my earlobe, my shoulder. Following the scoop neck of my tunic, his mouth kissed my collarbones, his tongue tracing the swell of each breast, delving into the valley between them. His free hand roamed beneath the fabric. I arched my back, pressing myself into his kneading hands as he rolled a nipple between forefinger and thumb.

Long, probing fingers slipped deep inside me. "Alrik." My head flung back, my hips strained forward.

He tugged at my trousers, and I pulled away from him long enough to loosen the cross garters that kept them from slipping to the floor. After some rather unbecoming hopping, I managed to step out from their tether.

"I want you." His breath was hot and heavy against my cheek.

"I want you too," I gasped between the thick, moist lips covering mine.

He pressed the tip of his arousal against me, rubbing it back and forth against swollen, quivering folds. I whimpered, needing more, and he drove inside me, filling me.

I cried out in muted desperation and grabbed a handful of his hair. My fingernails dug into his back. I wrapped my legs around his waist. Gods, if anyone were to come in and find us . . . Fear heightened the feverish, panicked pace, pushing our unbridled arousal to furious heights. With each thrust, he assaulted my womb. A mixture of pain and pleasure seized my body. I met him blow for blow, pushing my hips up to meet him, my passion clamping tightly around him, holding him to me, weakening him, possessing him.

A strangled cry contorted his features, his mouth held open in exquisite awe. His sounds, his pleasure, his need pushed me over the precipice, and my body convulsed. Waves of pleasure crashed over me, rippling with each final thrust. My legs shook, and my body melted as he shuddered and pulsed within me.

He leaned his forehead against the wall, and we remained frozen, our breath apace with each racing heartbeat for one last moment.

But too soon, he pulled away, and I disentangled my legs from around his waist. He fixed his breeches and tunic and inched closer to the door. I righted my own garments and sat on the bed. I waited, my hands resting on my lap. His face wore a mixture of euphoria, from the healthy glow of a man well satisfied, and sorrow. The fire in his eyes was diminished, his eyebrows heavy with our parting.

"I must go."

"I know."

He hesitated as if he didn't quite know what to do or say next.

"Thank you," I said. "For everything." My eyes glazed over, and my chest constricted.

He nodded. "I will be back as soon as I can, Seiðkana. You have my word." He stepped outside, leaving me to stare at the black iron latch as it clamped down, locking me in.

Halfdan proved a gracious captor, even providing me with a new kirtle, a comb, and a basin of rose-scented water to wash one morning. I hadn't bathed since Windsor and was grateful for the gift. Neither guard looked at me, let alone tried to touch me, when they shoved my meals through a sliver of open door. Halfdan was obviously taking Alrik's suggestions seriously, my virtue being considered a valuable asset.

After a while the days began to blur. I placed a notch in the dirt floor near the back corner of the cottage to keep track.

Despite Alrik's warning to sit and be patient, I wasn't about to wait to be rescued if I could devise a means of accomplishing the task myself. I assessed every possible opportunity. I couldn't take down the guards by hand—they were three times my size and fully armed. I tried dismantling the bed to use one of the larger posts as a makeshift club, but the frame wouldn't budge. Twice daily, food and ale were set inside the door, but the door was open only a slit, and each time I saw silhouettes of people milling around outside.

By the end of the third week, I grew increasingly anxious. A restless energy kept my legs bouncing when I sat. Surely, Alrik had reached Ealhswith by now. I wasn't sure how long it would take Alrik to find her, and I had no idea how he planned to meet with her. A Viking couldn't just walk straight into a village and ask to speak with the king's sister-in-law.

Trust him, I told myself firmly. But doubt hopped madly from shoulder to shoulder, mocking me. He had tried to come back in September, but circumstances out of his control prevented him from doing so. Who was to say something wouldn't stop him from returning this time as well?

Scooping away some dirt with my finger, I began to notch another day into the floor, but stopped as a thought struck me. The ground was soft here.

Reading was at the confluence of two rivers, the Thames and the Kennet, which protected the town on two sides from attack. The Vikings had overcome the remaining tactical weakness by digging a dyke around the exposed periphery and fortifying it with a wooden palisade. The wall of spiked tree trunks ran alongside the cottage I was being held in.

Perhaps I could dig my way out. If I broke out at night, emerging between the palisade and the cottage, I could keep to the shadows and slip down the riverbank when the way was clear. I wasn't sure if the shoreline was wide enough to allow passage, or if it was free of ice and debris, but despite the danger of being swept into the frigid water, I knew I had to try.

The latch on the door lifted.

"Hello, *wyrt-gaelstre*."

My blood waxed cold.

Halfdan and Gorm entered, followed by Ingvar, the Saxon from Alrik's crew, the man whose brother was killed.

"You are certain?" Gorm asked.

"That's her. I was with Alrik when he was fucking her."

Panic coursed through my veins.

"We found this on her when she was captured." Ingvar handed Alrik's knife to Halfdan.

Halfdan rolled the garnet-studded hilt in his palm.

"And you are certain she speaks Norse?" Gorm asked.

"Oh, she knows it, all right."

Halfdan nodded. "Gorm, place several lookouts along the river. When Alrik lands, see to it he does not make it back alive."

My knees buckled, and I stumbled backward, bumping up against the bed.

Gorm and Ingvar left.

Halfdan shut the door. "Let me show you what we do to spies," he said, and closed the distance between us.

TWENTY-ONE

"Bastard!" I cried out in Norse. Tears streamed down my face.

"You mistake me for Alrik," Halfdan said, switching the cat-o'-nine-tails across his leg. The whip had several corded ends, each tipped with a knot.

We were in a small sunken hut. The floor was dug a few feet into the earth. Plank walls and a thatched roof made up the portion aboveground. The rushes had been swept, mounding in piles around the periphery of the hut. A shoulder-high post near the back of the room was the only ornamentation. My neck had been forced into a chiseled-out split down the center of the post. A horizontal cross brace nailed into place behind my head ensured I couldn't move, and my hands were tied and bound to the front of the post. I was naked. My hair was thrown over my shoulders; the length hung loose, covering my hands. A woman sat on a small stool near the door, guiding wool onto a spindle. Her apparent job, beyond indifferent witness, was to tend the small fire burning in the central hearth. A variety of iron brands glowed red in the ashes.

Halfdan waited until I'd regained enough strength before continuing. Blood ran in rivulets down my back and snaked along my hips before drying thick and sticky down my legs.

"What is your relationship with Alrik?" He leaned his shoulder against the wall, watching me.

"I told you." My legs shook from the strain of trying to hold myself up. Whenever I collapsed, the weight of my body pulled my neck deeper into the wedge, and the rough edges razed my skin. "We met by accident. We haven't seen each other since last summer." My breath was strained. The words came in short spurts.

"Where is he?"

"I don't know."

"He stopped at York weeks ago, but has since disappeared."

"I don't know where he is."

"Do you care to know what I think?" He pushed off from the wall and walked behind me.

"Please," I begged.

He brought the whip down hard across the torn flesh of my back. My body convulsed from the pain, and my legs gave out. My scream was garbled as the wood dug into my throat.

"I think," he began, "that he has gone to tell your Saxon friends of our plans." He walked over to the fire and picked up a brand, the tip a fiery red.

I tried to find purchase with my bound hands on the post. I pushed myself higher. "He would never betray you. He respects you."

"He knows nothing of respect! He has dishonored me—spat on my father's name!" Spittle flew over the brand. It snapped and crackled as it evaporated.

Nothing I said made any difference. In Halfdan's eyes Alrik was a traitor and I was a spy. Alrik would be ambushed as soon as he landed, his life forfeit for a crime he didn't commit. And I would be tortured until Halfdan grew bored of my pleading, pathetic cries. He wouldn't kill me. My worth in gold was dependent on keeping me alive. We both knew that. But that didn't stop him from exacting pleasure in my pain.

He grabbed a handful of my hair and laid it across the brand. It sizzled, curled black, and caught fire. His fist closed around the flames, snuffing them out. The smell of burnt hair scorched my nostrils, churning my already panicked stomach. He held the brand inches away from my face, trailing the outline of my cheek. Heat radiated from the metal, searing my skin.

"Do you know what it's like to have your feet branded?" he asked conversationally. "Will make it harder to stand," he added.

"Please, I don't know where he is."

"You disappoint me." He moved behind and picked up my foot. I tried desperately to jerk it free of his grasp.

"Why do you protect him? He has left you here to take his punishment while he runs away like a cowering dog."

"I love him," I whispered.

He pushed the brand into the arch of my foot. I screamed, my body flailing to get away from the pain.

"Goddess," I called out in English between gasps. "Woden, Thunor, please save me."

He recognized the names of the gods and eyed me curiously. "You are not Christian." He set the brand back into the fire. "Who are you?"

"I'm a high priestess, daughter of the Goddess." I hiccuped through tears. "I cast the Ogham, symbols of magic and power like your runes. I prophesize."

The woman stood and pressed her back against the door. *"Völva!"* She pointed a grubby finger at me.

"Be still, Hilde," Halfdan roared. "She's no witch."

Hilde whimpered, clutching a talisman of Thor's hammer that hung from her neck. "She will curse us all!"

"I said be still!" Halfdan landed a strike across Hilde's cheek, which sent her staggering. The toe of her leather shoe scattered the glowing pokers across the dirt floor. She fell into a heap, cowering by the stool.

A thought, vague and unfocused, coalesced into inspiration. "Are you feeling well, Hilde? I will send an evil spirit to grip your belly with pain. Can you feel the demon possessing you, filling your blood with fever?"

Her hand flew to her stomach, and her eyes gaped in terror. Scrambling off the floor, she lunged for the door and ran screaming from the hut.

Halfdan stalked toward me. "Preying on the weak and simple-minded with your trickery will not help you, wench."

I lifted my eyes. "Goddess, I call upon thee. Come to your child, use my body, fill me with your power. Strike down my enemies."

His jaw was clenched. His teeth were bared beneath thin lips. "Enough!" He raised the whip as if to strike me, but stopped.

The crackle of something burning drew his attention back to the opened door. The rushes were alight. The flames licked at the roof above us.

The fire gave me courage and my voice grew steady. I raised it high. "Guide and guard Alrik the Bloodaxe, keep him safe from harm. Crone and Raven, grant Alrik strength and success in battle. Smite those who would stand against him." The hut began to fill with acrid black smoke.

"Stop now, witch!" He raged, but would step no closer.

I laughed, beyond caring what he would do to me, and borrowed Alrik's oath. "I swear on Odin's eye and Thor his son, I will bring about your ruin, Halfdan Ragnarsson." Using the last ounce of strength I had, I pulled myself up on trembling legs. My hair, drenched and matted, framed wild, crazed eyes as they locked with Halfdan's. "The more pain you inflict on me, the more I curse you in this life," I spat. "You will die a weak and useless man, Halfdan. You will never see Valhalla."

The last thing I saw before I fainted was Halfdan's face, ashen white, with eyes bulging in their sockets as the roof caught on fire.

I lay on my stomach on a nest of soft rushes. I smelt comfrey and something strong and astringent. My wounds had been treated.

"Up, wench," a gruff voice called in Norse.

A boot crashed into my side. I wheezed and whimpered.

"Up!" the voice repeated.

I was hauled to my feet, dragged, and thrown onto the ground outside. A brisk wind whipped around me and set my body shaking in violent tremors. A rope was secured to my wrists, and I was pulled, crawling and sliding, through the dirt to the back of a wagon. Taunts and insults hurtled at me, along with fistfuls of mud and refuse.

A figure knelt on one knee at my side. His hand reached out and yanked my hair, pulling my face to him. My head swam in pain and confusion. My eyes still hadn't adjusted to the brilliant sunlight, and I blinked, making out a dark hood trimmed in white ermine, dark laughing eyes, and a small smirking mouth.

"We are late for our wedding," he said cheerily. "Do try to keep up." Demas stood, brushing the dust from his trousers, and tied the rope to a post on the back of the wagon before disappearing around the front.

My senses, jumbled and disoriented, gradually came back to me, the courtyard rendering itself in stark relief. I was dressed in the tunic and trousers I'd had on the day I was captured. My hair had been braided and tied back with a leather thong. I didn't know who had administered to my wounds or took pains to tie my hair away from the sticky, gaping slashes on my back, but I was grateful. My gaze followed Halfdan as he approached the front of the wagon, giving me a wide berth. Demas reached out his hand and the two men clasped arms.

A raven flew overhead and perched on top of a sack of wool in the wagon, its large dark eyes regarding me silently. One of the horses snorted and stomped its feet. The bird took flight, disappearing into a thicket nearby.

I wondered if it had been sent by the Goddess to give me strength—to let me know she was still with me. But I didn't feel strong. I felt weak and horribly alone. Everything I had done, every step I had taken, led me back to the man about to cart me away. Fate was implacable. I was destined to live my life as Demas's captive. Had I just accepted the betrothal, none of this would have happened. Instead, I fought, I kicked, I screamed. I taunted fate. I goaded the Norns and their twisted game. I never had a choice. Warm tears rolled down the coolness of my cheeks, and I gave in to the inevitable. I surrendered my soul into fate's cruel hands.

"Time to leave, sweeting," Demas yelled back to me. "Best hold on."

The wagon jerked forward, pitching me face-first to the ground. I thrashed around, trying to gain footing. Where was I to find the energy to stand, let alone walk? I hadn't eaten or drunk anything since breakfast in the cottage when Ingvar came in. I had no idea how long ago that was, but several days must have passed since Halfdan's change of heart. The burn on the bottom of my foot was blistered over, and my back was tight and itchy with fresh scabs, though the recent movement had reopened a few tears. I could feel the blood oozing through the thick medicinal paste plastered to my back. Every part of my body hurt. My legs quaked, and my arms were weak and feeble in their attempts to set me right. I was sweating profusely, but my teeth chattered so hard my jaw ached. I suspected the chill had more to do with an emerging fever than with the temperature of the day.

"Avelynn!" A thundering growl erupted from somewhere behind me. I looked over my shoulder. Alrik charged toward me, his sword swinging wild, his tunic covered in blood. My heart leapt at seeing him, but then plummeted as all of Reading swarmed him.

"Another suitor, perhaps?" The amusement in Demas's voice cleaved my heart. "A shame he's too late." He laughed, the wagon set off, and I staggered onward. Merciless, insufferable fate pulled me farther away from the desperate sounds of battle behind.

We had come to an agreement, Demas and I, during the long journey to Wareham. After a short spurt of dragging my limp body along the old Roman road, he decided that my death was not advantageous and tossed me into the back of the wagon, the sacks of wool there a boon to my aching body. For my part, I decided that I would no longer fight my fate and became a complacent captive. On the second day, he provided me with a tent and a bed to sleep in, clean clothes and food.

Prior to my apparent rescue, Demas had approached Aethelred and offered to pay my ransom. The king, unwilling to pay such an exorbitant fee for my freedom, happily conceded the inconvenience onto someone else and granted his blessings to the exchange—and Demas's petition for marriage. The ceremony was to take place on the ides of March.

Having selflessly bought my freedom, despite my cruel treatment of his character at the Witan, Demas cemented the affection and respect of those around him. All the affluent people from

Somerset and Dorset would be present for our wedding feast. Aethelred, injured and recovering from the wound he suffered in the battle at Basing, would stay in Windsor, but Alfred and Ealh-swith would attend in his stead.

I scoffed. All his planning would be for naught. The future state of my conjugal affairs seemed irrelevant. By the time we reached Wareham, fever ravaged my body, and I was certain there wouldn't be a wedding. I was delirious. I wanted to die. I couldn't imagine a life without Alrik, but a thousand warriors against one ensured I would never again feel the soft wool of his tunic against my cheek or the strength of his solid arms around me. Instead, I would have Demas's foul hands touching my flesh. The thought repulsed me, and I welcomed the languid darkness pulling my soul to the underworld.

But when we passed through Wimborne, Demas retained the services of Father Anlaf, a prominent leech, who expertly tended the growing infection festering through the rancid poultices on my back. Despite my heavy heart and yearning desire to give up, Anlaf roused my body's traitorous instinct for survival. Fate, it seemed, was not finished baiting me.

I closed my eyes. I could feel the weight of Demas's body as he sat beside me on the down-filled mattress. I had been given a luxurious chamber in Wareham. The ornate poster bed was crowded with furs and finely woven linens. At the front of the room, closest to the door, stood a large table and several chairs, the legs intricately carved. Thick wall-clothing hung on the walls, each exquisite image painstakingly embroidered into the fabric and embellished with silver and gold thread. I had a fine bone comb to untangle my hair and sparkling glass horns for my wine. But it was only temporary—until the guests left after the wedding feast. I shuddered to think where he would dispose of me once the witnesses were gone.

"I see the good Father Anlaf has brought you back from death's door," Demas said.

"Not without a fight." I rolled over, my back to him.

"Now that I see you are back to your recalcitrant self, you have a host of guests wishing to speak with you. Foremost amongst them is the Archbishop of Canterbury. He wishes to ascertain for himself your consent to this marriage after what happened at the Witan in Winchester. He wants to know what has changed your mind."

"What do I tell him?"

"You tell him you were lying, and you pray that God will forgive your transgressions."

I heard the door to the chamber open and then close.

"Ah, wonderful! Come, come," Demas called jovially to whoever had just entered the room. "In keeping with tradition, my bride, I have a wedding gift for you."

"Avelynn?" a timid voice called out.

My eyes sprang open. I lifted my head. Edward shrugged off Gil's possessive hold and rushed in. Demas moved off the bed, and Edward crashed into my side, wrapping his arms around me. I sucked in a sharp breath and winced as pain shot through my back. It was the most glorious thing I had ever felt. I held him tight.

"Are you well?" he asked.

"I'm well," I said, half choking on the words. "And you?" I pulled away long enough to look into his dark blue eyes. I scanned his face, his full smiling mouth, the healthy, ruddy glow to his skin. *Dear gods, he's alive! He's real!*

"I'm well, sister."

I embraced him again, sobbing quietly into his soft wheaten hair.

We stayed clinging to each other until Adiva, my new chambermaid, interrupted our reunion. "The archbishop is waiting."

"Gil, see that Edward returns without incident to his room," Demas said.

Gil nudged Edward's shoulder, and Edward disentangled himself from my embrace, wiping his face with the back of his sleeve.

"I promised she would be treated well," Demas said.

Edward stiffened. "You kept your word."

"I remind you to keep yours." Demas nodded, and Gil led Edward from the room. Adiva followed, shutting the door behind her.

"I see your mind working," he said.

"What game are you playing at, Demas?"

"I am merely reminding the lad of our previous arrangement."

"And what arrangement is that?" I could feel the blood boil through my veins.

"That is between Edward and me."

"If you so much as harm him—"

"You'll what?" He laughed. "You are in no position to threaten me." He removed the knife from his belt and sat beside me. He admired the steel in the candlelight and then began to pick the dirt from beneath his fingernails with the deadly point. "No one knows Edward is alive, except a few of my closest friends. He is my collateral for your compliance. As long as you are willing and agreeable, he will remain alive."

It didn't make any sense. His whole purpose in marrying me was to gain control of my father's legacy. With Edward healthy and well, Demas would assume control over only half of Somerset. "What can you possibly gain from keeping him alive?"

"Well, let me put it this way." He leaned down, the knife's edge resting on my cheek, and whispered in my ear. "You will determine the manner of his death. If you are a well-behaved little girl, he will die quickly, without pain. If you so much as say one thing to thwart my plans, he will suffer interminably, and you, dear lady, will watch."

Rage coiled and burned, threatening to consume me. Demas's treachery and madness knew no bounds. He had kept Edward alive only to kill him when it suited his purposes.

I imagined grabbing Demas's knife and plunging it into his stomach, twisting and turning the blade until his intestines spilled onto the floor where I could step on them and grind them into the dirt.

He stood and straightened his tunic. "Have I made myself clear?"

"Perfectly."

"Excellent!" He clapped his hands together in satisfaction. "Then let's put your loyalty to the test, shall we." He pulled a scroll of parchment from beneath his tunic. "We will start by amending your will."

TWENTY-TWO

The procession began, each guest eager to view the spectacle—the girl who was tortured by Vikings and lived to tell the tale. I was never left alone with my visitors. Demas, or his spy Adiva, my faithful new lady-in-waiting, was always present.

Archbishop Aldulf was duly convinced of my contrition, Alfred relayed the king's sympathy and expressed his personal lament for my ordeal, ladies tittered as Demas wove a tale of depravity and torture, and men nodded when he pointed out that a shield wall was no place for a woman to begin with. I was a caged bear, poked and prodded, forced to do tricks for my audience.

Ealhswith hung back and waited until the others had been satisfactorily sated in my performance.

"How are you feeling?" she asked.

"Much better than I was."

She shook her head. "I don't believe it."

"Believe what?"

"This." She waved her hand, encompassing the room. "After all that has happened, how can you just lie there and accept this?" She locked her arms across her chest and glared at me.

I nodded my chin toward Adiva. "I've changed my mind." I shrugged. "Nothing left to fight about."

Ealhswith narrowed her eyes at Adiva, who sat on one of the chairs in the corner, embroidering a strip of silk. I followed her gaze. Long, auburn curls obscured her pale face as she bent forward. She couldn't have been more than fourteen. I wondered what Demas was threatening her with. Since she'd had the misfortune of seeing Edward alive, I suspected she wouldn't live to see the day after the wedding.

Father Anlaf bustled into the room and opened the shutters on the small window. The steady fire in the hearth snatched greedily at the fresh air. "Foul vapors carry disease," he admonished Adiva. "This window must be opened twice daily." Small, round, and dismal, he shooed her out. "Go fetch more cloths for your mistress's back."

She hesitated, looking from me to Ealhswith.

He frowned at her. "Go on."

She curtsied and left the room.

He turned his pointed glare to Ealhswith.

"I'll be staying," she said firmly.

Unable to tell the king's sister-in-law to leave, he nonetheless brusquely removed her from the bedside.

"How is my patient this afternoon?"

"Healing, unfortunately."

He ignored the bitterness in my voice and rolled me over. As if uncovering one of his precious relics, he gently removed layers of bandage. When he got down to the skin, I could hear Ealhswith inhale sharply.

" 'Tis not a place for a lady."

"I will stay with my friend."

He mumbled under his breath but continued about his work, poking and prodding the scarred and healing flesh.

"Dear God, Avelynn, it's a wonder you're still alive," she said quietly.

"Father Anlaf is to be credited for my current state of well-being."

"I will personally see to it that the monastery at Wimborne receives a generous gift from the king," she said in a low whisper.

This perked him up immeasurably. "A most gracious offer, my lady. May Christ reward you."

Adiva shuffled in with a basket full of cloth strips.

"I meant to tell you of a dream I had a fortnight ago," Ealhswith said, moving to the other side of the bed. She sat beside me. "A magnificent eagle landed upon my windowsill. He whispered in my ear where to find unfathomable treasure. He told me I was to rescue a beautiful maiden held ransom by a terrible dragon."

I turned my head and stared at her. Alrik?

"He flew away, perching high atop the mast of a merchant ship. It had the most striking red sail with a raven emblazed on the fabric."

Raven's Blood! My lower lip trembled. Gods, she had seen him, talked to him.

"Did you rescue the maiden?" Father Anlaf asked.

"No." She wrapped her hands around mine. "By the time I got there, some dark and sinister creature had gotten to her first."

"A dream to pray on, for sure," he said, looking up at her. "The Devil may be tempting you with material wealth, my lady. Perhaps you should add a personal donation to the Church yourself, to cleanse your soul."

"A considerate suggestion, Father. Thank you."

I squeezed her hand. "I fear the dragon has killed the eagle." Pain clenched my stomach, and tears sprang from a well, dark and deep.

"Nonsense," Anlaf said gruffly. "You are upsetting my patient, lady, with your fanciful talk. I ask you to leave."

"I'm sorry, Father," she said, and stood up. "I'll wait at the table until you're finished."

"Thank you, Ealhswith . . . for trying," I said.

Her eyebrows knitted together in sympathy, and she nodded.

Anlaf glared. Ealhswith frowned, but dutifully sat beside Adiva at the large table, her hands resting in mock contrition.

He clicked his tongue and went about his ministrations undisturbed. Scooping out some paste, he plastered my wounds with the thick salve. The herbs he used were pungently aromatic. I wondered what he was using and sighed. Muirgen would have known.

When he finished, he had me stand. I raised my arms, and he walked around me, winding me tight with the cloth strips. I felt like I was being encased in my death shroud, readied for burial, which I decided was only fitting. Life as I knew it would end tonight with the priest's "amen." Everything to this point—the loss of my parents, the loss of Alrik, the torture—all of it had been a fairy tale compared to what would come after I was married. I felt dead inside. After the "amen," my hell would begin.

Satisfied with his care, Anlaf straightened his rough woolen robe. "You will be able to stand at your wedding tonight."

Unbeknownst to him, I had been standing and walking a bit each day in an attempt to regain my strength. Going into my nuptials weak and immobile didn't appeal to me in the least.

He smiled broadly. Bushy brown eyebrows crested squinting little eyes. "Lord Demas will be pleased with your recovery."

"What's this? I believe I've heard my name," Demas called, entering the room.

"My lord." Father Anlaf bowed his head. "I was just mentioning to the lady that I believe her strong enough to stand for the ceremony." Anlaf lent me his hand and helped me back to the bed.

"Wonderful," Demas said, resting his hand on the monk's shoulder. "I cannot begin to thank you for your kind treatment of the mistress Avelynn."

"No trouble at all. I am happy to do God's will." He inclined his head and scampered out.

Demas bowed in a courtly flourish. "Lady Ealhswith, how lovely to see you again. I trust you have assured yourself of your friend's good treatment."

Ealhswith stood and placed herself bodily between the bed and Demas's smiling eyes. "I don't know what you're up to, Demas, but if anything should happen to Avelynn, I will personally ensure the king takes a vested interest in you. I doubt very much you will appreciate his scrutiny."

"What do I have to fear? You can see for yourself that she is being treated with the very best care. She is certainly not wanting."

Ealhswith leaned in closer to Demas, her voice a low whisper. "The lady Muirgen told me everything."

He straightened the gold brooch that held his cloak in place. "Many things revealed at the tribunal were not based in fact. Avelynn herself has recanted all her accusations."

Ealhswith narrowed her eyes at me. I merely shrugged my agreement.

She turned back to Demas. "Know, sir, that I will be watching you."

"I welcome the attention from such a beautiful lady." He bowed.

"We'll talk further, Avelynn," she promised, and stormed out.

Demas looked at the empty doorway for a moment before nodding to Adiva, who curtsied her way backward out of the room, shutting the door behind her.

"Your friend is troublesome." He rubbed his neatly trimmed beard with the back of his fingers.

"Might be hard to threaten the sister-in-law to the king," I said pointedly.

He smiled. "Everyone has a weakness, everyone a price." He

looked me over carefully. "The ceremony will start in two hours. Adiva is bringing you a basin to wash." He walked to the door. "I've had a dress brought in from Francia for you. Try not to sully it."

When he left, I closed my eyes, preparing myself for a perpetual state of misery, but the loud croak of a raven caught my attention. I blinked at the vision in front of my eyes. Sitting on the sill plate of the open window, the raven fluffed its glossy black feathers until its neck resembled a puffy mane. It croaked again, its thoughtful eyes regarding me, and then flew away. If only I could transform into a bird and soar through the window. My heart fluttered. I scanned the room. I was alone! I looked at the window carefully. I could certainly fit through it without problem. But where would I go? I wondered where Demas was holding Edward. Would I be able to find him? My strength had returned, but how far could I get before Adiva sounded the alarm?

As if on cue, my thoughts were interrupted by the entrance of the talebearer herself. Holding an exquisite white clay basin with intricate green twining vines, she smiled weakly. "It's time to get ready for your wedding, my lady."

The ceremony would be held in Demas's great hall. There were no decorations, nothing to belie a woman's touch. Stark and open, the benches were pushed against the wall. Guests stood in one somber mass, patiently waiting for the ceremony to end and the feasting to begin.

Dressed in a bright green tunic that set his hazel eyes swimming in a sea of deep green, his hair as shiny and slick as an otter's pelt, Demas looked every inch an affluent, gallant gentleman. I, in my white gown, shimmering with silver thread and accented with freshwater pearls, my long blond hair flowing softly down my back, looked every inch his opulent lady.

Archbishop Aldulf joined our hands together and placed a silk band over top. In his nasal drone, he intoned the words that would bind me to Demas forever. I thought of Edward, of his short life, and my part in his death. Dutifully, I repeated, "I take thee, Demas, to be my wedded husband, to have and to hold, from this day forward, for better and for worse, for richer and poorer, in sickness and health, to be bonny and buxom in bed and in board, till death do us part, and thereto plight thee my troth."

Demas repeated his lines in this tragic play with surgical precision. "I take thee, Avelynn, to be my wedded wife, to have and to hold, at bed and at board, for fairer and for fouler, for better and for worse, in sickness and health, till death do us part."

With a flourish, Demas produced a fine gold ring from a pouch hanging from his belt. He placed it over the top of the thumb of my left hand. "In the name of the Father," he said, and moved the ring to the first finger. "In the name of the Son." He moved the ring to the second finger. "In the name of the Holy Ghost." He placed the ring on the third finger. "Amen."

That last word echoed in my head like a hammer striking a bell.

"Who is to give the bride away?" Aldulf asked the crowd of witnesses.

"I am." Osric stepped forward.

My father wasn't here, so my uncle was in charge of my transfer. Marriage was a contract of ownership. The maiden, once under the control and administration of her father, was placed formally into her new husband's care. In the marriage contract, Demas must state clearly what my bride-price consists of—the prearranged worth of my value as a woman and wife. Most brides received land and tokens of wealth. I was under no such illusions. The ransom he paid the Vikings for my freedom assured that, on paper, he owed me nothing. In the wedding ceremony itself, the giving and receiving of the bride was played out figuratively.

Osric handed his knife to Demas. Demas walked behind me and grabbed hold of my hair. He tugged the strands roughly, causing my head to jerk back. He placed the knife against my back, just below my waist. He was careful to press hard enough for me to feel the steel's edge. Aldulf nodded and Demas sawed through my hair. Half its length fell to the rushes. Demas stepped over the fallen strands and waited in front of me.

Many took this next part of the festivities as a gesture of fun, and the task was completed with gentleness and humor. That was not to be my fate.

Osric slipped my right shoe off my foot. Bowing, he handed it to Demas. With all due ceremony, Demas struck me hard upside the head with the offending leather weapon, indicating the transference of ownership—as custom dictated—was completed. I staggered and leaned heavily on Aldulf for support.

Extricating himself from my shaking arms, Aldulf walked to the far right corner of the hall. Osric wrapped his arm around mine and followed. He pushed down forcibly on my shoulder, and I crumpled, kneeling before the archbishop for benediction. Without any acknowledged family in attendance to present him, Demas proceeded alone and knelt before Aldulf.

A tall, lanky man, dressed in simple monk's robes, stepped forward holding the care-cloth. He placed the veil over our heads while the priest prayed and blessed the union. We repeated this process in each corner. At the last, we were raised anew, two souls joined in the eyes of God and the Holy Church.

Aldulf led us solemnly from the hall to my bedchamber. He blessed the room and the marriage bed, and then placed a wreath of victory on my head. Made of myrtle leaves, early-blooming white wood anemone, and purple lesser periwinkle, the wreath symbolized my victory over the temptations of carnal sin, for I was of course a virgin. He produced the marriage charter, and we signed the contract. I was officially Demas's chattel.

Three beeswax candles—one tall and thin, two as thick around as my thigh—were set on a silver charger in the center of a small table near the foot of the bed. Aldulf lit the tall candle. It would burn until midnight. The two remaining candles would count down the hours of one day each. I would be spared the indignation of bedding Demas for sixty hours. As protocol demanded, we were to spend the first two nights in silent contemplation and prayer, each in separate chambers. It was not until the third night that we were expected to consummate the marriage. The consummation would wait, but the feasting would begin immediately.

Aldulf led us back into the hall. "In the name of the Father, the Son, and the Holy Ghost, I present to you, husband and wife."

The hall erupted into clapping and cheers, and we took our place at the head table. Pages scurried in with wooden platter heaving with food, while serving women bore clay pitchers of drink.

Demas had spent lavishly on the feast. Exotic wine, imported from the Continent, was poured into bottomless horns ornamented with sheet gold. Ale and mead flowed like the River Frome, which flanked the southern boundaries of the manor. Trays of food issued forth in a never-ending display of delicacies. Ten oxen alone had been roasting for days in pits strewn about the grounds to sate the guests' considerable hunger. For three days, their appetites were surfeited. For three days, their every thirst was quenched. Even the royal weddings of the past paled in comparison.

Servants dressed in fine clothes catered to every whim. Hunts were arranged. Horses were given as gifts. Gold and jewels were tossed about as tokens of appreciation. Demas dazzled the nobility of Wessex with finery.

I watched all this in detached fascination. The politics in play here were carefully calculated. Secret words, darting eyes, curt nods, and strong handshakes weaved amongst the pleasantries like snakes in the grass. Demas and Osric were forming powerful allegiances, beguiling their audience with forked tongue and sleight of hand. But to what purpose?

On the third night after the feast, a procession of half-awake drunk revelers sang and cheered us to the bedchamber. Demas gave strict instructions for Gil and Sigberht to remove the debris from the hall first thing in the morning. There was to be no one left in the manor after cock crow.

"The moment you have been waiting for has arrived," he said, staggering a bit to the large trestle table.

A wave of revulsion as thick as week-old pottage overcame me.

"Don't look so enthusiastic," he said dryly. "You are not my first choice either." He sat on one of the chairs and removed his cloak and shoes. "We have a little time to kill before we make this marriage official." He stretched out his feet, cracking his toes, and poured another hornful of wine.

I had been careful to meter out my consumption, thinking it prudent to keep my wits about me. Demas, with all the toasts he had to acknowledge and match horn for horn, was clearly drunk.

"You promised I would see Edward." I hadn't seen him since before the wedding ceremony, three days prior.

"And you shall, my wife, you shall. Once the greedy dogs pass out and stop draining me dry."

"You don't seem to have much affection for your fellow noblemen." I sat on the bed as far away from him as possible—though he gave no indication of wanting to come near me.

"They are a bunch of fools, following a weak, dying king and his useless brother. They will never defeat the Vikings. But all that will soon change."

My mind raced with questions, but my thoughts were halted

by the flicker of the day candle at the foot of my bed. A meager stump of wax was all that remained, floating in a puddle of hot liquid pooling around the quivering flame. I swallowed hard and looked up as someone knocked on the door.

"Ah, about time," Demas said, standing.

Gil walked in, leading Edward in front of his massive body.

"Come," Demas said, motioning to Edward with a crook of his finger.

Edward moved obediently to his side.

My arms ached to hold him, to protect him. But my feet were rooted. Anything I did or tried to do would only make matters worse. A tear ran cold down my cheek.

Demas stroked Edward's hair, which had been brushed to a brilliant shine, like fields of silken wheat under a full moon.

"Such a good lad, is he not, Gil?" Demas caught my gaze and smiled. "Pity."

Gil garbled his agreement; spittle dripped onto the rushes underfoot.

"Don't touch him," I warned, my voice low and menacing.

"Avelynn, don't," Edward pleaded. "It's all right."

"It is not all right!" I said, gasping.

"You see, Edward. I have not hurt her," Demas soothed.

Sigberht entered the room, carrying an axe. Gods, how could I stop them? It was now three against one!

Demas stepped away from Edward, and my heart stilled.

"Gil." Demas inclined his head behind him.

Gil walked over and grabbed hold of Edward. His trunk of an arm wrapped tightly around Edward's chest, and a knife appeared at his throat. A look of shock and confusion darted through Edward's trusting blue eyes.

"No," I yelped, and started forward.

"I wouldn't do that, wife," Demas called out.

Gil pressed the blade into Edward's throat. A small trickle of blood ran down his neck.

I couldn't do this. I didn't care what happened to me, but I could no longer sit here and just watch Edward die. I crouched, ready.

Demas shook his head and sighed. "I warned you any struggle on your part would result in Edward's suffering."

Grabbing the axe from Sigberht's outstretched hand, Demas moved in front of Edward and brought the full force of the shaft to bear on Edward's shin as he swung. The sound of bone shattering ripped through the small room. A scream rose from Edward's throat, but Gil moved his knife hand to Edward's mouth and efficiently silenced him. Edward's body shook, his eyes wide with terror as tears rolled down his face.

"Bastard!" I lunged at Demas, but Sigberht raised his knee, catching me in the stomach. I was pitched backward, colliding with the ground and curling onto my side, wheezing and gasping for breath.

Satisfied, Sigberht bound my hands, securing them to one of the posters of the bed. My lungs bucked and heaved as breath slowly trickled through my nose. Nausea built in my gut as pinpoints of light flickered across my vision. I strained through watery eyes to see Edward. His face was ashen, his eyes lolling in their sockets. He looked close to fainting.

An urgent knock at the door drew Sigberht away. He returned a moment later. "My lord, there is some sort of trouble in the courtyard."

Demas removed his belt, laying it across the back of one of the chairs. "I have a rather pressing matter to attend to here." He slipped his trousers off, kicking them onto the rushes beside him. He motioned to the axe. "You two take care of it. I need to consummate my marriage."

Gil released Edward, who dropped like a stone, and slipped out the door with Sigberht.

"Avelynn," Edward hiccupped through tears, as he crawled on hands and knee, dragging the one leg awkwardly behind him.

"Isn't this a cheery picture of domesticity," Demas said, stroking his erection, and stepped in front of Edward, blocking his progress. Demas yanked hard, lifting Edward by his hair, and placed a forearm around his neck. His hand covered Edward's mouth. "Do you know what it's like to feel pain, Avelynn? To have your heart cut out and mashed underfoot?"

"Yes." My eyes pleaded for mercy.

"You think Muirgen or your father count?" Edward struggled, squirming to break free. Demas grabbed his knife from the belt hanging on the back of the chair and struck Edward's temple with the iron hilt. Edward's body slackened. Demas searched my eyes. "I want you to feel firsthand the suffering you have caused me. I want you to live with the knowledge that I have taken away everything and everyone you have ever loved." His eyes, rimmed in red, glittered with tears, his gaze never leaving mine.

"I never meant to hurt anyone. Osric killed your friend. He is the enemy. Not me."

His face waxed white. "How do you know that?"

Admitting to witchcraft could in no way aid my cause now or in the future. "I saw the stag brooch. I know how much the young man meant to you. Osric is the only one capable of doing such a vicious thing."

He hesitated.

"Please."

Edward's limp body crumpled to the floor. Demas stepped away, wiping his nose with the back of his sleeve, and poured another glass of wine, slogging it down, his back to me.

Edward lay unconscious, but his chest moved with each precious breath.

Demas stumbled back to the bed. "You are right about Osric." He drained the cup and threw it at the hearth. It landed several feet from its target. "Your brother might yet prove useful. In the meantime, his life would secure your continued cooperation."

With my wrists still bound, he extricated me from the post and dragged me forward. He nudged Edward's side with his boot, earning a plaintive groan. "Such a handsome lad." He cocked his head to the side. "Since my young friend has been taken from me, perhaps your brother can serve in his place."

"He's only a child!"

"Ah, but he'll grow." His erection jerked and tightened. "I bet his mouth is tighter than your cunt."

Something snapped. I twisted out of his hold and lunged for the silver charger. I grasped it with my bound hands and threw the basin of hot wax into Demas's face. He yelped, dropping the knife as his hands clawed at his face, and fell backward, tripping over Edward. I grabbed the knife and then brought my foot down hard onto Demas's crotch. I stumbled to the table and held the hilt tight between my thighs, frantically sawing through the thick fibers binding my wrists.

I extricated myself from the rope and sent a prayer to the Goddess. Demas growled and lunged. I spun out of the way. He missed his target and fell, landing on his knees. I picked up one of the heavy, ornate chairs and brought it down over his head. Having momentarily dazed him, I used all the strength I could summon and connected my fist with the side of his jaw.

He tumbled sideways, rolling onto his back, his slackened arousal limp and harmless against his thigh.

If he thought he would find pity for his loss, his plight landed on deaf ears and a cold heart. Mad, blind hatred drove me forward. I raised the knife high in the air and brought it down swiftly and cleanly. "That was for my brother." His cock flopped lifeless onto the rushes between his legs. He howled and writhed, curling into a ball. But I wasn't finished.

I ran to the heavy plank table and dragged it between the door and the bed, a solid deterrent against anyone attempting to get in. I threw on Demas's cloak, fumbling with the brooch to secure it over my shoulder, and pulled on his shoes. Though large, they would serve to protect me better against the cold than the slippers I'd had on. Demas seemed close to fainting, and I wanted him wide awake. I grabbed the pitcher of wine and threw what was left of the contents in his face. He stirred and flashed me a look of venomous steel. I stepped behind him and yanked hard on his hair. He grabbed at my dress and tried to pull me down on top of him. My foot ground into the bleeding stump of his crotch and put a violent stop to his struggles. "That was for my father," I hissed in his ear.

I took the knife and cut deep across his forehead. "This is for my grandmother." I yanked hard, cleaving the skin in one fluid motion from his skull. Blood poured, covering his face, spilling into his sputtering mouth.

The door moved two inches and banged into the table.

"Lord?" It was Sigberht's voice. Our eyes connected. He took in the scene before him and rammed his body against the door. The bed jerked.

I hesitated, torn between a desire to rip Demas's heart out with my bare hands and a flicker of self-preservation.

The door heaved, and the bed slid an inch along the dirt floor.

As much as I wanted to finish Demas, survival won out.

I grabbed Edward, lifting him into my arms, and ran to the window. He moaned, stirring. I opened the shutters.

"Edward." I jostled him, trying to wake him. The door slammed against the table, the former creeping open another inch.

"Edward." I was near to panic. I tried to maneuver him gently through the window, but he fell from my grasp and landed with a gut-wrenching thud on the other side. He let out a pinched wail. "I'm so sorry," I whispered, and then jumped into the darkness after him.

TWENTY-THREE

I didn't think, I just moved. There were no consequences to my actions. I was pulled along by some unknown thread, an unseen hand pushing me beyond reason. What I had just done was suicide. It was only a matter of course before the entire manor knew what had happened and set out to bring me to justice.

I tucked my arm under Edward's knees, the other under his neck, and lifted him to my waist.

"Avelynn?" His voice was weak, infused with pain.

"It's okay. I've got you." I cradled him close. He whimpered as my hand cupped the knee of his broken leg. Anger flashed and boiled hard in my veins, and the rage fueled my resolve.

The sky burned an ominous orange. Muffled sounds flitted through the breeze. When the direction of the wind changed, I smelled smoke. Something nearby was on fire. I couldn't see the cause, but remembered the urgent knock on the door and Sigberht mentioning trouble. I thought of Ealhswith and Alfred, and the innocent people visiting and working within the manor. I sent a silent prayer to the Goddess for their safety, but as for Wareham itself, I hoped it went up in flames, taking Demas and Osric with it.

Harsh male voices, yelling and threatening, echoed in the haze. I hugged the tree line surrounding the manor, hoping to reach the River Frome. The river marked one of the manor's boundaries. If I could just keep to the shadows, perhaps we could make it. As I progressed farther from the hall, shadows flickered orange around me. Pillars of smoke rose into the starless sky, curling and choking the air. Several outbuildings were on fire, their wheat thatch fully engulfed. The warmth of the flames touched my bare arms and caressed my face, even as I passed several feet away. I didn't know how the fire had started. I only hoped the unfolding chaos would help to render Edward and me invisible.

Edward was a scant twig of a boy, but the limp weight of his body made my arms shake and my legs tremble. Lifting one knee to hold his back, my standing leg shook as I jostled him higher. He wrapped his arms around my neck, his head resting on my shoulder, trusting. I didn't know how far I would get. My only thoughts were to reach the river. But one thing was certain: if there was some possibility of escape, I would find it. I wouldn't stop until Edward was safe.

I stumbled upon a well-worn path leading to the river and stopped. I could hear the water's gentle sloshing nearby. The forest was cast in inky shadow, but the glow from the fires illuminated the path enough for me to discern moving shapes. There was not a soul in sight. No footfalls pounding against the ground as they ran for water. Surely, servants would be trying to collect river water in an attempt to quench the fires. I looked to the manor. A sense of foreboding, deep and innate, raised the hairs on my forearms and prickled along the back of my neck. Where was everyone?

I took a precious moment to catch my ragged breath, to slow the pounding of my frantic heart. My body was tiring fast, anger melting into exhaustion. My back ached. But the wind brought the specter of men's voices to my ears. I scrambled down the path.

The Frome was a wide river, but there had to be a narrow or calm enough section somewhere for me to cross. The water would be frigid. Ice along the banks would have retreated only a few weeks ago. I wasn't sure I could cross it, but what choice did I have? Either the river took us, or Demas would finish us off.

I stayed tight to the river's edge, but the shore quickly became choked with rushes and sedges, the ground spongy and wet. Bitter-cold water lapped at my ankles. Once soaked, Demas's leather shoes proved useless against the cold. The world was blanketed in muted darkness. The moon, pushing against the thick bank of clouds choking its light, did little to aid my course. The farther I struggled from the manor, the higher the riverbank rose away from me. I tried to clamber up the bank to the tree line above, but it was too slippery with mud. If I'd had two free hands I might have managed, but Edward and I had to find another way. Too afraid to turn back, I pressed onward.

In no time, water swirled around my knees. With each step, I sank a little deeper into the silt. Lifting my foot from the suctioning pull became increasingly difficult. I lost my balance and fell. Edward slipped from my arms. Frigid water engulfed me like arrows of ice. My breath caught in my throat. My chest constricted. I gasped, my entire body shaking.

"Avelynn." Edward flailed and sputtered, gasping for breath.

I trudged through the water, half crawling, half falling, and gathering him to my chest. "I've got you."

"I'm so cold." His teeth were chattering.

"It won't be long now." I pulled myself up, pushing onward with single-minded purpose.

"I'll find us someplace safe and warm and light a great fire."

His voice was weary, distant. "Do you promise?"

Tears slid down my cheeks. Goddess help us. "I promise."

I don't know how long I wandered. Time began to blur, each

dizzying moment followed by another, all my effort focused on placing one foot in front of the other. A lashing March wind nipped at my bare skin. The cold air gripped hard at my spine. Soaked with river water, the plaster on my back became slippery, and the cloth strips began to slide, bunching at my waist. Newly closed scabs chafed and tore against the back of my dress. Our progress had slowed considerably. Each step wracked my body, each breath strained.

"Let me walk." Edward pushed away from my hold, and I set him down, my body throbbing.

I stood panting. "But you're hurt."

"I will manage. Help me."

I nodded and wrapped his arm up and over my shoulder, his body leaning against mine. We hobbled through the bitter water, Edward sweating and wincing with the effort to stay upright. Demas's heavy wool cloak had absorbed half the river into its thick fibers, and it became an iron anchor dragging behind me. I released the clasp on my shoulder, giving my body up to exposure, and let the sodden mass go. Our steps were slow and heavy. We stumbled and fell, over and over. How long could we possibly keep doing this?

The clouds began to break apart. A waning gibbous moon skirted between fast-moving shadows, the wisps of clouds drifting across the brilliant surface like tendrils of smoke from Wareham's fires. I could see my breath. The moonlight cast my pale icy skin and white wedding gown into a ghostly beacon.

There was a jut in the shoreline up ahead. I struggled to keep us close to the embankment and thanked the Goddess—the steep overhang was tapering off. If we just kept going, we would soon be able to climb up onto solid ground. Using the last of my resources, I pressed forward, each muscle, each nerve, each fiber of my being protesting and quivering.

As we neared the crest of the bend, I heard male voices and froze.

We were downwind from them, and the cadence of their words reached me clearly. They spoke Norse.

We couldn't turn back. I gazed out over the water. The river was still too wide to try to ford. My heart sank into disbelief. How many Vikings were there? Would they move on? Did it matter? We couldn't stay there. My legs were numb. We were both freezing, and Edward was running out of strength. I had to find us shelter. We had to get out of the water.

Praying the breezes stayed on our side, keeping the sounds of our struggles upwind, we squelched through the rushes, their razor-sharp edges slicing across my arms. We rounded the jut in the shoreline, and I stared openmouthed at the sight before me. Even in the pale moonlight, *Raven's Blood* was unmistakable. The ship had been dredged up on shore, and its muted hues of red framed the shadow of a raven as the sail undulated in the breeze. I had never seen a more beautiful sight.

He was alive! He was here! I stumbled to the shore, pulling Edward with me. "Alrik!"

Edward fought hard against my hold, his eyes wide with panic. How could I explain to him they would help us?

"It's all right. I know these men."

"They are Vikings." His voice was a frantic whisper.

I spied a fair-size boulder peeking out from amongst the reeds near the bank and steered us in that direction. I set him on the rock, his body sagging. "I will be right back. It's okay."

He grabbed my skirt, fisting the fabric. "How can you say that? They are monsters. You are unarmed."

"Trust me." I pried his fingers loose and pushed through the cover of vegetation, clambering up the muddy bank, churned up by recent footsteps. I froze as I made eye contact with two Vikings. Both were savage looking and fully armed. We all stared at one another.

"Völva!" the taller of the two men said, before stepping backward.

His companion, shorter yet no less broad, stood his ground, a look of wary disbelief painted on his pale face.

I thought to explain myself, to ease their concern that I wasn't a witch, but didn't know how I could convince them otherwise. I had suddenly appeared from out of the river, wearing a flowing white gown stained with blood. "Where's Alrik?" I asked breathlessly instead.

The tall Viking continued to stay where he was, but his companion stepped closer. He studied me closely. "I remember you," he said slowly.

"Yes," I said, hopeful. "I was with Alrik when he visited England last summer. I blessed you for battle, shared your wine."

The tall Viking stepped forward. "You are the Saxon spy, the witch?"

I looked between the two men. Did I recognize either one of them? Dear gods, was Halfdan here? I remembered the handshake between Demas and the redheaded villainous scum. They were in business together. I stared at the red sail. This was Alrik's ship. He would never have given it up while there was still breath left in him. My heart sank. Alrik wasn't there. Halfdan was. My legs collapsed beneath me, and I dropped like a stone into the mud. Alrik was truly dead. I felt drained. The cold hit me with gale force, and I shivered uncontrollably.

The shorter Viking laughed and slapped his companion on the back in good cheer. "It is the lady herself." He threw his cloak over my shoulders. Pelts had been sewn onto a soft wool lining, and captured body heat radiated from the fabric. "Praise Thor! I didn't recognize you," he said. "My name is Cormac, and this lout is Olaf." Olaf nodded and stepped back into the shadows, guarding the ship, seemingly unconcerned and uninterested in the matter. Cormac continued, "I was with Alrik when he came to see you through the summer. I was with him when he landed in Reading. He has come a long way to find you, lady."

"Alrik's here?"

"Yes." He offered me his hand, and I took it, standing slowly, my head spinning.

"He's alive? But I saw him, swarmed and outnumbered. I feared him dead."

He laughed. "It would take more than an army to kill Alrik. Though it was his brother Ubbe who finally put an end to it. Half-dan was mad as a dog, but as Ubbe is the elder, he was obliged to leave off."

"They let Alrik go? Let him leave?" It seemed unbelievable. I wondered if I had fallen into the river, my life draining from me. If I hadn't been able to feel every ache in my body and hear the clicking of my teeth chattering, I might have pinched myself for a dream.

"Ubbe wouldn't permit the blood of their father to be shed. So"—he shrugged—"they sent Alrik into exile. Anyone wishing to sail with him could cast their lot with the traitorous scoundrel."

"Where is he?" The forest was silent and black around me.

"Waiting for you! Come, I will take you to him."

"My brother," I said helplessly, gesturing to the reeds. "He's badly hurt. I won't leave him."

"Olaf will put him aboard the ship and tend to his wounds."

"Thank you." I led them through the water back to the rock.

At our approach, Edward scrambled off the rock and stumbled backward, falling into water.

"Edward, please. These men will help you."

He stared wide-eyed at me. "What have you done?"

"I know this is difficult for you to understand, and I realize after all you've seen and experienced in Francia, you may not believe my words, but these men are not our enemy. They have come here to find me. Their leader is a powerful jarl; his name is Alrik. A man I have fallen in love with."

His mouth hung open.

Olaf grumbled, clearly impatient, and grabbed Edward by the scruff of his collar and lifted him up over his shoulder.

Edward immediately starting swinging his fists and flailing his body. Olaf grunted. "Tell him to be still or I'll make him complaisant."

I hesitated. I didn't want to frighten Edward further, but I didn't have time to make him understand. "Edward. If you do not be still, they will force the matter."

His jaw tightened and his eyes loosed arrows of hurt and betrayal my way, each one finding their mark on my heart.

"I'm sorry."

Olaf carried Edward back to the ship, his progress no longer hindered by signs of protest.

"Come; Alrik is waiting." Cormac roused my attention away from Edward. "He will be sorely pleased to see you. In his fury to take you away from this place, Alrik had us row like Jormungand was chasing us. Your brother will be on the ship waiting for your return."

Alrik was here! The aches in my body vanished, the fatigue disappeared, the shiver subsided, and the cold melted away. I looked upon Edward one last time and followed Cormac into a labyrinth of trees.

The farther we walked, the more I could see. An orange miasma hovered above the treetops ahead. I stopped dead. We were heading back to the manor! I looked in the direction of the ship. What if this Viking was leading me into a trap, his words a lie set to ensnare me? What if Halfdan was sitting at Demas's table just waiting for my deliverance? Had I not learned anything? After all that had happened, I was still quick to act without thinking.

Cormac sensed my hesitation and stopped.

"Why are you leading me back to the manor? Where's Halfdan?"

Even in the pale light, I could see Cormac's eyebrows draw together. "Halfdan is in Reading. Alrik is here with sixty men. He has laid siege to the manor."

I wanted to believe him, but my insides roiled and churned. I scanned the darkness, looking for the best means of escape. Where could I go? The sound of metal hissing across a scabbard brought my focus back to Cormac. I gripped the edges of the cloak, preparing to run.

"I am your sworn man, lady. Take the sword." He set the steel down in front of me, the moonlight catching on the broad flat surface. More metal slid against leather. "My knife is yours. Peace!" He placed it alongside the sword.

I lunged to grab the weapons, but rather than fight or try to stop me, Cormac knelt in the twigs and forest detritus and bowed his head. "I am your sworn man, lady. May Odin strike me down if I fail you."

He could have killed me, snapped my neck in two, forced me to the ground, raped me, tortured me, and brought me to Demas or Halfdan. Was he telling the truth? Gods, could I trust him? Could I trust anything?

In the silence of the forest, the wing beats of a large bird swooped over my head. A black outline perched on a black branch. The raven croaked. The world waited, watching.

"Alrik is here."

I blinked, uncertain if it was the raven or Cormac who had just spoken, and I stared at the bird. "Alrik is here." Gods! Why hadn't

I seen it sooner? The raven on the wagon at Reading told me Alrik was coming. The raven on the windowsill at Wareham told me Alrik was there. The raven in my dream, begging me to fly away with him—Alrik had asked me to marry him, to leave England. I looked into the sky. "Blessed Goddess, thank you." My heart beat in anticipation. Alrik was here!

"I will hold you to your oath, Cormac. May Odin and Thor banish you from Valhalla if you fail me."

He rose slowly. "I will not fail you."

Using the knife, I tore at the hem of my dress, pulling until a wide band of silk came loose. "Give me the scabbard for your knife." I held out my hand. He placed the worn leather in my palm. I threaded the band through the loop on the scabbard and secured the silk around my waist. I sheathed the knife and gripped the sword. "All right, take me to Alrik."

As we emerged from the forest, half the manor's buildings were in flames, but no one was rushing to tend to the blaze.

"Where is everyone?" I spoke under my breath.

"Alrik has them all detained. He is offering them as ransom for your freedom. The slaves and freemen are being held by the gates, the women in the stables."

"The women?" I turned, scanning the fury. "My friend Ealhswith is here!"

"He means to harm no one, save your betrothed."

I didn't bother mentioning that the priest had married us three days ago.

We skirted around the far side of the manor, opposite the route I had chosen for escape. Several armed Vikings stood sentry as we rounded the stables.

"Hail," Cormac called.

"Who's there?" one of the Vikings called.

"Cormac."

"Who's with you?" One of the guards stepped closer.

"Alrik's woman."

The guard stopped his forward momentum.

"Where's Alrik?" Cormac asked.

The Viking pointed ahead. "Can't miss him."

My heart pounded, my pulse racing ahead. We passed a weaving shed and a cow byre and then stopped. A line had clearly been drawn. Fully armed Saxons and Vikings stood apart from one another.

"Demas! Coward! Face me!" Alrik's deep, throaty voice boomed as he paced in front of the Viking line. He wasn't wearing a helmet. Blond hair brushed his shoulders as he moved. Chain mail, shining in the fire's light, strained to contain his broad chest. Widow Maker hung from his right hand. A round shield was gripped in his left. "I will destroy this maggot-infested dung heap. Bring me the woman Avelynn!"

"Alrik!" I ran. "Alrik!"

The large cloak flapped about my shoulders. My entire body trembled with each step, but it was no longer the cold causing me to quake. "Alrik!"

All eyes were trained on me. The sea of Vikings parted, and I ran headlong into the tallest, biggest Viking of them all. "Alrik," I cried, and collapsed into his arms.

"Avelynn?" He stared down at me as if I were an apparition. He set me away from him. His eyes traveled over my body. "Are you hurt?"

"I'm fine." I wanted to bury myself in his embrace, breathe his scent, take him into me until I dissolved in his arms.

"Avelynn?" Alfred shouldered his way to the front of the line. "I can't believe it!"

Osric rounded the wall of Saxons and threw the lifeless body of Adiva on the ground. "You killed your chambermaid and attempted to murder your husband. It wasn't enough that you tried to kill him with his own knife in your wedding bed, but you cast spells and spewed foul curses on his inert form."

"Lies!" I yelled.

"You are a traitor and a witch!" He spat in my direction. It fell far from my feet. "Viking whore!"

My blood boiled. I still had Cormac's sword, but Alrik put a stop to any rebuttal and pulled me sharply back, deftly unarming me, the sword slipping from my grasp.

"Let me go." I squirmed. He held me tight.

"You got what you came for, Viking; now leave," Osric said.

"I will take one of your women for safekeeping." He nodded to a Viking behind him.

"Ealhswith!" Alfred's panicked voice preceded his body as he lunged. Several men moved in to restrain him as the entire line of Vikings stepped forward.

Ealhswith had been gagged, her hands tied behind her back. In my shock, I had stopped struggling, and Alrik let me go. He grabbed Ealhswith's arm and placed his axe across her chest, the edge inches from her throat. "To ensure you do not follow, she will accompany us as far as your Christian house in Swanage. If we stay unmolested, that is where you shall find her." He pushed Ealhswith to a companion and lifted me in his arms.

"She's my friend!" I tried to get down, to help her.

He turned his back on the fuming, helpless Saxons and whistled. Several archers let loose a stream of fiery arrows into the surviving buildings.

"She is not in any danger. This was her idea," he whispered in my ear as we strode in front of a cheering, laughing band of pirates.

"Her idea?"

"When I came to find her, she felt it best to come up with an alternative plan, should the messenger not reach Halfdan in time."

Ealhswith and her plans! I had never been so happy in my life. I wrapped my arms around his neck. I never wanted to let him go.

The Vikings packed the ship with precious metals, livestock, kegs of ale, sacks of wheat, and crates of salted meat and bread. Apparently, Ealhswith and I were not the only Saxon property they were absconding with.

A tent was erected in the center of the ship, and Cormac led me inside to where Olaf had laid Edward. He was turned, his back to us, his breathing uneven. He was not asleep, though he pretended to be. I felt it best to leave matters alone for the moment.

Alrik placed another woolen blanket over him. "There is much to share," he said.

"Yes," I sighed. I didn't even know where to begin.

He lit an oil lamp and loosened some of the floor planks, exposing a crammed hold below. He rearranged several crates before settling on an ornate chest, which he placed on a squat wooden barrel. He lifted the lid and held up a pale yellow kirtle. He laid it upon the bed. As captain, Alrik slept on a raised bed in the center of the tent. His men slept where they rowed, each on a bench under the stars. He pulled out a heavy cloak lined with wolf pelts, woolen socks, and ankle-high leather boots.

"When you have changed, give the dress to Cormac. He will cut the pearls from the bodice and toss the rest overboard."

"Thank you."

He fingered my newly shorn hair.

"Is it done?" he asked.

"They were Christian words. The ceremony meant nothing to me."

"Did he . . . have you?"

"No."

He kissed my forehead. The tent flaps closed behind him, and he bellowed out orders, taking command of his ship. The sail was furled, and the oars dropped into the water. The boat surged forward, the sensation disorienting and exhilarating, and I planted my feet wide to maintain my balance as we pushed away from the shore.

I stared at the beautiful kirtle. I hoped Demas's wounds festered. I hoped he died an agonizing death, but if he did survive, I hoped to be there when he took his last breath, and I prayed to the Goddess it would be at the end of my sword that he fell.

I peeled the ruined wedding dress off my shivering body and stepped into the dry clothes. Fully dressed and wrapped in the cloak, I moved next to a cauldron hanging from chains attached to a beam jutting out from the mast overhead. The cauldron held a blistering fire and for the first time all night I felt myself warming.

Sometime later, I stood at the stern, watching the horizon until the faint light from the fires of Wareham faded into the night.

"Are you going to miss it?" Ealhswith asked. Her restraints had been removed as soon as we were well out of sight of the shore.

"There's nothing left here for me now." I forced a weak smile. "Are you well?" I looked her over. "Where's Aethelflaed?"

"She's safe and sound back in Windsor with the nursemaid." She sat on one of the many crates littering the deck. "And I'm fine. Alrik is a complete gentleman, as is his second-in-command." She waved flirtatiously at Tollak.

I gaped at her. "Ealhswith!"

"What? He's handsome."

I laughed and shook my head. She patted the space beside her, and I sat down. We were silent for some time, watching the dark shadows of the forest skim by.

"I'm sorry," she said quietly.

"For what?"

"Alrik had hoped to get here sooner. He could have stopped the wedding."

I hugged her fiercely. "I'm grateful he's here at all. I feared

Edward and I would both die tonight. I don't know how I can ever repay you."

She pulled away. "Repay me? I merely removed you from one fire to drop you into another. Both you and Alrik are homeless, traitors. I don't know where you can go, or what kind of life you'll have."

"I can't think of that yet."

Our first stop would be Swanage, to leave Ealhswith with the monks. Our second stop was Avalon. No one knew about the hidden island, though it was easily accessible by boat along the River Parrett, and they certainly wouldn't be expecting us to return to England. The Saxons would most likely assume we would head to Francia, as would the Vikings. The detour would buy us time. After that, only the gods knew our fate.

"But an exiled Viking and his crew are clanless—rogues—worse than fleas on a dog's back. Tollak left nothing to the imagination when he told me what could become of them." Ealhswith's eyes were pained. "Anyone who brings down an exiled traitor and his ship will bring honor and riches to his house. You will not be given a moment's reprieve."

I sighed. "No, I imagine not; yet the Vikings are only part of our concerns. Demas will not rest knowing that Edward and I are still alive. He risks losing Wedmore, and Osric all of Somerset, if the truth were to surface." Though in honesty, I didn't know how we could prove their deceptions. I'd already failed once to sway the Witan, and that was before I had absconded with the enemy. But land and holdings were only part of the perverse picture. After all the pain I'd inflicted on Demas, if he survived his wounds, he would hunt Edward and me to the ends of the earth. Nowhere would be far enough away for any of us. I shrugged, looking at Alrik. "We'll come up with something."

Even in the moon's faint glow, I could make out Alrik's strong cheekbones as the wind pulled the hair away from his face. We would have to face what lay ahead, but not tonight.

"And what of Edward?" she asked.

"I don't know."

"What if he came with me?"

"After everything I've done to protect him? I can't leave him here."

"But no one would know. To all but Demas, he's dead. I can hide him away, send him to my foster sister Angharad in Wales, or maybe to my aunt Godgifu in Mercia. I would make sure he is safe."

I had to concede to Ealhswith's point. Edward was only ten. What kind of life could I provide for him as Alrik and I ran from our enemies? Demas would assume Edward stayed with me. Perhaps he would be safer here, out of sight but deceptively close, right under his nose. The thought of sailing away without him made my stomach churn—to be unaware of his welfare, to face the harsh silence of uncertainty as I had when he'd been ill in Francia—I didn't know if I could go through that again. "I'll consider it." I squeezed her hand. "I'm truly grateful for everything you've done. Thank you."

"I wish I could have done more."

"I have my life, Edward is safe, and I have Alrik," I said, admiring his stature as he worked the steering board. "It's more than enough."

Alrik felt my gaze and without missing a beat, Tollak took his place at the helm.

"Can I interrupt?" Alrik said, resting his hand on my shoulder.

Ealhswith stood and arched her back, stretching. "I was just heading to bed." She looked back and forth between us and grinned. "Good night, Avelynn. Alrik," she said, bowing her head.

"Thank you," he said.

She squeezed my hand and slipped inside the tent where Alrik had set a cot for her beside Edward.

He sat beside me. "She is a good friend."

"Yes," I agreed. "She risked her life trying to save mine. If any-one were to find out her deception . . ."

"No one here will talk."

"You had a weasel on your ship before," I noted dryly.

He straightened. "Yes, and he lost his tongue before I drove my sword through his spine." He stood up. "Gods, woman, I don't know whether to shake you or kiss you." He ran his hand through his hair. "All that I have done, I risked for you. To know what my brother did to you and be unable to stop it, to know what that bastard Demas did and not be able to kill him with my bare hands! Aye, I had a traitor on my ship, and it was my fault that you suffered so." His gaze traveled over the sparkling water. Calm, as if it were a sheet of ice. His shoulders dropped in defeat. "I failed you."

"Gods." I scrambled up off the bench. Reaching out to him, I drew his face to me. "Alrik, you saved me. You didn't fail me. What I did, I did on my own. They were my choices, and I accept full responsibility for my actions and their consequences." I let my hands fall to my sides. "I've made so many mistakes. I wish I could re-tract them, but I can't, and dwelling on them doesn't serve me." I searched Alrik's face. "But when I needed you most, you were here. Against all odds, you came. You saved me."

He wrapped his strong, calloused hands around mine.

"Let's not dwell on the past," I pleaded. "There are far too many painful memories. I can't bear to look backward." Standing on tip-toes, I kissed his lips softly. "I thought you were dead, and I never want to feel like that again." I kissed each of his eyelids. "You were taken from me, and now I have you back." I kissed the bridge of his nose. "That's all that matters to me now." I pressed my mouth against his, inviting, offering absolution.

He opened his mouth to mine. Hunger, pain, loss, and fear, each emotion in turn played across our lips as words of yearning, forgiveness, relief, and surrender—unspoken yet acknowledged—coalesced around our bodies. He lifted me in his arms and cradled me close. I rested my head on his shoulder. No matter where we went, no matter what happened next, in this moment I was home.

By morning, we reached Swanage. The monks were reasonably flustered at the appearance of a Viking longship on their shore.

Ealhswith held my hands in hers. "Be careful."

"I will." I pulled her close. I would miss her terribly.

Edward hobbled out of the tent, a satchel slung over his shoulder. He cut a wide berth around the Vikings nearest him and stood beside Ealhswith.

I narrowed my eyes at him. He stood straighter, leaning on a staff. "I'm going with Ealhswith."

"You cannot possibly mean it. Demas will kill you if he finds you."

"I heard you and Ealhswith talking. I will go to her aunt in Mercia. I'll not sail another moment longer with the likes of them." He didn't bother hiding the vehemence in his voice or stares.

"Edward, please, try to understand."

"Help me to shore," he said to Ealhswith.

Alrik stood by my side. "Olaf and Cormac will see them both safely away."

I glared at him. "I can't leave him here."

"He is old enough to decide. Your friend will see to his protection. I can offer him no such security."

Ealhswith hugged me, her mouth next to my ear, her voice a whisper. "He will come to understand in time. I will make sure he knows the truth, about everything—your father, your grandmother. All of it."

I felt as though the world had collapsed, the force breaking me in two. "Edward."

"God keep you, sister."

Ealhswith's hand slid slowly out of mine, and I watched in silence as Edward and Ealhswith dropped over the side of the ship and were marched to shore.

"Gods keep you safe, Edward Eanwulfson. I love you."

The boat pulled away, and we headed out to sea. The weather was exceptionally fine, clear and sunny during the day, but at night the air teased the cold water until thick fog blanketed the ocean. Alrik kept a constant vigil, fearing an enemy ship would materialize out of the mists. It was a tense journey, as imagination played with shadows and sounds echoed in the night. We were all grateful to ride the tidal flow into the River Parrett.

We made Avalon by midmorning, and the men scattered, hunting fresh game and fish. Alrik strolled beside me as I sought my mother's grave.

The clearing opened before us and my mother's stone stood cold and barren in a sea of early-blooming bluebells. "I need to be alone," I said.

He surveyed the wilderness and unsheathed his knife. "Take this," he said, handing me the sharpened steel. "I will give you privacy, but I will not go far."

"Thank you."

He placed his hand on my shoulder, and I watched him disappear into the trees.

I read the Ogham symbols carved into the stone, *Here lies Aileen, daughter of the gods, loving wife of Eanwulf,* and felt a deep aching emptiness. I didn't know what to say. Was this the last time

I would look upon her grave? Would I come back to England? Would I ever see Edward again?

I fell, prostrating myself at the stone's base. "Mother, please, forgive me."

"There's nothing to forgive." A woman's gentle voice reached out from the past. I closed my eyes tight, fearing the whisper would fade away.

"You are my daughter. I love you."

Never in my life had I so desperately wanted to hear those words. My heart constricted, and tears slid down my cheeks.

I pulled myself up on trembling arms and knelt in the crushed flowers and fallen leaves. Slowly, I opened my eyes. It was the most beautiful vision I had ever seen. My mother, dressed in her finest gown of light blue linen, her dark curls cascading over her shoulders, stood before me.

"I've lost Edward. Father was taken from me, Muirgen—Mama. I'm so sorry."

"Edward must forge his own path. Your father and grandmother are here with me. We're watching and guiding you."

"I've let you all down. I should have married Demas. None of this would have happened."

"What would marrying Demas have accomplished? Do you think the men behind his actions would have stopped there? Once they had control, do you think you would still be alive? You kept your spirit, your heart, and your strength. You stayed true to yourself. I'm proud of you."

Words caught in my throat. I could barely see her translucent form through the veil of tears.

"The world needs your strength, Avelynn. Your people need you. Osric will order all the men who fought for you to surrender their lands. He will mark them as traitors and cast them out. All the

widowed women, all Wedmore's innocent children, will be homeless and penniless. Your people are coming home to Avalon."

"I can't help anyone. I'm a condemned traitor." I wiped the tears
with the back of my hand. "I'm here with Alrik—the enemy! He
has sixty Viking warriors with him. I can't stay."

"You must try to save the people of England from Osric's cruelty and ambitions. You have been chosen."

The vision flickered, and I jolted forward, my heart pounding,
knowing she would soon disappear.

"Please don't leave me."

"You must keep going. You must keep fighting."

"Mama." The vision flickered and disintegrated like dust motes
settling in a ray of light until there was nothing left. I fell to the
ground and wept. I wept for Edward, my father, Muirgen, my
mother. I wept for injustice, cruelty, and helplessness. My ribs heaved
and my chest ached with the grief rending me asunder. I held nothing in. Like a small child pleading for comfort, all the pain I had
buried deep inside burbled out in swells of grief. I pressed my forehead into the earth, my hands tight around clumps of loose soil.
Eventually, the tension melted from my body, and I rolled onto my
back, staring dry-eyed into a blue sky, my mind quieter, my breath
even.

A long time passed as I lay in the coarse grass. I sat up, peeling
away a crushed blade from my cheek. The sun was low on the horizon. It would soon be dusk. I leaned against the tree, feeling its
strong, silent support, and listened. Insects buzzed. Birds sang softly
in the branches overhead. My breath was deep and slow.

How could I convince Alrik to stay? How could I convince his
men? I plucked a shaft of grass and twirled it around my fingers.
There were plenty of wealthy villages along the southern and western
coasts of Wales. The Welsh were long an enemy of England, and

Alrik could make hasty attacks on their settlements and walk away with enough plunder to appease his men. And the women of Wedmore would need husbands. Men, whether Saxon or Viking, were always looking for women. Perhaps I could convince the Vikings to settle here. There was plenty of game and fish at hand.

Gods, I was being ridiculous.

Yet the idea persisted. What if it worked? Why should I run away like a coward with my tail between my legs? I had done nothing wrong. My predicament was the fault of two men, Osric and Demas.

I looked at my mother's grave. The bastards had taken away everything important to me—my family, my home, and my freedom—yet rather than fight, I was fleeing like a frightened rabbit hiding from the boar. I was not a rabbit. I had never been a rabbit. Somehow, I would prove my innocence and take back my freedom.

Catching movement, I turned my head to the right. Where once the boar had stood, snorting and pawing at the ground, a timid doe stepped into the fading sunlight. Her large, beautiful eyes met mine. Forgiveness, love, fortitude, and peace enveloped me. I was certain the doe smiled and nodded before she turned and disappeared into the bush.

"What are you staring at?" Alrik said, striding into the clearing.

I stood, smiling. "A gift from my mother."

He wrapped his arms around my waist. "Then you found what you came here for?"

"Yes," I said, letting him draw me close. "Faith and the strength to keep fighting."